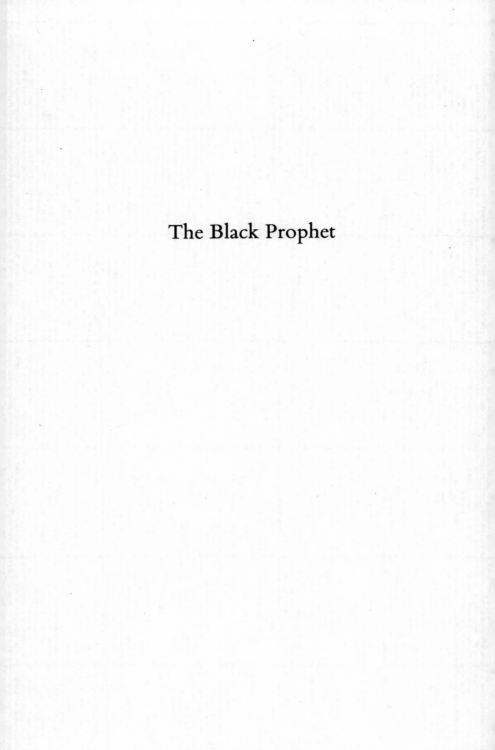

The Black Prophet

IRISH NOVELS SERIES
general editor: A. Norman Jeffares

The Black Prophet

A Tale of Irish Famine

by

WILLIAM CARLETON

Introduction by
Timothy Webb

IRISH UNIVERSITY PRESS
Shannon   Ireland

First edition Belfast and London 1847

This IUP reprint is a photolithographic facsimile

ISBN 0 7165 1798 1

Irish University Press   Shannon   Ireland
T. M. MacGlinchey   Publisher

PRINTED IN THE REPUBLIC OF IRELAND AT SHANNON
BY ROBERT HOGG PRINTER TO IRISH UNIVERSITY PRESS

INTRODUCTION

'And pray what language is that in which you have just addressed me?'

'It's the vernacular, sir, of a certain country, with whose history you are evidently unacquainted. Of a country, sir, whose inhabitants live upon a meal a month; keep very little—for sound reasons—between themselves and the elements, and where abstinence from food is the national diversion.'

'God bless me!' exclaimed the parson, 'That's very odd, very odd indeed, I shall take a note of that; how very like Ireland!'

This conversation provides a convenient perspective from which to survey William Carleton and his work. It is in some ways emblematic of Carleton himself, since both voices were at times his own. Like Randy the Irish-speaking peasant, Carleton sometimes spoke for the submerged Gaelic world of the cabins and the small farms, a world which was always poised on the edge of poverty and famine; this world was gradually disappearing during his earlier years and suffered its death blow from the Great Hunger of 1845–49. Thus Carleton was the spokesman and the historian of a community which was underprivileged and quite alien from the experience of the parson, Dr McClaret, and his like. Its special and separate identity was underlined by the fact that it had a language of its own, Gaelic (or Irish), which was still widely spoken in Carleton's boyhood. Carleton's own books were written in English but one can detect behind them a voice which was nurtured and enriched by Gaelic idiom. It was a new voice and it spoke of a new world, or rather of an old world which had so far been ignored or misrepresented in the English literature of his country. It is also symbolically appropriate that Randy is addressing himself to a Protestant clergyman, for Carleton needed an audience and his audience was largely Protestant, some of it unsympathetic to the world he described. This affected his writing in several ways which we shall consider later on.

Yet this equation between Carleton and Randy is too simple. The dialogue can be related to Carleton in a more complicated way since the second voice, the voice of Dr McClaret, was also one he used himself. McClaret's 'I shall take a note of that; how very like Ireland!' is the typical reaction of the English visitor and of a certain social class to which Carleton did not belong, yet it is also typical of Carleton in some of his moods. When he is McClaret he does not comprehend, he is critical, he forgets the meaning of the vernacular which Randy had understood so well. Here we are faced with another paradox. Even Carleton's best work is informed by a sense of the oddness of the Irish character. A recognition of the singularity of people is indispensable for the comic writer and this was responsible for much of Carleton's success. Yet the sense of the comic is never far removed from the outsider's 'how very like Ireland'; the balance is delicate and can easily be disturbed.

These complications and contradictions make better sense when seen in the context of Carleton's life and career. He was born in 1794 at Prillisk in County Tyrone, where he was brought up in relative prosperity. In his unfinished *Autobiography* he magnificently recreates the mood and flavour of that childhood, of a life based on the community and lived in harmony with nature. He studied under a series of hedge-schoolmasters, strange figures larger than life, some brutal, some incompetent, some magniloquent and versed in the 'seven languages'. When he was about fifteen he decided to go to Munster as a poor scholar to prepare himself for the priesthood. This was still almost the only road of advancement for the gifted peasant and for Carleton it seems to have had the ultimate attractions of power and prestige. However, his plans were soon abandoned though for what reason we do not know. For some years after that he lived an idle life at home where he soon became a village hero. On one occasion, before the assembled villagers, he jumped right across a river without wetting his heels; another time, he defeated the local miller in a contest at throwing a rock over a beam. He was also a champion dancer and master of all the traditional steps. Eventually when his family would support him no longer he took to the roads, living by his wits rather in the manner of a picaresque hero. The *Autobiography* details a long series of wanderings and disappointments in the course of which he was private tutor, hedge-schoolmaster and clerk in a Sunday School society. In the course of these struggles Carleton renounced the Catholic Church and became a Protestant, which helped him to achieve preferment. He settled in Dublin where he met the fanatical editor of the *Christian Examiner*, Caesar Otway, who printed his first sketches of peasant life. From that time Carleton was a controversial figure, a writer who succeeded in offending everybody during the course of his life. He contributed to journals so various as the *Dublin University Magazine*, the *Nation* and the *Irish Tribune*. He continued to produce stories and sketches. He also wrote a number of novels, most of which dealt with important aspects of Irish life and politics: the land question, Ribbonism, the Orange Order, the Catholic Church, the Great Hunger. He died in 1869.

The man at the centre of these biographical facts was a remarkable example of cultural schizophrenia. Catholic and Protestant, peasant and gentleman, countryman and town-dweller, Ulsterman and Dubliner, Irish speaker and writer of English prose, Carleton was in every way a divided man. This both enriches his work and confuses it. In that complexity we may find an image of the Irish condition. 'In his own chaotic and entangled soul he has mirrored all our own complications, has hinted at the chaos into which we plunged, almost to perish but ultimately to survive' (Benedict Kiely *Poor Scholar* [1947]). This complication is also an index of the difficulties which have faced the Irish writer at all times but particularly in Carleton's day. These factors can all be seen at work in one of his most famous novels, *The Black Prophet*.

In 1845 the Irish potato crop failed, but the authorities were not seriously alarmed. This had often happened before, though not on so extensive a scale. The following year *The Black Prophet: A Tale of Irish Famine* was published serially in the *Dublin University Magazine*. It was both a warning to the authorities, and an indictment. In that year the potato crop failed again and this time the extent of the disaster could not be disregarded. A population of over eight millions was threatened with extinction by starvation or by fever. Early in 1847 Carleton published his novel in book form with a dedication to Lord John Russell, Prime Minister of Great Britain and Ireland. Carleton made his didactic purposes quite explicit. In a brief preface he explained that the book was written in order 'to awaken those who legislate for us into something like a humane perception of a calamity that has been almost perennial in the country.'

Famine was a subject that haunted Carleton and it figures prominently in his works. As he tells us in the preface, some scenes in *The Black Prophet* are based in part on the lesser famines of 1817 and 1822, whose effects he witnessed on his early travels through Ireland. But famine was more than an occasional hazard for the Irish peasant; it was an annual reality:

> Much . . . is said . . . concerning what are termed 'Years of Famine,' but it is not generally known, that since the introduction of the potato into this country, no year has ever passed which, in some remote locality or other, has not been such to the unfortunate inhabitants. (*The Black Prophet*, p. 219)

The imagery of famine was grimly etched on Carleton's memory: wretched figures tearing up weeds for their children to eat, crawling in the ditches on their hands and knees, dying abandoned in fever huts by the side of the road; desperate mobs attacking provision carts on their way to the ports or to market, sitting in ditches or on the road as they gobbled the raw flour or oatmeal which they had stolen, bleeding the cows and heifers so they could drink the blood. Perhaps most horrible of all was the silence —the mobs unable to shout, the dogs too weak to bark. In *The Black Baronet* (1852) there is wild, hysterical laughter; the people are transformed into ghouls and vampires; starving fathers devour the corpses of their children. *The Squanders of Castle Squander* (1852) approaches the subject with a panoply of statistics but what remains in the memory is the body-cadgers and the visit of Lady Squander to her husband's grave, when she finds the graveyard strewn with half-eaten limbs and a dog munching a human head which he holds between his paws. Scenes like this give Carleton's work a lurid power yet they were written not merely for melodramatic effect but as the settings for stories with strong moral intentions.

The horrors described in these novels were to some extent remediable. In his official report on the famine Sir Charles

Trevelyan detected the Supreme Wisdom at work 'educing permanent good out of transient evil.' Carleton was neither so complacent nor so sanguine. Certain sections of the community were obviously to blame:

> Indeed, one would imagine, that after the many terrible visitations which we have had from destitution and pestilence, a legislature sincerely anxious for the health and comfort of the people, would have devoted itself, in some reasonable measure, to the humane consideration of such proper sumptuary and sanitary enactments, as would have provided not only against the recurrence of these evils, but for a more enlightened system of public health and cleanliness, and a better and more comfortable provision of food for the indigent and poor. (*The Black Prophet*, p.220)

Carleton's anger was also directed against two other kinds of people. The first category includes misers, profiteers, money-lenders and the provision dealers who combine to form monopolies: all of these are fused in the character of Darby Skinadre. Darby is granted none of the horrified sympathy with which Carleton approaches the central character of *Fardorougha the Miser*. The chapter in which Carleton details his extortions of money and goods from helpless peasants and ruined small farmers is an unflinching exposure of the iniquities of a whole social group. The second category is that of the landlords and their middleman. This category includes the Hendersons who rent out the estates to the small farmers, the agent who represents the landlord and, by implication, the landlord himself. Although the agent has a sense of justice, as we see when he restores the Daltons to their farm, he and his master are obviously guilty of negligence. It is through their indifference that the middlemen are allowed to profit from the misfortunes of the Daltons and their like. For Carleton, then, famine was a fact of nature but its effects were multiplied by human inefficiency and wickedness. As he says: the entrepreneurs created 'a kind of artificial famine in the country.' One is reminded of Frank O'Connor's indignant remark that in Irish terms, at any rate, *famine* is a terminological inexactitude:

> The word 'famine' itself is question-begging for it means 'an extreme and general scarcity of food', and to use it of a country with a vast surplus of food—cows, sheep, pigs, poultry, eggs and corn—is simply to debase language. (*The Backward Look* [1967], p. 141)

Such are the central themes and purposes of *The Black Prophet*. What else has the novel to offer? Carleton himself hoped that 'the workings of those passions and feelings which usually agitate human life, and constitute the character of those who act in it, will be found to constitute its chief attraction.' Few modern readers are susceptible to this attraction. The characters are of limited interest. Sarah, the prophet's daughter, is a strange mixture of violence and virtue; all her actions, both good and bad, are the result of passion. Mave Sullivan, sense to her sensibility, fairhaired to her black, shows a robustness which we might not expect in a Victorian heroine but for all that she is too angelically virtuous for this or any world. Donnel Dhu, the prophet, is a sinister presence. Carleton hints at some hidden and complex anguish of the soul but fails to develop it, so that Donnel remains a Gothic villain. All the characters are hampered by the plot, a melodramatic structure which forces them into traditional postures. Soliloquies are long and frequent; behaviour is generally theatrical. Darby Skinadre combines tears and religious insincerities in the manner of a conventional hypocrite. The prophet has an unpleasant experience not unlike that of Henry Irving in *The Bells*. He goes sleep-walking to the scene of a murder committed twenty years before. He conveniently fails to destroy the one remaining piece of incriminating evidence. The settings are over-coloured and gloomily romantic in the fashion of nineteenth-century prints. These burdens are too great for the novel to be a success. Its effect as a social document is also greatly weakened by the conventional framework which deprives it of credibility; nor has it the visionary force of a more concentrated work such as Defoe's *Journal of the Plague Year*. Yet the reasons for its failures are worth considering in more detail, for they tell us a great deal about Carleton and about the condition of Irish literature in his time.

In the first place, his didactic purposes obtrude themselves on the life of the novel. Carleton sometimes deviates from his narrative to address the ordinary reader or admonish the statesman. Sometimes he finds it necessary to prop up the imaginative truths of his novel with historical or medical footnotes. This didacticism also separates Carleton from the true source of his inspiration, the peasants. Take for example this sentence which describes the house of the dead Peggy Murtagh:

> The scene in her father's house on this melancholy night, was such as few hearts could bear unmoved, as well on account of her parents' grief as because it may be looked upon as a truthful exponent both of the destitution of the country, and of the virtues and sympathies of our people. (*The Black Prophet*, p. 133)

Here Carleton is standing outside the scene exhibiting it to his foreign readers. In another passage he talks of 'that piety which is characteristic of our peasantry.' This is not far

xii

removed from the perspective of Maria Edgeworth in the footnotes to *Castle Rackrent*. The important difference is that, of necessity, she was always on the outside examining the Irish with the eye and ear of a sympathetic anthropologist, while Carleton had once been on the inside from whence he had drawn his strength. Once he had left that intimate warmth his work suffered. It is not that he has lost sympathy with the people he is writing about: *The Black Prophet* is obviously the work of a compassionate man. What has happened is that by changing his perspective he has lost much of his vigour. He still writes with unrivalled knowledge of the realities of peasant life. He still has the advantage of being the first Irish writer in English who had been brought up in a peasant community. Yet, in spite of that, he is writing as Maria Edgeworth might have written, granted the special knowledge.

One obvious indication of this is the style of the novel. The language of *The Black Prophet* often moves stiffly, as if in borrowed clothes. Carleton is on his best behaviour, exhibiting the occasional foreign phrase as a sign of good breeding and affecting the manners of a gentleman. Take, for example, this description:

> . . . her eyes flashed and softened with an expression of brilliancy and tenderness that might be said to resemble the sky at night, when the glowing coruscations of the *Aurora Borealis* sweep over it like sheets of lightning, or fade away into those dim but graceful undulations, which fill the mind with a sense of such softness and beauty. (*The Black Prophet*, p. 98)

This is 'sophisticated' in the wrong kind of way; both the image and the style are affectations which are not in keeping with the subject. Nor does the dialogue exhibit the comic vigour of his best work in the *Traits and Stories of the Irish*

Peasantry. In these sketches of peasant life Carleton was able to give play to his own characteristic abilities. He was gifted with a faculty for seeing things clearly, for recreating places and characters in full and convincing detail. These places and characters were not imagined or invented, but were called up from the reserves of memory. In sad contrast, the characters in *The Black Prophet* are fictional stereotypes, whose reality is conditioned by the role they play in the scheme of the book. In this case, memory is conquered by literary decorum; the creative imagination fails to claim its rights.

The success of *Traits and Stories* indicates another limitation of *The Black Prophet*. In these stories Carleton most fully expressed himself through the comic, especially the comic potential of the spoken language. The *Traits and Stories* create (or recreate) a whole world in this way. Unforgettable characters like Denis O'Shaughnessy achieve identity through their comic manipulation of language. Their vitality is a verbal one, much of it derived from fruitful interplay between the Irish and English languages. This is missing from *The Black Prophet* and consequently so also is a good deal of Carleton's vitality.

This leads us to another crucial reason for the weakness of *The Black Prophet*. The novel was not a form which gave scope to Carleton's most recognizable talents. Most people would agree that his finest work is to be found in *Traits and Stories*. The novel demanded a kind of coherence which Carleton was not qualified to offer. Some of his conversational remarks can help us to understand why. When asked if his characters were imaginary he replied, 'I found them, and only gave them a linked embodiment. . . . ' On the subject of Denis O'Shaughnessy he had this to say:

. . . at the time I wrote this story I could appear to be

laconic and condemn all pride of the literary art, as I had found out by long and wearisome defeat and failure that the true road to acceptance is by following life and nature. (quoted in Thomas Flanagan, *The Irish Novelists 1800–1850*)

His preferences were no doubt conditioned by his father who was a renowned storyteller in the traditional style, and perhaps by Le Sage, whose picaresque novel *Gil Blas* was close to the pattern of his own early wanderings, and it was also a favourite of his. Thus, the kind of story to which Carleton was accustomed was relatively unsophisticated. Its basis was in the oral as much as in the written tradition. It was not an elegantly articulated structure in the manner of Jane Austen. Its emphasis was on character rather than pattern, on discovering rather than shaping.

In that case, why did Carleton turn to the novel? Very probably he failed to recognize the dangers since we know that he regarded *The Black Prophet* as his best book. In any case, he was always driven by two ineluctable needs—the need for money and the need to make himself acceptable to an admiring audience. Unfortunately it was difficult for him to achieve either of these ambitions without being in some way untrue to himself. To begin with, there were always the obvious dangers of propaganda. On the one hand there were the Caesar Otways who were eager for the harsh satire of 'The Lough Derg Pilgrim'; on the other hand there were the Young Irelanders who applauded the simplicities of books like *Paddy-Go-Easy*. Yet even Carleton must have realized that the absolutes of propaganda are never the truths of literature.

The greatest danger was much less obvious. The demands of literary taste were ill suited to Carleton's talents. Yet, if he were to survive, he would have to accommodate himself to that taste. Carleton had already changed his religion in the search for preferment; now, perhaps unconsciously, he changed his literary voice and manner. The people to whom he really belonged were not likely to read books and even less likely to buy them. The reading public was composed of the middle and upper class citizens of Dublin and London and writing for them meant adopting a pose and a vocabulary which they would recognize and sanction. It also meant adopting the form of the Victorian novel whose validity Carleton did not feel ready to question. His predicament might be best described as that of a literary middleman, representing the peasants to their social superiors, sometimes exploiting them a little, himself sandwiched none too comfortably between two classes, to neither of which he completely belonged. Yet Irish peasant society could not receive its fullest, most adequate expression in the form of the novel which was created to serve the needs of the urban English reading public. Behind *The Black Prophet* there is a visionary intensity, a violence, what Yeats called a 'clay-cold melancholy', which chafes against the conventional framework of the story. Perhaps this power might have been better expressed in poetry, drama or even the short story, or perhaps it required a different kind of novel for which the English language could not provide a model. One of Carleton's stories about his mother illustrates the point:

> I remember on one occasion, when she was asked to sing the English version of that touching melody, 'The Red-Haired Man's Wife', she replied, 'I will sing it for you; but the English words and the air are like a quarrelling man and wife: *the Irish melts into the tune, but the English doesn't.*' (General introduction to *Traits and Stories* [1843]).

Yet merely to put it this way is to underestimate the force

of *The Black Prophet*. Certainly the novel has shortcomings, but the whole is indisputably greater than the sum of the parts. The principal reason for this is the fatalistic atmosphere which Carleton so brilliantly evokes. *The Black Prophet* reveals in him a vein of dark poetry and a natural instinct for the macabre which one might not have suspected in the author of *Traits and Stories*. Though cramped and hindered by convention, Carleton has succeeded in creating a work of memorable and brooding intensity.

A letter of Maria Edgeworth's illustrates the courage and originality of this writing. In 1830 she wrote to her brother:

> It is impossible to draw Ireland as she now is in the book of fiction—realities are too strong, party passions too violent, to bear to see, or care to look at their faces in a looking glass. The people would only break the glass, and curse the fool who held the mirror up to nature—distorted nature in a fever. (quoted in Flanagan, *The Irish Novelists*)

Although she is referring to physical danger, Miss Edgeworth is really implying that she no longer has the means to transfer contemporary Irish society to the fictional realm. Her kind of literature is no longer adequate. Compare this with Carleton's statement in the preface to *The Black Prophet* that 'the strongest imagery of Fiction is frequently transcended by the terrible realities of Truth.' Unlike Miss Edgeworth, Carleton was willing to face those terrible realities as a writer. He met with the difficulties which must always face the pioneer, yet the way in which he responded to the challenge deserves to be saluted. It is perhaps one of the main reasons why he may claim to be the 'founder of Irish prose literature'.

A CHIERNAH: O, Lord!

A CHOLLEEN DHAS: my beautiful girl

A CHOLLEEN MACHREE: girl of my heart

ACHORA: my friend

ACHORA MACHREE: friend of my heart

ACUSHLA: my darling

ACUSHLA MACHREE: darling of my heart

ACUSHLA OGE: my young darling

AHAGUR: my love

A KAILLEY (to go): go on an evening visit or friendly call

ALANNA: my child

ALANNA DHAS: my beautiful child

AMIN A CHIERNAH: amen, O Lord!

ASTHORE: my treasure

A SUCHAR: my sweet, my love

AVILLISH: my darling

AVOURNEEN MACHREE: love of my heart

BANATH LATHT: goodbye (*lit.* blessing with you)

BODAGH: churl, vulgar upstart

BRINOGUE: 'a young fellow full of fun and frolic' (Carleton)

DUDEEN: short clay pipe

ERSHI MISHI: woe is me, alas!

FAREER GAIR: alas!

FEASTHALAGH: waste of time, nonsense

FULL BUT: with speed

KEOWT: low, contemptible fellow

KIND FATHER: inherited from the father

MA CHORP AN DIAOUL: my body to the devil!

MAVRONE: alas!

MAVOURNEEN: my love

PISHTHROGUE: charm, spell, witchcraft

PRASKEEN: apron
RATH: circular earthwork or mound
SEANACHIE: traditional story teller
SHIELING: hut of rough construction
SLANG: narrow strip of land along a stream, not suited to cultivation but grazed
SPRISSAUN: contemptible little person
THRANEEN: grass-stalk (i.e. very little)
VOTEEN: ostentatiously pious person

Note on the Text

The Black Prophet first appeared in the *Dublin University Magazine* from May to December 1846. The following year it was published in book form by Simms and M'Intyre of Belfast and London. Carleton did not make any changes in the text; in the preface he says that it was not 'in his power to revise or correct . . . in any way.' I have prepared this edition from the edition of 1899, which has a very small number of misprints and errors, but is substantially the same as the first edition.

TimothyWebb

University of Leeds.

LORD JOHN RUSSELL

MY LORD,—

Whenever I have dedicated any of my Works hitherto, I have always prefixed to them the name of some personal friend: in dedicating the following work to your Lordship, I would fain hope that I dedicate it to a friend of my country.

This is an Irish Book, my Lord, to which I would respect-fully solicit your Lordship's attention; it is painful to me to be obliged to add that it is written upon an exclusively Irish subject.

It is in your character of Prime Minister that I take the liberty of prefixing your Lordship's name to this " Tale of Irish Famine." Had Sir ROBERT PEEL been in office, I would have placed his name where that of your Lordship now stands. There is something not improper in this; for although I believe that both you and he are sincerely anxious to benefit our un-happy country, still I cannot help thinking that the man who, in his ministerial capacity, must be looked upon as a public exponent of those principles of Government which have brought our country to her present calamitous condition, by a long course of illiberal legislation and unjustifiable neglect, ought to have his name placed before a story which details with truth the sufferings which such legislation and neglect have entailed upon our people. This, my Lord, is not done from any want of respect to your Lordship, but because the writer trusts that, as it is the first Tale of Irish Famine that ever was dedicated to an English Prime Minister, your Lordship's enlarged and en-lightened policy will put it out of the power of any succeeding author ever to write another.

Permit me to say that your Lordship need not call in question the facts and circumstances depicted in it. It is, as I have stated, a tale of Irish suffering and struggle; and you may rest assured, my Lord, that there is no party in this country so well qualified to afford authentic information on this particular subject as those who have done most in giving an impulse to· and sustaining the literature of their country.

I have the honour to be, my Lord,

Your Lordship's obedient servant,

THE AUTHOR.

v

AUTHOR'S PREFACE

"A TALE of Irish Famine," published in a season of such unparalleled scarcity and destitution as the present, when our countrymen are perishing in thousands for want of food, ought, one would imagine, to excite a strong interest in the breasts of all those who can sympathize with them under sufferings so desolating and frightful. That the perusal of the present narrative may excite such an interest is not only the paramount wish of the author's heart, but constituted one of the purposes for which it was written. As it must, in this terrible crisis, be admitted that such a subject is one which involves the heart-rending consideration of life and death to an extent beyond all historic precedent, the author deems it necessary to state, at somewhat greater length, the motives which prompted him to select it. Having witnessed, last season, the partial, and in this the general failure of the potato crop, he anticipated, as every man must, the fearful visitation which is now almost decimating our wretched population; and it occurred to him that a narrative founded upon it, or, at all events, exhibiting through the medium of fiction an authentic detail of all that our unhappy and neglected country has suffered, during *past* privations of a similar kind, might be calculated to awaken those who legislate for us into something like a humane perception of a calamity that has been almost perennial in the country. Other motives mingled with this. He knew that the approaching destitution and misery would require all possible sympathy from every available source; and he hoped, as he has already said, that by placing before the eyes of those who had only heard of such inflictions faithful and unexaggerated pictures of all that the unhappy people suffer under them, he might, perchance, stir that sympathy into active and efficient benevolence, at a period when both were so wofully required. His object, however, went still farther. National inflictions of this kind pass away, and are soon forgotton by every one but those with whom they have left their melancholy memorials, to wit, the widow, the fatherless, the destitute, and all who look in vain around their desolate hearths for those on whose love and labour they had depended for the very means of sustaining life. Aware of this, then, and knowing besides, that the memory of our Legislature is as faithless on such a subject as that of the most heartless individual among us, the author deemed it an act of public usefulness to his countrymen, to re-

vii

cord in the following pages such an authentic history of those deadly periods of famine to which they have been so frequently subject, as could be relied upon with confidence by all who might feel an interest in placing them beyond the reach of this terrible scourge. In executing this task, the reader—especially if he be English or Scotch—may rest assured that the author has not at all coloured beyond the truth. The pictures and scenes represented are those which he himself witnessed in 1817, 1822, and other subsequent years; and if they be false or exaggerated, there are thousands still living who can come forward and establish their falsehood. They have been depicted, however, in the midst of living testimony, and they not only have escaped contradiction, but defy it. When the author refers to them in the *past* tense, it may be necessary to say that the contents of this volume appeared successively, during eight months, in the pages of the *Dublin University Magazine*, from which they are here collected, without—for so it happened—the author having had it in his power to revise or correct them in any way. But why talk of exaggeration or contradiction? Alas! do not the workings of death and desolation among us in the present time give them a fearful corroboration, and prove how far the strongest imagery of Fiction is frequently transcended by the terrible realities of Truth?

Let not the reader imagine, however, that the principal interest of this Tale is drawn from so gloomy a topic as famine. The author trusts that the workings of those passions and feelings which usually agitate human life, and constitute the character of those who act in it, will be found to constitute its chief attraction.

He has merely to say, in conclusion, that this work is the only item which he has been able to add to that Great Fund of Benevolence which the destitution of his country has called into existence, and to hope that the extensive circulation of this Tale of Famine among the higher and wealthier classes may, in the amplest sense, fulfil the objects for which it was written.

DUBLIN, *February 8th*, 1847.

INTRODUCTION

IT is a sad and significant commentary on the history of the past fifty years in Ireland that this reprint of *The Black Prophet*—a book first published in 1847, during a time of unexampled distress in Ireland, and written by Carleton with a view to calling public attention to the disastrous condition of the people—should appear just after a period when the most alarming reports were circulated of another impending famine which, according to some observers, threatened to almost equal that of "Black '47" in its effects. Whether well founded or not, the fear of such a calamity is an object-lesson in Irish misery. Carleton has not by any means exaggerated in this book (one of the most powerful stories he ever wrote) the appalling condition of the people who passed through the ghastly experiences of 1817 and 1822, therein described. Though written during the progress of the famine of 1846–47, his narrative concerns the earlier catastrophes. It was issued in a series called "The Parlour Library," and met with very great success, and it is passing strange that it was ever allowed to fall out of circulation. Such is the fact, however. For many years it has been unprocurable in any edition, and as its interest is perennial by reason of its subject alone, many readers will be glad to make or renew acquaintance with it. It has, moreover, distinct and absolute merits of its own. It is one of Carleton's best novels, and exhibits some of his cleverest natural descriptions and most powerful character-drawing. It has the additional advantage, too, of containing nothing offensive to any section of his countrymen, which is unusual in a writer who so frequently made use of the ambush of a story from which he could direct all the weapons suggested by viciousness against such of his countrymen, Protestant or Catholic, Nationalist or Loyalist, as he was temporarily opposed to. In *The Black Prophet* will be found neither sectarianism nor political propagandism. It is a genuine story of "hard times" in Ireland, by one who is admittedly supreme over all delineators of Irish life and character. Many other books by Carleton have gone out of print; some of them are rightly forgotten. *The Black Prophet*, however, and one or two others of the same period, such as *The Emigrants of Ahadarra*, are eminently worthy of a wide popularity. In no other Irish stories can such deep human interest, such mingled humour and pathos, irresistibly spontaneous and true, such masterly knowledge of the Irish peasantry, be met with. In many places these books suggest the immortal *Traits and Stories of the Irish Peasantry*, the work by which Carleton's name will be longest remembered, and even the *Traits and Stories* cannot show such intensely lurid descriptions as are to be found in one or two of the chapters on the famine in *The Black Prophet*, or more exquisite creations than the old patriarch and Dora McMahon in *The Emigrants of Ahadarra*.

The present novel attracted very great attention at the time of its publication, and much praise was awarded to it by the leading critical journals of the period; while its author was made the medium of various gifts of money towards the fund which was raised in England in aid of the peasantry's distress. Carleton expected great results from its popularity, in the direction of increased remuneration for his future works, and in the easier access to publishers, but he was oversanguine. In an unpublished letter, now lying before me, and dated from London three years after the publication of the novel, he writes to his daughter :—

"I called to Amen Corner, to Simms & McIntyre's [1] Lon-

---

[1] Simms & McIntyre, of Belfast and London, were the publishers of "The Parlour Library," in which series four of Carleton's novels appeared.

don establishment, and heard from an honest Englishman, who did not know who I was, that the sale of *my* works—especially *The Black Prophet*—is as extensive and active as when they first published them. This is a great advantage, and I hope before another year to have reached such a popularity as Dickens and Thackeray have at present, and consequently to have the English publishers at my feet and willing to come to my own terms." In another letter, he says, with some exaggeration : "You could not imagine my popularity, not only in London, but throughout England. My *Black Prophet* every one has read." So desirable a state of things from Carleton's point of view was unlikely to occur, and did not, in fact, occur. One or two London publishers did eventually issue books by him, but they were the works of his worst period, written when he had lost all his power, and their experiences with them were decidedly, and not unnaturally, discouraging. After 1848 Carleton wrote practically nothing worthy of his reputation. His work previous to that year had earned for him the proud titles of "a prose Burns," an "Irish Walter Scott," compliments which highly delighted him. His physical likeness to Scott was much more unmistakable than the similarity of his books to the "Waverley Novels"; but the title of "a prose Burns" might be sustained in many particulars. It is justified to a large extent by Carleton's strong human sympathies, his knowledge of the national life and idiom of his countrymen, his deep poetical feeling, his vigorous portraiture, and his inimitable and indomitable humour. The parallel might be still more closely drawn, perhaps, with regard to the character of the two men, for Carleton had all Burns' failings, but was without some of his good qualities. His career calls for a brief summary.

He was the youngest of fourteen children, and was born on February 20th (Shrove Tuesday), 1794, in the townland of Prillisk, and parish of Clogher, Co. Tyrone, where his father, a pious and excellent man, held a small farm. Both his parents were known far and wide for their extensive acquaintance with Irish legendary lore and minstrelsy, and their youngest son drank deep of their inexhaustible store of Irish tradition.[1] Hence the wonderful knowledge of Irish habits and phraseology, which, in after years, he turned to such good account. His earliest education was obtained at a hedge-school, but he eventually acquired considerable learning at one or two very good academies in his native county and in Louth. His father had set his heart upon one of his sons becoming a priest, and the future novelist was chosen for the sacred office. But Carleton had by this time formed certain views about the Catholic clergy, and even upon the religion of his fathers, which made it impossible to proceed further with the idea of making a priest of him. Soon after, his father died. Carleton had so far seen little of Ireland, the north-eastern portion of the country being the only part with which he could be said to have had any actual acquaintance. But the Carleton home was speedily broken up after the death of the father, and William Carleton soon set out on his travels, passing through all manner of rustic adventures, which are most graphically described in his deeply interesting *Autobiography* (published under the present writer's editorship in 1896), and were utilised largely by him in his stories. He had grown into a very tall, good-looking, athletic young fellow, famous for feats of daring and agility, noted as a dancer and as a wooer, and with, besides, a considerable reputation as a story-teller. In due time he found his way to Dublin, where, after some months of penury, he secured an appointment as tutor. While employed in this capacity, he met his future wife, a Miss Jane Anderson. He married on receiving an appointment as clerk in the offices of the Sunday School Society of Dublin, his salary then being what he considered the handsome one of £60 a year. It was during his stay in

---

[1] The original name of the family was O'Carolan.

this office that he began to write his earliest character-sketches and essays, which some of his friends pronounced admirable.

In 1827 he made the acquaintance of the Rev. Cæsar Otway, a picturesque writer upon Irish scenery and antiquities, but one who was warped by sour bigotry and a determined tendency to proselytism. Otway recognised Carleton's high intelligence, unequalled knowledge of the people, and saw that he would be of great service to him in his "No-Popery" crusade. Carleton, having definitely abandoned his early faith, entered into the plan with all the zeal of the apostate, and commenced a series of sketches of peasant life for a magazine conducted by Otway. Some of these, very considerably toned down in wiser moments by their author, and relieved of some of the acrid bitterness imported into them by Otway himself, or at his suggestion, formed, with a few unpublished sketches, the first series of the famous *Traits and Stories* published in two volumes in 1830. These tales immediately attracted special attention and a chorus of praise. Their success led to the publication of a second series, which came out in 1833, and was even more warmly received than the first, and [at once fixed his position as the greatest living authority on Irish peasant life. As an Irishman would say, one can almost smell the turf "off them."

English and Irish journals vied with each other in the praise they now bestowed upon Carleton, and he found several magazines open to his contributions. But he had a large family, and for many years was unable to live in even moderate comfort. Prices in Irish literary periodicals ruled very low, and it is very doubtful whether, with all his industry, Carleton earned £150 a year. The *Dublin University Magazine*, which was founded in 1833, welcomed all his contributions, and for a time paid for them at the rate of about sixteen guineas per sheet. That periodical was for many years the main resource of Carleton. Until 1838 he had written nothing but comparatively short stories or sketches of character, and now, despite the warnings of his friends that his genius was unfitted to cope with the novel proper, he began to write *Fardorougha the Miser*, which was completed and published in 1839. In this book, one of the best he ever wrote, the power and pathos displayed gave Carleton an easy triumph over those who had doubted his capacity for a more sustained flight than he had yet attempted. The novel was a conspicuous success, and even English critics, who hardly understood the emotional nature of the Celt, were greatly impressed by it. The *Athenœum*, in a comparison of Carleton's miser and Balzac's Père Grandet, admitted the greater truth to life of the Irish novelist's creation.

For the *Irish Penny Journal*, in 1840, Carleton wrote a most admirable series of Irish sketches called *Tales and Stories of the Irish Peasantry*. These were re-published later, with characteristic drawings by " Phiz," but have now been out of print for many years—a most inexplicable fact, for they are among Carleton's most humorous, most delightful writings. *Valentine McClutchy, Rody the Rover*, and *Paddy-go-Easy* followed the " Tales and Stories " very rapidly, and met with more or less success. But Carleton had, unfortunately, returned to his earlier habit of vituperation. *Valentine McClutchy*, which exhibits some of the most brilliant character-drawing in the whole range of Carleton's novels, and marvellous humour, is injured by the virulence of its attacks on the landlord class, whose enormities, great as they were, hardly justified such extreme venom as Carleton pours upon them. *Rody the Rover* is weak and ineffective, while *Paddy-go-Easy*, intended by its author to cure the indolence and recklessness of his countrymen, only exasperated them. They were, and are, highly offended at Carleton's implication that most Irishmen are like " Paddy-go-Easy." Nevertheless, there is a " power " of humour and of keen observation in the book. *The Black Prophet*, which Carleton always believed to be his best story,

and its successors, *The Emigrants of Ahadarra, The Tithe
Proctor,* and *Art Maguire, or The Broken Pledge,* complete
the list of the more notable works of this period of Carleton's
life. *Art Maguire* is a first-rate Temperance story, perhaps
the best that was ever written; but the *Tithe Proctor,* despite its occasional power, has done more to injure Carleton's
fame than anything he ever wrote. Chafing under what
he considered neglect by his countrymen, he assails them in
this book with all the violence at his command. He enumer-
ates all their genuine failings, exaggerates their few vices,
conceals or belittles all their virtues, and, in short, con-
tradicts and stultifies all his earlier record. This onslaught,
delivered just after Carleton had received a Civil List pension of £200 a year in answer to a petition from Ireland,
which was most influentially signed by people of all parties
and all religious beliefs, simply astounded the Irish public.
The explanation of what seems to be gross ingratitude is
that Carleton was mentally affected at the time. Constant
addiction to stimulants had undoubtedly weakened his brain,
and although some of the types in the novel are most deftly
handled, the book is, on the whole, a failure. It is useless
to disguise the fact that Carleton's greatest fault was his
weakness of principle. He was prepared to write for any or
every side provided he were paid for it. The one redeeming
feature about this moral blur upon him is that he so passion-
ately loved his family, so fondly doted upon his children,
that he was prepared to go to any lengths if, by doing so,
he could be in a position to meet their every want.

The remaining novels of Carleton do not call for mention,
with the possible exception of *Willy Reilly,* the most successful of all his writings, yet, in some measure, one of his
feeblest. It has run through at least fifty large editions.
But then it is founded upon an old romantic ballad which is
famous all over Ireland, and the remembrance of the loves
of Willy Reilly and his "dear Colleen Bawn" will sell
Carleton's novel to the end. *The Black Baronet, The*

Squanders of Castle Squander, etc., reflect no credit upon their author. They were written in times of decadence, and should be avoided by all who wish to get a favourable impression of Carleton's genius. He left behind him an unpublished novel, entitled *Anne Cosgrave*, which is a good deal better than much of his later published writings, and with careful pruning of the redundances and innuendoes characteristic of his worst books, might attract many readers.

Carleton died in Dublin on January 30th, 1869, and was buried in Mount Jerome Cemetery. He was not personally popular with any section of his countrymen, but all admired his genius. He was a peasant all his life, and never looked anything else. No writer has so intimately described Irish life—no other has ever known the people so thoroughly. The mystical side of the Celt has eluded his pen, but the every-day life of his native province is unapproachably delineated, especially in his *Traits and Stories*, of which one good critic has well said : " No one who does not know the things he tells knows Ireland," and which another, in the *Edinburgh Review* of many years ago, has most accurately described as " not only Irish, but thoroughly Irish, intensely Irish, exclusively Irish." " It is in his pages, and in his alone," says the same excellent writer, who has very severely criticised his faultier works, " that future generations must look for the truest and fullest, though still far from complete, picture of those who ere long will have passed away from that troubled land, from the records of history, and from the memory of man for ever."

D. J. O'DONOGHUE.

CHAPTER I

SOME twenty and odd years ago, there stood a little cabin at
the foot of a round hill that very much resembled a cupola
in shape, and which from its position and great height commanded a prospect of singular beauty. This hill was one of
a range that ran from north to south-west, but in consequence
of its standing, as it were, somewhat out of the ranks, its
whole appearance and character as a distinct feature of the
country were invested with considerable interest to a scienti-
fic eye, especially to' that of a geologist. An intersection or
abrupt glen divided it from those which constituted the range
or group we have alluded to ; through this, as a pass in the
country, and the only one for miles, wound a road into an
open district on the western side, which road, about half a
mile after its entering the glen, was met by a rapid torrent
that came down from the gloomy mountains that rose to the
left. The foot of this hill, which on the southern side was
green and fertile to the top, stretched off and was lost in the
rich land that formed the great and magnificent valley it
helped to bound, and to which the chasm we have described
was but an entrance ; the one bearing to the other, in size
and position, much the same relation that a small by-lane
in a country town bears to the great leading street which
constitutes its principal feature.

Noon had long passed, and the dim sun of a wet autumnal
day was sloping down towards the west through clouds and
gloom, when a young girl, about twenty-one or twenty-two
years of age, came out of the cabin we have mentioned, and
running up to the top of a little miniature hill or knoll

that rose beside it, looked round in every direction, as if anxious to catch a glimpse of some one whom she expected. It appeared, however, that she watched in vain; for, after having examined the country in every direction with an eye in which might be read a combined expression of eagerness, anger, and disappointment, she once more returned to the cabin with a slow and meditating step. This she continued to do from time to time for about an hour and a half, when at length a female appeared approaching, whom she at once recognized.

The situation of this hovel, for such, in fact, it must be termed, was not only strikingly desolate, but connected also with wild and supernatural terrors. From the position of the glen itself, a little within which it stood, it enjoyed only a very limited portion of the sun's cheering beams. As the glen was deep and precipitous, so was the morning light excluded from it by the north-eastern hills, as was that of evening by those which rose between it and the west. Indeed, it would be difficult to find a spot marked by a character of such utter solitude and gloom. Naturally barren, it bore not a single shrub on which a bird could sit or a beast browse, and little, of course, was to be seen in it but the bare gigantic projections of rock which shot out of its steep sides in wild and uncouth shapes, or the grey, rugged expanses of which it was principally composed. Indeed, we feel it difficult to say whether the gloom of winter or the summer's heat fell upon it with an air of lonelier desolation. It mattered not what change of season came, the place presented no appearance of man or his works. Neither bird, nor beast, was seen or heard, except rarely, within its dreary bosom, the only sounds it knew being the monotonous murmurs of the mountain torrent, or the wild echoes of the thunder-storms that pealed among the hills about it. Silence and solitude were the characteristics which predominated in it, and it would not be easy to say whether they were felt more during the gloom of November or the glare of June.

In the mouth of this glen, not far from the cabin we have described, two murders had been committed about twenty years before the period of our narrative, within the lapse of a month. The one was that of a carman, and the other of a man named Sullivan, who had also been robbed, as it was supposed the carman had been, for the bodies of both had been made away with, and were never found. This was evident—in the one case by the horse and cart of the carman remaining at the grey stone in question, on which the traces of blood were long visible; and in the other by the circumstance of Sullivan's hat and part of his coat having been found near the cabin in question on the following day, in a field through which his path home lay, and in which was a pool of blood, where his foot-marks were deeply imprinted, as if in a struggle for life and death. For this latter murder a man named Dalton had been taken up under circumstances of great suspicion, he having been the last person seen in the man's company. Both had been drinking together in the market, a quarrel had originated between them about money matters, blows had been exchanged, and Dalton was heard to threaten him in very strong language. Nor was this all. He had been observed following, or rather dogging, him on his way home, and although the same road certainly led to the residences of both, yet when his words and manner were taken into consideration, added to the more positive proof that the foot-marks left on the place of struggle exactly corresponded with his shoes, there could be little doubt that he was privy to Sullivan's murder and disappearance, as well probably as to his robbery. At all events the glen was said to be haunted by Sullivan's spirit, which was in the habit, according to report, of appearing near the place of murder, from whence he was seen to enter this chasm—a circumstance which, when taken in connection with its dark and lonely aspect, was calculated to impress upon the place the reputation of being accursed, as the scene of crime and supernatural appearances. We remember having played in it when young, and the feeling we experienced was one of awe and terror, to which might be added, on contemplating the "dread repose" and solitude around us, an impression that we were removed hundreds of miles from the busy on-goings and noisy tumults of life, to which, as if seeking protection, we generally hastened with a strong sense of relief, after having tremblingly gratified our boyish curiosity.

The young girl in question gave the female she had been expecting anything but a cordial or dutiful reception. In personal appearance there was not a point of resemblance between them, although the *tout ensemble* of each was singularly striking and remarkable. The girl's locks were black as the raven's wing; her figure was tall and slender, but elastic and full of symmetry. The ivory itself was not more white nor glossy than her skin; her teeth were bright and beautiful, and her mouth a perfect rosebud. It is unnecessary to say that her eyes were black and brilliant, for such ever belong to her complexion and temperament; but it *is* necessary to add that they were piercing and unsettled, and you felt that they looked into you rather than at you or upon you. In fact, her features were all perfect, yet it often happened that their general expression was productive of no agreeable feeling on the beholder. Sometimes her smile was sweet as that of an angel, but let a single impulse or whim be checked, and her face assumed a character of malignity that made her beauty appear like that which we dream of in an evil spirit.

The other woman, who stood to her in the relation of stepmother, was about the middle size. Her hair was sandy, or approaching to a pale red; her features were coarse, but regular; and her whole figure that of a well-made and powerful woman. In her countenance might be read a peculiar blending of sternness and benignity, each evidently softened down by an expression of melancholy—perhaps of suffering—as if some secret care lay brooding at her heart. The inside of the hovel itself had every mark of poverty and destitution

about it. Two or three stools, a pot or two, one miserable
standing-bed, and a smaller one gathered up under a rug
in the corner, were almost all that met the eye on entering
it ; and simple as these meagre portions of furniture were,
they bore no marks of cleanliness or care. On the contrary,
everything appeared to be neglected, squalid, and filthy ;
such, precisely, as led one to see at a glance that the inmates
of this miserable hut were contented with their wretched
state of life, and had no notion whatsoever that any moral
or domestic duty existed, by which they might be taught
useful notions of personal comfort or self-respect.

" So," said the young woman, addressing her stepmother
as she entered, " you're come back at last, an' a purty time
you tuck to stay away ! "

" Well," replied the other calmly, " I'm here now, at any
rate ; but I see you're in one of your tantrums, Sally, my
lady. What's wrong, I say ? In the meantime don't look
as you'd ait us widout salt."

" An' a bitther morsel you'd be," replied the younger, with
a flashing glance—" divil a more so. Here am I, sittin' or
runnin' out an' in these two hours, when I ought to be at
the dance in Kilnahushogue, before I go to Barney Gormly's
wake ; for I promised to be at both. Why didn't you come
home in time ? "

" Bekase, *achora*, it wasn't agreeable to me to do so. I'm
beginnin' to get ould an' stiff, an' it's time for me to take
care of myself."

" Stiffer may you be, then, soon, an' oulder may you never
be, an' that's the best I wish you ! "

" Aren't you afeard to talk to me that way ? " said the
elder of the two.

" No, not a bit. You won't flake me now as you used to
do. I am able an' willin' to give blow for blow at last, thank
goodness, an' will, too, if ever you thry that thrick."

The old woman gazed at her angrily, and appeared for a
moment to meditate an assault. After a pause, however,

during which the brief but vehement expression of rising
fury passed from her countenance, and her face assumed an
expression more of compassion than of anger, she simply said,
in a calm tone of voice,—

"I don't know that I ought to blame you so much for
your temper, Sarah. The darkness of your father's sowl is
upon yours; his wicked spirit is in you, an' may Heaven
above grant that you'll never carry about wid you, through
this unhappy life, the black an' heavy burden that weighs
down his heart! If God hasn't said it, you have his coorse,
or something nearly as bad, before you. Oh! go to the
wake as soon as you like, an' the dance, too. Find some
one that'll take you off my hands; that'll put a house over
your head, give you a bit to ait, an' a rag to put on you;
an' may God pity him that's doomed to get you! If the
woeful state of the counthry, an' the hunger an' the sickness
that's abroad, an' that's comin' harder an' faster on us every
day, can't tame you or keep you down, I dunna what will.
I'm sure the black an' terrible summer we've had ought to
make you think of how we'll get over all that's before us!
God pity you, I say agin, an' whatever poor man is to be
cursed wid you!"

"Keep your pity for them that wants it," replied the
other, "an' that's not me. As for God's pity, it isn't yours
to give, and even if it was, you stand in need of it yourself
more than I do: you're beginning to praich to us now that
you're not able to bate us; for that your praichments an'
your batins, may the divil pay you for all alike!—as he will
—an' that's my prayer."

A momentary gush of the stepmother's habitual passion
overcame her; she darted at her stepdaughter, who sprang
to her limbs, and flew at her in return. The conflict at first
was brief, for the powerful strength of the elder female soon
told. Sarah, however, quickly disengaged herself, and seizing an old knife which lay on a shelf that served as a dresser,
she made a stab at the very heart of her stepmother, panting

as she did it with an exulting vehemence of vengeance that
resembled the growl which a savage beast makes when
springing on its prey.

"Ha!" she exclaimed, "you have it now—you have it!
Call on God's pity now, for you will soon want it. Ha! ha!"

The knife, however, owing to the thick layers of cloth with
which the dress of the other was patched, as well as to the
weakness of the thin and worn blade, did not penetrate her
clothes, nor render her any injury whatsoever. The contest
was again resumed. Sarah, perceiving that she had missed
her aim, once more put herself in a posture to renew the
deadly attempt; and the consequence was, that a struggle
now took place between them which might almost be termed
one for life and death. It was indeed a fearful and unnatural struggle. The old woman, whose object was, if possible,
to disarm her antagonist, found all her strength—and it was
great—scarcely a match for the murderous ferocity which
was now awakened in her. The grapple between them consequently became furious; and such was the terrible impress
of diabolical malignity which passion stamped upon the features of this young tigress, that her stepmother's heart for a
moment quailed on beholding it, especially when associated
with the surprising activity and strength which she put
forth. Her dark and finely-pencilled eyebrows were fiercely
knit, as it were, into one dark line; her lips were drawn
back, displaying her beautiful teeth, that were now ground
together into what resembled the lock of death; her face was
pale with overwrought resentment, and her deep-set eyes
glowed with a wild and flashing fire that was fearful, whilst
her lips were encircled with the white foam of revengeful and
deadly determination; and what added most to the terrible
expression of her whole face was the exulting smile of cruelty
which shed its baleful light over it, resolving the whole contest, as it were, and its object—the murder of her stepmother
—into the fierce play of some beautiful vampire that was
ravening for the blood of its awakened victim.

After a struggle of some two or three minutes, the strength and coolness of the stepmother at length prevailed. She wrested the knife out of Sarah's hands, and, almost at the same moment, stumbled and fell. The other, however, was far from relaxing her hold. On the contrary, she clung to her fiercely, shouting out—

"I won't give you up yet—I love you too well for that— no, no, it's fond of you I'm gettin'. I'll hug you, mother dear; ay will I, and kiss you too, an' lave my mark behind me!" and, as she spoke, her stepmother felt her face coming in savage proximity to her own.

"If you don't keep away, Sarah," said the other, "I'll stab you. What do you mane, you bloody divil? Is it goin' to tear my flesh wid your teeth you are? Hould off! or, as Heaven's above us, I'll stab you with the knife."

"You can't," shouted the other: "the knife's bent, or you'd be done for afore this. I'll taste your blood for all that!" and, as the words were uttered, the stepmother gave a sudden scream, making at the same time a violent effort to disentangle herself, which she did.

Sarah started to her feet, and flying towards the door, exclaimed, with shouts of wild triumphant laughter—

"Ha, ha, ha! do you feel anything? I was near havin' the best part of one of your ears—ha, ha, ha!—but unfortunately I missed it; an' now look to yourself. Your day is gone, an' mine is come. I've tasted your blood, and I like it —ha, ha, ha!—an' if, as you say, it's kind father for me to be fond o' blood, I say you had better take care of yourself. And I tell you more: we'll take care of your fair-haired beauty for you—my father an' myself will—an' I'm to act against her, an' I will too; and you'll see what we'll bring your pet, *Gra Gal* Sullivan, to yet! There's news for you!"

She then went down to the river which flowed past, in whose yellow and turbid waters—for it was now swollen with rain—she washed the blood from her hands and face with an apparently light heart. Having meditated for some

time, she fell a-laughing at the fierce conflict that had just
taken place, exclaiming to herself—

"Ha, ha, ha! Well, now, if I had killed her—got the
ould knife into her heart—I might lave the counthry. If I
had killed her now, throth it 'ud be a good joke, an' all in a
fit of passion, bekase she didn't come home in time to let me
meet him. Well, I'll go back an' spake soft to her, or, afther
all, she'll give me a hard life of it."

She returned, and, having entered the hut, perceived that
the ear and cheek of her stepmother were still bleeding.

"I'm sorry for what I did," she said, with the utmost
frankness and good-nature. "Forgive me, mother; you
know I'm a hasty divil—for a divil's limb I am, no doubt of
it. Forgive me, I say—do now—here, I'll get somethin' to
stop the blood."

She sprang at the moment, with the agility of a wild cat,
upon an old chest that stood in the corner of the hut, exhibiting, as she did it, a leg and foot of surpassing symmetry
and beauty. By stretching herself up to her full length, she
succeeded in pulling down several old cobwebs that had been
for years in the corner of the wall; and in the act of doing
so, disturbed some metallic substance, which fell first upon
the chest, from which it trundled off to the ground, where it
made two or three narrowing circles and then lay at rest.

"Murdher alive, mother!" she exclaimed, "what is this?
Hallo! a tobaccy-box—a fine round tobaccy-box of iron, bedad
—an' what's this on it?—let me see; two letthers. Wait till
I rub the rust off; or stay, the rust shows them as well.
Let me see—P, an' what's the other? ay, an M. P.M.—
arrah, what can that be for? Well, divil may care; let it
lie on the shelf there. Here now—none of your cross looks,
I say—put these cobwebs to your face, an' they'll stop the
bleedin'. Ha, ha, ha!—well—ha, ha, ha!—but you *are* a
sight to fall in love wid this minute!" she exclaimed, laughing heartily at the blood-stained visage of the other. "You
won't spake, I see. Divil may care then, if you don't you'll

do the other thing—let it alone : but, at any rate, there's
the cobwebs for you, if you like to put them on; an' so *banath
lath*,[1] an' let that be a warnin' to you not to rise your hand
to me agin."

> " ' A sailor coorted a farmer's daughter,
> That lived contaygious to the Isle of Man,' " etc., etc.

She then directed her steps to the dance in Kilnahushogue,
where one would actually suppose, if mirth, laughter, and
extraordinary buoyancy of spirits could be depended on, that
she was gifted, in addition to her remarkable beauty, with
the innocent and delightful disposition of an angel.

The stepmother, having dressed the wound as well as she
could, sat down by the fire and began to ruminate on the
violent contest which had just taken place, and in which she
had borne such an unfortunate part. This was the first open
and determined act of personal resistance which she had
ever, until that moment, experienced at her stepdaughter's
hands; but now she feared that, if they were to live, as
heretofore, under the same roof, their life should be one of
perpetual strife—perhaps of ultimate bloodshed—and that
these domestic brawls might unhappily terminate in the
death of either. She felt that her own temper was none of
the best, and knew that so long as she was incapable of re-
straining it, or maintaining her coolness under the provoca-
tions to which the violent passions of Sarah would necessarily
expose her, so long must such conflicts as that which had
just occurred take place between them. She began now to
fear Sarah, with whose remorseless disposition she was too
well acquainted, and came to the natural conclusion, that a
residence under the same roof was by no means compatible
with her own safety.

"She has been a curse to me!" she went on, unconsciously
speaking aloud; "for when she wasn't able to bate me herself, her father did it for her. The divil is said to be fond of

---

[1] Good-night.

his own ; an' so does he doat on her, bekase she's his image
in everything that's bad. A hard life I'll lead between them
from this out, espeshially now that she has got the upper
hand of me. Yet what else can I expect or desarve ? This
load that's on my conscience is worse. Night and day I'm
sufferin' in the sight of God, an' actin' as if I wasn't to be
brought in judgment afore him. What am I to do ? I wish
I was in my grave! But then, again, how am I to face
death ?—and that same's not the worst; for afther death
comes judgment ! May the Lord prepare me for it, an' guide
an' direct me how to act ! One thing, I know, must be done
—aither she or I will lave this house ; for live undher the
same roof wid her I will not."

She then rose up, looked out of the door a moment, and,
resuming her seat, went on with her soliloquy—

" No ; he said it was likely he wouldn't be home to-night.
Wanst he gets upon his ould prophecies, he doesn't care how
long he stays away ; an' why he can take the delight he does
in prophesyin' and foretellin' good or evil, accordin' as it
sarves his purpose, I'm sure I don't know—espeshially
when he only laughs in his sleeve at the people for believin
him ; but what's that about poor *Gra Gal* Sullivan ? She
threatened her, and spoke of her father, too, as bein' in it.
Ah, ha ! I must watch him there ; an' you, too, my lady-divil
—for it 'ill go hard wid me if aither of you injure a hair of
her head. No, no, plaise God !—none of your evil doin's or unlucky prophecies for her, so long, any way, as I can presarve
her from them. How black the evenin' is gatherin' ! but,
God knows it's it that's the awful saison all out for harvest
weather—it is that—it is that ! "

Having given utterance to these sentiments, she took up
the tobacco-box which Sarah had, in such an accidental
manner, tumbled out of the wall, and surveying it for some
moments, laid it hastily on the chest, and, clasping her hands,
exclaimed—

" Saviour of life ! it's the same ! Oh, marciful God, it's

thrue! it's thrue! the very same I seen wid him that evenin'. I know it by the broken hinge an' the two letthers. The Lord forgive me my sins!—for I see now that do what we may, or hide it as we like, God is above all! Saviour of life, how will this end?—an' what will I do?—or how am I to act? But any way, I must hide this, and put it out of his reach."

She accordingly went out, and having ascertained that no person saw her, thrust the box up under the thatch of the roof in such a way that it was impossible to suspect, by any apparent disturbance of the roof, that it was there; after which, she sat down with sensations of dread that were new to her, and that mingled themselves as strongly with her affections as it was possible for a woman of a naturally firm and undaunted character to feel them.

CHAPTER II

THE BLACK PROPHET PROPHESIES

At a somewhat more advanced period of the same evening, two men were on their way from the market-town of Bally-nafail, towards a fertile portion of a country, named Aughamurran, which lay in a southern direction from it. One of them was a farmer, of middling, or rather of strug-gling, circumstances, as was evident from the traces of wear and tear that were visible upon a dress that had once been comfortable and decent, although it now bore the marks of careful, though rather extensive repair. He was a thin, placid-looking man, with something, however, of a careworn expression in his features, unless when he smiled, and then his face beamed with a look of kindness and good-will that could not readily be forgotten. The other was a strongly-built man, above the middle size, whose complexion and features were such as no one could look on with indifference, so strongly were they indicative of a two-fold character, or, we should rather say, calculated to make a twofold impression.

At one moment you might consider him handsome, and at another his countenance filled you with an impression of repugnance, if not of absolute aversion, so stern and inhuman were the characteristics which you read in it.   His hair, beard, and eyebrows were an ebon black, as were his eyes; his features were hard and massive; his nose, which was somewhat hooked, but too much pointed, seemed as if, whilst in a plastic state, it had been sloped by a trowel towards one side of his face, a circumstance which, whilst taken in connexion with his black whiskers that ran to a point near his mouth, and piercing eyes that were too deeply and narrowly set, gave him, aided by his heavy eyebrows, an expression at once of great cruelty and extraordinary cunning.   This man, whilst travelling in the same direction with the other, had suffered himself to be overtaken by him; in such manner, however, that their coming in contact could not be attributed to any particular design on his part.

" Why, then, *Donnel Dhu,*" said the farmer, " sure it's a sight for sore eyes to see you in this side of the counthry; an' now that I do see you, how are you ?"

" Jist the ould six-an'-eightpence, Jerry; and how is the Sullivan blood in you, man alive ? good an' ould blood it is, in troth; how is the family ?"

" Why, we can't —hut, what was I going to say ?" replied his companion; " we can't—complain—*ershi mishi !*—why, then, God help us, it's we that can complain, Donnel, if there was any use in it; but, *mavrone,* there isn't; so all I can say is, that we're just mixed midlin', like the praties in harvest, or hardly that same, indeed, since this woful change that has come on us."

" Ay, ay," replied the other ; " but if that change has come on you, you know it didn't come without warnin' to the counthry ; there's a man livin' that foretould as much—that seen it comin'—ay, ever since the pope was made prisoner, for that was what brought Bonaparte's fate—that's now the cause of the downfall of everything upon him."

" An it was the hard fate for us, as well as for himself,"
replied Sullivan; " little he thought, or little he cared, for
what he made us suffer, an' for what he's makin' us suffer
still, by the come-down that the prices have got."

" Well, but he's sufferin' himself more than any of us,"
replied Donnel; " however, that was prophesied too; it's read
of in the ould Chronicles. ' An eagle will be sick,' says St.
Columbkill, ' but the bed of the sick eagle is not a tree, but
a rock; an' there he must suffer till the curse of the Father [1]
is removed from him; an' then he'll get well, an' fly over the
world."

" Is that in the prophecy, Donnel ? "

" It's St. Columbkill's words I'm spakin'."

" Throth, at any rate," replied Sullivan, " I didn't care we
had back the war prices again; aither that or that the dear
rents wor let down to meet the poor prices we have now.
This woful saison, along wid the low prices and the high
rents, houlds out a black and terrible look for the counthry,
God help us ! "

" Ay," returned the Black Prophet, for it was he, " if you
only knew it."

" Why, was that, too, prophesied ? " inquired Sullivan.

" Was it ? No; but ax yourself *is* it. Isn't the Almighty,
in his wrath, this moment proclaimin' it through the heavens
and the airth ? Look about you, and say what is it you see
that doesn't foretell famine—famine—famine! Doesn't the
dark wet day, an' the rain, rain, rain, foretell it? Doesn't the
rottin' crops, the unhealthy air, an' the green damp foretell
it? Doesn't the sky without a sun, the heavy clouds, an' the
angry fire of the West foretell it? Isn't the airth a page of
prophecy, an' the sky a page of prophecy, where every
man may read of famine, pestilence, an' death? The airth is
softened for the grave, an' in the black clouds of heaven you
may see the death-hearse movin' slowly along—funeral afther

[1] That is—the Pope, in consequence of Bonaparte having imprisoned him.

funeral—funeral afther funeral—an' nothing to folly them but lamentation an' woe, by the widow an' orphan—the fatherless, the motherless, an' the childless—woe an' lamentation—lamentation an' woe."

Donnel Dhu, like every prophecy-man of his kind—a character in Ireland, by the way, that has nearly, if not altogether disappeared—was provided with a set of prophetic declamations suited to particular occasions and circumstances, and these he recited in a voice of high and monotonous recitative, that caused them to fall with a very impressive effect upon the minds and feelings of his audience. In addition to this, the very nature of his subject rendered a figurative style and suitable language necessary, a circumstance which, aided by a natural flow of words, and a felicitous illustration of imagery—for which, indeed, all prophecy-men were remarkable—had something peculiarly fascinating and persuasive to the class of persons he was in the habit of addressing. The gifts of these men, besides, were exercised with such singular delight, that the constant repetition of their oracular exhibitions by degrees created an involuntary impression on themselves, that ultimately rose to a kind of wild and turbid enthusiasm, partaking at once of imposture and fanaticism. Many of them were, therefore, nearly as much the dupies of the delusions that proceeded from their own heated imaginations as the ignorant people who looked upon them as oracles; for we know that nothing so much generates imposture as credulity.

" Indeed, Donnel," replied Sullivan, " what you say is unfortunately too thrue. Everything we can look upon appears to have the mark of God's displeasure on it; but if we have dearth and sickness now, what'll become of us this time twelvemonths, when we'll feel this failure most ? "

" I have said it," replied the prophet; " an' if my tongue doesn't tell the truth, the tongue that never tells a lie will."

" And what tongue is that ? " asked his companion.

" The tongue of the death-bell will tell it day after day to every parish in the land. However, we know that death's before us, an' the grave, afther all, is our only consolation."

" God help us ! " exclaimed Sullivan, " if we hadn't betther an' brighter consolation than the grave. Only for the hopes in our Divine Redeemer an' His mercy, it's little consolation the grave could give us. But, indeed, Donnel, as you say everything about us is enough to sink the heart within one— an' no hope at all of a change for the betther. However, God is good, an' if it's *His* will that we should suffer, it's our duty to submit to it."

The prophet looked around him with a gloomy aspect, and, truth to say, the appearance of everything on which the eye could rest, was such as gave unquestionable indications of wide-spread calamity to the country.

The evening, which was now far advanced, had impressed on it a character of such dark and hopeless desolation as weighed down the heart with a feeling of cold and chilling gloom that was communicated by the dreary aspect of every-thing around. The sky was obscured by a heavy canopy of low, dull clouds that had about them none of the grandeur of storm, but lay overhead charged with those wintry deluges which we feel to be so unnatural and alarming in autumn, whose bounty and beauty they equally disfigure and destroy. The whole summer had been sunless and wet—one, in fact, of ceaseless rain, which fell day after day, week after week, and month after month, until the sorrowful consciousness had arrived that any change for the better must now come too late, and that nothing was certain but the terrible union of famine, disease, and death which was to follow. The season, owing to the causes specified, was necessarily late, and such of the crops as *were* ripe had a sickly and unthriving look, that told of comparative failure, whilst most of the fields which, in other autumns, would have been ripe and yellow, were now covered with a thin, backward crop, so unnaturally green, that all hope of maturity was out of the question. Low meadows were in a state of inundation, and on alluvial soils the ravages of the floods were visible in layers of mud and gravel that were deposited over many of the prostrate corn-fields. The peat turf lay in oozy and neglected heaps, for there had not been sun enough to dry it sufficiently for use, so that the poor had want of fuel, and cold to feel, as well as want of food itself. Indeed, the appearance of the country, in consequence of this wetness in the firing, was singularly dreary and depressing. Owing to the difficulty with which it burned, or rather wasted away, without light or heat, the eye, in addition to the sombre hue which the absence of the sun cast over all things, was forced to dwell upon the long black masses of smoke which trailed slowly over the whole country, or hung, during the thick sweltering calms, in broad columns that gave to the face of nature an aspect strikingly dark and disastrous, when associated, as it was, with the destitution and suffering of the great body of the people. The general appearance of the crops was indeed deplorable. In some parts the grain was beaten down by the rain; in airier situations it lay cut but unsaved, and scattered over the fields, awaiting an occasional glimpse of feeble sunshine; and in other and richer soils whole fields, deplorably lodged, were green with the destructive exuberance of a second growth. The season, though wet, was warm; and it is unnecessary to say, that the luxuriance of all weeds and unprofitable productions was rank and strong, whilst an unhealthy fermentation pervaded everything that was destined for food. A brooding stillness, too, lay over all nature; cheerfulness had disappeared, even the groves and hedges were silent, for the very birds had ceased to sing, and the earth seemed as if it mourned for the approaching calamity, as well as for that which had been already felt. The whole country, in fact, was weltering and surging with the wet formed by the incessant overflow of rivers, whilst the falling cataracts, joined to a low, monotonous hiss, or what the Scotch term *sugh*, poured their faint but dismal murmurs on the gloomy silence which otherwise prevailed around.

Such was the aspect of the evening in question; but as the men advanced, a new element of desolation and dismay soon became visible. The sun, ere he sank among the dark western clouds, shot out over this dim and miserable prospect a light so angry, yet so ghastly, that it gave to the whole earth a wild, alarming, and spectral hue, like that seen in some feverish dream. In this appearance there were great terror and sublimity, for as it fell upon the black, shifting clouds, the effect was made still more awful by the accidental resemblance which they bore to coffins, hearses, and funeral processions, as observed by the prophecy-man, all of which seemed to have been lit up against the deepening shades of evening by some gigantic death-light that superadded its fearful omens to the gloomy scene on which it fell.

The sun as he then appeared might not inaptly be compared to some great prophet, who, clothed with the majesty and terror of an angry God, was commissioned to launch his denunciations against the iniquity of nations, and to reveal to them, as they lay under the shadow of his wrath, the terrible calamities with which he was about to visit their transgressions.

The two men now walked on in silence for some time, Donnel Dhu having not deemed it necessary to make any reply to the pious and becoming sentiments uttered by Sullivan. At length the latter spoke—

"Barrin' what we all know, Donnel, an' that's the saison an' the sufferin' that's in it, is there no news stirrin' at all? Is it thrue that ould Dick o' the Grange is drawin' near to his last account?"

"Not so bad as that; but he's still complainin'. It's one day up and another day down wid him—an' of coorse his laise of life can't be long now."

"Well, well," responded Sullivan, "it's not for us to pass judgment on our fellow-craturs; but by all accounts he'll have a hard reckonin'."

"That's his own affair, you know," said Donnel Dhu;

" but his son, Masther Richard, or ' Young Dick,' as they
call him, will be an improvement upon the ould stock."

" As to that, some says ay, an' some says no ; but I believe
myself, that he has, like his father, both good an' bad in
him ; for the ould man, if the maggot bit him, or that he
took the notion, would do one a good turn ; an' if he took a
likin' to you, he'd go any lin'th to sarve you ; but, then, you
were never sure of him—nor he didn't himself know this
minute what he'd do the next."

" That's thrue enough," replied Donnel Dhu ; " but lavin'
him to shift for himself, I'm of opinion that you an' I are
likely to get wet jackets before we're much oulder.　Ha !
Did you see that lightnin' ?　God presarve us ! it was terrible
—an' ay, there it is—the thundher at this hour is very fearful.　I would give a thrifle to be in my own little cabin, an'
indeed I'm afeard that I won't be worth the washin' when I
get there, if I can go back sich a night as it's goin' to be."

" The last few years Donnel, has brought a grievous
change on me and mine,'· replied Sullivan.　" The time was,
an' it's not long since, when I could give you a comfortable
welcome as well as a willin' one ; however, thank God, it
isn't come to sich a hard pass wid me yet that I haven't a
roof an' a bit to ait to offer you ; an' so to sich as it is you're
heartily welcome.　Home ! oh, you mustn't talk of home this
night.　Blood, you know, is thicker than wather, an' if it
was only on your wife Nelly's account you should be welcome.
Second an' third cousins by the mother's side we are, an' that's
purty strong.　Oh, no, don't talk of goin' home this night."

" Well," replied the other, " I'm thankful to you, Jerry,
an', indeed, as the night's comin' on so hard and stormy, I'll
accept your kind offer ; a mouthful of anything will do me,
an' a dry sate at your hearth till mornin'."

" Unfortunately, as I said," replied Sullivan, " ti's but
poor an' humble tratement I can give you ; but if it was
betther you should jist be as welcome to it, an' what more
can I say ? "

"What more can you say, indeed! I know your good
heart, Jerry, as who doesn't? Dear me, how it's powerin'
over there towards the south—ha, there it is again, that
thundher! Well, thank goodness, we haven't far to go, at
any rate, an' the shower hasn't come round this far yet. In
the mane time let us step out an' thry to escape it if we can."

"Let us cross the fields, then," said Sullivan, "an' get
up home by the *Slang*, an' then behind our garden; to be
sure, the ground is in a sad plash, but then it will save a
long twist round the road, an' as you say, we may escape the
rain yet."

Both accordingly struck off the highway, and took a short
path across the fields, whilst at every step the water spurted
up out of the spongy soil, so that they were soon wet nearly
to the knees, so thoroughly saturated was the ground with
the rain which had incessantly fallen. After toiling through
plashy fields, they at length went up, as Sullivan had said,
by an old unfrequented footpath, that ran behind his garden,
the back of which consisted of a thick elder hedge, through
which scarcely the heaviest rain could penetrate. At one
end of this garden, through a small angle, forming a *cul de
sac*, or point, where the hedge was joined by one of whitethorn, ran the little obsolete pathway alluded to, and as
another angle brought them at once upon the spot we are
describing, it would so happen that if any one had been
found there when they appeared, it would have been impossible to leave it if they wished to do so, without directly
meeting them, there being no other mode of egress from it
except by the footway in question.

In that sheltered nook, then, our travellers found a young
man about two or three-and-twenty, holding the unresisting
hand of a very beautiful and bashful-looking girl, not more
than nineteen, between his. From their position, and the
earnestness with which the young peasant addressed her,
there could be little doubt as to the subject matter of their
conversation. If a bolt from the thunder which had been

rolling a little before among the mountains, and which was still faintly heard in the distance, had fallen at the feet of the young persons in question, it could not have filled them with more alarm than the appearance of Sullivan and the prophet. The girl, who became pale and red by turns, hung her head, then covered her face with her hands; and after a short and ineffectual struggle, burst into tears, exclaiming—

"Oh, my God, it is my father!"

The youth, for he seemed scarcely to have reached maturity, after a hesitating glance at Sullivan, seemed at once to have determined on the course of conduct he should pursue. His eye assumed a bold and resolute look—he held himself more erect—and turning towards the girl, without removing his gaze from her father, he said in a loud and manly tone—

"Dear Mave, it is foolish to be frightened. What have you done that ought to make you aither ashamed or afeared? If there's blame anywhere, it's mine, not yours, an' I'll bear it."

Sullivan, on discovering this stolen interview—for such it was—felt precisely as a man would feel who found himself unexpectedly within the dart of a rattlesnake, with but one chance of safety in his favour, and a thousand against him. His whole frame literally shook with the deadly depth of his resentment; and in a voice which fully betrayed its vehemence, he replied—

"Blame! ay, shame an' blame—sin an' sorrow there is, an' ought to rest upon her for this unnatural an' cursed meetin! Blame! surely, an' as I stand here to witness her shame, I tell her that there would not be a just God in heaven, if she's not yet punished for houldin' this guilty discoorse with the son of the man that has her uncle's blood —my only brother's blood—on his hand of murdher——"

"It's false," replied the young fellow, with kindling eye; "it's false, from your teeth to your marrow. I know my father's heart an' his thought—an' I say, that whoever charges him with the murder of your brother, is a liar—a false and damnable li——"

He checked himself ere he closed the sentence.

"Jerry Sullivan," said he, in an altered voice, "I ax your pardon for the words—it's but natural you should feel as you do; but if it was any other man than yourself that brought the charge of blood against my father, I would tramp upon him where he stands."

"An' maybe murdher him, as my poor brother was murdhered. Dalton, I see the love of blood in your eye," replied Sullivan bitterly.

"Why," returned the other, "you have no proof that the man was murdered at all. His body was never found; and no one can say what became of him. For all that any one knows to the contrary, he may be alive still."

"Begone, sirra," said Sullivan, in a burst of impetuous resentment, which he could not restrain, "if I ever know you to open your lips to that daughter of mine—if the mane crature can be my daughter—I'll make it be the blackest deed but one that ever a Dalton did; an' as for you—go in at wanst—I'll make you hear me by-and-bye."

Dalton looked at him once more with a kindling, but a smiling eye.

"Spake what you like," said he—"I'll curb myself. Only, if you wish your daughter to go in, you had betther lave the way, and let her pass."

Mave—for such was her name—with trembling limbs, burning blushes, and palpitating heart, then passed from the shady angle where they stood; but ere she did, one quick and lightning glance was bestowed upon her lover, which, brief through it was, he felt a sufficient consolation for the enmity of her father.

The prophet had not yet spoken; nor indeed had time been given him to do so, had he been inclined. He looked on, however, with a surprise, which soon assumed the appearance, as well as the reality, of some malignant satisfaction, which he could not conceal. He eyed Dalton with a grin of peculiar bitterness.

" Well," said he, " it's the general opinion that if any one knows or can tell what the future may bring about, I can; an' if my knowledge doesn't desave me, Dalton, I think, while you're before me, that I'm looking at a man that was never born to be drowned at any rate. I prophesy that, die when you may, you'll live to see your own funeral."

" If you're wise," replied the young man, " you'll not provoke me now. Jerry Sullivan may say what he wishes —he's safe—an' he knows why; but I warn you, Donnel Dhu, to take no liberty with me—I'll not bear it."

" Troth, I don't blame Jerry Sullivan," rejoined the prophet. " Of coorse, no man would wish to have a son-in-law hanged. It's the prophecy that you'll go to the surgeons yet."

" Did you foresee in your prophecies this mornin', that you'd get yourself well drubbed before night?" asked Dalton, bristling up.

" No," said the other, " my prophecy seen no one able to do it."

" You an' your prophecy are liars, then," retorted the other; " an' in the doom you're kind enough to give me, don't be too sure but you meant yourself. There's more of murdher an' the gallows in your face than there is in mine. That's all I'll say, Donnel. Anything else you may get from me will be a blow; so take care of yourself."

" Let him alone, Donnel," said Sullivan; " it's not safe to meddle with one of his name. You don't know what harm he may do you."

" I'm not afeared of him," said the prophet, with a sneer; " he'll find himself a little mistaken, if he tries his hand. It won't be for me you'll hang, my lad."

The words were scarcely uttered, when a terrific blow on the eye, struck with the rapidity of lightning, shot him to the earth, where he lay for about half-a-minute, apparently insensible. He then got up, and after shaking his head, as if to rid himself of a sense of confusion and stupor, looked at Dalton for some time.

" Well," said he, " it's all over now—but the truth is, the fault was my own. I provoked him too much, an' without any occasion. I am sorry you struck me, Condy, for I was only joking all the time. I never had ill-will against you; an' in spite of what has happened, I haven't now."

A feeling of generous regret, almost amounting to remorse, instantly touched Dalton's heart; he seized the hand of Donnel, and expressed his sorrow for the blow which he had given him.

" My God ! " he exclaimed, " why did I strike you ? But no one could for a miuute suppose that you weren't in airnest."

" Well, well," said the other, " let it be a warnin' to both of us; to me, in the first place, never to carry a joke too far ; and to you, never to allow your passion to get the betther of you, afeared you might give a blow in anger that you'd have cause to repent of all the days of your life. My eye and cheek is in a frightful state; but no matther, Condy, I forgive you, especially in the hope that you'll mark my advice."

Dalton once more asked his pardon, and expressed his most unqualified sorrow for what had occurred; after which he again shook hands with Donnel, and departed.

Sullivan felt amazed at this *rencontre*, especially at the nature of its singular and unexpected termination ; he seemed, however, to fall into a meditative and gloomy mood, and observed, when Dalton had gone—

"If ever I had any doubt, Donnel, that my poor brother owed his death to a Dalton, I haven't it now."

"I don't blame you much for sayin' so," replied Donnel. "I'm sorry myself for what happened, and especially as you were present. I'm afeard, indeed, that a man's life would be but little in that boy's hands undher a fit of passion. I provoked him too much though."

" I think so," said Sullivan. " Indeed, to tell you the truth, I had as little notion that you wor jokin' as he had."

"That's my dhrame out last night at all events,"said Donnel.

"How is that?" asked Sulliyan, as they approached the door.

"Why," said he, "I dreamt that I was lookin' for a hammer at your house, an' I thought that you hadn't one to give me; but your daughter Mave came to me, and said 'Here's a hammer for you, Donnel, an' take care of it, for it belongs to Condy Dalton.' I thought I took it, an' the first thing I found myself doin' was drivin' a nail in what appeared was my own coffin. The same dhrame would alarm me, but that I know that dhrames go by contrairies, as I've reason to think this will."

"No man understands these things better than yourself, Donnel," said Sullivan; "but, for my part, I think, there's a dangerous kick in the boy that jist left us; an' I'm much mistaken or the world will hear of it, an' know it yet."

"Well, well," said Donnel Dhu, in a very Christian-like spirit, "I fear you're right, Jerry; but still let us hope for the best."

As he spoke they entered the house.

CHAPTER III

A FAMILY ON THE DECLINE—OMENS

JERRY SULLIVAN'S house and place had about them all the marks and tokens of gradual decline. The thatch on the roof had begun to get black, and in some places it was sinking into rotten ridges; the yard was untidy and dirty; the walls and hedges were broken and dismantled; and the gates were lying about, or swinging upon single hinges. The whole air of the premises was uncomfortable to the spectator, who could not avoid feeling that there existed in the owner either wilful neglect or unsuccessful struggle. The chimneys, from which the thatch had sunk down, stood up with the incrustations of lime that had been trowelled round their bases, projecting uselessly out from them; some of the quoins had fallen from the gable; the plaster came off the walls in several places, and the whitewash was sadly discoloured.

Inside, the aspect of everything was fully as bad, if not worse. Tables and chairs, and the general furniture of the house, had all that character of actual cleanliness and apparent want of care, which poverty superinduces upon the most strenuous efforts of industry. The floor was beginning to break up into holes; tables and chairs were crazy; the dresser, though clean, had a cold, hungry, and unfurnished look; and what was unquestionably the worst symptom of all, the inside of the chimney-brace, where formerly the sides and flitches of deep, fat bacon, grey with salt, were arranged in goodly rows, now presented nothing but the bare and dust-covered hooks, from which they had depended in happier times. About a dozen of herrings hung at one side of a worn salt-box, and at the other a string of onions that was now nearly stripped, both constituting the principal kitchen [1]—varied, perhaps, with a little buttermilk—which Sullivan's family were then able to afford themselves with their potatoes.

We cannot close our description here, however, for sorry we are to say that the severe traces of poverty were as visible upon the inmates themselves as upon the house and its furniture. Sullivan's family consisted of his eldest daughter, aged nineteen, two growing boys, the eldest about sixteen, and several younger children besides. These last were actually ragged—all of them scantily and poorly clothed; and if any additional proof were wanting that poverty, in one of its most trying shapes, had come among them, it was to be found in their pale, emaciated features, and in that languid look of care and depression which any diminution in the natural quantity of food for any length of time uniformly impresses upon the countenance. In fact, the whole group had a sickly and woe-worn appearance, as was evident from the unnatural dejection of the young, who, instead of exhibiting the cheerfulness and animation of youth, now moped about without gaiety, sat brooding in corners, or struggled for a warm place nearest the dull and cheerless fire.

[1] That is—condiment, savour.

"The day was, Donnel," said Sullivan, whilst he pointed, with a sigh, to the unfurnished chimney, "when we could give you—as I said a while agone—a betther welcome—in one sense—I mane betther tratement—than we can give you now ; but you know the times that is in it, an' you know the down-come we have got, an' that the whole counthry has got, so you must only take the will for the deed now ; to such as we have you're heartily welcome. Get us some dinner, Bridget," he added, turning to the wife ; " but, first and foremost, bring that girl into the room here, till she hears what I have to say to her ; and, Donnel, as you wor a witness to the disgraceful sight we seen a while agone, come in and hear, too, what I'm goin' to say to her. I'll have no black thraison in my own family against my own blood, an' against the blood of my lovin' brother, that was so thraicherously shed by that boy's father."

The persons he addressed immediately passed into the cold, damp room as he spoke ; Mave, the cause of all this anxiety, evidently in such a state of excitement as was pitiable. Her mother, who, as well as every other member of the family, had been ignorant of this extraordinary attachment, seemed perfectly bewildered by the language of her husband, at whom, as at her daughter, she looked with a face on which might be read equal amazement and alarm.

Mave Sullivan was a young creature, shaped with extraordinary symmetry, and possessed of great natural grace. Her stature was tall, and all her motions breathed unstudied ease and harmony. In colour, her long abundant hair was beautifully fair—precisely of that delightful shade which generally accompanies a pale but exquisitely clear and almost transparent complexion. Her face was oblong, and her features so replete with an expression of innocence and youth, as left on the beholder a conviction that she breathed of utter guilelessness and angelic purity itself. This was principally felt in the bewitching charm of her smile, which was irresistible, and might turn the hatred of a demon into love.

All her motions were light and elastic, and her whole figure, though not completely developed, was sufficiently rounded by the fulness of health and youth to give promise of a rich and luxuriant maturity. On this occasion she became deadly pale; but as she was one of those whose beauty only assumes a new phase of attraction at every change, her paleness now made her appear, if possible, an object of greater interest.

"In God's name, Jerry," asked her mother, looking from father to daughter in a state of much distress, "what is wrong, or what has happened to put you in sich a condition? I see by the anger in your eye an' the whiteness on your cheeks, barrin' the little red spot in the middle, that something out o' the way all out has happened to vex you."

"You may well say so, Bridget," he replied; "but when I tell you that I came upon that undutiful daughter of ours coortin' wid the son of the man that murdhered her uncle—my only brother—you won't be surprised at the state you see me in—coortin' wid a fellow that Dan M'Gowan here knows will be hanged yet, for he's jist afther tellin' him so."

"You're ravin', Jerry," exclaimed his wife, who appeared to feel the matter as incredible; "you don't mean to tell me that she'd spake to, or know, or make any freedoms whatsomever wid young Condy Dalton, the son of her uncle's murdherer? Hut, no, Jerry, don't say that at all events—any disgrace but that—death, the grave, or—or—anything—anything—but sich an unnatural curse as that would be."

"I found them together behind the garden not many minutes ago," replied Sullivan. "Donnel here seen them as well as I did—deny it she can't; an' now let her say what brought her there to meet him, or rather what brought him all the way there to meet her? Answer me that, you disgrace to the name—answer me at wanst!"

The poor girl trembled, and became so weak as to be scarcely able to stand; in fact, she durst not raise her eye to meet that of either parent, but stood condemned and incapable of utterance.

The night had now nearly set in, and one of her little sisters entered with a rush candle in her hand, the light of which, as it fell dimly and feebly on the group, gave to the proceedings a wild and impressive appearance. The prophecy-man, with his dark, stern look, peculiar nose, and black raven hair that fell thickly over his shoulders, contrasted strongly with the fair, artless countenance and beautiful figure of the girl who stood beside him, whilst over opposite them were Sullivan himself and his wife, their faces pale with sorrow, anxiety, and indignation.

"Give me that candle," proceeded her father—"hand it to me, child, and leave the room; then," he proceeded, holding it up to a great coat of frieze which hung against the wall—"there's his coat—there's my lovin' brother's coat; look upon it now, and ax yourself what do you desarve for meetin' against our will an' consint the son of him that has the murdher of the man that owned it on his hands an' on his heart? What do you desarve, I say?"

The girl spoke not, but the Black Prophet, struck by the words and the unexpected appearance of the murdered man's coat, started; in a moment, however, he composed himself, and calmly turned his eyes upon Sullivan, who proceeded to address his daughter,—

"You have nothing to say, then? You're guilty, an', of course, you have no excuse to make; however, I'll soon put an end to all this. Bring me a prayer-book. If your book-oath can bind you down against ever——"

He could proceed no further. On uttering the last words his daughter tottered, and would have fallen to the ground had not Donnel Dhu caught her in his arms. She had, in fact, become almost insensible from excess of shame and over-excitement, and, as Donnel carried her towards a bed that was in the corner of the room, her head lay over against his face.

It is unnecessary to say that Sullivan's indignation was immediately lost in alarm. On bringing the candle near her the first thing they observed were streaks of blood upon Donnel Dhu's face, that gave to it, in connection with the mark of the blow he had received, a frightful and hideous expression.

" What is this! " exclaimed her mother, seizing the candle, and holding it to the beautiful features of her trembling daughter, which were now also dabbled with blood—" in God's name, what ails my child? Oh, Mave, Mave, my darlin', what's come over you? Blessed Mother of Marcy, what blood is this? *Achora machree*, Mave, spake to me—to the mother that 'ud go distracted, and that will, too, if anything's wrong wid you. It was cruel in you, Jerry, to spake to her so harsh as you did, an' to take her to task before a sthranger in sich a cuttin' manner. Saivier of Airth, Mave, darlin', won't you spake to me—to your own mother? "

" Maybe I did spake to her too severely," said her father, now relenting, " an' if I did, may God forgive me, for sure you know, Bridget, I wouldn't injure a hair of my darlin's head. But this blood!—this blood!—oh, where did it come from? "

Her weakness, however, proved but of short duration, and their apprehension was soon calmed. Mave looked round her rather wildly, and no sooner had her eyes rested on Donnel Dhu, than she shrieked aloud, and turning her face away from him with something akin to fear and horror, she flung herself into her mother's arms, exclaiming, as she hid her face in her bosom,—

" Oh, save me from that man; don't let him near me; don't let him touch me. I can't tell why, but I'm deadly afraid of him. What blood is that upon his face? Father, stand between us! "

" Foolish girl! " exclaimed her father, " you don't know what you're sayin'. Of coorse, Donnel, you'll not heed her words, for, indeed, she hasn't come to herself yet. But, in God's name, where did this blood come from that's upon you and her? "

" You can't suppose, Jerry," said Donnel, " that the poor girl's words would make me take any notice of them. She has been too much frightened, and won't know, maybe, in a few minutes that she spoke them at all."

" That's thrue,', said her mother ; " but with regard to the blood——"

She was about to proceed, when Mave rose up, and requested to be taken out of the room.

" Bring me to the kitchen," said she ; " I'm afraid ; and see this blood, mother."

Precisely as she spoke a few drops of blood fell from her nose, which, of course, accounted for its appearance on Donnel's face, and probably for her terror also at his repulsive aspect.

" What makes you afeard of poor Donnel, *asthore* ? " asked her mother—" a man that wouldn't injure a hair of your head, nor of one belongin' to you, an' never did."

" Why, when my father," she returned, " spoke about the coat there, an' jist as Donnel started, I looked at it, an' seen it movin', an', I don't know why, but I got afeard of him."

Sullivan held up the candle mechanically, as she spoke, towards the coat, upon which they all naturally gazed : but, whether from its dim flickering light, or the force of imagination, cannot be determined, one thing was certain, the coat appeared actually to move again, as if disturbed by some invisible hand. Again, also, the prophet involuntarily started, but only for a single moment.

" Tut," said he, " it's merely the unsteady light of the candle ; show it here."

He seized the rushlight from Sullivan, and approaching the coat, held it so close to it, that had there been the slightest possible motion, it could not have escaped their observation.

" Now," he added, " you see whether it moves or not ; but, indeed, the poor girl is so frightened by the scowldin' she got, that I don't wondher at the way she's in."

Mrs. Sullivan kept still gazing at the coat, in a state of terror almost equal to that of her daughter.

"Well," said she, "I've often heard it said that one is sometimes to disbelieve their own eyes; an' only that I know the thing couldn't happen, I would swear on the althar that I seen it movin'."

"I thought so myself, too," observed Sullivan, who also seemed to have been a good deal perplexed and awed by the impression; "but, of coorse, I agree wid Donnel, that it was the unsteady light of the rush that made us think so; how-aniver it doesn't mather now; move or no move, it won't bring him that owned it back to us, so God rest him! and now, Bridget, thry an' get us something to ait."

"Before the girl laves the room," said the prophecy-man, "let me spake what I think, an' what I know. I've lost many a weary day an' night in studyin' the futhur, an' in lookin' into what's to come. I must spake, then, what I think, an' what I know, regardin' her. I must; for when the feelin' is on me, I can't keep the prophecy back."

"Oh! let me go, mother," exclaimed the alarmed girl; "let me go; I can't bear to look at him."

"One minute, *acushla*, till you hear what he has to say to you," and she held her back with a kind of authoritative violence, as Mave attempted to leave the room.

"Don't be alarmed, my purty creature," spoke the prophet; "don't be alarmed at what I'm goin' to say to you, an' about you, for you needn't. I see great good fortune before you. I see a grand and handsome husband at your side, and a fine house to live in. I see stairs, an' carpets, an' horses, an' hounds, an' yourself with jewels in your white little ears, an' silks an' satins on your purty figure. That's a wakin' dhrame I had, an' you may all mark my words, if it doesn't come out thrue: it's on the leaf, an' the leaf was open to me. Grandeur an' wealth is before her, for her beauty an' her goodness will bring it all about, an' so I read it."

"An' what about the husband himself?" asked her mother, whose affection caused her to feel a strong interest in anything that might concern the future interests of her daughter; "can you tell us nothing about his appearance, that we might give a guess at him?"

" No," replied M'Gowan, for such was the prophet's name, " not to you; to none but herself can I give the marks an' tokens that will enable her to know the man that is to be her husband when she sees him; and to herself, in the mornin', I will, before I go—that is, if she'll allow me—for what is written in the dark book ought to be read and expounded. Her beauty and her goodness will do it all."

The man's words were uttered in a voice so full of those soft and insinuating tones that so powerfully operate upon the female heart; they breathed, too, such an earnest spirit of good-will, joined to an evident admiration of the beauty and goodness he alluded to, that the innocent girl, notwithstanding her previous aversion, felt something like gratification at what he said, not on account of the prospects held out to her, but because of the singular charm and affectionate spirit which breathed in his voice; or, might it not have been that delicate influence of successful flattery which so gently insinuates itself into the heart of woman, and soothes that vanity which unconsciously lurks in the very purest and most innocent of the sex? So far from being flattered by his predictions, she experienced a strong sensation of disappointment, because she knew where her affection at that moment rested, and felt persuaded that if she were destined to enjoy the grandeur shadowed out for her, it never could be with him whom she then loved. Notwithstanding all this, she felt her repugnance against the prophet strongly counterbalanced by the strange influence he began to exercise over her; and with this impression she and they passed to the kitchen, where in a few minutes she was engaged in preparing food for him, with a degree of good feeling that surprised herself.

There is scarcely anything so painful to hearts naturally generous, like those of the Sullivans, as the contest between the shame and exposure of conscious poverty on the one hand,

and the anxiety to indulge in a hospitable spirit on the other. Nobody unacquainted with Ireland could properly understand the distress of mind which this conflict almost uniformly produces. On the present occasion it was deeply felt by this respectable but declining family; and Mave, the ingenuous and kind-hearted girl, felt much of her unaccountable horror of this man removed by its painful exercise. Still her aversion was not wholly overcome, although much diminished; for, ever as she looked at his swollen and disfigured face, and thought of the mysterious motions of the murdered man's coat, she could not avoid turning away her eyes, and wishing that she had not seen him that evening. The scanty meal was at length over; a meal on which many a young eye dwelt with those yearning looks that take their character from the hungry and wolfish spirit which marks the existence of "a hard year," as it is called in our unfortunate country, and which, to a benevolent heart, forms such a sorrowful subject for contemplation. Poor Bridget Sullivan did all in her power to prevent this evident longing from being observed by M'Gowan, by looking significantly, shaking her head, and knitting her brows, at the children; and when these failed she had recourse to threatening attitudes and all kinds of violent gestures; and on these proving also unsuccessful, she was absolutely forced to speak aloud,—

"Come, childhre, start out now and play yourselves; be off, I say, an' don't stand ready to jump down the daicent man's throat wid every bit he aits."

She then drove them abroad somewhere, but as the rain fell heavily the poor creatures were again forced to return, and resume their pitiable watch until the two men had finished their scanty repast.

Seated round the dull and uncomfortable fire, the whole family now forgot their hunger and care for a time, in the wild legends with which M'Gowan entertained them, until the hour of rest.

"We haven't the best bed in the world," observed Sullivan,

" nor the best bed-clothes aither, but, as I said before, I wish, for all our sakes, they were betther. You must take your chance wid these two slips o' boys to-night as well as you can. If you wish to tumble in now you may ; or, maybe you'd wish to join us in our prayers. We sthrive, God help us, to say a Rosary every night, for, afther all, there's nothin' like puttin' one's self undher the holy protection of the Almighty, blessed be His name ! Indeed, this sickness that's goin' is so rife and dangerous that it's good to sthrive to be prepared, as it is indeed, whatever comes, whether hunger or plenty, sickness or health ; an' may God keep us prepared always ! "

M'Gowan seemed for a moment at a loss, but almost immediately said in reply,—

" You are right, Jerry, but as for me, I say whatever prayers I do say, always by myself ; for I can then get my mind fixed upon them betther. I'll just turn into bed, then, for troth, I feel a little stiff and tired ; so you must only let me have my own way to-night. To-morrow night I'll pray double."

He then withdrew to his appointed place of rest, where, after having partially undressed himself, he lay down, and for some time could hear no other sounds than the solemn voices of this struggling and afflicted little fold, as they united, in offering up their pious and simple act of worship to that Great Being, in whose providential care they felt such humble and confiding trust.

When their devotions were concluded, they quietly, and in a spirit at once of resignation and melancholy, repaired to their respective sleeping-places, with the exception of old Sullivan himself, who, after some hesitation, took down the great coat already so markedly alluded to, and exclaiming, partly by way of soliloquy, and partly to those within hearing,—

" I don't know—but still there can't be any harm in it ; sure's it's betther that it should be doin' some good than hangin' up there idle, against the wall, sich a night as this. Here, Dan, for the first time since I put it up wid my own hands, except to shake the dust off it, I'm going to turn this big coat to some use. There," he added, spreading it over them ; " let it help to keep you warm to-night—for, God knows, you want it, you an' them poor *gorsoons.* Your coverin' is but light, an' you may hear the down-powrin' of rain that's in it ; an' the wind, too, is risin' fast, every minute —gettin' so strong, indeed, that I doubt it 'ill be a storm before it stops; an' Dan, if it 'udn't be too much, maybe you'd not object to offer up one *pather an' avy* for the poor sowl of him that owned it, an' that was brought to his account so suddenly and so terribly. There," he added, fixing it about them ; " it'll help to keep you warm at any rate ; an' it's surely betther to have it so employed than hangin' idle, as I have said, against the wall."

M'Gowan immediately sat up in the bed, and putting down his hands, removed the coat.

" We don't want it at all," he replied ; " take it away, Jerry—do, for Heaven's sake. The night's not at all so cowld as you think, an' we'll keep one another warm enough widout it, never fear."

" Troth you do want it," said Sullivan ; " for, *fareer gair,* it's the light coverin' that's over you an' them, poor boys. Heigh-ho, Dan, see what innocence is—poor things, they're sound already—an' may God pity them an' provide for them, or enable me to do it ! " And as he looked down upon the sleeping lads, the tears came so abundantly to his eyes, that he was forced to wipe them away. " Keep the coat, Dan," he added, " you do want it."

" No," replied the other. " The truth is, I couldn't sleep under it. I'm very timersome, an' a little thing frightens me."

" Oh," said Sullivan, " I didn't think of that ; but in troth, if you're timersome, it's more than the world b'lieves of you. Well, well—I'll hang it up again ; so good night,

an' a sound sleep to you, an' to every man that has a free
conscience in the sight of God!"

No response was given to this prayer, and his words were
followed by a deep and solemn silence, that was only broken
occasionally by the heavy pattering of the descending rain,
and the fitful gusts of the blast, as they rushed against the
house, and whistled wildly among the few trees by which it
and the garden were enclosed.

Every one knows that a night of wind and storm, if not
rising actually to a tempest or hurricane, is precisely that on
which sleep falls with its deepest influence upon men. Sullivan's family, on that which we are describing, were a proof
of this, at least until about the hour of three o'clock, when
they were startled by a cry for help, so loud and frightful
that in a moment he and the boys huddled on their dress, and
hurried to the bed in which the prophet lay. In a minute or
two they got a candle lit; and truly the appearance of the
man was calculated to drive fear and alarm into their hearts.
They found him sitting in the bed, with his eyes so wild and
staring that they seemed straining out of their sockets.
His hair was erect, and his mouth half open and drawn back,
whilst the perspiration poured from him in torrents. His
hands were spread, and held up, with their palms outwards,
as if in the act of pushing something back that seemed to
approach him. "Help," he shouted; "he's comin' on me—
he will have me powerless in a minute. He is gaspin' now,
as he——Stay back, stay back—here—help, help; it's the
murdhered man—he's upon me. Oh!—Oh, God! he's comin'
nearer and nearer. Help me—save me!"

Sullivan, on holding the candle to his face, perceived that
he was still asleep; and, suspecting the nature of his dream,
he awoke him at once. On seeing a portion of the family
about him, he started again, and looked for a moment so
completely aghast that he resembled horror personified.

"Who—what—what are you? Oh," he exclaimed, recovering, and striving to compose himself, " ha—Good God!

what a frightful dhrame I had. I thought I was murdherin'
a man—murdherin' the——" he paused, and stared wildly
about him.

"Murdherin' who?" asked Jerry.

"Murdherin'! eh—ha—why, who—who talks about murdherin'?"

"Compose yourself," added Sullivan; "you did; but you're
frightened. You say you thought you were murdherin' some
one; who was it?"

"Yes, yes," he replied; "it was myself. I thought the
murdhered man was—I mean, that the man was murdherin'
myself." And he looked with a terrible shudder of fear towards the great coat.

"Hut!" said Sullivan, "it was only a dhrame; compose
yourself; why should you be alarmed?—your hand is free
of it. So, as I said, compose yourself; put your trust in
God, an' recommend yourself to His care."

"It was a terrible dhrame," said the other, once more
shuddering; "but then it was a dhrame. Good God, yes!
However, I ax pardon for disturbin' you all, an' breakin' in
upon your sleep. Go to bed now—I'm well enough; only
jist set that bit of candle by the bedside for a while, till I
recover, for I did get a fearful fright."

He then laid himself down once more, and having wiped
the perspiration from his forehead, which was now cadaverous, he bade them good-night, and again endeavoured to
compose himself to rest. In this he eventually succeeded,
the candle burning itself out; and in about three-quarters
of an hour the whole family were once more wrapped in
sound and uninterrupted repose.

The next morning the Sullivan family rose to witness
another weary and dismal day of incessant rain, and to partake of a breakfast of thin stirabout, made and served up
with that woful ingenuity which necessity, the mother of
invention in periods of scarcity, as well as in matters of a
different character, had made known to the benevolent-

hearted wife of Jerry Sullivan ; that is to say, the victuals were made so unsubstantially thin, that in order to impose, if possible, on the appetite, it was deemed necessary to deceive the eye by turning the plates and dishes round and round several times, while the viands were hot, so as by spreading them over a larger surface, to give the appearance of a greater quantity. It is, Heaven knows, a melancholy cheat, but one with which the periodical famines of our unhappy country have made our people too well acquainted. Previous, however, to breakfast, the prophet had a private interview with Mave, or the *Gra Gal*, as she was generally termed, to denote her beauty and extraordinary power of conciliating affection, *Gra Gal* signifying the fair love, or to give the more comprehensive meaning which it implied, the fair-haired beauty whom all love, or who wins all love. This interview lasted at least a quarter of an hour, or it might be twenty minutes, but as the object of it did not then transpire, we can only explain the appearances which followed it, so far, at least, as the parties themselves were concerned. The *Gra Gal*, as we shall occasionally call her, seemed pleased, if not absolutely gratified, by the conversation which passed between them. Her eye was elated, and she moved about like one who appeared to have been relieved from some reflection that had embarrassed and depressed her ; still, it might have been observed that this sense of relief had nothing in it directly affecting the person of the prophet himself, on whom her eye fell from time to time with a glance that changed its whole expression of satisfaction to one of pain and dislike. On his part there also appeared a calm sedate feeling of satisfaction, under which, however, an eye better acquainted with human nature might easily detect a triumph. He looked, to those who could properly understand him, precisely as an able diplomatist would who had succeeded in gaining a point.

When breakfast was over, and previous to his departure, he brought Jerry Sullivan and his wife out to the barn, and in a tone and manner of much mystery, assuming at the same time that figurative and inflated style so peculiar to him, and also to his rival, the *Scanachie*, he thus addressed them—

"Listen," said he, " listen, Jerry Sullivan, and Bridget his wife ;—a child was born, and a page was written—the moon saw it, and the stars saw it ; but the sun did not, for he is dark to fate, an' sees nothing but the face of nature. Do you undherstand that, Jerry Sullivan, an' you, Bridget, his wife ? "

" Well, troth, we can't say we do yet," they replied ; " but how could we, you know, if it's regardin' prophecy you're spakin' ? "

" Undherstand it ! " he replied contemptuously, " you undherstand it !—no, nor Father Philemy Corcoran himself couldn't undherstand it, barrin' he fasted and prayed, and refrained from liquor, for that's the way to get the kay o' knowledge ; at laist, it's the way I got it first—however, let that pass. As I was sayin', a child was born and a page was written, and an angel from heaven was sent to Nebbychodanazor, the prophet, who was commanded to write. What will I write ? says Nebbychodanazor, the prophet. Write down the fate of a faymale child, by name Mave Sullivan, daughter to Jerry Sullivan and his wife Bridget, of Aughnamurrin. Amin, says the prophet ; fate is fate ; what's before is not behind, neither is what's behind before, and everything will come to pass that's to happen. Amin, agin, says the prophet, an' what am I to write ?—Grandeur an' wealth—upstairs and downstairs—silks an' satins—an inside car—bracelets, earrings, and Spanish boots, made of Morroccy leather, tanned at Cordovan. Amin, agin, says Nebbychodanazor, the prophet—this is not that, neither is that the other, but everything is everything—neither can something be nothing, nor nothing something to the end of time ; an' time itself is but cousin jarmin to eternity—as is recorded in the great book of fate, fortune, an' fatality. Write agin, says the angel.—What am I to write ? At the

name of Mabel Sullivan place along wid all the rest the two
great paragons of a woman's life, marriage and posterity—
write marriage happy, and posterity numerous—and so the
child's born, an' the page written—beauty and goodness, a
happy father, and a proud mother—both made wealthy
through her means."

"And so," he proceeded, dropping the recitative, and resuming his natural voice—

"Be kind and indulgent to your daughter, for she'll yet
live to make all your fortunes. Take care of her and yourselves till I see yez again."

And without adding another word he departed.

CHAPTER IV

A DANCE AND A DOUBLE DISCOVERY

THE dance to which Sarah M'Gowan went after the conflict
with her step-mother, was but a miserable specimen of what
a dance usually is in Ireland. On that occasion, there were
but comparatively few assembled ; and these few, as may be
guessed, consisted chiefly of those gay and frolicksome spirits
whom no pressure of distress, nor anything short of sickness
or death, could sober down into seriousness. The meeting,
in fact, exhibited a painful union of mirth and melancholy.
The season brought with it none of that relief to the peasantry which usually makes autumn so welcome. On the contrary, the failure of the potato crop, especially in its quality,
as well as that of the grain in general, was not only the
cause of hunger and distress, but also of the sickness which
prevailed. The poor were forced, as they too often are, to
dig their potatoes before they were fit for food ; and the consequences were disastrous to themselves in every sense.
Sickness soon began to appear ; but then it was supposed
that as soon as the new grain came in, relief would follow.
In this expectation, however, they were, alas ! most **wofully**

disappointed. The wetness of the summer and autumn had soured and fermented the grain so lamentably that the use of it transformed the sickness occasioned by the unripe and bad potatoes into a terrible and desolating epidemic. At the period we are treating of, this awful scourge had just set in, and was beginning to carry death and misery in all their horrors throughout the country. It was no wonder, then, that at the dance we are describing, there was an almost complete absence of that cheerful and light-hearted enjoyment which is, or at least which was, to be found at such meetings. It was, besides, owing to the severity of the evening, but thinly attended. Such a family had two or three members of it sick ; another had buried a fine young woman ; a third, an only son ; a fourth had lost the father ; and a fifth the mother of a large family. In fact, the conversation on this occasion was rather a catalogue of calamity and death than that hearty ebullition of animal spirits which throws its laughing and festive spirit into such assemblies. Two there were, however, who, despite of the gloom which darkened both the dance and the day, contrived to sustain our national reputation for gaiety and mirth. One of these was our friend Sarah, or, as she was better known, Sally M'Gowan, and the other a young fellow named Charley Hanlon, who acted as a kind of gardener and steward to Dick o' the Grange. This young fellow possessed great cheerfulness, and such an everlasting fund of mirth and jocularity as made him the life and soul of every dance, wake, and merry-meeting in the parish. He was quite a Lothario in his sphere — a lady-killer—and so general an admirer of the sex, that he invariably made love to every pretty girl he met, or could lure into conversation. The usual consequences followed. Nobody was such a favourite with the sex in general, who were ready to tear each other's caps about him, as they sometimes actually did ; and indeed this is not at all to be wondered at. The fellow was one of the most open, hardy liars that ever lived. Of shame he had heard ; but of what it meant, no earthly eloquence could give him the slightest perception ; and we need scarcely add, that his assurance was boundless, as were his powers of flattery. It is unnecessary to say, then, that a man so admirably calculated to succeed with the sex was properly appreciated by them, and that his false-hood, flattery, and assurance were virtues which enshrined the vagabond in their hearts. In short, he had got the character of being a rake ; and he was necessarily obliged to suffer the agreeable penalty of their admiration and favour in consequence. The fellow, besides, was by no means ill-looking, nor ill-made, but had just enough of that kind of face and figure which no one can readily either find fault with or praise.

This gallant and Sally M'Gowan were, in fact, the life of the meeting ; and Sally, besides, had the reputation of being a great favourite with him—a circumstance which consider-ably diminished her popularity with her own sex. She her-self felt towards him that kind of wild, indomitable affection, which is as vehement as it is unregulated in such minds as hers. For instance, she made no secret of her attachment to him, but on the contrary gloried in it, even to her father, who, on this subject, could exercise no restraint whatsoever over her. It is not our intention to entertain our readers with the history of the occurrences which took place at the dance, as they are, in fact, not worth recording. Hanlon, at its close, proposed to see Sally home, as is usual.

" You may come with me near home," she replied : " but I'm not goin' home to-night."

" Why," he asked, " where the dickens are you goin', then ? "

" To Barney Gormly's wake ;—there 'ill be lots of fun there, too," she replied. " But come—you can come wid me as far as the turn-up to the house ; for I won't go in, nor go home neither, till after the berril, to-morrow."

" Do you know," said he, rather gravely, " the Grey Stone that's at the mouth of the Black Glen—or Glen Dhu ? "

"I ought," said she; "sure that's where the carman was found murdhered."

"The same," added Hanlon. "Well, I must go that far to-night," said he.

"And that's jist where I turn off to the Gormlys."

"So far, then, we'll be together," he replied.

"But why that far only, Charley—eh?"

"That's what you could never guess," said he, "and very few else aither; but go I must, an' go I will. At all events, I'll be company for you in passin' it. Are you never afeard at night, as you go near it?"

"Divil a taste," she replied; "what 'ud I be afeard of? My father laughs at sich things; although," she added, musing, "I think he's sometimes timorous for all that. But I know he's often out at all hours, and he says he doesn't care about ghosts—I know I don't."

The conversation now flagged a little, and Hanlon, who had been all the preceding part of the evening full of mirth and levity, could scarcely force himself to reply to her observations, or sustain any part in the dialogue.

"Why, what the sorra's comin' over you?" she asked, as they began to enter into the shadow of the hill at whose foot her father's cabin stood, and which here, for about two hundred yards, fell across the road. "Is it gettin' afeard you are?"

"No," he replied; "but I was given to undherstand, last night, that if I'd come this night to the Grey Stone, I'd find out a saicret that I'd give a great deal to know."

"Very well," she replied, "we'll see that; an' now raise your spirits. Here we're in the moonlight, thank goodness, such as it is. Dear me, thin, but it's an awful night, and the wind's risin'; and listen to the flood, how it roars in the glen below, like a thousand bulls!"

"It is," he replied; "but hould your tongue now for a little, and as you're here stop wid me for a while, although I don't see how I'm likely to come by much knowledge in sich a place as this."

They now approached the Grey Stone, and as they did the moon came out a little from her dark shrine of clouds, but merely with that dim and feeble light which was calculated to add ghastliness and horror to the wildness and desolation of the place.

Sally could now observe that her companion was exceedingly pale and agitated; his voice, as he spoke, became disturbed and infirm; and as he laid his hand upon the Grey Stone he immediately withdrew it, and taking off his hat he blessed himself, and muttered a short prayer with an earnestness and solemnity for which she could not account. Having concluded it, both stood in silence for a short time, he awaiting the promised information,—for which on this occasion he appeared likely to wait in vain,—and she without any particular purpose beyond her natural curiosity to watch and know the event.

The place at that moment was, indeed, a lonely one, and it was by no means surprising that, apart from the occurrence of two murders, one on, and the other near, the spot where they stood, the neighbouring peasantry should feel great reluctance in passing it at night. The light of the moon was just sufficient to expose the natural wildness of the adjacent scenery. The glen itself lay in the shadow of the hill, and seemed to the eye so dark that nothing but the huge outlines of the projecting crags, whose shapes appeared in the indistinctness like gigantic spectres, could be seen, whilst all around, and where the pale light of the moon fell, nothing was visible but the muddy gleams of the yellow flood as it rushed, with its hoarse and incessant roar, through a flat country on whose features the storm and the hour had impressed a character of gloom, and the most dismal desolation. Nay, the still appearance of the Grey Stone, or rock, at which they stood, had, when contrasted with the moving elements about them, and associated with the murder committed at its very foot, a solemn appearance that was of itself calculated to fill the mind with awe and terror. Hanlon felt this, as, indeed, his whole manner indicated.

" Well," said his companion, alluding to the short prayer he had just concluded, " I didn't expect to see you at your prayers like a *voteen* this night, at any rate. Is it fear that makes you so pious upon our hands? Troth, I doubt there's a white feather—a cowardly drop—in you, still an' all."

" If you can be one minute serious, Sally, do, I beg of you. I am very much disturbed, I acknowledge, an' so would you, maybe, if you knew as much as I do."

" You're the colour of death," she replied, putting her fingers upon his cheek; " an' my God! is it paspiration I feel, sich a night as this? I declare to goodness it is! Give me that white pocket-handkerchy that you say Peggy Murray gave you. Where is it?" she proceeded, taking it out of his pocket. " Ay, ay, I have it; stoop a little; take care of your hat, here now," and while speaking she wiped the cold perspiration from his forehead. " Is this the one she made you a present of it, an' put the letthers on?"

" It is," he replied, " the very same; but she didn't make me a present of it, she only hemmed it for me."

" That's a lie of you," she replied, fiercely: " she bought it for you out of her own pocket. I know that much. She tould Kate Duffy so herself, an' boasted of it; but, wait."

" Well," replied Hanlon, anxious to keep down the gust of jealousy which he saw rising, " and if she did, how could I prevent her?"

" What letthers did she put on it?"

" P. and an M.," he replied, " the first two letthers of my name."

" That's another lie," she exclaimed, " they're not the two first letthers of your name, but of her own; there's no M in Hanlon. At any rate, unless you give the same hand-kerchy to me I'll make it be a black business to her."

" Keep it, keep it, wid all my heart," said he, glad to get

rid of a topic which at that moment came on him so powerfully and unseasonably. " Do what you like wid it."

" You say so willingly now—do you ? "

" To be sure I do; an' you may tell the whole world that
I said so, if you like."

" P. M.—oh, ay, that's for Peggy Murray—maybe the
letthers I saw on the ould tobaccy-box I found in a hole of
the wall to-day were for Peggy Murray. Ha ! ha ! ha ! Oh,
maybe I won't have a brag over her ! "

" What letthers ? " asked Hanlon eagerly ; " a tobaccy-
box, did you say ? "

" Ay did I—a tobaccy-box. I found it in a hole in the
wall in our house to-day ; it tumbled out while I was gettin'
some cobwebs to stop a bleedin'."

" Was it a good one ? " asked Hanlon, with apparent care-
lessness ; " could one use it ? "

" Hardly; but no, it's all rusty, an' has but one hinge."

" But one hinge ! " repeated the other, who was almost
breathless with anxiety ; " an' the letthers—what's this you
say they wor ? "

" The very same that's on your handkerchy," she replied—
" a P and an M."

" Great God ! " he exclaimed, " is this possible ! Heavens !
what is that ? Did you hear anything ? "

" What ails you ? " she inquired. " Why do you look so
frightened ? "

" Did you hear nothing ? " he again asked.

" Ha ! ha !—hear ! " she replied, laughing—" hear ; I
thought I heard something like a groan ; but sure 'tis only
the wind. Lord ! what a night ! Listen how the wind and
storm growls, an' tyrannizes, and rages down in the glen
there, an' about the hills. Faith, there'll be many a house
stripped this night. Why, what ails you ? Afther
all, you're but a hen-hearted divil, I doubt ; sorra thing
else."

Hanlon made her no reply, but took his hat off, and once

more offered up a short prayer, apparently in deep and most extraordinary excitement.

" I see," she observed, after he had concluded, " that you're bent on your devotions this night, an' the divil's own place you've pitched upon for them."

" Well, now," replied Hanlon, " I'll be biddin' you good-night; but, before you go, promise to get me that tobaccy-box you found; it's the least you can give me for Peggy Murray's handkerchy."

" Hut! " returned Sally, " it's not worth a *thraneen* : you couldn't use it even if you had it; sure it's both rusty and broken."

" No matther for that," he replied; " I want to play a thrick on Peggy Murray wid it, so as to have a good laugh against her—the pair of us—you wid the handkerchy, and me wid the tobaccy-box."

" Very well," she replied. " Ha! ha! ha!—that'll be great. At any rate, I've a crow to pluck wid the same Peggy Murray. Oh, never fear, you must have it; the minnit I get my hands on it I'll secure it for you."

After a few words more of idle chat they separated; he to his master's house, which was a considerable distance off; and this extraordinary creature—unconscious of the terrors and other weaknesses that render her sex at once so dependent on and so dear to man, full only of delight at the expected glee of the wake—to the house of death where it was held.

In the country parts of Ireland it is not unusual for those who come to a wake-house from a distance to remain there till the funeral takes place; and this also is frequently the case with the nearest door neighbours. There is generally a solemn hospitality observed on the occasion, of which the two classes I mention partake. Sally's absence, therefore, on that night, or for the greater portion of the next day, excited neither surprise nor alarm at home. On entering their miserable shieling, she found her father, who had just returned, and her stepmother, in high words; the cause of which, she soon learned, had originated in his account of the interview between young Dalton and Mave Sullivan, together with its unpleasant consequences to himself.

"What else could you expect," said his wife, "but what you got? You're ever an' always too ready wid your divil's grin an' your black prophecy to thim you don't like. I wondher you're not afeard that some of them might come back to yourself, an' fall upon your own head. If ever a man tempted Providence you do."

"Ah, dear me!" he exclaimed, with a derisive sneer, rendered doubly repulsive by his now hideous and disfigured face, "how pious we are! Providence, indeed! Much I care about Providence, you hardened jade, or you aither, whatever puts the word into your purty mouth. Providence! oh, how much we regard it, as if Providence took heed of what we do. Go an' get me somethin' to put to this swellin', you had betther; or if it's goin' to grow religious you are, be off out o' this; we'll have none of your cant or *pishthrogues* here."

"What's this?" inquired Sarah, seating herself on a three-legged stool, "the ould work is it? bell-cat, bell-dog—Ah, you're a blessed pair, an' a purty pair, too; you, wid your swelled face, an' blinkin' eye—*arrah*, what daicent man gave you that? and you," she added, turning to her stepmother, "wid your cheeks poulticed, an' your eye blinkin' on the other side—what a pair o' beauties you are, ha! ha! ha!—I wouldn't be surprised if the divil an' his mother fell in consate wid you both—ha! ha! ha!"

"Is that your manners, afther spendin' the night away wid yourself?" asked her father, angrily. "Instead of stealin' into the house thremblin' with fear, as you ought to be, you walk in with your brazen face, ballyraggin' us like a Hecthor."

"Devil a taste I'm afeard," she replied, sturdily—"I did nothing to be afeard or ashamed of, an' why should I?"

"Did you see Mr. Hanlon on your travels—eh?"

"You needn't say 'eh' about it," she replied; "to be sure I did; it was to meet him I went to the dance—I have no saicrets."

"Ah, you'll come to a good end yet, I doubt," said her father.

"Sure she needn't be afeard of Providence, anyhow," observed his wife.

"To the devil wid *you* at all events," he replied; "if you're not off out o' this to get me something for this swellin' I'll make it worse for you."

"Ay, ay, I'll go," she said, looking at him with peculiar bitterness, "an' wid the help of the same Providence that you laugh at, I'll take care that the same roof won't cover the three of us long. I'm tired of this life, an' come or go what may I'll look to my sowl, an' lead it no longer."

"Do you mane to break our hearts?" he replied, laughing, "for sure we couldn't do less afther her, Sally; eh? ha! ha! ha! Before you lave us, anyhow," he added, "go an' get me some *casharrawan* roots to bring down this swellin'; I can't go to the Grange wid sich a face as this on me."

"You'll have a blacker an' a worse one on the day of judgment," replied Nelly, taking up an old spade as she spoke, and proceeding to look for the *casharrawan* (dandelion) roots which he wanted.

When she had gone, the prophet, assuming that peculiar sweetness of manner, for which he was so remarkable when it suited his purpose, turned to his daughter, and putting his hand in his waistcoat pocket, pulled out a tress of fair hair, whose shade and silky softness were exquisitely beautiful.

"Do you see that," said he; "isn't that purty?"

"Show," she replied, and taking the tress into her hand, she looked at it.

"It is lovely; but isn't that aiquil to it?" she continued, letting loose her own of raven black and equal gloss and

softness—"what can it brag over that, eh?" and as she compared them her black eye flashed, and her cheek assumed a
rich glow of pride and conscious beauty, that made her look
just such a being as an old Grecian statuary would have
wished to model from.

" It is aiquil to her's any day," replied her father, softened
into affection as he contemplated her; " and, indeed, Sally,
I think you're her match every way except—except—no
matter, troth are you."

" What are you going to do wid it?" she asked; " is it to
the Grange it's goin'?"

" It is; an' I want you to help me in what I mentioned to
you. If I get what I'm promised we'll lave the country,
you and I, and as for that ould vagabond, we'll pitch her to
ould Nick. She's talkin' about devotion, and has nothin' but
Providence in her lips!"

" But isn't there a Providence?" asked his daughter, with
a sparkling eye.

" Devil a much myself knows or cares," he replied, with
indifference, " whether there is or not."

" Bekase, if there is," she said, pausing—" if there is, one
might as well——"

" She paused again, and her fine features assumed an intel-
lectual meaning—a sorrowful and meditative beauty, that
gave a new and more attractive expression to her face than
her father had ever witnessed on it before.

" Don't vex me, Sarah," he replied, snappishly. " Maybe
it's goin' to imitate her you are. The clargy knows these
things maybe—an' maybe they don't. I only wish she'd
come back with the *casharrawan*. If all goes right, I'll
pocket what'll bring yourself an' me to America. I'm beginnin' somehow to get unaisy; an' I don't wish to stay in
this country any longer."

Whilst he spoke, the sparkling and beautiful expression
which had lit up his daughter's countenance passed away,
and with it probably the moment in which it was pos-

sible to have opened a new and higher destiny to her existence.

Nelly, in the meantime, having taken an old spade with her to dig the roots she went in quest of, turned up Glendhu, and kept searching for some time in vain, until at length she found two or three bunches of the herb growing in a little lonely nook that lay behind a projecting ledge of rock, where one would seldom think of looking for herbage at all. Here she found a little, soft, green spot, covered over with dandelion ; and immediately she began to dig it up. The softness of the earth and its looseness surprised her a good deal ; and moved by an unaccountable curiosity, she pushed the spade farther down, until it was met by some substance that felt rather hard. From this she cleared away the earth as well as she could, and discovered that the spade had been opposed by a bone ; and on proceeding to examine still further, she discovered that the spot on which the dandelions had grown, contained the bones of a full-grown human body.

CHAPTER V

THE BLACK PROPHET IS STARTLED BY A BLACK PROPHECY

HAVING satisfied herself that the skeleton was a human one, she cautiously put back the earth, and covered it up with the green sward, as graves usually are covered, and in such a way that there should exist, from the disturbed appearance of the place, as little risk as possible of discovery. This being settled, she returned with the herbs, and laying aside the spade, from off which she had previously rubbed the red earth, so as to prevent any particular observation, she sat down, and locking her fingers into each other, swayed her body backwards and forwards in silence, as a female does in Ireland when under the influence of deep and absorbing sorrow, whilst from time to time she fixed her eyes on the prophet, and sighed deeply.

"I thought," said he, "I sent you for the casharrawan—
where is it?"

"Oh," she replied, unrolling it from the corner of her
apron, "here it is—I forgot it—ay, I forgot it—and no wondher—oh, no wondher indeed!—Providence! You may
blasphayme Providence as much as you like; but he'll take
his own out o' you yet; an' indeed it's comin' to that—it is,
Donnel, an' you'll find it so."

The man had just taken the herbs into his hand, and was
about to shred them into small leaves for the poultice, when
she uttered the last words. He turned his eyes upon her;
and in an instant that terrible scowl for which he was so remarkable when in a state of passion, gave its deep and
deadly darkness to his already disfigured visage. His
eyes blazed, and one half of his face became ghastly with
rage.

"What do you mane?" he asked—"what does she mane,
Sarah? I tell you wanst for all, you must give up ringin'
Providence into my ears, unless you wish to bring my hand
upon you, as you often did—mark that!"

"Your ears," she replied, looking at him calmly, and without seeming to regard his threat; "oh, I only wish I could
ring the fear of Providence into your heart—I wish I could;
but I'll do for yourself what you often pretend to do for others,
I'll give you warnin'. I tell you now that Providence
himself is on your track—that his judgment's hangin' over
you—and that it'll fall upon you before long;—this is my
prophecy, and a black one you'll soon find it."

That Nelly had been always a woman of some good-nature,
with gleams of feeling and humanity appearing in a character
otherwise apathetic, hard, and dark, M'Gowan well knew;
but that she was capable of bearding him in one of his worst
and most ferocious moods, was a circumstance which amazed
and absolutely overcame him. Whether it was the novelty
or the moral elevation of the position she so unexpectedly
assumed, or some lurking conviction within himself which

echoed back the truth of her language, it is difficult to say.
Be that, however, as it might, he absolutely quailed before
her, and instead of giving way to headlong violence or outrage, he sat down, and merely looked on her in silence and
amazement.

Sarah certainly thought he was unnecessarily tame on the
occasion, and that Nelly's phophecy ought not to have been
listened to in silence. The utter absence of all fear, however,
on the part of the elder female, joined to the extraordinary
union of determination and indifference with which she spoke,
had something morally impressive in it; and Sarah, who
felt, besides, that there seemed a kind of mystery in the
words of the denunciation, resolved to let the matter rest between them, at least for the present.

A silence of some time now ensued, during which she looked
from the one to the other with an aspect of uncertainty. At
length, she burst into a hearty laugh—

"Ha, ha, ha!—well," said he, "it's a good joke at any
rate to see my father bate wid his own weapons. Why, she
has frightened you more wid her prophecy than ever you did
any one wid one of your own. Ha, ha, ha!"

To this sally neither replied, nor seemed disposed to
reply.

"Here," added Sarah, handing her stepmother a cloth,
"remimber you have to go to Darby Skinadre's for meal.
I'd go myself, an' save you the journey, but that I'm afraid
you might fall in love wid one another in my absence. Be
off now, you old step-devil, an' get the meal; or, if you're
not able to go, I will."

After a lapse of a few minutes, the woman rose, and taking
the cloth, deliberately folded it up, and asked him for money
to purchase the meal she wanted.

"Here," said he, handing her a written paper, "give him
that, an' it will do as well as money. He expects Master
Dick's interest for Dalton's farm, an' I'll engage he'll attend
to that."

She received the paper, and looking at it, said—

"I hope this is none of the villainy I suspect."

"Be off, he replied; "get what you want, and that's all you have to do."

"What's come over you?" asked Sarah of her father, after the other had gone. "Did you get afeared of her?"

"There's something in her eye," he replied, "that I don't like, and that I never seen there before."

"But," returned the other, a good deal surprised, "what can there be in her eye that you need care about? You have nobody's blood on your hands, an' you stole nothin'. What made you look afeard that time?"

"I didn't look afeard."

"But I say you did, an' I was ashamed of you."

"Well, never mind—I may tell you something some o' these days about that same woman. In the meantime, I'll throw myself on the bed, an' take a sleep, for I slept but little last night."

"Do so," replied Sarah; "but at any rate, never be cowed by a woman. Lie down, an' I'll go over a while to Tom Cassidy's. But first, I had betther make the poultice for your face, to take down that ugly swellin'."

Having made and applied the poultice, she went off, light-hearted as a lark, leaving her worthy father to seek some rest if he could.

She had no sooner disappeared, than the prophet, having closed and bolted the door, walked backwards and forwards in a moody and unsettled manner.

"What," he exclaimed to himself, "can be the matther with that woman, that made her look at me in sich a way a while agone? I could not mistake her eye. She surely knows more than I thought, or she would not fix her eye into mine as she did. Could there be anything in that dhrame about Dalton an' my coffin? Hut! that's nonsense. Many a dhrame I had that went for nothing. The only thing she could stumble on is the *box*, an' I don't think she would be

likely to find that out, unless she went to throw down the
house; but anyhow it's no harm to thry."

He immediately mounted the old table, and, stretching up,
searched the crevice in the wall where it had been, but, we
need not add, in vain. He then came down again, in a state
of dreadful alarm, and made a general search for it in every
hole and corner visible, after which his agitation became wild
and excessive.

"She has got it!" he exclaimed—"she has stumbled on it,
aided by the devil—an' may she soon be in his clutches!—
and it the only thing I'm afeared of! But then," he added,
pausing, and getting somewhat cool, "does she know how it
might be brought against me, or who owned it? I don't
think she does; but still, where can it be, and what could
she mane by Providence trackin' me out?—an' why did she
look as if she knew something? Then that dhrame—I can't
get it out o' my head this whole day—and the terrible one I
had last night, too! But that last is aisily accounted for.
As it is, I must only wait an' watch her; an' if I find
she can be dangerous, why—*it'll be worse for her*—that's
all."

He then threw himself on the wretched bed, and, despite
of his tumultuous reflections, soon fell asleep.

CHAPTER VI

A RUSTIC MISER AND HIS ESTABLISHMENT

THERE is to be found in Ireland, and, we presume, in all
other countries, a class of hardened wretches, who look forward to a period of dearth as to one of great gain and advantage, and who contrive, by exercising the most heartless and
diabolical principles, to make the sickness, famine, and general desolation which scourge their fellow-creatures, so many
sources of successful extortion and rapacity, and consequently
of gain to themselves. These are country misers, or money-

lenders, who are remarkable for keeping meal until the arrival of what is termed a hard year, or a dear summer, when
they sell it out at enormous or usurious prices, and who, at
all times and under all circumstances, dispose of it only at
terms dictated by their own griping spirit, and the crying
necessity of the unhappy purchasers.

The houses and places of such persons are always remarkable for a character in their owners of hard and severe
saving, which at a first glance has the appearance of that
rare virtue in our country called frugality—a virtue which,
upon a closer inspection, is found to be nothing with them
but selfishness, sharpened up into the most unscrupulous
avarice and penury.

About half-a-mile from the residence of the Sullivans, lived
a remarkable man of this class, named Darby Skinadre. In
appearance he was lank and sallow, with a long, thin,
parched-looking face, and a miserable crop of yellow beard,
which no one could pronounce as anything else than "a
dead failure;" added to this were two piercing ferret eyes,
always sore and fiery, and with a tear standing in each, or
trickling down his fleshless cheeks; so that, to persons disposed to judge only by appearances, he looked very like a
man in a state of perpetual repentance for his transgressions,
or, what was still farther from the truth, who felt a most
Christian sympathy with the distresses of the poor. In his
house, and about it, there was much, no doubt, to be com-
mended, for there was much to mark the habits of the saving
man. Everything was neat and clean, not so much from any
innate love of neatness and cleanliness, as because these
qualities were economical in themselves. His ploughs and
farming implements were all snugly laid up and covered, lest
they might be injured by exposure to the weather; and his
house was filled with large chests and wooden hogsheads,
trampled hard with oatmeal, which, as they were never
opened unless during a time of famine, had their joints and
crevices festooned by innumerable mealy-looking cobwebs,

which description of ornament extended to the dresser itself, where they might be seen upon most of the cold-looking shelves, and those neglected utensils, that in other families are mostly used for food. His haggard was also remarkable for having in it, throughout all the year, a remaining stack or two of oats or wheat, or perhaps one or two large ricks of hay, tanned by the sun of two or three summers into a tawny hue—each or all kept in the hope of a failure and a famine.

In a room from the kitchen, he had a beam, a pair of scales, and a set of weights, all of which would have been vastly improved by a visit from the lord mayor, had our mealmonger lived under the jurisdiction of that civic gentleman. He was seldom known to use metal weights when disposing of his property; in lieu of these he always used round stones, which, upon the principle of the Scottish proverb, that "many a mickle makes a muckle," he must have found a very beneficial mode of transacting business.

If anything could add to the iniquity of his principles, as a plausible but most unscrupulous cheat, it was the hypocritical prostitution of the sacred name and character of religion to his own fraudulent impositions upon the poor and the distressed. Outwardly, and to the eye of men, he was proverbially strict and scrupulous in the observation of its sanctions, but outrageously severe and unsparing upon all who appeared to be influenced either by a negligent or worldly spirit, or who omitted the least tittle of its forms. Religion and its duties, therefore, were perpetually in his mouth, but never with such apparent zeal and sincerity as when enforcing his most heartless and hypocritical exactions upon the honest and struggling creatures whom necessity or neglect had driven into his meshes.

Such was Darby Skinadre; and certain we are that the truth of the likeness we have given of him will be at once recognised by our readers as that of the roguish hypocrite, whose rapacity is the standing curse of half the villages of the country, especially during seasons of distress, or failure of crops.

Skinadre, on the day we write of, was reaping a rich harvest from the miseries of the unhappy people. In a lower room of his house, to the right of the kitchen as you entered it, he stood over his scales, weighing out with a dishonest and parsimonious hand, the scanty pittance which poverty enabled the wretched creatures to purchase from him; and in order to give them a favourable impression of his piety, and consequently of his justness, he had placed against the wall a delf crucifix, with a semi-circular receptacle at the bottom of it for holding holy water. This was as much as to say, " How could I cheat you with the image of our Blessed Redeemer before my eyes to remind me of my duty, and to teach me, as He did, to love my fellow-creatures? " And with many of the simple people, he actually succeeded in making the impression he wished; for they could not conceive it possible, that any principle, however rapacious, could drive a man to the practice of such sacrilegious imposture.

There stood Skinadre, like the very Genius of Famine, surrounded by distress, raggedness, feeble hunger, and tottering disease, in all the various aspects of pitiable suffering, hopeless desolation, and that agony of the heart which impresses wildness upon the pale cheek, makes the eye at once dull and eager, parches the mouth, and gives to the voice of misery tones that are hoarse and hollow. There he stood, striving to blend consolation with deceit, and, in the name of religion and charity, subjecting the helpless wretches to fraud and extortion. Around him was misery, multiplied into all her most appalling shapes. Fathers of families were there, who could read in each other's faces, too truly, the gloom and anguish that darkened the brow and wrung the heart. The strong man, who had been not long before a comfortable farmer, now stood dejected and apparently broken - down, shorn of his strength without a trace of either hope or spirit; so wofully shrunk away too, from his superfluous apparel, that the spectators actually wondered to think that this was the large man, of such powerful frame, whose feats of strength had so often heretofore filled them with amazement. But, alas! what will not sickness and hunger do?

There, too, was the aged man—the grandsire himself—bent with a double weight of years and sorrow — without food until that late hour; forgetting the old pride that never stooped before, and now coming with the last feeble argument, to remind the usurer that he and his father had been schoolfellows and friends, and that although he had refused to credit his son, and afterwards his daughter-in-law, still, for the sake of old times, and of those who were now no more, he hoped he would not refuse to his grey hairs and tears, and for the sake of the living God besides, that which would keep life in his son and his daughter-in-law, and his famishing grandchildren, who had not a morsel to put in their mouths nor the means of procuring it on earth—if he failed them.

And there was the widower, on behalf of his motherless children, coming with his worn and desolate look of sorrow, almost thankful to God that his Kathleen was not permitted to witness the many-shaped miseries of this woful year; and yet experiencing the sharp and bitter reflection, that now, in all their trials—in his poor children's want and sickness— in their moanings by day and their cries for her by night, they have not the soft affection of her voice nor the tender touch of her hand to soothe their pain—nor has he that smile, which was ever his, to solace him now, nor that faithful heart to soothe him with its affection, or to cast its sweetness into the bitter cup of his affliction. Alas! no; he knows that that heart will beat for him and them no more; that that eye of love will never smile upon them again; and so he feels the agony of her loss superadded to all his other sufferings, and in this state he approaches the merciless usurer.

And the widow—emblem of desolation and dependence— how shall she meet and battle with the calamities of this fearful season? She out of whose heart these very calamities draw forth the remembrances of him she has lost, with such vividness that his past virtues are added to her present sufferings; and his manly love as a husband—his tenderness as a parent—his protecting hand and ever kind heart, crush her solitary spirit by their memory, and drag it down to the uttermost depths of affliction. Oh! bitter reflection!—" if her Owen were now alive, and in health, she would not be here; but God took him to Himself, and now unless he—the miser—has compassion on her, she and her children—her Owen's children—must lie down and die! If it were not for their sakes, poor darlings, she would wish to follow him out of such a world; but now she and the Almighty are all that they have to look to, blessed be His name!"

Others there were whose presence showed how far the general destitution had gone into the heart of society, and visited many whose circumstances had been looked upon as beyond its reach. The decent farmer, for instance, whom no one had suspected of distress, made his appearance among them with an air of cheerfulness that was put on to baffle suspicion. Sometimes he laughed as if his heart were light, and again expressed a kind of condescending sympathy with some poor person or other to whom he spoke kindly, as a man would do who knew nothing personally of the distress which he saw about him, but who wished to encourage those who did with the cheering hope that it must soon pass away. Then affecting the easy manner of one who was interesting himself for another person, he asked to have some private conversation with the usurer, to whom he communicated the immediate want that pressed upon himself and his family.

It is impossible, however, to describe the various aspects and claims of misery which presented themselves at Skinadre's house. The poor people flitted to and fro, silently and dejectedly, wasted, feeble, and sickly — sometimes in small groups of twos and threes, and sometimes a solitary individual might be seen hastening with earnest but languid speed, as if the life of some dear child or beloved parent, of a hus-

band or wife, or, perhaps, the lives of a whole family, depended
upon her or his arrival with food.

CHAPTER VII

A PANORAMA OF MISERY

SKINADRE, thin and mealy, with his coat off, but wearing a
waistcoat to which were attached flannel sleeves, was busily
engaged in the agreeable task of administering to their necessities. Such was his smoothness of manner, and the singular
control which a long life of hypocrisy had given him over his
feelings, that it was impossible to draw any correct distinc-
tion between that which he only assumed and that which he
really felt. This consequently gave him an immense advantage over every one with whom he came in contact, especially
the artless and candid, and all who were in the habit of expressing what they thought. We shall, however, take the
liberty of introducing him to the reader, and allow honest
Skinadre to speak for himself.

"They're beggars—thim three—that woman and her two
childre; still my heart bleeds for them, bekase we should
love our neighbours as ourselves; but I have given away
as much meal in charity, an' me can so badly afford it,
as would—I can't now, indeed, my poor woman! Sick—
throth they look sick, an' you look sick yourself. Here,
Paddy Lenahan, help that woman and her two poor childre
out of that half-bushel of meal you've got; you won't miss a
handful for God's sake."

This he said to a poor man who had just purchased some
oatmeal from him; for Skinadre was one of those persons
who, however he may have neglected works of mercy himself, took great delight in encouraging others to perform
them.

"Troth it's not at your desire I do it, Darby," replied the
old man; "but bekase she and they wants it, God help them!

Here, poor creature, take this for the honour of God ; an'
I'm only sorry, for both our sakes, that I can't do more."

" Well, Jemmy Duggan," proceeded the miser, addressing
a new-comer, " what's the news wid you ? They're hard
times, Jemmy ; we all know that, an' feel it, too, an' yet we
live, most of us, as if there wasn't a God to punish us."

" At all events," replied the man, " we feel what sufferin'
is now, God help us ! Between hunger and sickness, the
counthry was never in sich a state widin the memory of man.
What, in the name o' God, will become of the poor people,
I know not. The Lord pity them, an' relieve them ! "

" Amen, amen, Jemmy ! Well, Jemmy, can I do anything for you ? But, Jemmy, in regard of that, the thruth
is, we have brought all these scourges on us by our sins and
our thransgressions ; thim that sins, Jemmy, must suffer."

" There's no one denyin' it, Darby ; but you're axin' me
can you do anything for me, an' my answer to that is, that
you can, if you like."

" Ah ! Jemmy, you wor ever an' always a wild, heedless,
heerum-skeerum rake, that never was likely to do much good ;
little religion ever rested on you, an' now I'm afeared so sign's
on it."

" Well, well, who's widout sin ? I'm sure I'm not. What
I want is, to know if you'll credit me for a hundred of meal
till the times mends a trifle. I have the six o'them at home
widout their dinner this day, an' must go widout it, if you
refuse me. When the harvest comes round, I'll pay you."

" Jemmy, you owe three half-years' rent ; an' as for the
harvest an' what it'll bring, only jist look at the day that's
in it. It goes to my heart to refuse you, poor man ; but,
Jemmy, you see that you have brought this on yourself. If
you had been an attentive, industrious man, an' minded your
religion, you wouldn't be as you are now. Six you have at
home, you say ? "

" Ay, not to speak of the woman an' myself. I know you
won't refuse them, Darby, bekase if we're hard pushed now,

it's a'most everybody's case as well as mine. Be what I may, you know I'm honest."

"I don't doubt your honesty, Jemmy; but, Jemmy, if I sell my meal to a man that can pay and won't, or if I sell my meal to a man that would pay and can't, by which do I lose most ? There it is, Jemmy—think o' that, now. Six in family, you say ? "

"Six in family, wid the woman an' myself."

" The sorra man livin' feels more for you than I do, an' I would let you have the meal if I could ; but the truth is, I'm makin' up my rent—an' Jemmy, I lost so much last year by my own foolish good-nature, an' I gave away so much on trust, that now I'm brought to a hard pass myself. Throth I'll fret enough this night for havin' to refuse you. I know it was rash of me to make the promise I did ; but still, God forbid that ever any man should be able to throw it in my face, an' say that Darby Skinadre ever broke his promise."

" What promise ? "

" Why never to sell a pound of meal on trust."

"God help us, then !—for what to do or where to go I don't know."

" It goes to my heart, Jemmy, to refuse you—six in family, an' the two of yourselves. Throth it does, to my very heart itself; but stay, maybe we may manage it. You have no money you say ? "

"No money now, but won't be long so, plaise God."

" Well, but haven't you value of any kind ?—sure, God help them, they can't starve, poor creatures—the Lord pity them ! "

Here he wiped away a drop of villainous rheum which ran down his cheek, and he did it with such an appearance of sympathy, that almost any one would have imagined it was a tear of compassion for the distresses of the poor man's family.

" Oh ! no, they can't starve. Have you no value of any

kind, Jemmy?—ne'er a beast now, or anything that way?"

"Why, there's a young heifer; but I'm strugglin' to keep it to help me in the rent. I was obliged to sell my pig long ago, for I had no way of feedin' it."

"Well, bring me the heifer, Jemmy, an' I won't let the crathurs starve. We'll see what can be done when it comes here. An' now, Jemmy, let me ax you if you wint to hear mass on last Sunday?"

"Throth I didn't like to go in this trim. Peggy has a web of frieze half-made this good while; it'll be finished some time, I hope."

"Ah! Jemmy, Jemmy, it's no wondher the world's the way it is, for indeed there's little thought of God or religion in it. You passed last Sunday like a haythen, an' now see how you stand to-day for the same."

"You'll let me bring some o' the meal home wid me now," said the man; "the poor cratures tasted hardly anything to-day yet, an' they wor cryin' whin I left home. I'll come back wid the heifer *full but*. Throth they're in outher misery, Darby."

"Poor things!—an' no wondher, wid sich a haythen of a father; but, Jemmy, bring the heifer here first, till I look at it; an' the sooner you bring it here the sooner they'll have relief, the crathurs."

It is not our intention to follow up this iniquitous bargain any farther; it is enough to say that the heifer passed from Jemmy's possession into his, at about the fourth part of its value.

To those who had money he was a perfect honeycomb, overflowing with kindness and affection, expressed in such a profusion of warm and sugary words, that it was next to an impossibility to doubt his sincerity.

"Darby," said a very young female, on whose face was blended equal beauty and sorrow, joined to an expression that was absolutely deathlike, "I suppose I needn't ax you for credit?"

He shook his head.

"It's for the ould couple," she added, "an' not for myself. I wouldn't ax it for myself. I know my fault, an' my sin, an' may God forgive myself in the first place, an' him that brought me to it, an' to the shame that followed it! But what would the ould couple do now widout me?"

"An' have you no money? Ah, Margaret Murtagh! sinful creature—shame, shame, Margaret. Unfortunate girl that you are, have you no money?"

"I have not, indeed; the death of my brother Alick left us as we are; he's gone from them now; but there was no fear of me goin' that wished to go. Oh, if God in His goodness to them had took me an' spared him, they wouldn't be sendin' to you this day for meal to keep life in them till things comes round."

"Throth I pity them—from my heart I pity them, now that they're helpless an' ould—especially for havin' sich a daughter as you are; but if it was my own father an' mother, God rest them, I couldn't give meal out on credit. There's not in the parish a poorer man than I am. I'm done wid givin' credit now, thank goodness; an' if I had been so long ago it isn't robbed, an' ruined, an' beggared by rogues I'd be this day, but a warm, full man, able an' willin' too, to help my neighbours; an' it is not empty-handed I'd send away any messenger from your father or mother, as I must do, although my heart bleeds for them this minute."

Here once more he wiped away the rheum, with every appearance of regret and sorrow. In fact, one would almost suppose that by long practice he had trained one of his eyes —for we ought to have said that there was one of them more sympathetic than the other—to shed its hypocritical tear at the right place, and in such a manner, too, that he might claim all the credit of participating in the very distresses which he refused to relieve, or by which he amassed his wealth.

The poor heart-broken looking girl, who by the way carried an unfortunate baby in her arms, literally tottered out of the room, sobbing bitterly, and with a look of misery and despair that it was woeful to contemplate.

"Ah, then, Harry Hacket," said he, passing to another, "how are you? an' how are all you over in Derrycloony, Harry? not forgettin' the ould couple?"

"Throth middlin' only, Darby. My fine boy, Dennis, is down wid this illness, an' I'm wantin' a barrel of meal from you till towards Christmas."

"Come inside, Harry, to this little nest here, till I tell you something; an', by the way, let your father know I've got a new prayer that he'll like to larn, for it's he that's the pious man, an' attinds to his duties—may God enable him! an' every one that has the devotion in the right place; *amin a Chiernah!*"

He then brought Hacket into a little out-shot behind the room in which the scales were, and, shutting the door, thus proceeded in a sweet, confidential kind of whisper—

"You see, Harry, what I'm goin' to say to you is what I'd not say to ever another in the parish, the divil a one— God pardon me for swearin'—*amin a Chiernah!* I'm ruined all out—smashed down, an' broke horse an' foot; there's the Slevins that wint to America, an' I lost more than thirty pounds by them."

"I thought," replied Hacket, "they paid you before they went; they were always a daicent an' an honest family, an' I niver heard any one spake an ill word o' them."

"Not a penny, Harry."

"That's odd, then, bekase it was only Sunday three weeks that Murty Slevin, their cousin, if you remimber, made you acknowledge that they paid you, at the chapel green."

"Ay, an' I do acknowledge; bekase, Harry, one may as well spake charitably of the absent as not; it's only in private to you that I'm lettin' out the truth."

"Well, well," exclaimed the other, rather impatiently, "what have they to do wid us?"

" Ay have they ! it was what I lost by them an' others—
see now don't be gittin' onpatient, I bid you—time enough
for that when you're refused—that prevints me from bein'
able to give credit as I'd wish. I'm not refusin' you, Harry;
but *achora*, listen : you'll bring me your bill at two months,
only I must charge you a thrifle for trust, for chances, or
profit an' loss, as the schoolmasther says ; but you're to keep
it a saicret from livin' mortual, bekase if it 'ud get known
in these times that I'd do sich a thing, I'd have the very
flesh ait off o' my bones by others wantin' the same thing ;
bring me the bill, then, Harry, an' I'll fill it up myself, only
be dhe husth [1] about it."

Necessity forces those who are distressed to comply with
many a rapacious condition of the kind; and the consequence
was that Hacket did what the pressure of the time compelled
him to do, passed his bill to Skinadre at a most usurious
price, for the food which was so necessary to his family.

It is surprising how closely the low rustic extortioner and
the city usurer upon a larger scale resemble each other in
the expression of their sentiments—in their habits of business
—their plausibility—natural tact— and especially, in that
hardness of heart and utter want of all human pity and sympathy, upon which the success of their black arts of usury
and extortion essentially depends. With extortion in all
its forms Skinadre, for instance, was familiar. From those
who were poor but honest he got a bill such as he exacted
from Hacket, because he knew that, cost what it might to
them, he was safe in their integrity. If dishonest, he still
got a bill and relied upon the law and its cruel list of haras-
sing and fraudulent expenses for security. From others he
got property of all descriptions : from some butter, yarn, a
piece of frieze, a pig, a cow, or a heifer. In fact, nothing that
possessed value came wrong to him, so that it is impossible
to describe adequately the web of mischief which this blood-
sucking old spider contrived to spread around him, especially

---

[1] Hold your tongue.

for those whom he knew to be too poor to avail themselves of a remedy against his villainy.

"Molly Cassidy, how are you?" he said, addressing a poor-looking woman, who carried a parcel of some description rolled up under her cloak; "how are all the family, *achora*?"

"Glory be to God for it, they can scarcely be worse," replied the woman, in that spirit of simple piety and veneration for the Deity, which in all their misery characterizes the Irish people; "but sure we're only sufferin' like others, an' indeed not so bad as many—there's Mick Kelly has lost his fine boy, Lanty; an' his other son, young Mick, isn't expected —an' all wid this sickness, that was brought on them, as it is everywhere, wid bad feedin'."

"They're miserable times, Molly—at laist I find them so —for I dunna how it happens, but every one's disappointment falls upon me, till they have me a'most out of house an' home—throth it ud' be no wondher I'd get hard-hearted some day, wid the way I'm thrated an' robbed by every one—ay, indeed—bekase I'm good-nathured, they play upon me."

The poor creature gave a faint smile, for she knew the man's character thoroughly.

"I have a dish of butther here, Darby," she said, "an' I want meal instead of it."

"Butther, Molly—why thin, Molly, sure it isn't to me you're bringin' butther—me that has so much of it lyin' on my hands here already. Sure, any way, it's down to dirt since the wars is over—butther is—if it was anything else but butther, Molly; but it's of no use—I've too much of it."

"The sorra other thing I have, then, Mr. Skinadre; but sure you'd betther look at it, an' you'll find it's what butther ought to be—firm, clane, an' sweet."

"I can't take it, *achora;* there's no market for it now."

"Here, as we're distressed, take it for sixpence a pound,

and that's the lowest price—God knows if we worn't as we are, it isn't for that you'd get it."

"Troth, I dar' say, you're ill off—as who isn't in these times?—an' it's worse they're gettin' an' will be gettin' every day—throth, I say, my heart bleeds for you—but we can't dale—oh, no!—butther, as I said, is only dirt now."

"For God's sake, then," exclaimed the alarmed creature, "take it for whatever you like."

"It 'ud go hard wid me to see your poor family in a state of outther want," he replied, "an' it's not in my nature to be harsh to a strugglin' person—so whether I lose or gain, I'll allow you threepence a pound for it."

A shade of bitterness came across her features at this iniquitous proposal; but she felt the truth of that old adage, in all its severity, that necessity has no law.

"God help us," she exclaimed, "threepence a pound for sich butther as this!—however, it's the will o' God, sure an' it can't be helped—take it."

"Ay, it's aisy said, take it; but not so aisy to say what 'll I do wid it, when I have it; however, that's the man I am, an' I know how it 'ill end wid me—sarvin' every one, workin' for every one, an' thinkin' of every one but myself, an' little thanks or gratitude for all—I know I'm not fit for sich a world—but still it's a consolation to be doin' good to our fellow-cratures when we can; and that's what lightens my heart."

A woman now entered, whose appearance excited general sympathy, as was evident from the subdued murmurs of compassion which were breathed from the persons assembled, as soon as she entered the room. There was something about her, which, in spite of her thin and worn dress, intimated a consciousness of a position, either then or at some previous time, above that of the common description of farmers' wives. No one could mistake her for a highly-educated woman, but there was in her appearance that decency of manner resulting from habits of independence and from moral feeling, which, at a first glance, whether it be accompanied by superior dress or not, indicates something which is felt to entitle its proprietor to unquestionable respect. The miser, when she entered, had been putting away the dish of butter into the outshot we have mentioned, so that he had not yet an opportunity of seeing her, and ere he returned to the scales, another female possessing probably not less interest to the reader, presented herself—this was Mave or Mabel, the young and beautiful daughter of the pious and hospitable Jerry Sullivan.

Skinadre, on perceiving the matron who preceded her, paused for a moment, and looked at her with a wince in his thin features which might be taken for an indication of either pleasure or pain. He closed the sympathetic eye, and wiped it; but this not seeming to satisfy him, he then closed both, and blew his nose with a little skeleton mealy handkerchief, that lay on a sack beside him for the purpose.

"Hem—a-hem! why thin, Mrs. Dalton, it isn't to my poor place I expected you would come."

"Darby," she replied, "there is no use for any length of conversation between you and me—I'm here contrary to the wishes of my family—but I am a mother, an' cannot look upon their destitution without feelin' that I shouldn't allow my pride to stand between them and death—we are starving, I mean—they are—and I'm come to you to ask for credit— if we are ever able to pay you, we will; if not, it's only one good act done to a family that often did many to you when they thought you grateful."

"I'm the worst in the world—I'm the worst in the world," replied Skinadre; "but it wasn't 'till I knew that you'd be put out o' your farm that I offered for it, and now you've taken away my correcther, and spoke ill o' me everywhere, an' said I bid for it over your heads—ay, indeed; an' that it was your husband that set me up, by the way—oh, yes— an' supposin' it was—an' I'm not denyin' it, but is that any raison that I'd not bid for a good farm, when I knew that yez 'ud be put out of it."

"I am now spakin' about the distress of our family," said Mrs. Dalton, "you know that sickness has been among us, an' is among us—poor Tom is just able to be up, but that's all!"

"Throth an' it 'ud be well for you all, an' for himself too, that he had been taken away afore he comes to a bad end, what he will come to, if God hasn't said it—I hope he feels the affliction he brought on poor Ned Murray an' his family by the hand he made of his unfortunate daughter."

"He does feel it. The death of her brother and their situation has touched his heart, and he's only waitin' for better health and better times to do her justice; but now, what answer do you give me?"

"Why this: I'm harrished by what I've done for every one—an'—an'—the short and the long of it is, that I've neither male nor money to throw away. I couldn't afford it, and I can't. I'm a rogue, Mrs. Dalton—a ¦miser, an extortioner, an ungrateful knave, an' everything that's bad an' worse than another—an' for that raison, I say, I have neither male nor money to throw away. That's what I'd say if I was angry; but I'm not angry. I do feel for you an' them; still, I can't afford to do what you want, or I'd do it, for I like to do good for evil, bad as I am. I'm strivin' to make up my rent, an' to pay an unlucky bill that I have due to-morrow, and doesn't know where the money's to come from to meet both.

"Mave Sullivan, *achora*, what can I——"

Mrs. Dalton, from her position in the room, could not have noticed the presence of Mave Sullivan, but even had she been placed otherwise, it would have been somewhat difficult to get a glimpse at the young creature's face. Deeply did she participate in the sympathy which was felt for the mother of her lover, and so naturally delicate were her feelings, that she had drawn up the hood of her cloak, lest the other might have felt the humiliation to which Mave's presence must have exposed her by the acknowledgment of their distress. Neither was this all the gentle and generous girl had to suffer. She experienced, in her own person, as well as Mrs. Dalton did, the painful sense of degradation which necessity occasions, by a violation of that hereditary spirit of decent pride and independence which the people consider as the prestige of high respect, and which, even whilst it excites compassion and sympathy, is looked upon, to a certain extent, as diminished by even a temporary visitation of poverty. When the meal-man, therefore, addressed her, she unconsciously threw the hood of her cloak back, and disclosed to the spectators a face burning with blushes, and eyes filled with tears. The tears, however, were for the distress of Mrs. Dalton and her family, and the blushes for the painful circumstances which compelled her at once to witness them, and to expose those which were felt under her own care-worn father's roof. Mrs. Dalton, however, on looking round and perceiving what seemed to be an ebullition merely of natural shame, went over to her with a calm but mournful manner, that amounted almost to dignity.

"Dear Mave," said she, "there is nothing here to be ashamed of. God forbid that the struggle of an honest family with poverty should bring a blot upon either your good name or mine. It does not, nor it will not—so dry your tears, my darlin' girl—there are better times before us all, I trust. Darby Skinadre," she added, turning to the miser, "you are both hard-hearted and ungrateful, or you would remember, in our distress, the kindness we showed you and yours. If you can cleanse your conscience from the stain of ingratitude, it must be by a change of life."

"Whatever stain may be on my ungrateful conscience," he replied, turning up his red eyes, as it were with thanksgiving, "there's not the stain of blood and murdher on it— that's one comfort."

Mrs. Dalton did not seem to hear him, neither did she look in the direction of where he stood. As the words were uttered, she had been in the act of extending her hand to Mave Sullivan, who had hers stretched out to receive it. There now occurred, however, a mutual pause. Her hand was withdrawn, as was that of Mave also, who had suddenly become pale as death.

"God bless you, my darlin' girl!" exclaimed Mrs. Dalton, sighing, as if with some hidden sorrow—"God bless you and yours, prays my unhappy heart this day!"

And with these words she was about to depart, when Mave, trembling and much agitated, laid her hand gently and timidly upon hers—adding, in a low, sweet, and tremulous voice—

"My heart is free from that suspicion—I can't tell why—but I don't believe it."

And while she spoke, her small hand gradually caught that of Mrs. Dalton, as a proof that she would not withhold the embrace on that account. Mrs. Dalton returned her pressure, and at the same moment kissed the fair girl's lips, who sobbed a moment or two in her arms, where she threw herself. The other again invoked a blessing upon her head, and walked out, having wiped a few tears from her pale cheeks.

The miser looked upon this exhibition of feeling with some surprise; but as his was not a heart susceptible of the impressions it was calculated to produce, he only said, in a tone of indifference,—

"Well, to be sure now, Mave, I didn't expect to see you shakin' hands wid and kissin' Condy Dalton's wife, at any rate—considherin' all that happened atween the families. However, it's good to be forgivin'—I hope it is—indeed, I know that; for it comes almost to a failin' in myself. Well, achora, what am I to do for you?"

"Will you let me speak to you inside, a minute?" she asked.

"Will I? Why, then, to be sure I will—an' who knows but it's my daughter-in-law I might have you yet, avillish!

Yourself and Darby's jist about an age. Come inside, *ahagur*."

Their dialogue was not of a very long duration. Skinadre, on returning to the scales, weighed two equal portions of oatmeal, for one of which Mave paid him.

"I will either come or send for this," she said, laying her hand upon the one for which she had paid. "If I send any one, I'll give the token I mentioned."

"Very well, *a suchar*—very well," he replied, "it's for nobody livin' but yourself I'd do it; but sure now that I must begin to coort you for Darby, it won't be aisy to refuse you anything in raison."

"Mind, then," she observed, as she seized one of the portions, in order to proceed home—"mind," said she, laying her hand upon that which she was leaving behind her— "mind it's for this one I have paid you."

"Very well, *achora*—it makes no differ; sure a kiss o' them red, purty lips o' yours to Darby will pay the intherest for all."

Two other females now made their appearance, with one of whom our readers are already acquainted. This was no other than the prophet's wife, who had for her companion a woman whom neither she herself nor any one present knew.

"Mave Sullivan, darlin'," exclaimed the former, "I'm glad to see you. Are you goin' home now?"

"I am, Nelly," replied Mave, "just on my step."

"Well, thin, if you stop a minute or two, I'll be part o' the way home wid you. I have something to mention as we go along."

"Very well, then," replied Mave, "make as much haste as you can, Nelly, for I'm in a hurry"; and an expression of melancholy settled upon her countenance as she spoke.

The stranger was a tall, thin woman, much about the age and height of the prophet's wife, but neither so lusty nor vigorous in appearance. She was but indifferently dressed, and though her features had evidently been handsome in her younger days, yet there was now a thin, shrewish expression about the nose, and a sharpness about the compressed lips, and those curves which bounded in her mouth, that betokened much firmness, if not obstinacy of character, joined to a look which might as well be considered an indication of trial and sufferings as of a temper naturally none of the best.

On hearing Mave Sullivan's name mentioned, she started, and looked at her keenly, and for a considerable time; after which she asked for a drink of water, which she got in the kitchen, where she sat, as it seemed, to rest a little.

Nelly, in the mean time, put her hand in a red, three-cornered pocket that hung by her side, and pulling out a piece of writing, presented it to the meal-man. That worthy gentleman, on casting his eyes over it, read it as follows:—

"DARBY SKINADRE,—Give Daniel M'Gowan, otherwise the Black Prophet, any quantity of meal necessary for his own family, which please charge—and you know why—to your friend,
"DICK o' THE GRANGE, Jun."

Skinadre's face, on perusing this document, was that of a man who felt himself pulled in different directions by something at once mortifying and pleasant. He smiled at first— then bit his lip—winked one eye—then another—looked at the prophet's wife with complacency—but immediately checked himself, and began to look keen and peevish. This, however, appeared to be an error on the other side; and the consequence was, that, after some comical alternations, his countenance settled down into its usual expression.

"Troth," said he, "that same Dick o' the Grange, as he calls himself, is a quare young gintleman—as much male as you want—a quare, mad—your family's small, I think?"

"But sharp an' active," she replied, with a hard smile, as of one who cared not for the mirth she made, "as far as we go."

"Ay," said he, abruptly, "divil a much—God pardon me for swearin'—ever they wor good for that had a large appetite. It's a bad sign of either man or woman. There never was a villain hanged yet that didn't ait more to his last breakfast than ever he did at a meal in his life before. Howanever, one may as well have a friend : so I suppose we must give you a thrifle."

When her portion was weighed out, she and Mave Sullivan left this scene of extortion together, followed by the strange women, who seemed, as it were, to watch their motions, or at least to feel some particular interest in them.

He had again resumed his place at the scales, and was about to proceed in his exactions, when the door opened and a powerful young man, tall, big-boned, and broad-shouldered, entered the room, leading or rather dragging with him the poor young woman and her child, who had just left the place in such bitterness and affliction. He was singularly handsome, and of such resolute and manly bearing, that it was impossible not to mark him as a person calculated to impress one with a strong anxiety to know who and what he might be. On this occasion his cheek was blanched and his eye emitted a turbid fire which could scarcely be determined as that of indignation or illness.

" Is it thrue," he asked, " that you've dared to refuse to this—this—unfor—is it thrue that you've dared to refuse this girl and her starvin' father the meal she wanted? Is this thrue, you hard-hearted ould scoundrel?—bekase if it is, by the blessed sky above us, I'll pull the windpipe out of your throat, you infernal miser ! "

He seized unfortunate Skinadre by the neck as he spoke, and almost at the same moment forced him to project his tongue about three inches out of his mouth, causing his face, at the same time, to assume by the violence of the act, an expression of such comic distress and terror, as it was difficult to look upon with gravity.

" Is it thrue," he repeated in a voice of thunder, " that you've dared to do so scoundrelly an act, an' she, the unfortunate creature, famishin' wid hunger herself ? "

Whilst he spoke, he held Skinadre's neck as if in a vice—
firm in the same position—and the latter, of course, could
do nothing more than turn his ferret eyes round as well as
he could, to entreat him to relax his grip.

"Don't choke him, Brian," exclaimed Hacket, who came
forward to interpose; "you'll strangle him—as heaven's
above, you will."

"An' what great crime would that be?" answered the
other, relaxing his awful grip of the miser. "Isn't he, and
every mealmonger like him, a curse an' a scourge to the
counthry?—an' hasn't the same counthry curses and scourges
enough, widout either him or them? Answer me now," he
proceeded, turning to Skinadre, "why did you send her away
widout the food she wanted?"

"My heart bled for her—but——"

"It's a lie, you born hypocrite—it's a lie—your heart never
bled for anything or anybody."

"But you don't know," replied the miser, "what I lost
by——"

"It's a lie, I say," thundered out the gigantic young fellow, once more seizing the unfortunate mealmonger by the
throat, when out again went his tongue, like a piece of
machinery touched by a spring, and again were the red
eyes, now almost starting out of his head, turned round,
whilst he himself was in a state of suffocation, that rendered
his appearance ludicrous beyond description—"it's a lie, I
say, for you have neither thruth nor heart—that's what we
all know."

"For heaven's sake let the man go," said Hacket, "or
you'll have his death to answer for"—and as he spoke he
attempted to unclasp the young man's grip—"Tom Dalton,
I say, let the man go."

Dalton, who was elder brother to the lover of Mave Sullivan, seized Hacket with one of his hands, and spun him like
a child to the opposite end of the room.

"Keep away," he exclaimed, " till I settle wid him—here

now, Skinadre, listen to me: you refused my father credit when we wanted it, although you knew we were honest—you refused him credit when we were turned out of our place, although you knew the sickness was among us—well, you know whether we that wor yer friends, an'—my father, at least—the makin' of you "—and, as he spoke, he accompanied every third word by a shake or two, as a kind of running commentary upon what he said; "ay—you did—you knew it well, an' I could bear all that ; but I can't bear you to turn this unfortunate girl out of your place widout what she wants, an' she sinkin' wid hunger herself. If she's in distress, 'twas I that brought her to it, an' to shame an' to sorrow too—but I'll set all right for you yet, Margaret dear —an' no one has a betther right to spake for her."

"Tom," said the young woman, with a feeble voice, "for the love of God let him go, or he'll drop."

"Not," replied Dalton, "till he gives you what you came for. Come, now," he proceeded, addressing the miser, "weigh her—how much will you be able to carry, Margaret ? "

"Oh, never mind now, Tom," she replied, "I don't want any, it's the ould people at home—it's them—it's them."

"Weigh her out," continued the other, furiously; "weigh her out a stone of male, or by all the lies that ever came from your lips, I'll squeeze the breath out o' your body, you deceitful ould hypocrite."

"I will," said the miser, panting, and adjusting his string of a cravat; "I will, Tom; here, I amn't able, weigh it yourself—I'm not—indeed I'm not able," said he, breathless, "an' I was thinkin' when you came in of sendin' afther her, bekase, when I heard of the sickness among them, that I mayn't sin, but I found my heart bleedin' inwar——"

Tom's clutches were again at his throat. "Another lie," he exclaimed, "an' you're a gone man !—do what I bid you."

Skinadre appeared, in point of fact, unable to do so, and Dalton, seeing this, weighed the unhappy young woman a stone of oatmeal, which, on finding it to be too heavy for her feeble strength, he was about to take up himself, when he put his hands to his temples, then staggered, and fell.

They immediately gathered about him to ascertain the cause of this sudden attack, when it appeared that he had become insensible. His brow was now pale and cold as marble, and a slight dew lay upon his broad forehead; his shirt was open, and exposed to view a neck and breast which, although sadly wasted, were of extreme whiteness and great manly beauty.

Margaret, on seeing him fall, instantly placed her baby in the hands of another woman, and, flying to him, raised his head and laid it upon her bosom; whilst the miser, who had now recovered, shook his head, lifted his hands, and looked as if he felt that his house was undergoing pollution. In the meantime, the young woman bent her mouth down to his ear, and said, in tones that were wild and hollow, and that had more of despair than even of sorrow in them—

"Tom, oh, Tom, are you gone?—hear me—"

But he replied not to her.

"Ah! there was a day," she added, looking with a mournful smile around, "when he loved to listen to my voice; but that day has passed for ever."

He opened his eyes as she spoke; hers were fixed upon him. He felt a few warm tears on his face, and she exclaimed in a low voice, not designed for other ears—

"I forgive you all, Tom dear—I forgive you all!"

He looked at her, and, starting to his feet, exclaimed—

"Margaret, my own dear Margaret, hear me! She is dyin'!" he shouted, in a hoarse and excited voice—"she is dyin' with want! I see it all. She's dead!"

It was too true: the unhappy girl had passed into another life; but whether from a broken heart, caused by sin, shame, and desertion, or from famine and the pressure of general destitution and distress, could never properly be ascertained.

"I see!" exclaimed Dalton, his eyes again blazing, and his voice hollow with emotion—"I see—there she lies; an'

who brought her to that? But I intended to set all right.
Ay—there she lies. An' again, how are we at home?—
brought low—down, down to a mud cabin! Now, Dick o'
the Grange, an' now, Darby Skinadre—now for revenge.
The time is come. I'll take my place at the head of them,
an' what's to be done, must be done. Margaret Murtagh,
you're lyin' dead before me, and by the broken heart you died
of——"

He could add no more: but with these words, tottering
and frantic, he rushed out of the miser's house.

"Wid the help o' God, the young savage is as mad as a
March hare," observed Skinadre, coolly; " but as it's all over
wid the unfortunate crathur, I don't see why an honest man
should lose his own, at any rate."

Whilst uttering the words, he seized the meal, and deliberately emptied it back into the chest from which young
Dalton had taken it.

CHAPTER VIII

A MIDDLEMAN AND MAGISTRATE—MASTER AND MAN

HAVING mentioned a strange woman who made her appearance at Skinadre's, it may be necessary, or, at least, agreeable to the reader, that we should account for her presence
under the roof of that worthy individual, especially as she is
likely to perform a part of some interest in our tale. We
have said already that she started on hearing Mave Sullivan's
name mentioned, and followed her and the Black Prophet's
wife like a person who watched their motions, and seemed to
feel some peculiar interest in either one or both. The reader
must return, then, to the Grey Stone already alluded to,
which to some of the characters in our narrative will probably prove to be a " stone of destiny."

Hanlon having parted from Sarah M'Gowan in a state of
deep and powerful excitement, wended his way along a
lonely and dreary road, to the residence of his master, Dick

o' the Grange. The storm had increased, and was still increasing at every successive blast, until it rose to what might be termed a tempest. It is, indeed, a difficult thing to describe the peculiar state of his feelings as he struggled onwards, sometimes blown back to a standstill, and again driven forward by the gloomy and capricious tyranny of the blast, as if he were its mere plaything. In spite, however, of the conflict of the external elements as they careered over the country around him, he could not shake from his imagination the impression left there by the groan which he had heard at the Grey Stone. A supernatural terror, therefore, was upon him, and he felt as if he were in the presence of an accompanying spirit—of a spirit that seemed anxious to disclose the fact that murder would not rest; and so strongly did this impression gain upon him, that in the fitful howlings of the storm, and in its wild wailings and dying sobs among the trees and hedges, as he went along, he thought he could distinguish sounds that belonged not to this life. Still he proceeded, his terrors thus translating, as it were, the noisy conflict of the elements into the voices of the dead, or thanking heaven that the strong winds brought him to a calmer sense of his position, by the necessity that they imposed of preserving himself against their violence. In this anomalous state he advanced, until he came to a grove of old beeches that grew at the foot of one of the hill-ranges we have described, and here the noises he heard were not calculated to diminish his terrors. As the huge trees were tossed, and swung about in the gloomy moonlight, his ears were assailed by a variety of wild sounds which had never reached them before. The deep and repeated crashes of the tempest, as it raged among them, were accompanied by a frightful repetition of hoarse moanings, muffled groans, and wild, unearthly shrieks, which encountered him from a thousand quarters in the grove, and he began to feel that horrible excitement which is known to be occasioned by the mere transition from extreme cowardice to reckless indifference.

Still he advanced homewards, repeating his prayers with singular energy, his head uncovered notwithstanding the severity of the night, and the rain pouring in torrents upon him, when he found it necessary to cross a level of rough land, at all times damp and marshy but in consequence of the rains of the season, now a perfect morass. Over this he had advanced about half-a-mile, and got beyond the frightful noises of the wood, when some large object rose into the air from a clump of plashy rushes before him, and shot along the blast, uttering a booming sound, so loud and stunning that he stood rivetted to the earth. The noise resembled that which sometimes proceeds from a humming-top, if a person could suppose one made upon such a gigantic scale as to produce the deep and hollow buzz which this being emitted. Nothing could now convince him that he was not surrounded by spirits, and he felt confident that the voice of undiscovered murder was groaning on the blast—shrieking, as it were, for vengeance in the terrible voice of the tempest. He once more blessed himself, repeated a fresh prayer, and struggled forward, weak and nearly exhausted, until at length he reached the village adjoining which his master, Dick o' the Grange, resided.

The winds now, and for some minutes previously, had begun to fall, and the lulls in the storm were calmer and more frequent, as well as longer in duration. Hanlon proceeded to his master's, and, peering through the shutters, discovered that the servants had not yet retired to rest; then bending his steps farther up the village, he soon reached a small isolated cabin, at the door of which he knocked, and in due time was admitted by a thin, tall female, who held a rush-light in her hand.

"God protect us, dear, you're lost!—blessed father, sich a night! Oh! my, my! Well, well; sit near the spark o' fire, sich as it is; but, indeed, it's little you'll benefit by it. Any way, sit down."

Hanlon sat on a stool, and laying his hat beside him on

the floor, he pressed the rain as well as he could out of his drenched hair, and for some time did not speak, whilst the female, squatted upon the ground, somewhat like a hare in her form, sat with the candle in her hand, which she held up in the direction of his face, whilst her eyes were rivetted on him with a look of earnest and solemn inquiry.

"Well," she at length said, "did your journey end, as I told you it would, in nothing? And yet, God presarve me, you look—eh!—what has happened?—you look like one that was terrified, sure enough. Tell me at wanst, did the dhrame come out thrue?"

"I'll not have a light heart this many a day," he replied; "let no one say there's not a Providence above us to bring murdher to light."

"God of glory be about us:" she exclaimed, interrupting him; "something has happened! Your looks would frighten one, an' your voice isn't like the voice of a livin' man. Tell me—and yet for all so curious as I feel, I'm thremblin' this minute—but, tell me, did the dhrame come out thrue, I say?"

"The dhrame came out thrue," he replied solemnly. "I know where the tobaccy-box is that he had about him— the same that thransported my poor uncle, or that was partly the means of doin' it."

The woman crossed herself, muttered a short ejaculatory prayer, and again gathered her whole features into an expression of mingled awe and curiosity.

"Did you go to the place you dhreamt of?" she asked.

"I went to the Grey Stone," he replied, "an' offered up a prayer for his sowl, afther puttin' my right hand upon it in his name, jist as I did on yestherday; an' afther I had got an account of the tobbacy-box, I heard a groan at the spot—as heaven's above me, I did."

"Savior of earth, *gluntho shin*?"[1]

"But that wasn't all. On my way home, I heard, as I

[1] Do you hear that.

was passin' the ould trees at the Rabbit Bank, things that I can't find words to tell you of."

" Well, *acushla*, glory be to God for everything! it's all His will, blessed be His name? What did you hear, *avic*? —but wait till I throw a dhrop o' the holy water that I have hangin' in the little bottle at the bedpost upon us."

She rose whilst speaking, and getting the bottle alluded to, sprinkled both herself and him, after which she hung it up again in its former position.

" There, now, nothin' harmful, at any rate, can come near us after that, blessed be His name! Well, what did you hear comin' home?—I mean at the Rabbit Bank. *Wurrah*," she added, shuddering, " but it's it that's the lonely spot afther night! What was it, dear? "

"Indeed I can scarcely tell you—sich groanins, an' wild shoutins, an' shrieks man's ears never hard in this world, I think; there I hard them as I was comin' past the trees, an' afther I passed them; an' when I left them far behind me, I could hear, every now and then, a wild shriek that made my blood run cowld. But there was still worse as I crossed the Black Park; something got up into the air out o' the rushes before me, an' went off wid a noise not unlike what Jerry Hamilton of the Band makes when he rubs his middle finger up against the tambourine."

" Heaven be about us! " she exclaimed, once more crossing herself, and uttering a short prayer for protection from evil; " but tell me, how did you know it was his box, and how did you find it out? "

" By the letters P. M. and the broken hinge," he replied.

" Blessed be the name of God! " she exclaimed again— " *He* won't let the murdher lie, that's clear. But what I want to know is, how did your goin' to the Grey Stone bring you to the knowledge of the box? "

He then gave her a more detailed account of his conversation with Sarah M'Gowan, and of the singular turn which it chanced to take towards the subject of the handkerchief, in the first instance; but when the coincidence of the letters was mentioned, together with Sarah's admission that she had the box in her possession, she clasped her hands, and looking upwards, exclaimed—

"Blessed be the name of the Almighty for that! Oh, I feel there is no doubt now but the hand of God is in it, an' we'll come at the murdherer or the murdherers yet."

"I hope so," he replied; "but I'm lost wid wet an' cowld; so in the meantime I'll be off home, an' to my bed. I had something to say to you about another matther, but I'll wait till mornin'; for, dear knows, I'm in no condition to spake about anything else to-night. This is a snug little cabin; but, plaise God, in the coorse of a week or so, I'll have you more comfortable than you are. If my own throuble was over me, I wouldn't stop long in the neighbourhood; but as the hand of God seems to be in this business, I can't think of goin' till it's cleared up, as cleared up it will be, I have no doubt, an' can have none, afther what has happened this awful night."

Hanlon was a clever, active, ingenious fellow, who could, as they say in the country, put a hand to anything, and make himself useful in a great variety of employments. He had, in the spring of that year, been engaged as a common labourer by Dick o' the Grange, in which capacity he soon attracted his employer's notice, by his extraordinary skill in almost everything pertaining to that worthy gentleman's establishment. It is true he was a stranger in the country, of whom nobody knew anything—for there appeared to be some mystery about him; but as Dick cared little for either his place of birth or his pedigree, it was sufficient for him to find that Hanlon was a very useful, not to say valuable, young man about his house, that he understood everything, and had an eye and hand equally quick and experienced. The consequence was, that he soon became a favourite with the father and a kind of *sine quâ non* with the son, into whose rustic gallantries he entered with a spirit that satisfied the

latter of his capacity to serve him in that respect as well as
in others. Hanlon, in truth, was just the person for such a
master, and for such an establishment as he kept. Dick o'
the Grange was not a man who, either by birth, education,
or position in society, could entertain any pretensions to rank
with the gentry of the surrounding country. It is true he
was a magistrate, but then he was a middleman, and as such
found himself an interested agent in the operation of one of
the worst and most cruel systems that ever cursed either the
country or the people. We, of course, mean that which
suffered a third party to stand between the head landlord,
and those who in general occupied the soil. Of this system,
it may be with truth said, that the iniquity lay rather in the
principle on which it rested, than in the individual who ad-
ministered it; because it was next to an impossibility that a
man anxious to aggrandize his family—as almost every man
is—could, in the exercise of the habits which enabled him
to do so, avoid such a pressure upon those who were under
him as amounted to great hardship and injustice. The system
held out so many temptations to iniquity in the management
of land, and in the remuneration of labour, that it required
an amount of personal virtue and self-denial to resist them,
that was scarcely to be expected from any one, so difficult
was it to overlook or neglect the opportunities for oppression
and fraud which it thus offered.

Old Dick, although bearing the character of being a violent
and outrageous man, was, however, one of those persons of
whom there will be always somebody found to speak favourably. Hot and ungovernable in temper he unquestionably
was, and capable of savage and cruel acts; but at the same
time his capricious and unsteady impulses rendered him
uncertain, whether for good or evil; so much so, indeed, that
it was impossible to know when to ask him for a favour; nor
was it extraordinary to find him a friend this day to the
man whose avowed enemy he proclaimed himself yesterday
and this same point of character was as true the other way—

for whilst certain that you had him for a friend, perhaps you found him hard at work to oppress or overreach you if he could. The consequence of this peculiarity was, that he had a twofold reputation in the country. Some were found to abuse him, and others to mention many acts of generosity and kindness which he had been known to perform under circumstances where they were least to be expected. This, perhaps, was one reason why they made so strong an impression upon the people, and were so distinctly remembered to his advantage. It is true he was a violent party man, but then he wanted coolness to adjust his resentment to his principles, and thus make them subservient to his private interests. For this reason, notwithstanding his strong and outspoken prejudices, it was a well-known fact that the Roman Catholic population preferred him as a magistrate to many who were remarkable for a more equal and even tenor of life, and in whom, under greater plausibility of manner, there existed something which they would have readily exchanged for his violent abuse of them and their creed.

Such was Dick o' the Grange, a man who, as a middleman and a magistrate, stood out a prominent representative of a class that impressed themselves strongly upon their times, and who, whether as regards their position or office, would not find at the present day in the ranks of any party in Ireland, a single man who could come forward and say that they were not an oppressive evil to the country.

Dick o' the Grange, at this period of our narrative, was far advanced in years, and had for some time past begun to feel what is known in men who have led a hard convivial life, as that breaking down of the constitution which is generally the forerunner of dissolution. On this account he had for some time past resigned the management of his property altogether to his son, Young Dick, who was certainly wild and unreflecting, but neither so impulsively generous nor so habitually violent as his father. The estimate of his charac-

ter which went abroad, was such as might be expected—
many thought him worse, but more thought him better than
the old man. He was the youngest son and a favourite--two
circumstances which probably occasioned his education to be
neglected as it had been. All his sisters and brothers having
been for some years married and settled in life, he and his
father, who was a widower, kept a bachelor's house, where
we regret to say the paternal *surveillance* over his morals
was not so strict as it ought to have been. Young Dick
was handsome, and so exceedingly vain of his person, that
any one wishing to gain a favour, either from himself or
his worthy sire, had little more to do than dexterously apply
a strong dose of flattery to this his weakest point, and the
favour was sure to be granted, for his influence over Old Dick
was boundless.

In this family, then, it was that Hanlon held the situation
we have described—that is, partly a gardener, and partly a
steward, and partly a labouring man. There was a rude and
riotous character in and about Dick's whole place, which
marked it at once as the property of a person below the
character of a gentleman. Abundance there was, and great
wealth; but neither elegance nor neatness marked the house
or furniture. His servants partook of the same equivocal
appearance, as did the father and son, and the " Grange " in
general; but, above all and everything in his establishment
must we place, in originality and importance, Jemmy Branigan, who, in point of fact, ought to receive credit for the
greater portion of old Dick's reputation, or at least for all
that was good of it. Jemmy was his old and confidential—
enemy—for more than forty years, during the greater portion
of which period it could scarcely be said with truth that,
in Jemmy's hands, Dick o' the Grange ought to be looked
upon as a responsible person. When we say "enemy," we
know perfectly well what we mean; for if half a dozen battles
between Jemmy and his master every day during the period
above mentioned constituted friendship, then, indeed, the

reader may substitute the word *friend*, if he pleases. In
fact, Dick and Jemmy had become notorious through the
whole country ; and we are certain that many of our readers
will, at a first glance, recognize these two remarkable originals.
Truly, the ascendancy which Jemmy had gained over the
magistrate was surprising; and nothing could be more
amusing than the interminable series of communications,
both written and oral, which passed between them, in the
shape of dismissals from service on the one side, and notices
to leave it on the other ; each of which, whether written or
oral, was treated by the party noticed with the most thorough
contempt. Nothing was right that Jemmy disapproved of,
and nothing wrong that had his sanction, and this without
any reference whatsoever to the will of his master, who, if
he happened to get into a passion about it, was put down by
Jemmy, who got into a greater passion still; so that, after a
long course of recrimination and Billingsgate on both sides,
delivered by Jemmy in an incomparably louder voice, and
with a more consequential manner, Old Dick was finally
forced to succumb.

The worthy magistrate and his son were at breakfast next
morning, when young "Masther Richard," as he was called,
rang the bell, and Jemmy attended—for we must add, that
Jemmy discharged the duties of butler, together with any
other duty that he himself deemed necessary, and that without leave asked or given.

"Where's Hanlon, Jemmy?" he asked.

"Hanlon—throth it's little matther where he is, an' divil
a one o' myself cares."

"Well, but I care, Jemmy, for I want him. Where is
he ? "

"He's gone up to that ould *streel's*, that lives in the
cabin above there. I don't like the same Hanlon—nobody
here knows anything about him, nor he won't let them know
anything about him. He's as close as Darby Skinadre, and
deep as a dhraw-well. Altogether, he looks as if there was

a weight on his conscience, for all his lightness an' fun—an'
if I thought so, I'd discharge him at wanst."

"And I agree with you for once," observed his master—
"there is some cursed mystery about him. I don't much
like him either, to say the truth."

"An' why don't you like him?" asked Jemmy, with a
contemptuous look.

"I can't say—but I don't."

"No! you can't say? I know you can't say anything, at
all events, that you ought to say," replied Jemmy, who, like
his master, would have died without contradiction; "but *I*
can say why you don't like him—it's bekase he's the best
sarvint ever was about your place—that's the raison you
don't like him. But what do you know about a good sarvint
or a bad one—or about anything else that's useful to you,
God help you."

"If you were near my cane, you old scoundrel, I'd pay you
for your impertinence—ay, would I."

"Ould scoundrel, is it? Oh, hould your tongue—I'm not
of your blood, thank God!—and don't be fastenin' your name
upon me. Ould scoundrel, indeed! Throth, we could spare
an odd one now an' then out of our little establishment."

"Jemmy, never mind," said the son, "but tell Hanlon I
want to speak to him in the office after breakfast."

"If I see him I will, but the divil an inch I'll go out of
my way for it—if I see him I will, an' if I don't I
won't. Did *you* put the fresh bandage to your leg, to keep
in them *pharisee* [1] veins o' yours, as the docthor ordered
you?"

This, in fact, was the usual style of his address to the old
magistrate, when in conversation with him.

"Damn the quack!" replied his master: "no, I didn't."

"An' why didn't you?"

"You're beginning this morning," said the other, losing
temper. "You had better keep quiet, I tell you! If you

---

[1] Varicose, presumably.

don't keep quiet, keep your distance, if you're wise—that's all."

"Why didn't you, I ax," continued Jemmy, walking up to him, with his hands in his coat pockets, and looking coolly, but authoritatively in his face. "I tell you, you must put on the clane bandage; for if you don't know how to take care of yourself, I do, and I will. I'm all that's left over you' now; an' in spite of all I can do, it's a purty account I'd be able to give of you, if I was called on."

"This to my face!" exclaimed Dick—"this to my face, you villain!"—and, as he spoke, the cane was brandished over Jemmy's head, as if it would descend every moment.

"Aye," replied Jemmy, without budging, "ay, indeed—an' a purty face it is—a nice face hard drinkin' an' a bad life has left you. Ah! do if you dare," he added, as the other swung his staff once or twice, as if about to lay it down in reality; "throth, if you do, I'll know how to act."

"What would you do, you ould cancer—what would you do if I did?"

"Troth, what you'll force me to do some day. I know you will, for heaven an' earth couldn't stand you; an' if I do, it's not me you'll have to blame for it. Ay, the same step you will drive me to—I see that."

"What will you do, you old viper, that has been like a blister to me my whole life—what will you do?"

"Send you about your business," replied Jemmy, coolly, but with all the plenitude of authority in his manner; "send you from about the place, an' then I'll have a quiet house. I'll send you to your youngest daughter's, or somewhere, or anywhere, out of this. So now that you know my determination, you had betther keep yourself cool, unless, indeed, you wish to thravel. Oh, then, heavens above, but you wor a bitther sight to me, an' but it was the unlucky day that ever the divil druv you acrass me!"

"Dick," said the father, "as soon as you go into the office, write a discharge, as bad a one for that ould vagabond as the

English language can enable you to do—for, by the light of
heaven, he shan't sleep another night under this roof."

"Sha'n't I?—we'll see that, though. To the divil I pitch
yourself and your discharge—an' now mark my words. I'll
be no longer throubled wid you ; you've been all my life a
torment an' a heartbreak to me—a blisther of French flies
was swan's-down compared to you ; but, by the book, I'll end
it at last—ay, will I—I give you up—I surrindher you as a
bad bargain—I wash my hands out o' you—this is Tuesday
mornin', God bless the day, an' the weather—an' woful
weather it is—but sure it's betther than you desarve, an' I
don't doubt but it's you an' the likes o' you that brings it on
us ! Ay, this is Tuesday mornin,' an' I now give you warnin'
that on Sathurday next you'll see the last o' me—an' don't
think that this warnin' is like the rest, or that I'll relent
agin, as I was foolish enough to do often before. No—my
mind's made up—an' indeed—" here his voice sank to a tone
of great calmness and philosophy, like a man who was now
above all human passion,-and who could consequently talk
in a voice of cool and quiet determination—" an', indeed," he
added, " my conscience was urgin' me to this for some time
past—so that I'm glad things has taken this turn."

"I hope you'll keep your word, then," said his master,
" but before you go, listen to me."

" Listen to you—to be sure I will; God forbid I wouldn't ;
let there be nothing, at any rate, but civility between us
while we're together ; what is it ? "

" You asked me last night to let Widow Leary's cow out
o' the pound."

" Ay, did I ! "

" And I swore I wouldn't."

" I know you did. Who would doubt that, at any rate ? "

" Well, before you leave us, be off now and let the animal
out o' the pound."

" Is that it ? Oh, God help you ! what'll you do when
you'll be left to yourself, as you will be on Sathurday next ?

' Let her out,' says you. Throth, the poor woman had her
cow safe and sound at home wid her before she went to bed
last night, and her poor childre had her milk to 'kitchen' their
praties, the craythurs. Do you think I'd let her stay in till
the maggot bit you ? Oh, ay, indeed'! In the mane time,
as soon as you're done breakfast, I want you in the study,
to put the bandage on that ould, good-for-nothin' leg o' yours;
an' mark my words, let there be no shirkin' now, for on it
must go, an' will, too. If I see that Hanlon, I'll tell him you
want him, Masther Richard ; an' now that I'm on it, I had
betther say a word to you before I go ; bekase, when I do go,
you'll have no one to guide you, God help you, or to set you a
Christian patthern. You see that man sittin' there wid that
bad leg, stretched out upon the chair ? "

" I do, Jemmy—ha, ha, ha ! Well, what next ? "

" That man was the worst patthern ever you had. In one
word, don't folly his example in anything—in any one single
thing ; an' then there may be some chance o' you still. I'll
want you by-an'-by in the study, I tould you."

These last words were addressed to his master, at whom he
looked as one might be supposed to do at a man whose case,
in a moral sense, was hopeless ; after which, having uttered
a groan that seemed to intimate the woful affliction he was
doomed, day by day, to suffer, he left the room.

It is not our intention, neither is it necessary, that we
should enter into the particulars of the interview which
Hanlon had that morning with young Dick. It is merely
sufficient to state that they had a private conversation in
the old magistrate's office, at which the female whom Hanlon
had visited the night before, was present. When this was
concluded, Hanlon walked with her a part of the way, evidently holding serious and interesting discourse touching a
subject which we may presume bore upon the extraordinary
proceedings of the previous night. He closed by giving her
directions how to proceed on her journey ; for it seemed she
was not acquainted with the way, being, like himself, but a

stranger in the neighbourhood:—" You will go on," said he,
" till you reach the height at Aughindrummon; from that
you will see the trees at the Rabbit Bank undher you; then
keep the road straight till you come to where it crosses the
ford of the river: a little on this side, and where the road
turns to your right, you will find the Grey Stone, an' jist
opposite that you will see the miserable cabin where the
Black Prophet lives."

" Why do they call him the Black Prophet ? "

" Partly, they tell me, from his appearance, and partly
bekase he delights in prophesyin' evil."

" But could he have anythin' to do wid the murdher ? "

" I was thinkin' about that," he replied. " and had some
talk this mornin' wid a man that's livin' a long time—indeed,
that was born—a little above the place—and he says, that
the Black Prophet, or M'Gowan, did not come to the neighbourhood till afther the murdher. I wasn't myself cool
enough last night to ask his daughter many questions about
it ; an' I was afraid, besides, to appear over anxious in the
business. So now that you have your instructions in that
and the other matthers, you'll manage everything as well as
you can."

Hanlon then returned to the Grange, and the female proceeded on her mission to the house, if house it could be called,
of the Black Prophet, for the purpose, if possible, of collecting such circumstances as might tend to throw light upon a
dark and mysterious murder.

When Sarah left her father, after having poulticed his
face, to go a kailey, as she said, to a neighbour's house, she
crossed the ford of the river, and was proceeding in the same
direction that had been taken by Hanlon the preceding night,
when she met a strange woman, or rather she found her
standing, apparently waiting for herself, at the Grey Stone.
From the position of the stone, which was a huge one, under
one ledge of which, by the way, there grew a little clump of
dwarf elder, it was impossible that Sarah could pass her

without coming in tolerably close contact; for the road was
an old and narrow one, though perfectly open and without
hedge or ditch on either side of it.

"Maybe you could tell me, young woman, whereabouts
here a man lives that they call Donnel Dhu, or the Black
Prophet; his real name is M'Gowan, I think?"

"I ought to be able to tell you, at any rate," replied
Sarah; "I'm his daughter."

The strange woman, on surveying Sarah more closely,
looked as if she never intended to remove her eyes from her
countenance and figure. She seemed for a moment, as it
were, to forget every other object in life—her previous conversation with Hanlon—the message on which she had been
sent—and her anxiety to throw light upon the awful crime
that had been committed at the spot whereon she stood.
At length she sighed deeply, and appeared to recover her
presence of mind, and to break through the abstraction in
which she had been wrapped.

"You're his daughter, you say?"

"Ay, I do say so."

"Then you know a young man by name Pierce—och,
what am I sayin'?—by name Charley Hanlon?"

"To be sure I do—I'm not ashamed of knowin' Charley
Hanlon."

"You have a good opinion of him, then?"

"I have a good opinion of him; but not so good as I had,
though."

"*Musha*, why, then, might one ax?"

"I'm afeared he's a cowardly crathur, and rather unmanly
a thrifle. I like a man to be a man, an' not to get as white
as a sheet, an' as cowld as a tombstone, bekase he hears what
he thinks to be a groan at night, an' it may be nothin' but
an ould cow behind a ditch. Ha! ha! ha!"

"An' where did he hear the groan?"

"Why, here where we're standin'. Ha! ha! ha! I was
thinkin' of it since, and I did hear somethin' very like a

groan; but what about it? Sich a night as last night would make any one groan that had a groan in them."

"You spoke about ditches, but sure there's no ditches here."

"Divil a matther—who cares what it was? What did you want wid my father?"

"It was yourself I wanted to see."

"Faix an' you've seen me, then, an' the full o' your eye you've tuck out o' me. You'll know me again, I hope."

"Is your mother livin'?"

"No."

"How long is she dead, do you know?"

"I do not: I hardly remimber anything about her. She died when I was a young clip—a mere child, I believe. Still," she proceeded rather slowly, musing, and putting her beautiful and taper fingers to her chin—"I think that I *do* remimber—it's like a dhrame to me, though, an' I dunna but it is one—still, it's like a dhrame to me, that I was wanst in her arms, that I was cryin' an' that she kissed me—that she kissed me! If she had lived, it's a different life maybe I'd lead, an' a different crature I'd be to-day maybe; but I never had a mother."

"Did your father marry a second time?"

"He did."

"Then you have a stepmother?"

"Ay, have I."

"Is she kind to you, an' do you like her?"

"Middlin'—she's not so bad—betther than I deserve, I doubt. I'm sorry for what I did to her; but then I have the divil's temper, an' have no guide o' myself when it comes on me. I know, whatever she may be to me, I'm not the best stepdaughter to her."

The strange female was evidently much struck with the appearance and singularly artless disposition of Sarah, as well as with her extraordinary candour. And, indeed, no wonder; for as this neglected creature spoke, especially with

reference to her mother, her eyes flashed and softened with
an expression of brilliancy and tenderness that might be said
to resemble the sky at night, when the glowing coruscations
of the *Aurora Borealis* sweep over it like sheets of lightning,
or fade away into those dim but graceful undulations, which
fill the mind with a sense of such softness and beauty.

" I don't know," observed her companion, sighing and
looking at her affectionately, " how any stepmother could be
harsh to you."

" Ha ! ha ! ha ! don't you, indeed ? Faix, then, if you had
me, maybe you wouldn't think so—I'm nothin' but a born
divil when the fit's on me."

" Charley Hanlon," proceeded the strange woman, " bid
me ax you for the ould tobaccy-box you promised him last
night."

" Well, but he promised me a handkerchy ; have you got
it ? "

" I have," replied the other, producing it ; " but then I'm
not to give it to you, unless you give me the box for it."

" But I havn't the box now," said Sarah ; " how-and-ever
I'll get it for him."

" Are you sure that you can an' will ? " inquired the other.

" I had it in my hand yesterday," she said, " an' if it's to
be had I'll get it."

" Well then," observed the other, mildly, " as soon as you
get him the box, he'll give you this handkerchy ; but not till
then."

" Ha ! " she exclaimed, kindling, " is that his bargain ;
does he think I'd thrick him or cheat him ?—hand it here."

" I can't," replied the other; " I'm only to give it to you
when I get the box."

" Hand it here, I say," returned Sarah, whose eyes flashed
in a moment ; " it's Peggy Murray's rag, I suppose—hand it
here, I bid you."

The woman shook her head, and replied, " I can't—not till
you get the box."

Sarah replied not a word, but sprang at it, and in a minute had it in her hands.

"I would tear it this minute into ribands," she exclaimed, with eyes of fire and glowing cheeks, " an' thramp it undher my feet, too; only that I want it to show her, that I may have the advantage over her."

There was a sharp, fierce smile of triumph on her features as she spoke ; and altogether her face sparkled with singular animation and beauty.

" God bless me!" said the strange woman, looking at her with a wondering yet serious expression of countenance ; " I wanst knew a face like yours, an' a temper the aquil of it— at any rate, my good girl, you don't pay much respect to a stranger. Is your stepmother at home ? "

" She is not, but my father is ; however, I don't think he'd see you now. My stepmother's gone to Darby Skinadre, the mealmonger's."

" I'm goin' there."

" An' if you see her," replied the other, " you'll know her by a score on her cheek—ha! ha! ha! an' when you see it, maybe you'll thank God I'm not your stepdaughter."

" Isn't there a family named Sullivan that lives not far from Skinadre's ? "

" There is ; Jerry Sullivan ; it's his daughter that's the beauty—*Gra Gal* Sullivan. Little she knows what's preparin' for her ! "

" How am I to go to Skinadre's from this ? " asked the woman.

" Up by that road there ; any one will tell you as you go along."

"Thank you, dear," replied the woman, tenderly ; " God bless you ; you are a wild girl, sure enough; but, above all things, afore I go, don't forget the box for—for—och, for— Charley Hanlon. God bless you, *a colleen machree*, an' make you what you ought to be ! "

Sarah, during many a long day, had not heard herself ad-

dressed in an accent of kindness or affection ; for it would
be wrong to bestow upon the rude attachment which her
father entertained for her, or his surly mode of expressing
it, any term that could indicate tenderness, even in a remote
degree. She looked, therefore, at the woman earnestly, and
as she did so her whole manner changed to one of melancholy
and kindness. A soft and benign expression came like the
dawn of breaking day over her features, her voice fell into
melody and natural sweetness, and approaching her companion, she took her hand and exclaimed—

" May God bless *you* for thim words ! " it's many a day
since I heard the voice o' kindness. I'll get the box, if it's
to be had, if it was only for your own sake."

She then passed on to her neighbour's house, and the next
appearance of her companion was that in which the reader
caught a glimpse of her in the house of Darby Skinadre,
from which she followed Nelly M'Gowan and Mave Sullivan
with an appearance of such interest.

CHAPTER IX

MEETING OF STRANGERS—MYSTERIOUS DIALOGUES.

GRA GAL SULLIVAN and the prophet's wife, having left the
miser's meal-shop, proceeded in the direction of Aughamur-
an, evidently in close, and, if one could judge by their gestures, deeply important conversation. The strange woman
followed them at a distance, meditating, as might be perceived
by her hesitating manner, upon the most seasonable moment
of addressing either one or both, without seeming to interrupt
or disturb their dialogue. Although the actual purport of
the topic they discussed could not be known by a spectator,
yet, even to an ordinary observer, it was clear that the elder
female uttered something that was calculated to warn or
alarm the younger. She raised her extended forefinger,
looked earnestly into the face of her companion, then upwards

solemnly, and clasping her hands with vehemence, appeared to close her assertion by appealing to heaven in behalf of its truth; the younger looked at her with wonder, seemed amazed, paused suddenly on her step, raised her hands, and looked as if about to express terror; but, checking herself, appeared as it were perplexed by uncertainty and doubt. After this the elder woman seemed to confide some secret or sorrow to the other, for she began to weep bitterly, and to wring her hands as if with remorse, whilst her companion looked like one who had been evidently transformed into an impersonation of pure and artless sympathy, She caught the rough hand of the other, and ere she had proceeded very far in her narrative, a few tears of compassion stole down her youthful cheek; after which she began to administer consolation in a manner that was at once simple and touching. She pressed the hand of the afflicted woman between hers, then wiped her eyes with her own handkerchief, and soothed her with a natural softness of manner that breathed at once of true tenderness and delicacy.

As soon as this affecting scene had been concluded, the strange woman imperceptibly mended her pace, until her proximity occasioned them to look at her with that feeling which prompts us to recognise the wish of a person to address us, as it is often expressed, by an appearance of mingled anxiety and diffidence, when they approach us. At length Mave Sullivan spoke—

" Who is that strange woman that is followin' us, an' wants to say something, if one can judge by her looks ? "

" Well, I don't know," replied Nelly; " but whatsomever it may be, she wishes to speak to either you or me, no doubt of it."

" She looks like ' a poor woman,' " [1] said Mave, " an' yet she didn't ask anything in Skinadre's, barrin' a drink of water; but God pity her if she's comin' to us for relief, poor crature! At any rate, as she appears to have care and distress in her face, I'll spake to her."

[1] A common and compassionate name for a person forced to ask alms.

She then beckoned the female to approach them, who did so; but they could perceive, as she advanced, that they had been mistaken in supposing her to be one of those unhappy beings whom the prevailing famine had driven to mendicancy. There was visible in her face a feeling of care and anxiety certainly, but none of that supplicating expression which is at once recognised as the characteristic of the wretched class to which they supposed her to belong. This circumstance considerably embarrassed the inexperienced girl, whose gentle heart at the moment sympathized with the stranger's anxieties, whatever they may have been, and she hesitated a little, when the woman approached, in addressing her. At length she spoke—

" We wor jist sayin' to one another," she observed, " that it looked as if you wished to spake to either this woman or me."

" You're right enough, then," she replied; " I have something to say to her, and a single word to yourself, too."

" An' what is it you have to say to me? " asked Nelly; " I hope it isn't to borry money from me, bekase if it is, my banker has failed, an' left me poor as a church mouse."

" Are you in distress, poor woman? " inquired the generous and kind-hearted girl. " Maybe you're hungry; it isn't much we can do for you; but little as it is, if you come home with me, you'll come to a family that won't scruple to share the little they have *now* with any one that's worse off than themselves."

" Ay, you may well say ' now,' " observed the Prophet's wife; " for until now it's they that could always afford it; an' indeed it was the ready an' the willin' bit was ever at your father's table."

The stranger looked upon the serene and beautiful features of Mave with a long gaze of interest and admiration; after which she added, with a sigh—

" And you, I believe, are the girl they talk so much about for the fair face and the good heart? Little pinetration it takes to see that you have both, my sweet girl. If I don't mistake, your name is Mave Sullivan, or *Gra Gal*, as the people mostly call you."

Mave, whose natural delicacy was tender and pure as the dew-drop of morning, on hearing her praises thus uttered by the lips of a stranger, blushed so deeply, that her whole neck and face became suffused with the delicious crimson of modesty, unconscious that, in doing so, she was adding fresh testimony to the impressions which had gone so generally abroad of her extraordinary beauty, and the many unostentatious virtues which adorned her humble life.

" Mave Sullivan is my name," she replied, smiling through her blushes; " as to the other nickname, the people will call one what they like, no matther whether it's right or wrong."

" The people's seldom wrong, then, in givin' names of the kind," returned the stranger; " but in your case they're right at all events, as any one may know that looks upon you: that sweet face an' them fair looks is seldom ever found with a bad heart. May God guard you, my purty and innocent girl, an' keep you safe from all evil, I pray His holy name this day ! "

The Prophet's wife and Mave exchanged looks as the woman spoke, and Mave said,—

" I hope you don't think there's any evil before me ? "

" Who is there," replied the stranger, " that can say there's not ? Sure it's before us and about us every hour in the day; but in your case, darlin', I jist say—be on your guard, an' don't trust or put belief in any one that you don't know well. That's all I can say, an' indeed all I know."

" I feel thankful to you," replied Mave; " and now that you wish me well—for I'm sure you do—maybe you'd grant me a favour ? "

" If it's widin the bounds of my power I'll do it," returned the other, " but it's little I can do, God help me ! "

" Nelly," said Mave, " will you go on to the cross-roads there, an' I'll be with you in a minute."

The cross-roads alluded to were only about a couple of hundred yards before them. The Prophet's wife proceeded, and Mave renewed the conversation.

"What I want you to do for me is this—that is if you can do it—maybe you could bring a couple of stone o' meal to a family of the name of—of——" Here she blushed again, and her confusion became so evident that she felt it impossible to proceed until she had recovered in some degree her composure. "Only two or three years agone," she continued, "they were the daicentest farmers in the parish; but the world went against them, as it has of late a'most against every one, owin' to the fall of prices, and now they're out of their farm, very much reduced, and there's sickness among them as well as want. They've been livin'," she proceeded, wiping away the tears which were now fast flowing, "in a kind of cabin or little cottage not far from the fine house an' place that was not long ago their own. Their name," she added, after a pause, in which it was quite evident that she struggled strongly with her feelings, "is—is—Dalton."

"Was the young fellow one of them," asked the woman, "that was so outrageous awhile ago in the miser's? I think I heard the name given to him."

"Oh, I have nothing to say for him," replied Mave; "he was always wild, but they say never bad-hearted; it's the rest of the family I'm thinkin' about—an' even that young man isn't more than three or four days up out o' the fever. What I want you to do is to bring the meal I'm spakin' of to that family—any one will show you their little place—an' to lave it there about dusk this evenin', so that no one will ever know you do it; an', as you love God an' hope for mercy, don't breathe my name in the business at all."

"I will do it for you," replied the other; "but, in the meantime, where am I to get the meal?"

"Why, at the miser's," replied Mave; "an' when you go there, tell him that the person who tould him they wouldn't forget it to him sent you for it, an' you'll get it."

"God forbid I'd refuse you that much," said the stranger; "an' although it'll keep me out longer than I expected, still I'll manage it for you, an', come or go what will, widout mentioning your name."

"God bless you for that," said Mave, "an' grant that you may never be brought to the same hard pass that they're in, an' keep you from ever havin' a heavy or a sorrowful heart."

"Ah, *acushla oge*," replied the woman," with a profound sigh, "that prayer's too late for me; anything else than a heavy an' a sorrowful heart I've seldom had; for the last twenty years and upwards little but care an' sorrow has been upon me."

"Indeed, one might easily guess as much," said Mave; "you have a look of heart-break an' sorrow, sure enough. But answer me this—how do you know that there's evil before me or about me?"

"I don't know much about it," returned the other, "but I'm afeard there's something to your disadvantage planned or a-plannin' against you. When I seen you a while ago, I didn't know who you were till I heard your name; I'm a stranger here, not two weeks in the neighbourhood, an' know hardly anybody in it."

"Well," observed Mave, who had fallen back upon her own position, and the danger alluded to by the stranger, "I'll do nothin' that's wrong myself, an', if there's danger about me, as I hear there is, it's a good thing to know that God can guard me in spite of all that any one can do against me."

"Let that be your principle, *ahagur*; sooner or later the hand o' God can an' will make everything clear, an', afther all, dear, He is the best protection, blessed be His name!"

They had now reached the cross-roads already spoken of, where the Prophet's wife again joined them for a short time, previous to her separation from Mave, whose way from that point lay in a direction opposite to theirs.

"This woman," said Mave, "wishes to go to Condy Dalton's in the coorse o' the evenin', an' you, Nelly, can show her from the road the poor place they now live in, God help them!"

"To be sure," replied the other, "an' the house where they did live when they wor *at* themselves, full, an' warm, an' daicent; an' it is a hard case on them, God knows, to be turned out like beggars from a farm that they spent hundreds on, an' to be forced to see the lan'lord, ould Dick o' the Grange, now settin' it at a higher rent, an' puttin' into his own pocket the money that they laid out upon improvin' it an' makin' it valuable for him an' his; throth, it's open robbery, an' nothin' else."

"It *is* a hard case upon them, as everybody allows," said Mave; "but it's over now, an' can't be helped. Good-bye, Nelly, an' God bless you; an' God bless you, too," she added, addressing the strange woman, whose hand she shook and pressed. "You are a great deal oulder than I am, an', as I said, every one may read care an' sorrow upon your face. Mine doesn't show it yet, I know, but, for all that, the heart within me is full of both, an' no likelihood of it's ever bein' otherwise with me."

As she spoke the tears again gushed down her cheeks; but she checked her grief by an effort, and, after a second hurried good-bye, she proceeded on her way home.

"That seems a mild girl," said the strange woman, "as she is a lovely crathur to look at."

"She's betther than she looks," returned the Prophet's wife, "an' that's a great deal to say for her."

"That's but truth," replied the stranger, "an' I believe it, for indeed she has goodness in her face."

"She has, an' in her heart," replied Nelly; "no wondher, indeed, that every one calls her the *Gra Gal*, for it's she that well desarves it; "you are bound for Condy Dalton's, then?" she added.

"I am," said the other.

"I think you must be a sthranger in the counthry, otherwise I'd know your face," continued Nelly; "but maybe you're a relation of theirs."

"I'm a sthranger," said the other, "but no relation."

"The Dalton's," proceeded Nelly, "are daicent people, but hot an' hasty, as the sayin' is. It's the blow before the word wid them always."

"Ay, but they say," returned her companion, "that a hasty heart was never a bad one."

"Many a piece o' nonsense they say as well as that," rejoined Nelly; "I know them that 'ud put a knife into your heart hastily enough—ay, an' give you a hasty death into the bargain. They'll first break your head—cut you to the skull, an' then, indeed, they'll give you a plasther. That was iver an' always the correcthur of the same Daltons ; an', if all accounts be thrue, the hand o' God is upon them, an' will be upon them till the bloody deed is brought to light."

"How is that ? " inquirêd the other, with intense interest, whilst her eyes became suddenly rivetted upon Nelly's hard features.

"Why, a murdher that was committed betther than twenty years ago in this neighbourhood."

"A murdher ! " exclaimed the stranger. "Where?—when ?—how ? "

"I can tell you where, an' I can tell you when," replied Nelly, "but there I must stop, for, unless I was at the committin' of it, you might know very well I couldn't tell you how."

"Where, then ? " she asked, and, whilst she did so, it was by a considerable effort that she struggled to prevent her agitation from being noticed by the Prophet's wife.

"Why, near the Grey Stone, at the cross-roads of Mallybenagh—that's the where."

"An' now for the when," asked the stranger, who almost panted with anxiety as she spoke.

"Let me see," replied Nelly, "fourteen and six makes twenty, an' two before that, or nearly—I mane the year o'

the rebellion. Why, it's not all out two-and-twenty years,
I think."

"Aisy," said the other, "I'm but very weak an' feeble;
will you jist wait till I rest a minute on this green bank by
the road?"

"What ails you?" asked Nelly; "you look as if you'd got
suddintly ill."

"I did get a little ill, but it'll soon pass away," she answered; "thrue enough," she added in a low voice, as if in
a soliloquy, "God is a just judge—He is—He is! Well, but
—oh, I'll soon get betther—well, but listen, what became
of the murdhered man?—was the body ever got?"

"Nobody knows that—the body was never got—that is to
say, nobody knows where it's now lyin'—snug enough too."

"Ha!" thought the stranger, eyeing her furtively—
"snug enough!—there's more knowledge where that came
from. What do you mane by snug enough?" she asked,
abruptly.

"Mane!" replied the other, who at once perceived the
force of the unguarded expression she had used—"mane,
why what could I mane, but that whoever did the deed
hid the body where very few would be likely to find it?"

Her companion now stood up, and, approaching the Prophet's wife, raised her hand, and said, in a tone that was
both startling and emphatic—

"I met you this day, as you may think, by accident;
but, take my word for it, and as sure as we must both
account for our acts, it was the hand o' God that brought
us together. I now look into your face, an' I tell you that
I see guilt an' throuble there—ay, an' the dark work of
a conscience that's gnawin' your heart both night an' day."

While speaking, she held her face within about a foot
of Nelly's, into which she looked with an expression so
searching and dreadful in its penetration, that the other
shrunk back, and felt for a moment as if subdued by a
superior spirit. It was, however, only for a moment; the

sense of her subjection passed away, and she resumed that
hard and imperturbable manner, for which she had been all
her life so remarkable, unless when, like Etna or Vesuvius,
she burst out of this seeming coldness into fire and passion.
There, however, they stood, looking sternly into each other's
faces, as if each felt anxious that the other should quail
before her gaze—the stranger, in order that her impressions
might be confirmed ; and the Prophet's wife, that she should,
by the force of her strong will, fling off those traces of
inquietude which she knew very well were often too legible
in her countenance.

"You are wrong," said Nelly, "an' have only mistaken
my face for a lookin'-glass. It was your own you saw,
an' it was your own you wor spakin' of—for if ever I
saw a face that publishes an ill-spent life on the part
of its owner, yours is it."

"Care an' sorrow I have had," replied the other, "an'
the sin that causes sorrow, I grant ; but there's knowledge
in your hollow eye of somethin' that's weighin' down your
heart, an' that won't let you rest until you give it up.
You needn't deny it, for you can't hide it—hard your eye
is, but it's not clear, an' I see that it quivers, an' is unaisy
before mine."

"I said you're mistaken," replied the other ; "but even
supposin' you wor not, how is it your business whether
my mind is aisy or not ? You won't have my sins to
answer for."

"I know that," said the stranger ; "an' God sees my
own account will be too long an' too heavy, I doubt. I
now beg of you, as you hope to meet judgment, to think
of what I said. Look into your own heart, an' it will
tell you whether I am right or whether I am wrong.
Consult your husband, an' if he has any insight at all
into futurity, he must tell you that, unless you clear your
conscience, you'll have a hard death-bed of it."

"You're goin' to Condy Dalton's," replied Nelly, with

much coolness, but whether assumed or not it is difficult
to say; "look into his face, an' thry what you can find
there. At any rate, report has it that there's blood upon
his hand, an' that the downfall of himself an' his family
is only the vengeance of God, an' the curse of murdher
that's pursuin' him an' them."

"Why," inquired the other, eagerly, "was he accused
of it?"

"Ay, an' taken up for it; but bekase the body wasn't
found, they could do nothin' to him."

"May Heaven assist me!" exclaimed the stranger; "but
this day is—however, God's will be done, as 'it *will* be
done! Are you goin'?"

"I'm goin'," replied Nelly; "by crossin' the fields here,
I'll save a great deal of ground; an' when you get as far
as the broken bridge, you'll see a large farm-house without
any smoke from it; about a quarter of a mile or less beyant
that you'll find the house you're lookin' for—the house
where Condy Dalton lives."

Having thus directed the stranger, the Prophet's wife
entered a gap that led into a field, and proceeded on her
way homewards, having, ere she departed, glanced at her
with a meaning which rendered it extremely difficult to
say whether the singular language addressed to her had
left behind it any such impression as the speaker wished
it to produce. Their glances met and dwelt on each other
for a short time; the strange woman pointed solemnly
towards the sky, and the Prophet's wife smiled carelessly;
but yet, by a very keen eye, it might have been noticed
that, under this natural or affected indifference, there lurked
a blank or rather an unquiet expression, such as might
intimate that something within her had been moved by the
observations of her strange companion.

CHAPTER X

THE BLACK PROPHET MAKES A DISCLOSURE

THE latter proceeded on her way home, having marked the miserable hovel of Condy Dalton. At present our readers will accompany us once more to the cabin of Donnel Dhu, the Prophet.

His wife, as the reader knows, had been startled into something like remorse, by the incidents which had occurred within the last two days, and especially by the double discovery of the dead body and the tobacco-box. Sarah, her stepdaughter, was now grown, and as she very reasonably concluded, her residence in the same house with this fiery and violent young female was next to an impossibility. The woman herself was naturally coarse and ignorant; but still there was mixed up in her character a kind of apathetic or indolent feeling of rectitude or vague humanity, which rendered her liable to occasional visitations of compunction for whatever she did that was wrong. The strongest principle in her, however, was one which is frequently to be found among her class—I mean such a lingering impression of religious feeling as is not sufficiently strong to prevent the commission of crime, but yet is capable by its influence to keep the conscience restless and uneasy under its convictions. Whether to class this feeling with weakness or with virtue, is indeed difficult; but to whichsoever of them it may belong, of one thing we are certain, that many a mind, rude and hardened by guilt, is weak or virtuous only on this single point. Persons so constituted are always remarkable for feelings of strong superstition, and are easily influenced by the occurrence of slight incidents, to which they are certain to attribute a peculiar significance, especially when connected with anything that may occasion them uneasiness for the time, or which may happen to occupy their thoughts, or affect their own welfare or interests.

The reader need not be surprised, therefore, on learning that this woman, with all her apathy of character on the general matters of life, was accessible to the feeling or principle we have just described, nor that the conversation she had just had with the strange woman both disturbed and alarmed her.

On returning, she found her husband and stepdaughter both at home; the latter hacking up some whitethorn wood with an old hatchet, for the fire, and the other sitting with her head leaning gloomily upon his hand, as if ruminating upon the vicissitudes of a troubled or ill-spent life.

Having deposited her burthen, she sat down, and drawing a long breath, wiped her face with the corner of a blue *praskeen* which she always wore, and this she did with a serious and stern face, intimating, as it were, that her mind was engaged upon matters of deep interest, whatever they might have been.

"What's that you're doin'?" she inquired of Sarah, in a grave, sharp voice.

"Have you no eyes?" replied the other; "don't you see what I'm doin'?"

"Where did you get them whitethorns that you're cuttin' up?"

"Where did I get them, is it?"

"Ay; I said so."

"Why, where they grew—ha! ha! ha! There's information for you."

"Oh, God help you! how do you expect to get through life at all?"

"Why, as well as I can—although not, maybe, as well as I wish."

"Where did you cut them thorns, I ax?"

"An' I tould you; but since that won't satisfy you, I cut them on the *Rath* above there."

"Heavens presarve us! You hardened jade, have you no fear of anything about you?"

" Divil a much that I know of, sure enough."

" Didn't you know that them thorns belongs to the fairies, and that some evil will betide any one that touches or injures a single branch o' them? "

" Divil a single branch I injured," replied Sarah, laughing; " I cut down the whole tree at wanst."

" My sowl to glory, if I think it's safe to live in the house wid you, you hardened divil."

" Throth I think you may well say so, afther yesterday's escape," returned Sarah; " an' I have no objection that you should go to glory, body an' sowl; an' a purty piece o' goods will be in glory when you're there—ha ! ha! ha ! "

" Throw out them thorns, I bid you."

" Why so ? Don't we want them for the fire ? "

" No matther for that; we don't want to bring the ' good people '—this day's Thursday, the Lord stand between us an' harm—amin !—about our ears. Out wid them ! "

" No, the sorra branch."

" Out wid them, I say. Are you afeard of neither God nor the divil ? "

" Not overburdened wid much fear of either o' them," replied the daring young creature.

" Aren't you afeard o' the good people, then ? "

" If they're good people, why should we be afeard o' them ? No, I'm not."

" Put the thorns out, I bid you again."

" Divil a chip, mother dear; if your own evil conscience or your dirty cowardice makes you afeard o' the fairies, I don't think I am : I don't care that about them. These same thorns must boil the dinner in spite of all the fairies in Europe ; so don't fret either yourself or me on the head o' them."

" Oh ! I see what's to come ! There's a doom over this house, that's all, an' over some, if not all o' them that's in it. Everything's leadin' to it; an' come it will."

" Why, mother dear, at this rate you'll lave my father

nothin' to say. You're keepin' all the black prophecies to
yourself. Why don't you rise up, man alive," she added,
turning to him, " and let her hear how much of the divil's
lingo you can give. It's hard, if you can't prophesy as much
evil as she can. Shake yourself, ruffle your feathers, or clap
your wings three times in the divil's name, an' tell her she'll
be hanged; or, if you wish to soften it, say she'll go to heaven on a string—ha, ha, ha!"

At this moment, a poor, famine-struck looking woman,
with three or four children, the very pictures of starvation
and misery, came to the door, and in that voice of terrible
destitution which rings feeble and hollow from an empty and
exhausted frame, she implored them for some food.

" We haven't it for you, honest woman," said Nelly, in her
cold, indifferent voice—" it's not for you now."

The hope of relief was nearly destroyed by the unfeeling
tone of the voice in which she was answered. She looked,
however, at her famishing children, and once more returned
to the door, after having gone a few steps from it.

" Oh, what will become of these? " she added, pointing to
the children. " I don't care about myself—I think my cares
will soon be over."

" Go to the divil out o' that! " shouted the prophet, " don't
be tormentin' us wid yourself an' your brats."

" Didn't you hear already," repeated his wife, " that you
got your answer? We're poor ourselves, and we can't help
every one that comes to us. It's not for you now."

" Don't you hear that there's nothing for you? " again cried
the prophet, in an angry voice; " yet you'll be botherin' us! "

" Indeed we haven't it, good woman," repeated Nelly; " so
take your answer."

" Don't you know that's a lie? " said Sarah, addressing her
stepmother. " You have it, if you wish to give it."

" What's a lie? " said her father, starting, for he had again
relapsed into his moodiness—" what's a lie?—who—who's a
liar? "

" You are," she replied, looking him coolly and contemptuously in the face; "you tell the poor woman that there's nothing for her. Don't you know that's a lie. It may be very well to tell a lie to them that can bear it—to a rich *bodagh*, or his proud lady of a wife—although it's a mean thing even to them; but to tell a lie to that heartbroken woman an' her poor childre—her childre—aren't they her own?—an' who would spake for them if she wouldn't? If every one treated the poor that way, what would become of them? Ay, to look in her face, where there's want an' hunger, and answer distress wid a lie—it's cruel—cruel!"

"What a kind-hearted creature she is!" said her stepmother, looking towards Donnel Dhu—"isn't she?"

"Come here, poor woman," said Sarah, calling her back; "it is for you. If these two choose to let you an' your childre die or starve, I won't"; and she went to the meal to serve them as she spoke.

The woman returned, and looked with considerable surprise at her; but Nelly went also to the meal, and was about to interpose, when Sarah's frame became excited, and her eyes flashed, as they always did when in a state of passion.

"If you're wise, don't prevent me," she said. "Help these creatures I will. I'm your match now, an' more than your match, thank God; so be quiet."

"If I was to die for it, you won't have your will now, then," said Nelly.

"Die when you like, then," replied Sarah; "but help that poor woman an' her childre I will."

"Fight it out," said Donnel Dhu; "it's a nice quarrel, although Sal has the right on her side."

"If you prevent me," said she, disregarding him, and addressing her stepmother, "you'll rue it quickly; or hould—I'm beginnin' to hate this blackguard kind of quarrellin'—here, let her have as much meal as will make my supper; I'll do widout any, for the sake o' the childre this night."

This was uttered in a tone of voice more mitigated, but at

the same time so resolute, that Nelly stepped back and left her to pursue her own course. She then took a wooden trencher, and with a liberal hand assisted the poor creatures, who began to feel alarmed at the altercation which their distress had occasioned in the family.

"You're starvin', childre," said she, whilst emptying the meal into the poor woman's bag.

"May the blessin' of God rest upon you," whispered the woman, "you've saved my orphans"; and as she uttered the words, her hollow eyes filled, and a few tears ran slowly down her cheeks.

Sarah gave a short loud laugh, and snatching up the youngest of the children, stroked its head, and patted its pale cheek, exclaiming—

"Poor thing, you won't go without your supper this night, at any rate."

She then laughed again in the same quick, abrupt manner, and returned into the house.

"Why, then," said her stepmother, looking at her with mingled anger and disdain, "is it tears you're sheddin'?—cryin' no less! Afther that mericles will never cease."

Sarah turned towards her hastily; the tears in a moment were dried upon her cheeks, and as she looked at her hard, coarse, but well-shaped features, her eyes shone with a brilliant and steady light for more than a minute. The expression was at once lofty and full of strong contempt, and as she stood in this singular but striking mood, it would, indeed, be difficult to conceive a finer type of energy, feeling, and beauty, than that which was embodied in her finely-turned and exquisite figure. Having thus contemplated the old woman for some time, she looked upon the ground, and her face passed rapidly into a new form and expression of beauty. It at once became soft and full of melancholy, and might have been mistaken for an impersonation of pity and sorrow.

"Oh, no!" she exclaimed, in a low voice, that was melody itself, "I never got it from either the one or the other—the kind or soft word—an' it's surely no wondher that I am as I am."

And as she spoke she wept. Her heart had been touched by the distresses of her fellow-creatures, and became, as it were, purified and made tender by its own sympathies, and so she wept. Both of them looked at her; but as they were utterly incapable of understanding what she felt, this natural struggle of a great but neglected spirit excited nothing on their part but mere indifference.

At this moment the prophet, who seemed labouring under a fierce but gloomy mood, rose suddenly up, and exclaimed—

"Nelly!—Sarah!—I can bear this no longer; the saicret must come out. I am a——"

"Stop," screamed Sarah, "don't say it—don't say it! Let me lave the counthry. Let me go somewhere—anywhere—let me—let me—die first!"

"I am——" said he.

"I know it," replied his wife—"a MURDHERER! I know it now—I knew it since yestherday mornin'."

"Give him justice," said Sarah, now dreadfully excited, and seizing him by the breast of his coat—"give him common justice—give the man justice, I say. You are my father, aren't you? Say how you did it. It was a struggle—a fight; he opposed you—he did, and your blood riz, and you stabbed him for fear he might stab you. That was it. Ha! ha! I know it was; for you are my father, and I am your daughter; and that's what I would do, like a man. But you never did it—ah! you never did it—in cold blood, or like a coward."

There was something absolutely impressive and commanding in her sparkling eyes, and the energetic tones of her voice, whilst she addressed him.

"Donnel," said the wife, "it's no saicret to me; but it's enough now that you've owned to it. This is the last night that I'll spend with a murdherer. You know what I have to answer for on my own account; and so, in the name of God, we'll part in the mornin'."

"Ha!" exclaimed Sarah, "you'd lave him now, would you? You'd desart him now — now that all the world will turn against him—now that every tongue will abuse him—that every heart will curse him—that every eye will turn from him with hatred;—now that shame, an' disgrace, an' guilt is all upon his head, you'd lave him, would you, and join the world against him? Father, on my knees I go to you "—and she dropped down as she spoke—" here on my knees I go to you, an' before you spake, mark, that through shame, an' pain, an' sufferin', an' death, I'll stay by you, an' with you. But, I now kneel to you—what I hardly ever did to God— an' for His sake—for God's sake—I ask you—oh! say—say that you did not kill the man in cowld blood; that's all! Make me sure of *that*, and I'm happy!"

"I think you're both mad," replied Donnel. "Did I say that I was a murdherer? Why didn't you hear me out?"

"You needn't," returned Nelly, "I knew it since yestherday mornin'."

"So you think," he replied; "an' it's but natural you should. I was at the place this day, and seen where you dug the *casharrawan*. I have been strugglin' for years to keep this saicret, an' now it must come out; but I'm not a murdherer."

"What saicret, father, if you are not a murdherer?" asked Sarah; "what saicret—but there is not murdher on you; do you say that?"

"I do say it; there's neither blood nor murdher on my head! but I know who the murdherer is, an' I can keep the saicret no longer."

Sarah laughed, and her eyes sparkled up with singular vividness—"that'll do," she exclaimed—"that'll do—all's right now; you're not a murdherer, you killed no man, aither in cold blood or otherwise—ha, ha—you're a good father— you're a good father; I forgive you all now—all ever you did."

Nelly stood contemplating her husband with a serious, firm, but dissatisfied look; her chin was supported upon her forefinger and thumb, and instead of seeming relieved by the disclosure she had just heard, which exonerated him from the charge of blood, she still kept her eyes rivetted upon him with a stern and incredulous aspect.

"Spake out then," she observed, coolly, "an' tell us all, for I am not convinced."

Sarah looked as if she would have sprung at her.

"You are not convinced," she exclaimed—"you are not convinced! do you think he'd tell a lie on sich a subject as this?" But no sooner had she uttered the words than she started as if seized by a spasm. "Ah, father," she exclaimed, "it's now your want of truth comes against you; but still— still I'll believe you."

"Tell us all about it," said Nelly, coldly—"let us hear all."

"But you both promise solemnly in the sight of God never to breathe this to a human being till I give yez lave."

"We do—we do," replied Sarah; "in the sight of God we do."

"You don't spake," said he, addressing Nelly.

"I promise it."

"In the sight of God?" he added, "for I know you."

"Ay," said she, "in the sight of God, since you must have it so."

"Well then," said he, "the common report is right; the man that murdhered him is Condy Dalton. I have kept it till I can bear it no longer. It's my intention to go to a magistrate as soon as my face gets well. For near two-an'-twenty years now, this saicret is lyin' hard upon me; but I'll aise my mind, and let justice take its coorse. Bad I have been, but never so bad as to take my fellow-crature's life."

"Well, I'm glad to hear it," said his wife; "an' now I can undherstand you."

"And I'm both glad and sorry," observed Sarah; "sorry

for the sake of the Daltons.   Oh, who would suppose it! and
what will become of them ? "

"I have no peace," her father added; "I have not had a
minute's peace ever since it happened ; for sure, they say,
any one that keeps their knowledge of murdher saicret and
won't tell it, is as bad as the murdherer himself.   There's
another thing I have to mention," he added, after a pause,
" but I'll wait for a day or two; it's a thing I lost, an' as
the case stands now, I can do nothing widout it."

"What is it, father? " asked Sarah, with animation, "let
us know what it is."

"Time enough yet," he replied ; "it'll do in a day or two ;
in the mean time it's hard to tell but it may turn up somewhere or other ; I hope it may, for if it got into any hands
but my own——"

He paused, and bent his eyes with singular scrutiny, first
upon his wife, and then upon Sarah, who had not the most
distant apprehension of his meaning.   Not so Nelly, who
felt convinced that the allusion he made was to the tobacco-
box, and her impression being that it was mixed up in some
way with an act of murder, she determined to wait until he.
should explain himself at greater length upon the subject.
Had Sarah been aware of its importance she would at once
have disclosed all she knew concerning it, together with
Hanlon's anxiety to get it into his possession.   But of this
she could know nothing, and for that reason there existed no
association in her mind to connect it with the crime which
the Prophet seemed resolved to bring to light.

When Donnel Dhu had laid himself down upon the bed
that day, he felt that by no effort could he shake a strong
impression of evil from off him.   The disappearance of the
box surprised him so much, that he resolved to stroll out and
examine a spot with which the reader is already acquainted.
On inspecting the newly disturbed earth, he felt satisfied
that the body had been discovered, and this circumstance,
joined with the disappearance of the tobacco-box, precipitated

his determination to act as he was about to do ; or, perhaps, altogether suggested the notion of taking such steps as might bring Condy Dalton to justice.

CHAPTER XI

PITY AND REMORSE

THE public mind, though often obtuse and stupid in many matters, is in others sometimes extremely acute and penetrating. For some years previous to the time laid in our tale, the family of Condy Dalton had begun to decline very perceptibly in their circumstances. There had been unpropitious seasons—there had been failure of crops and disease among the cattle—and, perhaps, what was the worst scourge of all, there existed a bad landlord in the person of Dick o' the Grange. So long, ,however, as they continued prosperous, their known principles of integrity and strict truth caused them to be well spoken of and respected, in spite of the imputation which had been made against them as touching the murder of Sullivan. In the course of time, however, when the evidences of struggle succeeded those of comfort and independence, the world began to perceive the just judgments of God as manifested in the disasters which befell them, and which seemed to visit them as with a judicial punishment. Year after year, as they sank in the scale of poverty, did the almost forgotten murder assume a more prominent and distinct shape in the public mind, until at length it became too certain to be doubted, that the slow but sure finger of God's justice was laid upon them as an additional proof that crime, however it may escape the laws of men, cannot veil itself from the all-seeing eye of the Almighty.

There was, however, an individual member of the family, whose piety and many virtues excited a sympathy in her behalf, as general as it was deep and compassionate. This was Mrs. Dalton, towards whom only one universal impression of good-will, affection, and respect prevailed. Indeed it

might be said, that the whole family were popular in the
country; but, notwithstanding their respectability both individually and collectively, the shadow of crime was upon
them; and as long as the people saw that everything they
put their hand to failed, and that a curse seemed to pursue
them, as if in attestation of the hidden murder, so long did
the feeling that God would yet vindicate his justice by their
more signal punishment, operate with dreadful force against
them, with the single exception we have mentioned.

Mrs. Dalton, on her return home from her unsuccessful
visit to the miser's, found her family in the same state of
grievous privation in which she had left them. 'Tis true
she had not mentioned to any of them her intention of appealing to the gratitude or humanity of Skinadre; yet they
knew, by an intuitive perception of her purpose, that she had
gone to him, and although their pride would not allow them
to ask a favour directly from him, yet they felt pleased that
she had made the experiment, and had little doubt that the
miser, by obliging her in the request she went to prefer,
would gladly avail himself of the circumstance to regain
their good-will, not so much on their own account as for the
sake of standing well with the world, in whose opinion he
knew he had suffered by his treachery towards them in the
matter of their farm. She found her husband seated in an
old arm-chair, which, having been an heir-loom in the family
for many a long year, had, with one or two other things,
been purchased in at the sheriff's sale. There was that chair,
which had come down to them from three or four generations; an old clock, some smaller matters, and a grey sheep,
the pet of a favourite daughter, who had been taken away
from them by decline during the preceding autumn. There
are objects, otherwise of little value, to which we cling for
the sake of those unforgotten affections and old mournful
associations that invest indifferent things with a feeling of
holiness and sorrow by which they are made sacred to the
heart.

Condy Dalton was a man tolerably well stricken in years; his face was pale but not unhealthy looking; and his hair, which rather flowed about his shoulders, was almost snow-white—a circumstance which, in this case, was not attributed to the natural progress of years, but to that cankered remorse which turns the head grey before its time. Their family now consisted of two sons and two daughters, the original number having been two sons and three daughters—one of the latter having fallen a victim to decline, as we have already stated. The old man was sitting in the arm-chair, in which he leant back, having his chin at the same time on his breast, a position which gave something very peculiar to his appearance.

As Mrs. Dalton had occupied a good deal of time in unsuccessfully seeking for relief from other sources, it is unnecessary to say that the day had now considerably advanced, and the heavy shadows of this dismal and unhealthy evening had thrown their gloom over the aspect of all nature, to which they gave an appearance of desolation that was in painful keeping with the sickness and famine that so mercilessly scourged the kingdom at large. A pot of water hung upon a dark slow fire, in order that as little time as possible might be lost in relieving their physical wants on Mrs. Dalton's return with the relief which they expected.

" Here's my mother," said one of her daughters, looking with a pale cheek and languid eye out of the door ; for she, too, had been visited by the prevailing illness; " an', my God, she's comin' as she went—empty-handed! "

The other sister and Con, her brother, went also to look out, and there she was, certainly without relief.

" She isn't able to carry it herself," said their father ; " it will be sent afther her ; or maybe she's comin' to get one of you—Con, I suppose—to go for it. Bad as Skinadre is, he wouldn't have the heart to refuse us a lock o' meal to keep the life in us. Oh, no ! he'd not do that."

In a few moments Mrs. Dalton entered, and after looking

upon the scene of misery about her, she sat down and burst into tears.

"Mother," said the daughter, "there's no relief then? You came as you went, I see."

"I come as I went, Nancy; but there is relief. There's relief for the poor of this world in heaven; but on this earth, an' in this world, there is none for us, glory be to the name of God still."

"So Skinadre refused, then?" said her husband; "he wouldn't give the meal?"

"No," she replied, "he would not; but the truth is, our woeful state is now so well known that nobody will trust us; they know there's no chance of ever bein' paid, an' they all say they can't afford it."

"I'm not surprised at what Tom says," observed our friend, young Con, "that the mealmongers and strong farmers that keep the provisions up on the poor desarves to be smashed and tramped under foot; an' indeed they'll get it, too, before long, for the people can't stand this, especially when one knows that there's enough, ay, and more than enough in the country."

"If I had tobacco," said the old man, "I didn't care—that would keep the hunger off o' me; but it's poor Mary here, now recoverin' from the sickness, that I pity; don't cry, Mary, dear; come here, darlin', come here and turn up that ould *creel*, and sit down beside me. It's useless to bid you not to cry, *avourneen machree*, bekase we all know what you feel; but you have one comfort, you are innocent—so are you all—there's nothing on any of your minds—no dark thought to lie upon your heart—oh, no—no; an' if it was only myself that was to suffer, I could bear it, but to see them that's innocent sufferin' along wid me is what kills me. This is the hand of God that's upon us, an' that has been upon us; an' that will be upon us, an' I knew it would be so, for ever since that black night, the thought—the thought of what happened!—ay, it's that that's in me, an' upon me—

it's that that has put wrinkles in my cheek before their time, an' that has made my hair white before it's time, and that has——"

"Con dear," observed his wife, "I never wished you to be talkin' of that before them ; sure you did as much as man could do ; you repented an' were sorry for it, an' what more could be expected from you ? "

"Father dear," said Mary, drying, or struggling to dry her tears, "don't think of me, or of any of us, nor don't think of anything that will disturb your mind—don't think of me, at any rate ; I'm very weak, but I'm not so hungry as you may think; if I had one mouthful of anything just to take this feelin' that I have inwardly an' this weakness away, I would be satisfied—that would do me ; an' although I'm cryin', it's more to see your misery, father dear, an' all your miseries, than for what I'm sufferin' myself ; but there's a kiss for you, it's all I have to give you."

"Mary dear," said her sister, smitten to the heart by her words, "you are sufferin' more than any of us, you an' my father," and she encircled her lovingly and mournfully in her arms as she spoke, and kissed her worn lips, after which she went to the old man, and said in a voice of compassion and consolation that was calculated to soothe any heart—"Oh, father dear, if you could only banish all uneasy thoughts from your mind,—if you could only throw that darkness that's so often over you, off you, we could bear anything—anything—oh, anything, if we seen you aisy in your mind and happy ! "

Mrs. Dalton had dried her tears, and sat upon a low stool musing and silent, and apparently revolving in her mind the best course to be pursued under such distressing circumstances. It was singular to observe the change that had taken place in her appearance even within a few hours ; the situation of her family, and her want of success in procuring them food, had so broken down her spirits and crushed her heart, that the lines of her face were deepened, and her features sharpened and impressed with the marks of suffering as strongly as if they had been left there by the affliction of years. Her son leant himself against a piece of broken wall that partly divided their hut into something like two rooms, if they could be called so, and from time to time he glanced about him, now at his father, then at his poor sisters, and again at his heart-broken mother, with an impatient agony of spirit that could scarcely be conceived.

" Well," said he, clenching his hands and grinding his teeth, " is it expected that people like us will sit tamely undher sich thratement as we have resaved from Dick o' the Grange? Oh, if we had now the five hundhre good pounds that we have spent upon our farm—spent, as it turned out, not for ourselves, but to enable that ould villain of a landlord to set it to Darby Skinadre—for I b'lieve it's he that's to get it, with strong inthrest goin' into his pocket for all our improvements. If we had now," he continued, his passion rising, " if we had that five hundhre pounds now—or one hundhre—or one pound, Great God !—ay, or one shillin' now, wouldn't it save some of you from starvin'? "

This reflection, which in the young man excited only wrath, occasioned the female part of the family to burst into fresh sorrow ; not so the old man—he arose hastily, and paced up and down the floor in a state of gloomy indignation and fury, which far transcended that of his son.

" Oh," said he, " if I was a young man, as I was wanst— but the young men now are poor, pitiful, cowardly—I would —I would "—he paused suddenly, however, looked up, and clasping his hands, exclaimed—" forgive me, oh God !—forgive the thought that was in my unhappy heart ! Oh, no— no—never, never allow yourself, Con dear, to be carried away by anger, for fraid you might do in one minute, or in a short fit of anger, what might make you pass many a sleepless night, an' maybe banish the peace of God from your heart for ever ! "

" God bless you for them last words, Condy ! " exclaimed

his wife; "that's the way I wish you always to spake—but what to do, or where to go, or who to turn to, unless to God Himself, I don't know."

"We're come to it at last," said the other daughter, Peggy; "little we thought it, but at all events, it's betther to do that than to do worse—betther than to rob or steal, or do an ondaicent act of any kind. In the name of God, then, rather than you should die of hunger, Mary—you, an' my father, an' all of yez—I'll go out and beg from the neighbours."

"Beg!" shouted the old man with a look of rage—"beg!" he repeated, starting to his feet and seizing his staff—"beg! you shameless and disgraceful strap. Do you talk of a Dalton goin' out to beg?—take that."

And as he spoke, he struck her over the arm with a stick which he always carried.

"Now, that will teach you to talk of beggin'. No!—die —die first—die at wanst; but no beggin' for any one wid the blood of a Dalton in their veins. Death—death a thousand times sooner!"

"Father—oh, father, father, why did you do that?" exclaimed his son; "to strike poor, kind an' heart-broken Peggy, that would shed her blood for you, or for any of us. Oh, father, I'm sorry to see it!"

The sorrowing girl turned pale at the blow, and a few tears came down her cheeks; but she thought not of herself, nor of her sufferings. After a pause, occasioned by the pain, she ran to him, and, throwing her arms about his neck, exclaimed, in a gush of sorrow that was perfectly heart-rending to witness,—

"Oh, father dear, forgive me—your own poor Peggy; sure it was chiefly on your account an' Mary's I was goin' to do it. I won't go, then, since you don't wish it; but I'll die with you."

The old man flung the stick from him, and, clasping her in his arms, he sobbed and wept aloud.

"My darlin' child!" he exclaimed, "that never yet gave

one of us a bad word or an angry look—will you forgive your unhappy father, that doesn't know what he's doin'? Oh! I feel that this state we're in—this outher desolation an' misery we're in—will drive me mad! But that hasty blow, avourneen machree—that hasty blow an' the hot temper that makes me give it—is my curse yet, has been always my curse, an' ever will be my curse; it's that curse that's upon me now, an' upon all of us this minute—it is, it is!"

"Condy," said his wife, "we all know you're not as bad as you make yourself. Within the last few years your temper has been sorely tried, an' your heart too, God knows; for our trials an' our downcome in this world has been great. In all these trials, however, an' sufferins, it's a consolation to us that we never neglected to praise an' worship the Almighty—we are now brought almost to the very last pass— let us go to our knees, then, an' throw ourselves upon His mercy, an' beg of Him to support us, an', if it is His holy will, to aid us an' send us relief."

"Oh, Mary, dear!" exclaimed her husband, "but you are the valuable an' faithful wife! If ever woman was a protectin' angel to man, you wor to me. Come, childre, in the name of the merciful God, let us kneel an' pray."

The bleak and depressing aspect of twilight had now settled down upon the sweltering and deluged country, and the air was warm, thick, moist, and, consequently, unhealthy. The cabin of the Daltons was placed in a low, damp situation, but fortunately it was approached by a remnant of one of these old roads or causeways which had once been peculiar to the remote parts of the country, and also of very singular structure, the least stone in it being considerably larger than a shilling loaf. This causeway was nearly covered with grass, so that, in addition to the antique and desolate appearance which this circumstance gave it, the footsteps of a passenger could scarcely be heard as they fell upon the thick, close grass with which its surface was mostly covered.

Along this causeway, then, at the very hour when the

Daltons, moved by that piety which is the characteristic of our
peasantry, had gone to prayer, was the strange woman, whom
we have already noticed, proceeding with that relief which, it
may be, God in His goodness had ordained should reach them in
answer to the simple but trustful spirit of their supplications.

On reaching the miserable-looking cabin, she paused,
listened, and heard their voices blend in those devout tones
that always mark the utterance of prayer among the people.
They were, in fact, repeating a Rosary, and surely it is not
for those who differ with them in creed, or for any one who
feels the influence of true charity, to quarrel with the form
of prayer, when the heart is moved, as theirs were, by earnestness and humble piety.

The strange woman, on approaching the door more nearly,
stood again for a minute or two, having been struck more
forcibly by something which gave a touching and melancholy
character to this simple act of domestic worship. She observed, for instance, that their prayers were blended with
many sighs, and, from time to time, a groan escaped from one
of the men, which indicated either deep remorse or a sense of
some great misery. One of the female voices, too, was so
feeble as scarcely to be heard, yet there ran through it, she
felt, a spirit of such tender and lowly resignation, mingled
with such an expression of profound sorrow, as almost moved
her to tears. The door was open, and the light so dim, that
she could not distinctly see their persons—two circumstances
which for a moment induced her to try if it were possible to
leave the meal there without their knowledge. She determined
otherwise, however; and, as their prayers were almost immediately concluded, she entered the house. The appearance
of a stranger in the dusky gloom, carrying a burden, caused
them to suppose that it was some poor person coming to ask
charity, or permission to stop for the night.

"Who is this?" asked Condy. "Some poor person, I
suppose, axin' charity," he added. "But God's will be done,

we haven't it to give this many a long day. Glory be to His
name!"

"This is Condy Dalton's house?" said the strange woman,
in a tone of inquiry.

"Sich as it is, it's his house, an' the best he has, my poor
crathur. I wish it was betther, both for his sake an' yours,"
he replied, in a calm and resigned voice, for his heart had
been touched and solemnized by the act of devotion which had
just concluded.

Mrs. Dalton, in the mean time, had thrown a handful of
straw on the fire, to make a temporary light.

"Here," said the stranger, " is a present of meal that a
friend sent you."

"Meal!" exclaimed Peggy Dalton, with a faint scream of
joy; "did you say meal?" she asked.

"I did," replied the other; "a friend that hard of your
present distress, and thinks you don't desarve it, sent it to
you."

Mrs. Dalton raised the burning straw, and looked for about
half-a-minute into her face, during which the woman carried
the meal over, and placed it on the hearth.

"I met you to-day, I think," said Mrs. Dalton, "along with
Donnel Dhu's wife, on your way to Darby Skinadre's?"

"You might," replied the woman; "for I went there part
o' the road with her."

"An' who are we indebted to for this present?" she asked
again.

"I'm not at liberty to say," replied the other; "barrin'
that it's from a friend an' well-wisher."

Mrs. Dalton clasped her hands, and, looking with an appearance of abstraction on the straw as it burned in the fire,
said, in a voice that became infirm by emotion—

"Oh, I know it; it can be no other. The friend she
spakes of is the girl—the blessed girl—whose goodness is
in every one's mouth—*Gra Gal* Sullivan. I know it—I
feel it."

"Now," said the woman, "I must go, but before I do, I wish to look upon the face of Condy Dalton."

"There's a bit of rush on the shelf there," said Mrs. Dalton to one of her daughters; "bring it over and light it."

The girl did so; and the strange woman, taking the little taper in her hand, approached Dalton, and looked with a gaze almost fearfully solemn and searching into his face.

"You are Condy Dalton?" she asked.

"I am," said he.

"Answer me now," she proceeded, "as if you were in the presence of God at judgment, are you happy?"

Mrs. Dalton, who felt anxious, for many reasons, to relieve her unfortunate husband from this unexpected and extraordinary catechist, hastened to reply for him.

"How, honest woman, could a man be happy, who is in a state of such destitution, or who has had such misfortunes as he has had?" and, as she spoke, her eyes filled with tears of compassion for her husband.

"Don't break in upon me," said the woman, solemnly, "but let me ax my question, an' let him give his answer. In God's name an' presence, are you a happy man?"

"I can't spake a lie to that, for I must yet meet my Judge —I AM NOT."

"You have one particular thought that makes you unhappy?"

"I have one particular thought that makes me unhappy."

"How long has it made you unhappy?"

"For near two-an'-twenty years."

"That's enough," she replied; "God's hand is in it all—I must now go. I have done what I was axed to do; but there's a higher will at work. Honest woman," she added, addressing Mrs. Dalton, "I wish you an' your childre good-night!"

The moment she went they almost ceased to think of her. The pot still hung on the fire, and little time was lost in preparing a meal of food.

From the moment *Gra Gal* Sullivan's name was mentioned,

the whole family observed that young Con started, and appeared to become all at once deeply agitated; he walked backwards and forwards—sat down, and rose up—applied his hands to his forehead—appeared sometimes flushed, and again pale—and altogether seemed in a state which it was difficult to understand.

" What is the matter with you, Con ? " asked his mother, " you seem dreadfully uneasy."

" I am ill, mother," he replied—" the fever that was near takin' Tom away is upon me; I feel that I have it by the pains that's in my head an' the small o' my back."

" Lie down a little, dear," she added—" it's only the pain, poor boy, of an empty stomach—lie down on your poor bed, God help you, an' when the supper's ready you'll be betther."

" It's her," he replied—" it's her—I know it "—and, as he uttered the words, touched by her generosity, and the consciousness of his own poverty, he wept bitterly, and then repaired to his miserable bed, where he stretched himself in pain and sorrow.

" Now, Con," said his wife, in a tone of consolation and encouragement, " will you ever despair of God's mercy, or doubt His goodness, after what has just happened ? "

" I'm an unhappy man, Nancy," he replied; " but it never went to that with me, thank God—but where is that poor wild boy of ours, Tom—oh, where is he now, till he gets one meal's mate ? "

" He is up at the Murtaghs'," said his sister, " an' I had betther fetch him home; I think the poor fellow's a'most out of his senses since Peggy Murtagh's death—that an' the dregs of the fever has him that he doesn't know what he's doin', God help him ! "

CHAPTER XII.

FAMINE, DEATH, AND SORROW

It has never been our disposition, either in the living life we lead, or in the fictions, humble and imperfect as they are, which owe their existence to our imagination, to lay too heavy a hand upon human frailty, any more than it has been to countenance or palliate vice, whether open or hypocritical. Peggy Murtagh, with whose offence and death the reader is already acquainted, was an innocent and affectionate girl, whose heart was full of kind, generous, and amiable feelings. She was very young and very artless, and loved not wisely but too well; whilst he who was the author of her sin, was nearly as young and artless as herself, and loved her with a first affection. She was, in fact, one of those gentle, timid, and confiding creatures who suspect not evil in others, and are full of sweetness and kindness to every one. Never did there live—with the exception of her offence—a tenderer daughter or a more affectionate sister than poor Peggy, and for this reason, the regret was both sincere and general, which was felt for her great misfortune. Poor girl! she was but a short time released from her early sorrows, when her babe followed her, we trust, to a better world, where the tears were wiped from her eyes, and the weary one was at rest.

The scene in her father's house on this melancholy night, was such as few hearts could bear unmoved, as well on account of her parents' grief as because it may be looked upon as a truthful exponent both of the destitution of the country, and of the virtues and sympathies of our people.

Stretched upon a clean bed in the only room that was off the kitchen, lay the fair but lifeless form of poor Peggy Murtagh. The bed was, as is usual, hung with white, which was simply festooned about the posts and canopy, and the coverlid was also of the same spotless colour, as were the death-clothes in which she was laid out. To those who are beautiful—and poor Peggy had possessed that frequently fatal gift—death, in its first stage, bestows an expression of mournful tenderness that softens while it solemnizes the heart. In her case, there were depicted all the innocence and artlessness that characterized her brief and otherwise spotless life. Over this melancholy sweetness lay a shadow that manifested her early suffering and sorrow, made still more touching by the presence of an expression which was felt by the spectator to have been that of repentance. Her rich auburn hair was simply divided on her pale forehead, and it was impossible to contemplate the sorrow and serenity which blended into each other upon her young brow, without feeling that death should disarm us of all our resentments, and teach us a lesson of pity and forgiveness to our poor fellow-creatures, who, whatever may have been their errors, will never more offend either God or man. Her extreme youthfulness was touching in the highest degree, and to the simplicity of her beauty was added that unbroken stillness which gives to the lifeless face of youth the only charm that death has to bestow, whilst it fills the heart to its uttermost depths with the awful conviction that that is the slumber which no human care nor anxious passion shall ever break. The babe, thin and pallid from the affliction of its young and unfortunate mother, could hardly be looked upon, in consequence of its position, without tears. They had placed it by her side, but within her arm, so that by this touching arrangement all the brooding tenderness of the mother's love seemed to survive and overcome the power of death itself. There they lay, victims of sin, but emblems of innocence, and where is the heart that shall, in the inhumanity of its justice, dare to follow them out of life, and disturb the peace they now enjoy by the heartless sentence of unforgiveness ?

It was, indeed, a melancholy scene. The neighbours, having heard of her unexpected death, came to the house, as is customary, to render every assistance in their power to the bereaved old couple, who were now left childless. And here, too, might we read the sorrowful impress of the famine and illness which desolated the land.   The groups around the poor departed one were marked with such a thin and haggard expression as general destitution always is certain to leave behind it.   The skin of those who, with better health and feeding, had been fair and glossy as ivory, was now wan and flaccid;—the long bones of others projected sharply, and as it were offensively, to the feelings of the spectators—the overlapping garments hung loosely about the wasted and feeble person, and there was in the eyes of all a dull and languid motion, as if they turned in their sockets by an effort.   They were all mostly marked also by what appeared to be a feeling of painful abstraction, which, in fact, was nothing else than that abiding desire for necessary food, which in seasons of famine keeps perpetually gnawing, as they term it, at the heart, and prevades the system by that sleepless solicitation of appetite, which, like the presence of guilt, mingles itself up, whilst it lasts, with every thought and action of one's life.

In this instance, it may be remembered, that the aid which the poor girl had come to ask from Skinadre was, as she said, " for the ould couple," who had, indeed, been for a long time past their *last meal*, a very common thing during such periods, and were, consequently, without a morsel of food. The appearance of her corpse, however, at the house, an event so unexpected, drove, for the time, all feelings of physical want from their minds ; but this is a demand which will not be satisfied, no matter by what moral power or calamity it may be opposed, and the wretched couple were now a proof of it.   Their conduct to those who did not understand this, resembled insanity or fatuity more than anything else.   The faces of both were ghastly, and filled with a pale, vague expression of what appeared to be horror, or the dull staring stupor which results from the fearful conflict of two great opposing passions in the mind—passions, which in this case were the indomitable ones of hunger and grief. After dusk, when the candles were lighted, they came into the room where their daughter was laid out, and stood for some time contemplating herself and her infant in silence. Their visages were white and stony as marble, and their eyes, now dead and glassy, were marked by no appearance of distinct consciousness, or the usual expression of reason. They had no sooner appeared, than the sympathies of the assembled neighbours were deeply excited, and there was nothing heard for some minutes, but groans, sobbings, and general grief. Both stood for a short time, and looked with amazement about them. At length, the old man, taking the hand of his wife in his, said—

"Kathleen, what's this?—what ails me? I want something."

"You do, Brian—you do. There's Peggy there, and her child, poor thing; see how quiet they are; Oh! how she loved that child; an' see, darlin'—oh, see how she keeps her arm about it, for fear anything might happen it, or that any one might take it away from her; but that's her, all over—she loved everything."

"Ay," said the old man, "I know how she loved it; but, somehow, she was ever and always afeard, poor thing, of seemin' over fond of it before us, or before strangers, bekase, you know, the poor unhappy—what was I going to say? oh, ay, an' I'll tell you, although I didn't let on to her, still I loved the poor little thing myself—ay, did I. But, ah! Kathleen, wasn't she the good and lovin' daughter?"

The old woman raised her head, and looked searchingly around the room. She seemed uneasy, and gave a ghastly smile which it was difficult to understand. She then looked into her husband's face, after which she turned her eyes upon the countenances of the early dead who lay before her, and going over to them, stooped and looked closely into their still but composed faces. She then put her hand upon her daughter's forehead, touched her lips with her fingers, carried her hand down along her arm, and felt the pale features of the baby with a look of apparent wonder; and whilst she did this, the old man left the room and passed into the kitchen.

"For God's love, an' take her away," said a neighbouring woman, with tears in her eyes; no one can stand this."

"No, no," exclaimed another; "its best to let her have her own will; for until they both shed plenty of tears, they won't get the betther of the shock her unexpected death gave them."

"Is it thrue that Tom Dalton's gone mad, too?" asked another; for it's reported he is."

"No; but they say he's risin' the counthry, to punish Dick o' the Grange and Darby Skinadre—the one, he says, for puttin' his father and themselves out o' their farm, and the other for bein' the death, he says, of poor Peggy there and the child, an' for takin' or offerin' to take the farm over their heads."

The old woman then looked around, and asked—

"Where is Brian? Bring him to me—I want him here. But wait," she added; "I will find him myself."

She immediately followed him into the kitchen, where the poor old man was found searching every part of the house for food.

"What are you lookin' for, Brian?" asked another of his neighbours.

"Oh," he replied, "I am dyin' wid fair hunger—wid fair hunger, and I want somethin' to ait;" and as he spoke, a spasm of agony came over his face. "Ah," he added, "if Alick was livin'—if Alick was livin' wid us, it isn't this way we'd be, for what can poor Peggy do for us, afther her 'misfortune?' However, she is a good girl—a good daughter to us, an' will make a good wife, too, for all that has happened yet; for sure they were both young and foolish, an' Tom is to marry her. She is now all we have to depend on, poor thing, an' it wrings my heart to catch her in lonesome places, cryin', as if her heart would break; for, poor thing, she's sorry—sorry for her fault, an' for the shame an' sorrow it has brought her to; an' that's what makes her pray, too, so often as she does; but God's good, an' He'll for-. give her, bekase she has repented."

"Brian," said the wife, "come away; come away till I show you something."

As she spoke she led him into the other room.

"There," she proceeded, "there is our dearest and our best—oh, I am hungry too; but I don't care for that—sure the mother's love is stronger than hunger or want either; but there she is, that was wanst our pride, an' our delight, an' what is she now? She needn't cry now, the poor heart-broken child,—she needn't cry now,—all her sorrow, an' all her shame, an' all her sin is over. She'll hang her head no more, nor her pale cheek won't get crimson at the sight of any one who knew her before her fall; but for all her sin in that one act, did her heart ever fail to you or me? Was there ever such love, an' care, an' respect, as she paid us? an' we wouldn't tell her that we forgave her; we wor too hard-hearted for that, an' too wicked to say that one word that she longed for so much—oh, an' she our only one—but now—daughter of our hearts—now we forgive you when it's too late—for, Brian, there they are! there they lie in their last sleep—the sleep they will never awaken from; an' it's well for them, for they'll waken an' rise no more to care, an' throuble, an' sorrow, an' shame! There they lie—see how quiet an' calm they both lie there, the poor broken branch an' the little withered flower!"

The old man's search for food in the kitchen had given to the neighbours the first intimation of their actual distress, and in a few minutes it was discovered that there was not a single mouthful of anything in the house, nor had they tasted a morsel since the morning before, when they took a little gruel, which their daughter had made for them. In a moment, with all possible speed, the poor creatures about them either went or sent for sustenance, and in many a case, almost the last morsel was shared with them, and brought, though scanty and humble, to their immediate assistance. In this respect there is not in the world any people so generous and kind to their fellow-creatures as the Irish, or whose sympathies are so deep and tender, especially in periods of sickness, want, or death. It is not the tear alone they are willing to bestow—oh, no!—whatever can be done—whatever aid can be given—whatever kindness rendered—or consolation offered, even to the last poor shilling, or "the very bit out of the mouth," as they say themselves, will be given with a good will, and a sincerity that might in vain be looked for elsewhere. But, alas! they know what it is to want this consolation and assistance themselves, and hence their promptitude and anxiety to render them to others. The old man, touched a little by the affecting language of his wife, began to lose the dull stony look we have described, and his eyes turned upon those who were about him with something like meaning, although ' at that moment it could be scarcely called so.

"Am I dhramin'?" he asked. "Is this a dhrame? What brings the people all about us? Where's Alick from us— an' stay—where's her that I loved best, in spite of her folly? Where's Peggy from me—there's something wrong wid me— and yet she's not here to take care o' me!"

"Brian, dear," said a poor, famished-looking woman, approaching him, "she's in a betther place, poor thing."

"Go long out o' that," he replied, "and don't put your hands on me. It's Peggy's hands I want to have about me, an' her voice. Where's Peggy's voice, I say? 'Father, forgive me,' she said, 'forgive me, father, or I'll never be happy more'—but I wouldn't forgive her, although my heart did at the same time; still I didn't say the word;—bring her here," he added, "tell her I'm ready now to forgive her all; for she, it's she that was the forgivin' creature herself; tell her I'm ready now to forgive her all, an' to give her my blessin' wanst more."

It was utterly impossible to hear this language from the

stunned and heart-broken father, and to contemplate the fair
and lifeless form of the unhappy young creature as she lay
stretched before him in the peaceful stillness of death, without being moved even to tears. There were, indeed, few dry
eyes in the house as he spoke.

"Oh, Brian dear," said her weeping mother, "we helped
ourselves to break her heart, as well as the rest. We
wouldn't forgive her; we wouldn't say the word, although
her heart was breakin' bekase we did not. Oh Peggy!" she
commenced in Irish, "oh, our daughter—girl of the *one
fault!* the kind, the affectionate, and the dutiful child, to
what corner of the world will your father an' myself turn
now that you're gone from us? You asked us often an' often
to forgive you, an' we would not. You said you were sorry,
in the sight of God an' of man, for your fault—that your
heart was sore, an' that you felt our forgiveness would bring
you consolation; but we would not. Ould man," she exclaimed, abruptly, turning to her husband, "why didn't you
forgive our only daughter? Why, I say, didn't you forgive
her her one fault—you wicked ould man, why didn't you
forgive her?"

"Oh, Kathleen, I'll die," he replied, mournfully, "I'll die
if I don't get something to ait. Is there no food? Didn't
Peggy go to thry Darby Skinadre, an' she hoped, she said,
that she'd bring us relief; an' so she went upon our promise
to forgive her when she'd come back wid it."

"I wish, indeed, I had a drop o' gruel or something myself," replied his wife, now reminded of her famished state
by his words.

At this moment, however, relief, so far as food is concerned, did come. The compassionate neighbours began, one
by one, to return each with whatever could be spared from
their own necessities, so that in the course of a little time
this desolate old couple were supplied with provisions sufficient to meet the demands of a week or fortnight.

It is not our intention to describe, or rather to attempt to describe, the sorrow of Brian Murtagh and his wife, as soon as a moderate meal of food had awakened them, as it were, from the heavy and stupid frenzy into which the shock of their unhappy daughter's death, joined to the pangs of famine, had thrown them. It may be sufficient to say, that their grief was wild, disconsolate, and hopeless. She was the only daughter they had ever had; and when they looked back upon the gentle and unfortunate girl's many virtues, and reflected that they had, up to her death, despite her earnest entreaties, withheld from her their pardon for her transgression, they felt, mingled with their affliction at her loss, such an oppressive agony of remorse as no language could describe.

Many of the neighbours now proposed the performance of a ceremony, which is frequently deemed necessary in cases of frailty similar to that of poor Peggy Murtagh—a ceremony which, in the instance before us, was one of equal pathos and beauty. It consisted of a number of these humble, but pious and well-disposed people joining in what is termed the Litany of the Blessed Virgin, which was an earnest solicitation of mercy, through her intercession with her Son, for the errors, frailties, and sins of the departed; and, indeed, when her youth and beauty, and her artlessness, and freedom from guile, were taken into consideration, in connexion with her unexpected death, it must be admitted that this act of devotion was as affecting as it was mournful and solemn. When they came to the words, "Mother most pure, Mother most chaste, Mother undefiled, Mother most loving, pray for her!"—and again to those, "Morning Star, Health of the Weak, Refuge of Sinners, Comfortress of the Afflicted, pray for her!"—their voices faltered, became broken, and, with scarcely a single exception, they melted into tears. And it was a beautiful thing to witness these miserable and half-famished creatures, shrunk and pinched with hunger and want, labouring, many of them, with incipient illness, and several only just recovered from it, forgetting their own distresses and afflictions, and rendering all the aid and consolation in their power to those who stood in more need of them than themselves. When these affecting prayers for the dead had been concluded, a noise was heard at the door, and a voice which in a moment hushed them into silence and awe. The voice was that of him whom the departed girl had loved with such fatal tenderness.

" In the name of God," exclaimed one of them, " let some o' you keep that unfortunate boy out; the sight of him will kill the ould couple." The woman who spoke, however, had hardly concluded, when Tom Dalton entered the room, panting, pale, tottering through weakness, and almost frantic with sorrow and remorse. On looking at the unhappy sight before him, he paused, and wiped his brow, which was moistened by excitement and over-exertion. There was now the silence of death in the room so deep, that the shooting of a spark from one of the death-candles was heard by every one present, an incident which, small as it was, deepened the melancholy interest of the moment.

"An' that's it," he at last exclaimed, in a voice which, though weak, quivered with excess of agony—" that's it, Peggy dear—that's what your love for me has brought you to! An' now it's too late; I can't help you now, Peggy dear. I can't bid you hould your modest face up, as the darlin' wife of him that loved you betther than all this world besides, but that left you, for all that, a stained name an' a broken heart! Ay, an' there's what your love for me brought you to! What can I do for you, Peggy dear? All my little plans for us both—all that I dreamt of an' hoped to come to pass, where are they now, Peggy dear? And it wasn't I, Peggy, it was poverty—oh, you know how I loved you!—it was the down-come we got—it was Dick o' the Grange that oppressed us—that ruined us—that put us out without house or home—it was he, and it was my father— my father that they say has blood on his hand, an' I don't doubt it, or he wouldn't act the part he did—it was he, too, that prevented me from doin' what my heart encouraged me to do for you!' Oh, blessed God," he exclaimed, "what will become of me! when I think of the long, sorrowful, implorin' look she used to give me, I'll go mad—I'll go mad!—I've killed her—I've murdhered her, and there's no one to take me up an' punish me for it! An' when I was ill, Peggy dear—when I had time to think on my sick bed of all your love, and all your sorrow, and distress, and shame, on my account, I thought I'd never see you in time to tell you what I was to do, an' to give consolation to your breakin' heart ; but all that's now over ; you are gone from them all—you are gone from me, an' like the lovin' creathur you ever wor, you brought our baby along wid you! An' when I think of it—oh, God! when I think of it, before your shame, my heart's delight, how your eye felt proud out of me, an' how it smiled when it rested on me. Oh! little you thought I'd hould back to do you justice—me that you doted on—an' yet it was I that sullied you!—ay, me! Here," he shouted, "here, is there no one to seize a murdherer?—no one to bring him to justice ? "

Those present now gathered about him, and attempted, as best they might, to soothe and pacifiy him ; but in vain.

" Oh ! " he proceeded, " if she was only able to upbraid me —but what am I sayin'—upbraid! Oh! never, never was her harsh word heard—oh, nothing ever to me but that long look of sorrow, that will either drive me mad, or leave me a broken heart! That's the look that'll always, always be before me, an' that, till death's day, will keep me from ever bein' a happy man."

He now became exhausted, and received a drink of water, after which he wildly kissed her lips, and bathed her inani-mate face, as well as that of their infant, with tears.

" Now," said he, at length ; " now, Peggy dear, listen— may God never prosper me, if I don't work bitther vengeance on them that, along wid myself, was the means of bringin'

you to this—Dick o' the Grange an' Darby Skinadre, for if
Darby had given you what you wanted, you might be yet a
livin' woman. As for myself, I care not what becomes of
me; you are gone, our child is gone, and now I have nothing
in this world that I'll ever care for—there's nothing in it
that I'll ever love again."

He then turned to leave the room, and was in the act of
going out of it, when her father, who had nearly recovered
the use of his reason, said—

"Tom Dalton, you are lavin' this house, an' may the curse
of that girl's father, broken-hearted as you've left him, go
along wid you."

"No," exclaimed his wife, "but may the blessin' of her
mother rest upon you for the sake of the love she bore you!"

"You've spoken late, Kathleen Murtagh," he replied,
"the curse of her father is on me, an' will folly me; I feel it."

His sister then entered the room to bring him home,
whither he accompanied her, scarcely conscious of what he
did, and ignorant of the cloud of vengeance which was so
soon to break upon his wretched father's head.

CHAPTER XIII

SARAH'S APPEAL FOR A MURDERER

OUR readers are not, perhaps, in general aware that a most
iniquitous usage prevailed among middlemen landlords,
whenever the leases under which their property was held
were near being expired. Indeed, as a landed proprietor,
the middleman's position differed most essentially from that
of the man who held his estate in fee. The interest of the
latter is one that extends beyond himself and his wants, and
is consequently transmitted to his children and more remote
descendants; and on this account he is, or ought to be, bound
by ties of a different and higher character, to see that it shall
not pass down to them in an impoverished or mutilated con-

dition. The middleman, on the contrary, feels little or none of this, and very naturally endeavours to sweep from off the property he holds, whilst he holds it, by every means possible, as much as it can yield, knowing that his tenure of it is but temporary and precarious. For this reason, then, it too frequently happened that on finding his tenants' leases near expiring, he resorted to the most unscrupulous and oppressive means to remove from his land those who may have made improvements upon it, in order to let it to other claimants at a rent high in proportion to these very improvements.

Our readers know that this is not an extreme case, but a plain, indisputable fact, which has, unfortunately, been one of the standing grievances of our unhappy country, and one of the great curses attending the vicious and unsettled state of property in Ireland.

Dick o' the Grange's ejectment of Condy Dalton and his family, therefore, had, in the eyes of many of the people, nothing in it so startlingly oppressive as might be supposed. On the contrary, the act was looked upon as much in the character of a matter of right on his part, as one of oppression to them. Long usage had reconciled the peasantry to it, and up to the period of our tale, there had been no one to awaken and direct public feeling against it.

A fortnight had now elapsed since the scene in which young Dalton had poured out his despair and misery over the dead body of Peggy Murtagh, and during that period an incident occurred, which, although by no means akin to the romantic, had produced, nevertheless, a change in the position of Dick o' the Grange himself, without effecting any either in his designs or inclinations. His own leases had expired, so that, in one sense, he stood exactly in the same relation to the head landlord in which his own tenants did to him. Their leases had dropped about a twelvemonth or more before his, and he now waited until he should take out new ones himself, previous to his proceeding any further in the disposition and readjustment of his property.

Such was his position and theirs, with reference to each other, when one morning, about a fortnight or better subsequent to his last appearance, young Dick, accompanied by the Black Prophet, was seen to proceed towards the garden —both in close conversation. The Prophet's face was now free from the consequences of young Dalton's violence, but it had actually gained in malignity more than it had lost by the discoloration and disfigurement resulting from the blow. There was a calm, dark grin visible when he smiled, that argued a black and satanic disposition; and whenever the lips of his hard, contracted, and unfeeling mouth expanded by his devilish sneer, a portion of one of his vile side fangs became visible, which gave to his features a most hateful and viper-like aspect. It was the cold, sneering, cowardly face of a man who took delight in evil for its own sake, and who could neither feel happiness himself nor suffer others to enjoy it.

As they were about to enter the garden, Donnel Dhu saw approaching him at a rapid and energetic pace, his daughter Sarah, whose face, now lit up by exercise, as well as by the earnest expression of deep interest which might be read in it, never before appeared so strikingly animated and beautiful.

"Who is this lovely girl approaching us?" asked the young man, whose eyes at once kindled with surprise and admiration.

"That is my daughter," replied Donnel, coldly; "what can she want with me now, and what brought her here?"

"Upon my honour, Donnel, that girl surpasses anything I have seen yet. Why she's perfection—her figure is—is— I haven't words for it—and her face—good heavens! what brilliancy and animation!"

The Prophet's brow darkened at his daughter's unseasonable appearance in the presence of a handsome young fellow of property, whose character for gallantry was proverbial in the country.

"Sarah, my good girl," said he, whilst his voice, which

at once became low and significant, quivered with suppressed rage—"what brought you here, I ax? Did any one send for you? or is there a matter of life and death on hands that you tramp afther me in this manner—eh?"

"It may be life an' death for anything I know to the contrairy," she replied; "you're angry at something, I see," she proceeded,—"but to save time, I want to spake to you."

"You must wait till I go home, then, for I neither can nor will spake to you now."

"Father, you will—you must," she replied—"and in some private place, too. I won't detain you long, for I haven't much to say, and if I don't say it now, it may be too late."

"What the deuce, M'Gowan!" said Dick, "speak to the young woman—you don't know but she may have something of importance to say to you."

She glanced at the speaker, but with a face of such indifference, as if she had scarcely taken cognizance of him beyond the fact that she found some young man there in conversation with her father.

Donnel, rather to take her from under the libertine gaze of his young friend, walked a couple of hundred yards to the right of the garden, where, under the shadow of some trees that overhung a neglected fish-pond, she opened the purport of her journey after him to the Grange.

"Now, in the divil's name," he asked, "what brought you here?"

"Father," she replied, "hear me, and do not be angry, for I know—at laste I think—that what I'm goin' to say to you is right."

"Well, madam, let us hear what you have to say."

"I will—an' I must speak plain, too. You know me;—that I cannot think one thing and say another."

"Yes, I know you very well—go on—ay, and so does your unfortunate stepmother."

"Oh—well!" she replied—"yes, I suppose so—ha! ha!"
In a moment, however, her face became softened with deep

feeling. "Oh, father," she proceeded, "maybe you don't know me, nor she either; it's only now I'm beginnin' to know myself. But listen—I have often observed your countenance, father—I have often marked it well. I can see by you when you are pleased or angry—but that's aisy; I can tell, too, when the bad spirit is up in you by the pale face but black look that scarcely any one could mistake. I have seen everything bad, father, in your face—bad temper, hatred, revenge—an' but seldom anything good. Father, I'm your daughter, an' don't be angry!"

"What, in the devil's name, are you drivin' at, you brazen jade?"

"Father, you said this mornin', before you came out, that you felt your conscience troublin' you for not discoverin' the murdher of Sullivan; that you felt sorry for keepin' it to yourself so long—sorry!—you said you were sorry, father!"

"I did, and I was."

"Father, I have been thinkin' of that since; no, father— your words were false; there was no sorrow in your face, nor in your eye—no, father, nor in your heart. I know that—I feel it. Father, don't look so; you may bate me, but I'm not afraid."

"Go home out o' this," he replied—"be off, and carry your cursed madness and nonsense somewhere else."

"Father, here I stand—your own child—your only daughter; look me in the face—let your eye look into mine, if you can. I challenge you to it! Now, mark my words— you are goin' to swear a murdher against the head of a poor and a distressed family—to swear it—and, father, you know he never murdhered Sullivan!"

The Prophet started and became pale, but he did not accept the challenge.

He looked at her, however, after a struggle to recover his composure, and there she stood firm, erect; her beautiful face animated with earnestness, her eyes glowing with singu-

lar lustre, yet set, and sparkling in the increasing moisture
which a word or thought would turn into tears.

"What do you mane, Sarah?" said he, affecting coolness—
"what do you mane? I know! Explain yourself."

"Father, I will. There was a bad spirit in your face and
in your heart when you said you were sorry—that you
repented for consalin' the murdher so long; there was, father,
a bad spirit in your heart, but no repentance there."

"An' did you come all the way from home to tell me this?"

"No, father, not to tell you what I have said,—but,
father dear, what I am goin' to say; only first answer me.
If he did murdher Sullivan, was it in his own defence?—
was it a cool murdher?—a cowardly murdher?—because if
it was, Condy Dalton is a bad man. But still listen: it's
now near two-an'-twenty years since the deed was done. I
know little about religion, father—you know that—but still
I have heard that God is willin' to forgive all men their sins
if they repent of them—if they're sorry for them. Now,
father, it's well known that for many a long year Condy
Dalton has been in great sorrow of heart for something or
other; can man do more?"

"Go home out o' this, I say—take yourself away."

"Oh, who can tell, father, the inward agony and bitther
repentance that that sorrowful man's heart, maybe, has suffered? Who can tell the tears he shed, the groans he
groaned, the prayers for mercy he said, maybe, an' the
worlds he would give to have that man that he killed—only
by a hasty blow, maybe—again alive and well! Father,
don't prosecute him—lave the poor heart-broken ould man
to God! Don't you see that God has already taken him an'
his into His hands—hasn't He punished them a hundred ways
for years? Hav'nt they been brought down, step by step,
from wealth an' respectability, till they're now, like poor
beggars, in the very dust? Oh, think, father—dear father
—think of his white hairs—think of his pious wife that every
one respects—think of his good-hearted, kind daughters—

think of their poverty, and of all they have suffered so long—an' above all, oh, think, father dear, of what they will suffer if you are the manes of takin' that sorrowful white-haired ould man out from the middle of his poor, but lovin', and daicent, and respected family, and hangin' him for an act that he has repented for, maybe, and that we ought to hope the Almighty Himself has forgiven him for. Father, I go on my knees to you to beg that you won't prosecute this ould man —but lave him to God!"

As she uttered the few last sentences, the tears fell in torrents from her cheeks ; but when she knelt—which she did—her tears ceased to flow, and she looked into her father's face with eyes kindled into an intense expression, and her hands clasped as if her own life and everlasting salvation depended upon his reply.

"Go home, I desire you," he replied, with a cold sneer— for he had now collected himself, and fell back into his habitual snarl—"Go home, I desire you, or maybe you'd wish to throw yourself in the way of that young profligate that I was spakin' to when you came up. Who knows, afther all, but that's your real design, and neither pity nor compassion for ould Dalton ? "

"Am I his daughter ? " she replied, whilst she started to her feet, and her dark eyes flashed with disdain—" Can I be his daughter ? "

"I hope you don't mean to cast a slur upon your——" He paused a moment, and started as if a serpent had bitten him ; but left the word " mother " unuttered.

Again she softened, and her eyes filled with tears. "Father, I never had a mother!" she said.

"No," he replied; "or if you had, her name will never come through my lips."

She looked at him with wonder for a few moments, after which she turned, and, with a face of melancholy and sorrow, proceeded with slow and meditating steps in the direction of their humble cabin.

Her father, who felt considerably startled by some portions
of her appeal, though by no means softened, again directed
his steps towards the garden gate, where he had left young
Dick standing. Here he found this worthy young gentleman
awaiting his return, and evidently amazed at the interview
between him and his daughter; for although he had been at
too great a distance to hear their conversation, he could and
did see, by the daughter's attitudes, that the subject of their
conversation was extraordinary and important.

On approaching him, the Prophet now, with his usual
coolness, pulled out the tress which he had, in some manner,
got from *Gra Gal* Sullivan, and holding it for a time, placed
it in Dick's hands.

"There's one proof," said he, alluding to a previous part
of their conversation, "that I wasn't unsuccessful, and indeed, I seldom am, when I set about a thing in earnest."

"But is it possible," asked the other, "that she actually
gave this lovely tress willingly—you swear that? "

"As heaven's above me," replied the Prophet, "there
never was a ringlet sent by woman to man with more love
than she sent that. Why, the purty creature actually shed
tears, and begged of me to lose no time in givin' it. You
have it now, at all events—an' only for young Dalton's outrage, you'd have had it before now."

"Then there's no truth in the report that's she's fond of
him ? "

"Why—ahem!—n—no—oh no—not now—fond of him she
was, no doubt; an' you know, it's never hard to light a
half-burned turf—or a candle that was lit before. If they
could be got out of the counthry, at all events—these Daltons
—it would be so much out of your way, for between you an
me, I can tell you that your life won't be safe when he comes
to know that you have put his nose out of joint with the
Gra Gal."

"It's strange, however, that she should change so soon! "

"Ah, Masther Richard! how little you know of woman,

when you say so. They're a vain, uncertain, selfish crew—women are—there's no honesty in them, nor I don't think there's a woman alive that could be trusted, if you only give her temptation and opportunity—none of them will stand that."

"But how do you account for the change in her case, I ask ? "

" I'll tell you that. First an' foremost, you're handsome—remarkably handsome."

" Come, come, no nonsense, Donnel—get along, will you, ha! ha! ha!—handsome, indeed!—never you mind what the world says—well! "

" Why," replied the other, gravely, " there's no use in denyin' it, you know; it's a matter that tells for itself, an' that a poor girl with eyes in her head can judge of as well as a rich one—at any rate, if you're not handsome, you're greatly belied ; an' every one knows that there's never smoke without fire."

" Well, confound you!—since they'll have it so, I suppose I may as well admit it—I believe I am a handsome dog, and I have reason to know that—that——" here he shook his head and winked knowingly ;—" oh, come, Donnel, my boy, I can go no further on that subject—ha! ha! ha!"

" There is no dispute about it," continued Donnel, gravely ; " but still I think, that if it was not for the mention I made of the dress, an' grandeur, an' state that she was to come to, she'd hardly turn round as she did. Dalton, you know, is the handsomest young fellow, barrin' yourself, in the parish ; an' troth, on your account an' hers, I wish he was out of it. He'll be crossin' you—you may take my word for it—an' a dangerous enemy he'll prove—that I know."

" Why ?—what do you mean ? "

Here the Prophet, who was artfully endeavouring to fill the heart of his companion with a spirit of jealousy against Dalton, paused for about a minute, as if in deep reflection, after which he sighed heavily.

"Mane!" he at length replied—"I'm unhappy in my mind, an' I know I ought to do it—an' yet I'm loth now afther sich a length of time. Mane, did you say, Masther Richard?"

"Yes, I said so, and I say so—what do you mean by telling me that young Dalton will be a dangerous enemy to me?"

"An' so he will—an' so he would to any one that he or his bore ill-will against. You know there's blood upon their hands?"

"No, I don't know any such thing; I believe he was charged with the murder of Mave Sullivan's uncle, but as the body could not be found, there were no grounds for a prosecution. I don't therefore know that there's blood upon his hand."

"Well, then, if you don't—may God direct me!" he added, "an' guide me to the best—if you don't, Masther Richard—heaven direct me agin!—will I say it? Could you get that family quietly out of the counthry, Masther Richard? Bekase, if you could, it would be betther, maybe, for all parties."

"You seem to know something about these Daltons, M'Gowan?" asked Dick, "and to speak mysteriously of them?"

"Well, then, I do," he replied; "but what I have to say, I ought to say to your father, who is a magistrate."

The other stared at him with surprise, but said nothing for a minute or two.

"What is this mystery?" he added at length. "I cannot understand you; but it is clear that you mean something extraordinary."

"God pardon me, Masther Richard, and you are right enough, no—I can't keep it any longer. Listen to me, sir, for I am goin' to make a strange and a fearful discovery—I know who it was that murdhered Sullivan—I'm in possession of it for the last two-an'-twenty years—I have travelled everywhere—gone to England, to Wales, Scotland, an'

America, but it was all of no use, the knowledge of the murdher and the murdherer was here "—he laid his hand upon his heart as he spoke—" an' durin' all that time I had peace neither by night nor by day."

His companion turned towards him with amazement, and truly his appearance was startling, if not frightful : he looked as if it were into vacancy—his eyes had become hollow and full of terror—his complexion assumed the hue of ashes—his voice got weak and unsteady, and his limbs trembled excessively, whilst from every pore the perspiration came out, and ran down his ghastly visage in large drops.

" M'Gowan," said his companion, "this is a dreadful business. As yet you have said nothing, and from what I see, I advise you to reflect before you proceed further in it —I think I can guess the nature of your secret; but even if you went to my father, he would tell you that you are not bound to say anything to criminate yourself."

The Prophet, in the meantime, had made an effort to recover himself, which, after a little time, was successful.

" I believe you think," he added, with a gloomy and a bitter smile, " that it was I who committed the murdher— oh, no ! if it was, I wouldn't be apt to hang myself, I think. No !—but I must see your father, as a magistrate; an' I must make the disclosure to him. The man that did murdher Sullivan is livin', and that man is Condy Dalton. I knew of this, an' for two-an'-twenty years let that murdherer escape ; an' that is what made me so miserable an' unhappy. I can prove what I say, an' I know the very spot where he buried Sullivan's body, an' where it's lyin' to this very day."

" In that case, then," replied the other, "you have only one course to pursue, and that is, to bring Dalton to justice."

" I know it," returned the Prophet ; " but still I feel that it's a hard case to be the means of hangin' a fellow-crature ; but of the two choices, rather than bear any longer what I have suffered, an' am still sufferin,' I think it betther to prosecute him."

"Then go in and see my father at once about it, and a devilish difficult card you'll have to play with him—for my part, I think he is mad ever since Jemmy Branigan left him. In fact, he knows neither what he is saying or doing without him, especially in some matters ; for to tell you the truth," he added, laughing, "Jemmy, who was so well acquainted with the country and every one in it, took much more of the magistrate on him than ever my father did ; and now the old fellow, when left to himself, is nearly helpless in every sense. He knows he has not Jemmy, and he can bear nobody else near him or about him."

"I will see him, then, before I lave the place ; an' now, Masther Richard, you know what steps you ought to take with regard to *Gra Gal* Sullivan. As she is willin' herself, of coorse there is but one way of it."

"Of course I am aware of that," said Dick ; "but still I feel that it's devilish queer she should change so soon from Dalton to me."

"That's bekase you know nothing about women," replied the Prophet. "Why, Master Richard, I tell you that a weathercock is constancy itself compared to them. The notion of you, an' your wealth, an' grandeur, an' the great state you're to keep her in—all turned her brain ; an' as a proof of it, there you have a lock of her beautiful hair that she gave me with her own hands. If that won't satisfy you, it's hard to say what can ; but, indeed, I think you ought to know by this time o' day how far a handsome face goes with them. Give the divil himself but that, an' they'll take his horns, hooves, an' tail into the bargain—ay, will they."

This observation was accompanied by a grin so sneering and bitter, that his companion, on looking at him, knew not how to account for it, unless by supposing that he must, during the course of his life, have sustained some serious or irreparable injury at their hands.

"You appear not to like the women, Donnel ; how is that ? "

"Like them!" he replied, and as he spoke, his face, which had been, a little before, ghastly with horror, now became black and venomous—"ha! ha! how is that, you say?—oh, no matther now—they're angels—angels of perdition; their truth is traichery, an' their—but no matther. I'll now go in an' spake to your father on this business; but I forgot to say that I must see *Gra Gal* soon, to let her know our plans; so do you make your mind aisy, and lave the management of the whole thing in my hands."

CHAPTER XIV

A MIDDLEMAN MAGISTRATE OF THE OLD SCHOOL AND HIS CLERK

DICK o' the Grange—whose name was Henderson—at least such is the name we choose to give him—held his office, as many Irish magistrates have done before him, in his own parlour; that is to say, he sat in an arm-chair at one of the windows, which was thrown open for him, whilst those who came to seek justice, or, as they termed it, law, at his hands, were compelled to stand uncovered on the outside, no matter whether the weather was stormy or otherwise. We are not now about to pronounce any opinion upon the constitutional spirit of Dick's decisions, inasmuch as nineteen out of every twenty of them were come to by the only "Magistrates' Guide" he ever was acquainted with—to wit, the redoubtable Jemmy Branigan. Jemmy was his clerk, and although he could neither read nor write, yet in cases where his judgments did not give satisfaction, he was both able and willing to set his mark upon the discontented parties in a fashion that did not allow his blessed signature to be easily forgotten. Jemmy, however, as the reader knows, was absent on the morning we are writing about, having actually fulfilled his threat of leaving his master's service— a threat, by the way, which was held out and acted upon

at least once every year since he and the magistrate had
stood to each other in the capacity of master and servant.
Not that we are precisely correct in the statement we have
made on this matter, for sometimes his removal was the
result of dismissal on the part of his master, and sometimes
the following up of the notice which he himself had given
him to leave his service. Be this as it may, his temporary
absences always involved a trial of strength between the
parties, as to which of them should hold out, and put a
constraint upon his inclinations the longest; for since the
truth must be told of Jemmy, we are bound to say that he
could as badly bear to live removed from the society of his
master, as the latter could live without him. For many
years of his life he had been threatening to go to America,
or to live with a brother that he had in the Isle of *White*,
as he called it, and on several occasions he had taken formal
leave of the whole family (always in the presence of his
master, however), on his departure for either the one place
or the other, whilst his real abode was a snug old garret,
where he was attended and kept in food by the family and
his fellow-servants, who were highly amused at the outrageous distress of his master, occasioned sometimes by
Jemmy's obstinate determination to travel, and sometimes
by his extreme brotherly affection.

Donnel, having left the son cracking a long whip which
he held in his hand, and looking occasionally at the tress
of Mave Sullivan's beautiful hair, approached the hall door,
at which he knocked, and on the appearance of a servant,
requested to see Mr. Henderson. The man wafted his hand
towards the space under the window, meaning that he should
take his stand there, and added,—

"If it's law you want, I'm afeard you'll get more abuse
than justice from him now, since Jemmy's gone."

The knowing grin, and the expression of comic sorrow
which accompanied the last words, were not lost upon the
Prophet, who, in common with every one in the neighbour-

hood for a circumference of many miles, was perfectly well aware of the life which master and man both led.

"Is that it?" said the Prophet; "however, it can't be helped. Clerk or no clerk, I want to see him on sarious business, tell him; but I'll wait, of coorse, till he's at leisure."

"Tom," said Henderson from within, "who's there?—is that him? If it is, tell him, confound him! to come in, an' I'll forgive him. If he'll promise to keep a civil tongue in his head, I'll forget all, say. Come in, you old scoundrel, I'm not angry with you; I want to speak to you, at all events."

"It's not him, sir; it's only Donnel M'Gowan, the Black Prophet, that wants some law business."

"Send him to the devil for law business. What brings him here now? Tell him he shall have neither law nor justice from me. Did you send to his brother-in-law? Maybe he's there!"

"We did, sir. Sorra one of his seed, breed, or generation, but we sent to. However, it's no use—off to Ameriky he's gone, or to the Isle o' White, at any rate."

"May the devil sink America and the Isle of White both in the ocean, and you, too, you scoundrel, and all of you! Only for the cursed crew that's about me, I'd have him here still—and he the only man that understood my wants and my wishes, and that could keep me comfortable and easy."

"Troth, then, he hadn't an overly civil tongue in his head, sir," replied the man; "for, when you and he, your honour, were together, there was little harmony to spare between you."

"That was my own fault, you cur. No servant but himself would have had a day's patience with me. He never abused me but when I deserved it—did he?"

"No, your honour; I know he didn't, in troth."

"You lie, you villain, you know no such thing. Here am

I with my sore leg, and no one to dress it for me. Who's
to help me upstairs or downstairs?—who's to be about me?
or who cares for me, now that he's gone? Nobody—not
a soul."

"Doesn't Masther Richard, sir?"

"No, sir; Master Richard gives himself little trouble
about me. He has other plots and plans on his hands—other
fish to fry—other irons in the fire. Master Richard, sirra,
doesn't care a curse if I was under the sod to-morrow, but
would be glad of it; neither does any one about me—but
he did; and you infernal crew, you have driven him away
from me!"

"We, your honour?"

"Yes, all of you; you put me first out of temper by your
neglect and your extravagance; then I vented it on him,
because he was the only one among you I took any pleasure
in abus——in speaking to. However, my mind's made up—
I'll call an auction—sell everything—and live in Dublin
as well as I can. What does that black hound want?"

"Some law business, sir; but I dunna what it is."

"Is the scoundrel honest, or a rogue?"

"Throth, it's more than I'm able to tell your honour, sir.
I don't know much about him. Some spakes well, an' some
spakes ill of him—jist like his neighbours—ahem!"

"Ay, an' that's all you can say of him? but if he was
here, I could soon ascertain what stuff he's made of, and
what kind of a hearing he ought to get. However, it doesn't
matter now—I'll auction everything—in this Grange I won't
live; and to be sure but I was a precious old scoundrel to
quarrel with the best servant a man ever had."

Just at this moment, who should come round from a back
passage, carrying a small bundle in his hand, but the object
of all his solicitude. He approached quietly upon tiptoe,
with a look in which might be read a most startling and ludicrous expression of anxiety and repentance.

"How is he?"—said he—"how is his poor leg? Oh, thin,

blessed saints, but I was the double-distilled villain of the
airth to lave him as I did to the crew that was about him!
The best masther that ever an ould vagabond like me was
ongrateful to!   How is he, Tom ?"

"Why," replied the other, "if you take my advice, you'll
keep from him at all events. He's cursin' and abusin' you
ever since you went, and won't allow one of us even to name
you."

"Troth, an' it only shows his sense; for I desarved nothin'
else at his hands.   However, if what you say is thrue, I'm
afeard he's not long for this world, and that his talkin' sense
at last is only the lightenin' before death, poor gintleman!
I can stay no longer from him, anyhow, let him be as he
may; an' God pardon me for my ongratitude in desartin' him
like a villain as I did."

He then walked into the parlour; and as the Prophet was
beckoned as far as the hall, he had an opportunity of witnessing the interview which took place between this extraordinary
pair. Jemmy, before entering, threw aside his bundle and
his hat, stripped off his coat, and in a moment presented
himself in the usual striped cotton jacket, with sleeves, which
he always wore. Old Dick was in the habit of letting fly an
oath at something, when Jemmy, walking in, just as if nothing
had happened, exclaimed,—

"Why, thin, Mother o' Moses, is it at the ould work I find
you ?   Troth, it's past counsel, past grace wid you—I'm
afraid you're too ould to mend. In the mane time, don't
stare as if you seen a ghost—only tell us how is that unfortunate leg of yours?"

"Why—eh?—ay,—oh, ay,—you're back, are you?—an'
what the devil brought you here again, eh?"

"Come, now, keep yourself quiet, you onpenitent ould
sinner, or it'll be worse for you. How is your leg?"

"Ah, you provokin' old rascal—eh?—so you are back?"

"Don't you see I am—who would stick to you like myself, afther all? Troth, I missed your dirty tongue, bad as it

is—divil a thing but rank peace and quietness I was in ever
since I seen you last."

"And devil a scoundrel has had the honesty to give me a
single word of abuse to my face since you left me."

"And how often did I tell you that you couldn't depind
upon the crew that's about you—the truth's not in them—an'
that you ought to know. However, so far as I am consarned,
dont't fret—God knows I forgive you all your folly and *feasthalagh*,[1] in hopes always that you'll mend your life in many
respects. You had myself before you as an example, though
I say it, that oughtn't to say it; but you know you didn't
take patthern by me as you ought.'

"Shake hands, Jemmy—I'm glad to see you again—you
were put to expense since you went?"

"No, none—no, I tell you."

"But I say you were."

"There, keep yourself quiet now—no, I wasn't—an' if I
was, too, what is it to you ? "

"Here, put that note in your pocket."

"Sorra bit, now," replied Jemmy, "to plaise you"—grip-
ping it tightly at the same time as he spoke—"do you want
to vex me agin?"

"Put it in your pocket, sirra, unless you wish me to break
your head."

"Oh, he would," said Jemmy, looking, with a knowing
face of terror, towards Tom Booth and the Prophet—"it's
the weight of his cane I'd get, sure enough—but it's an ould
sayin' an' a true one, that where the generosity's in, it must
come out. There now, I've put it in my pocket for you—
an' I hope you're satisfied. Divil a sich a tyrant in Europe,"
said he loudly, "when he wishes—an' yet, afther all," he
added, in a low, confidential voice, just loud enough for his
master to hear—"where 'ud one get the like of him? Tom
Booth, desire them to fetch warm wather to the study, till I
dress his poor leg, and make him fit for business."

[1] Nonsense.

"Here is Donnel Dhu," replied Booth, "waitin' for law business."

"Go to the windy, Donnel," said Jemmy, with an authoritative air—"go to your ground; but before you go let *me* know what you want."

"I'll do no such thing," replied the Prophet—"unless to say that it's a matter of life an' death."

"Go out," repeated Jemmy, with brief and determined authority, "an' wait till it's his honour's convanience—his full convanience—to see you. As dark a rogue, sir,"—he continued, having shoved the Prophet outside, and slapped the door in his face—"and as great a schamer as ever put a coat on his back. He's as big a liar, too, when he likes, as ever broke bread; but there's far more danger in him when he tells truth, for then you may be sure that he has some divil's design in view."

Dick o' the Grange, though vulgar and eccentric, was by no means deficient in shrewdness and common sense; neither was he, deliberately, an unjust man; but, like too many in the world, he generally suffered his prejudices and his interests to take the same side. Having had his leg dressed, and been prepared by Jemmy for the business of the day, he took his place as usual in the chair of justice, had the window thrown open, and desired the Prophet to state the nature of his business.

The latter [told him that the communication must be a private one, as it involved a matter of deep importance, being no less than an affair of life and death.

This startled the magistrate, who, with a kind of awkward embarrassment, ordered, or rather, requested Jemmy to withdraw, intimating that he would be sent for, if his advice or opinion should be deemed necessary.

"No matther," replied Jemmy, "the loss will be your own; for sure I know the nice hand you make of law, when you're left to yourself. Only before I go, mark my words; there you stand, Donnel Dhu, an' I'm telling him to be on his guard against you—don't put trust, plaise your honour, in either his word or his oath—an' if he's bringin' a charge against any one, give it in favour of his enemy, whoever he is. I hard that he was wanst tried for robbery, an' I only wondher it wasn't for murdher, too; for, in troth and sowl, if ever a man has both one and the other in his face, he has. It's known to me that he's seen now an' then *colloguin* an' skulkin' behind the hedges, about dusk, wid red Roddy Duncan, that was *in* twiste[1] for robbery. Troth it's birds of a feather wid them—an' I wouldn't be surprised if we were to see them both swing from the same rope yet. So there's my correcthor of you, you villain," he added, addressing M'Gowan, at whom he felt deeply indignant, in consequence of his not admitting him to the secret of the communication he was about to make.

Henderson, when left alone with the Prophet, heard the disclosures which the latter made to him with less surprise than interest. He himself remembered the circumstances perfectly well, and knew that on the occasion of Condy Dalton's former arrest, appearances had been very strongly against them. It was then expected that he would have disclosed the particular spot in which the body had been concealed, but as he strenuously persisted in denying any knowledge of it, and as the body consequently could not be produced, they were obliged, of necessity, to discharge him, but still under strong suspicions of his guilt.

The interview between Henderson and M'Gowan was a long one; and the disclosures made were considered of too much importance for the former to act without the co-operation and assistance of another magistrate. He accordingly desired the Prophet to come to him on the following day but one, when he said he would secure the presence of a Major Johnston, who was also in the commission, and by whose warrant old Condy Dalton had been originally arrested on suspicion of the murder. It was recommended that every-

---

[1] Twice.

thing that had transpired between them should be kept
strictly secret, lest the murderer, if made acquainted with
the charge which was about to be brought home to him,
should succeed in escaping from justice. Young Dick, who
had been sent for by his father, recommended this, and on
those terms they separated.

CHAPTER XV

A PLOT AND A PROPHECY

OUR readers cannot forget a short dialogue which took
place between Charley Hanlon and the strange female who
has already borne some part in the incidents of our story.
It occurred on the morning she had been sent to convey the
handkerchief which Hanlon had promised to Sarah M'Gowan,
in lieu of the tobacco-box of which we have so frequently
made mention, and which, on that occasion, she expected to
have received from Sarah. After having inquired from
Hanlon why Donnel Dhu was called the Black Prophet, she
asked—

" But could he have anything to do with the murdher ? "

To which Hanlon replied that—" he had been thinkin'
about that, an' had some talk, this mornin', wid a man that's
livin' a long time—indeed, that was born—a little above the
place, an' he says that the Black Prophet, or M'Gowan, did
not come to the neighbourhood till afther the murdher."

Now this person was no other than red Roddy Duncan, to
whom our friend Jemmy Branigan made such opprobrious
allusion in the character he gave of the Black Prophet to
Dick o' the Grange. This man, who was generally known
by the *sobriquet* of Red Roddy, had been for some time looking after the situation of bailiff or driver to Dick o' the
Grange ; and as Hanlon was supposed to possess a good
deal of influence with Young Dick, Duncan very properly
thought he could not do better than cultivate his acquain-

ance. This was the circumstance which brought them together at first, and it was something of a dry, mysterious manner which Hanlon observed in this fellow, when talking about the Prophet and his daughter, that caused him to keep up the intimacy between them.

When Donnel Dhu had closed his lengthened conference with Henderson, he turned his step homewards, and had got half-way through the lawn, when he was met by Red Roddy. He had, only a minute or two before, left Young Dick, with whom he held another short conversation ; and as he met Roddy, Dick was still standing within about a hundred yards of them, or rather lounging about, cracking his whip with that easy indolence and utter disregard of everything but his pleasures, which chiefly constituted his character.

"Don't stand to speak to me here," said the Prophet; "that young scoundrel will see us. Have you tried Hanlon yet, and will he do?—yes or no ?"

"I hav'nt tried him, but I'm now on my way to do so."

"Caution!"

"Certainly—I'm no fool, I think. If we can secure him, the business may be managed aisily ; that is, provided the two affairs can come off on the same night."

"Caution, I say again."

"Certainly—I'm no fool, I hope. Pass on."

The Prophet and he passed each other very slowly during this brief dialogue ; the former, when it was finished, pointing naturally towards the Grange or Young Dick, as if he had been merely answering a few questions respecting some person about the place that the other was going to see. Having passed the Prophet, he turned to the left, by a back path that led to the garden, where, in fact, Hanlon was generally to be found, and where, upon this occasion, he found him. After a good deal of desultory chat, Roddy at last inquired if Hanlon thought there existed any chance of his procuring the post of bailiff.

"I don't think there is, then, to tell you the truth," replied Hanlon; "ould Jemmy is against you bitterly, an' Masther Richard's interest in this business isn't as strong as his."

"The blackguard ould villain!" exclaimed Roddy; "it would be a good job to give him a dog's knock some night or other."

"I don't see that either," replied Hanlon; "ould Jemmy does a power of good in his way; and, indeed, many an act of kindness the masther himself gets credit for that ought to go to Jemmy's account."

"But you can give me a lift in the drivership, Charley, if you like."

"I'm afeared not, so long as Jemmy's against you."

"Ay, but couldn't you thry and twist that ould scoundhrel himself in my favour?"

"Well," replied the other, "there is something in that, and whatever I can do with him I will, if you'll thry an' do me a favour."

"Me!—name it, man—name it, and it's done, if it was only to rob the Grange. Ha! ha! ha! An', by the way, I dunna what puts robbin' the same Grange into my head!"

As he spoke, his eye was bent with an expression of peculiar significance on Hanlon.

"No," replied Hanlon, with indifference, "it is not to rob the Grange. I b'lieve you know something about the man they call the Black Prophet?"

"Donnel Dhu? Why—ahem—a little—not much; nobody, indeed, knows or cares much about him. However, like most people, he has his friends and his enemies."

"Don't you remember a murdher that was committed here about two-an'-twenty years ago?"

"I do."

"Was that before or afther the Black Prophet came to live in this counthry?"

"Afther it—afther it. No, no," he replied, correcting himself; "I am wrong; it was before he came here."

"Then he could have no hand in it?"

"Him! is it him? Why, what puts sich a thing as that into your head?"

"Faith, to tell you the thruth, Roddy, his daughter Sarah an' myself is beginnin' to look at one another; an' to tell you the truth again, I'd wish to know more about the same Prophet before I become his son-in-law, as I have some notion of doin'."

"I hard, indeed, that you wor pullin' a string wid her, an' now that I think of it, if you give me a lift with ould Jemmy, I'll give you one there. The bailiff's berth is jist the thing for me; not havin' any family of my own, you see I could have no objection to live in the Grange, as their bailiff always did; but aren't you afeared to tackle yourself in that divil's clip, Sarah?"

"Well, I don't know," replied the other; "I grant it's a hazard, by all accounts."

"An' yet," continued Roddy, "she's a favourite with every one; an' indeed there's not a more generous or kind-hearted creature alive this day than she is. I advise you, however, not to let her into your saicrets, for if it was the knockin' of a man on the head, and that she knew it, and was asked about it, out it would go, rather than she'd tell a lie."

"They say she's handsomer than *Gra Gal* Sullivan," said Hanlon; "an' I think myself she is."

"I don't know—it's a dead tie between them; however, I can give you a lift with her father, but not with herself, for somehow she doesn't like a bone in my skin."

"She and I made a swop," proceeded Hanlon, "some time ago, that 'ud take a laugh out o' you: I gave her a pocket-handkerchy, and she was to give me an ould tobaccy-box; but she says she can't find it, although I have sent for it, an' axed it myself several times. She thinks the step-mother has thrown it away or hid it somewhere."

Roddy looked at him inquiringly: "A tobaccy-box," he exclaimed; "would you like to get it?"

"Why," replied Hanlon, "the poor girl has nothin' else to give, an' I'd like to have somethin' from her, even if a ring was never to go on us, merely as a keepsake."

"Well, then," replied Duncan, with something approaching to solemnity in his voice, "mark my words: you promise to give me a lift for the drivership with ould Jemmy and the two Dicks?"

"I do."

"Well, then, listen: if you will be at the Grey Stone to-morrow night at twelve o'clock—midnight—I'll engage that Sarah will give you the box there."

"Why, in troth, Roddy, to tell you the truth, if she could give it to me at any other time an' place, I'd prefer it. That Grey Stone is a wild place to be in at midnight."

"It is a wild place; still it's there, an' nowhere else that you must get the box. And now that that bargain's made, do you think it's thrue that this ould Hendherson "—here he looked very cautiously about him—"has as much money as they say he has?"

"I b'lieve he's very rich."

"Is it thrue that he airs the bank notes in the garden here, and turns the guineas in the sun, for fraid—for fraid —they'd get blue-mowlded?—is it?"

"It may, for all I know; but it's more than I've seen yet."

"An' now, between you and me, Charley—whisper—I say, isn't it a thousand pities—nobody could hear us, surely?"

"Nonsense: who could hear us?"

"Well, isn't it a thousand pities, Charley, avic, that daicent fellows, like you an' me, should be as we are, an' that mad ould villain havin' his house full o' money?— eh, now?"

"It's a hard case," replied Hanlon, "but still we must put up wid our lot. His father, I'm tould, was as poor in the beginnin' as either of us."

"Ay, but it's the son we're spakin' about—the ould tyrannical villain that dhrives an' harries the poor! He has loads of money in the house, they say—eh?"

"Divil a know myself knows, Roddy; nor—not makin' you an' ill answer—divil a hair myself cares, Roddy. Let him have much, or let him have little, that's your share an' mine of it."

"Charley, they say America's a fine place; talkin' about money—wid a little money there, they say a man could do wondhers."

"Who says that?"

"Why, Donnel Dhu, for one; an' he knows, for he was there."

"I b'lieve that Donnel was many a place; over half the world, if all's thrue."

"Augh! the same Donnel's a quare fellow—a deep chap —a 'cute fellow; hut! I know more about him than you think—ay, do I."

"Why, what do you know?"

"No matther—a thing or two about the same Donnel; an' by the same token, a better fellow never lived—an' whisper—you're a strong favourite wid him, that I know, for we wor talkin' about you. In the mean time, I wish to goodness we had a good *scud* o' cash among us, an' we safe an' snug in America! Now, shake hands and good-bye —an' mark me, if you dhrame of America an' a long purse any o' these nights, come to me an' I'll riddle your dhrame for you."

He then looked Hanlon significantly in the face, wrung his hand, and left him to meditate on the purport of their conversation.

The latter, as he went out, gazed at him with a good deal of surprise.

"So," thought he, "you were feelin' my pulse, were you? I don't think it's hard to guess whereabouts you are; however, I'll think of your advice at any rate, an' see what

good may be in it. But, in the name of all that's wonderful,
how does it come to pass that that red ruffian has sich
authority over Sarah M'Gowan as to make her fetch me
the very thing I want?—that tobaccy-box—an' at sich a
place, too, an sich an hour! An' yet he says she doesn't
like a bone in his skin, which I b'lieve! I'm fairly in the
dark here; however, time will make it all clear, I hope;
an' for that we must wait."

He then resumed his employment.

Donnel Dhu, who was a man of much energy, and activity
whenever his purposes required it, instead of turning his
steps homewards, directed them to the house of our kind
friend Jerry Sullivan, with whose daughter, the innocent
and unsuspecting Mave, it was his intention to have another
private interview. During the interval that had elapsed
since his last journey to the house of this virtuous and hospitable family, the gloom that darkened the face of the country had become awful, and such as wofully bore out to the
letter the melancholy truth of his own predictions. Typhus
fever had now set in, and was filling the land with fearful
and unexampled desolation. Famine, in all cases the source
and origin of contagion, had done, and was still doing, its
work. The early potato crop, so far as it had come in, was a
pitiable failure—the quantity being small, and the quality
watery and bad. The oats, too, and all early grain of that
season's growth, were still more deleterious as food, for they
had all fermented and become sour, so that the use of them,
and of the bad potatoes, too, was the most certain means of
propagating the pestilence which was sweeping away the
people in such multitudes. Scarcely anything presented
itself to him, as he went along, that had not some melancholy
association with death or its emblems. To all this, however,
he paid little or no attention. When a funeral met him, he
merely turned back three steps in the direction it went, as
was usual; but unless he happened to know the family from
which death had selected its victim, he never even took the

trouble of inquiring who it was they bore to the grave—a
circumstance which strongly proved the utter and heartless
selfishness of the man's nature. On arriving at Sullivan's,
however, he could not help feeling startled, hard and without sympathy as was his heart, at the wild and emaciated
evidences of misery and want which a couple of weeks' severe
suffering had impressed upon them. The gentle Mave, herself, patient and uncomplaining as she was, had become thin
and cheerless; yet of such a character was the sadness which
rested on her, that it only added a mournful and melancholy
charm to her beauty—a charm that touched the heart of the
beholder at once with love and compassion. As yet there had
been no sickness among them; but who could say to-day that
he or she might not be stricken down at once before to-morrow.

"Donnel," said Sullivan, after he had taken a seat, "how
you came to prophesy what would happen, an' what has happened, is to me a wondher; but sure enough, *fareer gair*,[1]
it has all come to pass!"

"I can't tell myself," replied the other, "how I do it; all
I know is, that the words come into my mouth, an' I can't
help spakin' them. At any rate, that's not surprisin'. I'm
the seventh son of the seventh son, afther seven generations;
that is, I'm the seventh son that was in our family; an' you
must know that the knowledge increases as they go on. Every
seventh son knows more than thim that wint before him till
it comes to the last, an' he knows more than thim all. There
were six seventh sons before me, so that I'm the last; for it
was never known since the world began that ever more than
seven afther one another had the gift of prophecy in the
same family. That's the raison, you see, that I have no sons
—the knowledge ends wid me."

"It's very strange," replied Sullivan, "an' not to be accounted for by any one but God—glory be to His name!"

"It is strange—an' when I find that I'm goin' to foretell
anything that's bad or unlucky, I feel great pain an' unaisi-

[1] Bitter misfortune.

ness in my mind—but, on the other hand, when I am to prophesy what's good, I get quite light-hearted and aisy—I'm
all happiness. An' that's the way I feel now, an' has felt
for the last day or two."

"I wish to God, Donnel," said Mrs. Sullivan, "that you
could prophesize something good for us."

"Or," continued her charitable and benevolent husband,
"for the thousands of poor crathurs that wants it more still
that we do—sure it's thankful to the Almighty we ought to
be, an' is, I hope—that this woful sickness hasn't come upon
us yet. Even Condy Dalton an' his family—ay, God be
praised for givin' me the heart to do it—I can forgive him
and them."

"Don't say them, Jerry, *ahagur*," observed his wife ; "we
never had any bad feelin' against them."

"Well, well," continued the husband, "I can forgive him
an' all o' them now—for, God help them, they're in a state
of the most heart-breakin' distitution, livin' only upon the
bits that the poor starvin' neighbours is able to crib from
their own hungry mouths for them ! " And here the tears—
the tears that did honour not only to him, but to human nature and his country—rolled slowly down his emaciated
cheeks, for the deep distress to which the man that he believed to be the murderer of his brother had been brought.

"Indeed, Donnel," said Mrs. Sullivan, "it would be a
hard an' uncharitable heart that wouldn't relent if it knew
what they're sufferin'. Young Con is jist risin' out of the
faver that was in the family, and it would wring your——"

A glance at Mave occasioned her to pause. The gentle
girl, upon whom the Prophet had kept his eye during the
whole conversation, had been reflecting, in her wasted but
beautiful features, both the delicacy and depth of the sympathy that had been expressed for the unhappy Daltons.
Sometimes she became pale as ashes, and again her complexion assumed the subdued hue of the wild rose ; for—alas
that we must say it—sorrow and suffering—in other words,

want, in its almost severest form, had thrown its melancholy
hue over the richness of her blush—which, on this occasion,
borrowed a delicate grace from distress itself. Such, indeed,
was her beauty, and so gently and serenely did her virtues
shine through it, that it mattered not to what condition of
calamity they were subjected; in every situation they seemed
to shed some new and unexpected charm upon the eyes of
those who looked upon her. The mother, we said, on glancing at her, paused—but the chord of love and sorrow had
been touched, and poor Mave, unable any longer to restrain
her feelings, burst out into tears, and wept aloud on hearing
the name and sufferings of her lover. Her father looked at
her, and his brow got sad; but there was no longer the darkness of resentment or indignation there; so true is it that
suffering chastens the heart into its noblest affections, and
purges it of gloomier and grosser passions.

"Poor Mave," he exclaimed, "when I let the tears down
for the man that has my brother's blood on his hands, it's no
wondher that you should cry for him you love so well."

"Oh, dear father," she exclaimed, throwing herself into
his arms, and embracing him tenderly, "I feel no misery nor
sorrow now—the words you have spoke have made me happy.
All these sufferin's will pass away; for it cannot be but God
will, sooner or later, reward your piety and goodness. Oh,
if I could do anything for—for—for any one," and she blushed
as she spoke: "but I cannot. There is nothing here that I
can do at home; but if I could go out an' work by the day,
I'd do it an' be happy, in ordher to help the—that—family
that's now brought so low, and that's so much to be pitied!"

We have already said that the prophet's eye had been
bent upon her ever since he came into the house, but it was
with an expression of benignity and affection which, notwithstanding the gloomy character of his countenance, no one
could more plausibly or winningly assume.

Mave, in the meantime, could scarcely bear to look upon
him; and it was quite clear from her manner that she had,

since their last mysterious interview, once more fallen back into those feelings of strong aversion with which she had regarded him at first. M'Gowan saw this, and without much difficulty guessed at the individual who had been instrumental in producing the change.

"God pardon an' forgive me," he exclaimed, as if giving unconscious utterance to his own reflections—"for what I had thoughts of about that darlin' an' lovely girl; but sure I'll make it up to her; an' indeed, I feel the words of the goodness that's to befall her breakin' out o' my lips. *A colleen dhas*, I had some private discourse wid you when I was here last, an' will you let me spake a few words to you by ourselves agin!"

"No," she replied, "I'll hear nothing from you—I don't like you—I can't like you, an' I'll hold no private discoorse with you."

"Oh, thin, but that voice is music itself, an' you are, by all accounts, the best of girls; but sure we have all turned over a new leaf—poor child. I discovered how I was taken in an' desaved; but sure I can't ait you—an' a sweet morsel you'd be, *a lanna dhas*—nor I can't run away wid you—an' I seen the day that it's not my heart would hinder me to do that same. Oh, my goodness, what a head o' hair!—an' talkin' about that—you undherstand—I'd like to have a word or two wid yourself."

"Say whatever you have to say before my father and mother, then," she replied; "I have no——" she paused a moment, and seemed embarrassed. The Prophet, who skilfully threw in the allusion to her hair, guessed the words she was on the point of uttering, and availing himself of her difficulty, seemed to act as if she had completed what she was about to say.

"I know, dear," he added, "you have no saicrets from them—I'm glad to hear it, an' for that raison I'm willin' to say what I had to say in their presence—so far as I'm consarned, it makes no difference."

The allusion to her hair, added to his last observations, reminded her that it might be possible he had some message from her lover, and she consequently seemed to waver a little, as if struggling against her strong instinctive abhorrence of him.

"Don't be afeared, Mave dear," said her mother, "sure poor, honest Donnel wishes you well, an' won't prophesize any harm to you. Go with him."

"Do, *achora*," added the father; "Donnel can have nothing to say to you that can have any harm in it—go for a minute or two, since he wishes it."

Reluctantly, and with an indomitable feeling against the man, she went out, and both stood under the shelter of a little elder hedge that adjoined the house.

"Now, tell me," she asked quickly, "what is it you have to say to me?"

"I gave young Condy Dalton the purty ringlet of hair you sent him."

"What did he say?" she inquired.

"Not much," he replied, "till I tould him it was the last token that ever you could send him afther what your father said to you."

"Well?"

"Why, he cursed your father, an' said he desarved to get his neck broke."

"I don't believe that," she replied; "I know he never said them words, or anything like them. Don't mislead me, but tell me what he did say."

"Ah! poor Mave," he replied, "you little know what hot blood runs in the Daltons' veins. He said very little that was creditable to himself—an' indeed I won't repate it—but it was enough to make any girl of spirit have done wid him."

"An' don't you know," she replied mournfully, "that I have done with him, an' that there never can be anything but sorrow and good-will between us? Wasn't that my message to him by yourself?"

"It was, dear, an' I hope you're still of the same mind."

"I am," she said; "but you are not tellin' me the truth about him. He never spoke disrespectfully of my father or me."

"No, indeed, *asthore*, he did not then—oh, the sorra syllable—oh, no; if I said so, don't believe me." And yet the very words he uttered, in consequence of the meaning which they received from his manner, made an impression directly the reverse of their natural import.

"Well, then," she said, "that's all you have to say to me?"

"No," he replied, "it is not: I want to know from you when you'll be goin' to your uncle's at Mullaghmore."

"To-morrow," replied the artless and unsuspicious girl, without a moment's hesitation.

"Well, then," said he, "you pass the Grey Stone, at the foot of Mallybenagh—of coorse, I know you must. Now, my dear Mave, I want to show you that I have some insight into futurity. What hour will you pass it at?"

"About three o'clock, as near as I think—it may be a little more or a little less."

"Very well, *acushla*; when you pass the Grey Stone, about a few hundred yards on the right-hand side, the first person you meet will be a young man, well-made and very handsome. That young man will be the person, whoever he is —an' I don't know myself—that will bring you love, and wealth, and happiness, an' all that a woman can wish to have with a man. Now, dear, if this doesn't happen, never b'lieve anything I say again; but if this does happen, I hope you'll have good sense, *acushla machree*, to be guided by one that's your true friend—an' that's myself. The first person you meet, afther passin' the Grey Stone, on your right-hand side —remember the words. I know there's great luck an' high fortune before you; for, indeed, your beauty an' goodness well desarves it, and they'll get both."

They then returned into the house, Mave somewhat sur-

prised, but no way relieved, whilst the Prophet seemed rather
in better spirits by the interview.

"Now, Jerry Sullivan," said he, " an' you, Bridget, his
wife, lend your ears an' listen. The heart of the Prophet is
full of good to you and yours, and the good must come to his
lips, and flow from them when it comes. There are three
books known to the wise, the Book of Marriage, the Book of
Death, and the Book of Judgment. Open a leaf, says the
Angel of Marriage—the Garden Angel of Jericho—where he
brings all love, happiness, and peace to; open a leaf, says the
Angel of Marriage—him that has one head and ten horns—
and read us a page of futurity from the Prophecy of St. Nebbychodanazor the divine. The child is a faymale child, says
the angel with one head and ten horns, by name Mabel Sullivan, daughter to honest Jerry Sullivan an' his daicent wife
Bridget, of Aughnamurrin. Amin, says the Prophet. Time
is not tide, nor is tide time; an' neither will wait for man.
Three things will happen. A girl, young and handsome,
will walk forth upon the highway, and there she will meet a
young man, young an' handsome, too, who will rise her to
wealth, happiness, and grandeur. So be it, says the Book
of Marriage, an' amin, agin, says the Prophet. Open a new
leaf, says Nebbychodanazor the divine—a new leaf in the
Book of Judgment, and another in the Book of Death. A
man was killed, an' his body hid, an' a man lived with his
blood upon him. Fate is fate, an' justice is near. For years
he will keep the murdher to himself, till a man's to come that
will bring him to judgment. Then will judgment be passed,
and the Book of Death will be opened. Read, says the Prophet—it is done at last—Judgment is passed, and Death
follows—the innocent is set free, and the murdherer that
consaled the murdher so long swings at last; and all these
things is to be found by the Wise in the Books of Marriage,
Death, and Judgment." He then added, as he had done at
the conclusion of his former prophecy,—

"Be kind and indulgent to your daughter, for she'll soon

make all your fortunes ; an' take care of her and yourselves till I see yez again."

As before, he gave them no further opportunity of asking for explanations, but immediately departed ; and as if he had been moved by some new impulse or after-thought, he directed his steps once more to the Grange, where he saw young Henderson, with whom he had another private interview, of the purport of which our readers may probably form a tolerably accurate conjecture.

CHAPTER XVI

MYSTERIOUS DISAPPEARANCE OF THE TOBACCO-BOX

M'GOWAN'S mind, at this period of our narrative, was busily engaged in arranging his plans—for we need scarcely add here, that, whether founded in justice or not, he had more than one ripening. Still there preyed upon him a certain secret anxiety, from which, by no effort, could he succeed in ridding himself. The disappearance of the tobacco-box kept him so ill at ease and unhappy, that he resolved, on his way home, to make a last effort at finding it out, if it could be done ; and many a time did he heartily curse his own stupidity for ever having suffered it to remain in his house or about it, especially when it was so easy to destroy it. His suspicions respecting it most certainly rested upon Nelly, whom he now began to regard with a feeling of both hatred and alarm. Sarah, he knew, had little sympathy with him ; but then he also knew that there existed less in common between her and Nelly. He thought, therefore, that his wisest plan would be to widen the breach of ill-feeling between them more and more, and thus to secure himself, if possible, of Sarah's co-operation and confidence, if not from affection or good-feeling towards himself, at least from ill-will towards her step-mother. For this reason, therefore, as well as for others of equal, if not of more importance, he came to the determination of taking, to a certain extent, Sarah into his confidence, and thus making not only her quickness and activity, but her impetuosity and resentments, useful to his designs. It was pretty late that night when he reached home; and as he had devoted the only portion of time that remained between his arrival and bed-time to a description of the unsettled state of the country, occasioned by what were properly called the Famine Outrages, that were then beginning to take place, he made no allusion to anything connected with his projects to either Nelly or his daughter, the latter of whom, by the way, had been out during the greater part of the evening. The next morning, however, he asked her to take a short stroll with him along the river, which she did; and both returned after having had at least an hour's conversation—Sarah, with a flushed cheek and indignant eye, and her father with his brow darkened, and his voice quivering from suppressed resentment; so that, so far as observation went, their interview and communication had not been very agreeable on either side. After breakfast, Sarah put on her cloak and bonnet, and was about to go out when her father said,—

"Pray, ma'am, where are your goin' now?"

"It doesn't signify," she replied; "but at all evints you needn't ax me, for I won't tell you."

"What kind of an answer is that to give me? Do you forget that I am your father?"

"I wish I could, for indeed I'm sorry you are."

"Oh, you know," observed Nelly, "she was always a dutiful girl—always a quiet, good crathur. Why, you onbiddable sthrap, what kind of an answer is that to give to your father?"

Ever since their stroll that morning, Sarah's eyes had been turned from time to time upon her stepmother with flash after flash of burning indignation, and now that she addressed her, she said,—

"Woman, you don't know how I scorn you! Oh, you mane an' wicked wretch, had you no pride durin' all your life ! It's but a short time you an' I will be undher the same roof together—an' so far as I am consarned, I'll not stoop even to bandy abuse or ill-tongue with you again. I know only one other person that is worse an' meaner still than you are—an' there, I am sorry to say, he stands, in the shape of my father."

She walked out of the cabin with a flushed cheek, and a step that was full of disdain and a kind of natural pride that might almost be termed dignity. Both felt rebuked ; and Nelly, whose face got blanched and pale at Sarah's words, now turned upon the Prophet with a scowl.

" Would it be possible," said she, " that you'd dare to let out anything to that madcap ? "

" Now," said he, " that the coast is clear, I desire you to answer me a question that I'll put to you—an' mark my words—by all that's above us, an' undher us, an' about us, if you don't spake thruth, I'll be apt to make short work of it."

" What is it ? " she inquired, looking at him with cool and collected resentment, and an eye that was perfectly fearless.

" There was a tobaccy-box about this house, or in this house ; do you know anything about it ? "

" A tobaccy-box—is it ? "

" Ay, a tobaccy-box."

" Well, an' what about it ? What do you want wid it ? An ould rusty tobaccy-box ; *musha,* is that what's throublin' you this mornin' ? "

" Come," said he, darkening, " I'll have no humbuggin'— answer me at wanst. Do you know anything about it ? "

" Is it about your ould rusty tobaccy-box ? Arrah, what 'ud I know about it ? What the sorra would a man like you do wid a tobaccy-box that doesn't ever smoke ? Is it mad or ravin' you are ? Somehow I think the stroll you had wid that vagabond gipsy of a daughter of yours hasn't put you into the best of temper, nor her either. I hope you didn't act the villain on me ; for she looks at me as if she could ait me widout salt. But. indeed, she's takin' on her own hand finely of late ; she's gettin' too proud to answer me now when I ax her a question."

" Well, why don't you ax her as you ought ? "

" She was out all yestherday evenin', and when I said, ' You idle sthrap, where wor you ? ' she wouldn't even think worth her while to give me an answer, the vagabone."

" Do you give me one in the mane time. What about the box I want ? Spake truth, if your regard your health."

"I know nothing about your box, an' I wish I could say as much of yourself. However, I won't long throuble you, that I can tell you—ay, an' her too. She needn't fear that I'll be long undher the same roof wid her. I know, any way, I wouldn't be safe ; she'd only stick me in one of her fits now that's she's able to fight me."

" Now, Nelly," said the Prophet, deliberately shutting the door, " I know you to be a hardened woman, that has little fear in your heart. I think you know me, too, to be a hardened and determined man. There, now, I have shut an boulted the door, an' by Him that made me, you'll never lave this house, nor go out of that door a livin' woman, unless you tell me all you know about that tobaccy-box. Now, you know my mind an' my coorse—act as you like now."

"Ha, ha, ha ! Do you think to frighten me ? " she asked, laughing derisively. " Me !—oh, how much you're mis-taken, if you think so ! Not that I don't b'lieve you to be dangerous, an' a man that one ought to fear, but I have no fear of you."

" Answer me quickly," he replied ; and, as he spoke, he seized the very same knife from which she had so narrowly escaped in her conflict with Sarah, " answer me, I say ; an' mark, I have no raison to wish you alive."

And as he spoke, the glare in his eye flashed and became fearful.

" Ay," said she, " there's you're daughter's look, an' the same knife, too, that was near doin' for me wanst. Well, don't think that it's fear makes me say what I'm goin' to say; but that's the same knife; an' besides I dhramed last night that I was dressed in a black cloak—an' a black cloak, they say, is death! Ay, death!—an' I know I'm not fit to die, or to meet judgment, an' you know that, too. Now, then, tell me what it is you want wid that box."

"No," he replied sternly and imperatively, "I'll tell you nothin' about it; but get it at wanst, before my passion rises higher an' deadlier."

"Well, then, mark me, I'm not afraid of you—but I have the box."

"An' how did you come by it?" he asked.

"Sarah was lookin' for a cobweb to stop the blood where she cut me in our fight the other day, an' it came tumblin' out of a cranny in the wall."

"An' where is it now?"

"I'll get it for you," she replied; "but you must let me out first."

"Why so?"

"Because it's not in the house."

"An' where is it? Don't think you'll escape me."

"It's in the thatch of the roof."

The Prophet deliberately opened the door, and catching her by the shoulder, held her a prisoner, as it were, until she should make her words good. The roof was but low, and she knew the spot too well to make any mistake about it.

"Here," said she, "is the cross I scraped on the stone undher the place."

She put up her hand as she spoke, and searched the spot —but in vain. There certainly was the cross as she had marked it, and there was the slight excavation under the thatch where it had been; but as for the box itself, all search for it was fruitless—it had disappeared.

CHAPTER XVII

NATIONAL CALAMITY—SARAH IN LOVE AND SORROW

THE astonishment of the Prophet's wife on discovering that the tobacco-box had been removed from the place of its concealment was too natural to excite any suspicion of deceit or falsehood on her part, and he himself, although his disappointment was dreadful on finding that it had disappeared, at once perceived that she had been perfectly ignorant of its removal. With his usual distrust and want of confidence, however, he resolved to test her truth a little further, lest by any possibility she might have deceived him.

"Now, Nelly," said he sternly, "mark me;—is this the way you produce the box? You acknowledge that you had it—that you hid it even—an' now when I tell you I want it, an' that it may be a matther of life an' death to me—you purtend it's gone, an' that you know nothin' about it—now, I say agin, mark me well—produce the box!"

"Here," she replied, chafed and indignant, as well at its disappearance as at the obstinacy of his suspicions—" here's my throat—dash your knife into it, if you like—but as for the box, I tell you, that although I did put it in there, you know as much about it now as I do."

"Well," said he, "for wanst I believe you—but mark me still—this box must be gotten, an' it's to you I'll look for it. That's all—you know me."

"Ay," she replied, "I know you."

"Eh—what do you mane by that?" he asked—"what do you know? come now; come, I say, what do you know?"

"That you're a hardened an' a bad man;—oh, you needn't brandish your knife—nor your eyes needn't blaze up that way, like your daughther's," she added—"except that you're hard, an' dark, an' widout one spark o' common feelin', I know nothin' particularly wicked about you—but, at the same time, I suspect enough."

"What do you suspect, you hardened vagabond?"

"It doesn't matther what I suspect," she answered; "only I think you'd have a bad heart for anything—so go about your business, for I want to have nothin' more either to do or say to you—an' I wish to glory I had been always of that way o' thinkin', *a chiernah!*—many a scalded heart I'd a missed that I got by you."

She then walked into the cabin, and the Prophet slowly followed her with his fixed, doubtful, and suspicious eye, after which he flung the knife on the threshold, and took his way, in a dark and disappointed mood, to Glendhu.

It is impossible for us here to detail the subject-matter of his reflections, or to intimate to our readers how far his determination to bring Condy Dalton to justice originated in repentance for having concealed his knowledge of the murder, or in some other less justifiable state of feeling. At this moment, indeed, the family of the Daltons were in anything but a position to bear the heavy and terrible blow which was about to fall upon them. Our readers cannot forget the pitiable state in which we left them, during that distressing crisis of misery when the strange woman arrived with the oatmeal, which the kind-hearted Mave Sullivan had so generously sent them. On that melancholy occasion her lover complained of feeling ill, and, unfortunately, the symptoms were, in this instance, too significant of the malady which followed them. Indeed, it would be an infliction of unnecessary pain to detail here the sufferings which this unhappy family had individually and collectively borne. Young Condy, after a fortnight's prostration from typhus fever, was again upon his legs, tottering about, as his father had been, in a state of such helplessness between want of food on the one hand, and illness on the other, as it is distressing even to contemplate. If, however, the abstract consideration of it, even at a distance, be a matter of such painful retrospect to the mind, what must not the actual endurance of that and worse have been to the thousands upon thousands of families who were obliged, by God's mysterious dispensation, to encounter these calamities in all their almost incredible and hideous reality.

At this precise period, the state of the country was frightful beyond belief ; for it is well known that the mortality of the season we are describing was considerably greater than that which even cholera occasioned in its worst and most malignant ravages. Indeed, the latter was not attended by such a tedious and lingering train of miseries as that which, in so many woful shapes, surrounded typhus fever. The appearance of cholera was sudden, and its operations quick, and although, on that account, it was looked upon with tenfold terror, yet for this very reason the consequences which it produced were by no means so full of affliction and distress, nor presented such strong and pitiable claims on human aid and sympathy as did those of typhus. In the one case, the victim was cut down by a sudden stroke, which occasioned a shock or moral paralysis both to himself and the survivors— especially to the latter—that might be almost said to neutralize its own inflictions. In the other, the approach was comparatively so slow and gradual, that all the sympathies and afflictions were allowed full and painful time to reach the utmost limits of human suffering, and to endure the wasting series of these struggles and details which long illness, surrounded by destitution and affliction, never fails to inflict. In the cholera, there was no time left to feel—the passions were wrenched and stunned by the blow, which was over, one may say, before it could be perceived ; whilst, in the wide-spread but more tedious desolation of typhus, the heart was left to brood over the thousand phases of love and misery which the terrible realities of the one, joined to the alarming exaggerations of the other, never failed to present. In cholera, a few hours, and all was over ;—but in the awful fever which then prevailed, there was the gradual approach—the protracted illness—the long nights of racking pain—day after day of raging torture—and that dark period of uncertainty when the balance of human life hangs in the terrible equilibrium of suspense—all requiring the exhibition of constant attention—of the eye whose affection never sleeps—the ear that is deaf only to every sound but the moan of pain—the touch whose tenderness is felt as a solace, so long as suffering itself is conscious—the pressure of the aching head—the moistening of the parched and burning lips—and the numerous and indescribable offices of love and devotedness, which always encompass, or should encompass, the bed of sickness and of death. There was, we say, all this, and much more than the imagination itself, unaided by a severe acquaintance with the truth, could embody in its gloomiest conceptions.

In fact, Ireland, during the season, or rather the year we are describing, might be compared to one vast lazar-house filled with famine, disease, and death. The very skies of heaven were hung with the black drapery of the grave, for never since, nor within the memory of man before it, did the clouds present shapes of such gloomy and funereal import. Hearses, coffins, long funeral processions, and all the dark emblems of mortality were reflected, as it were, on the sky, from the terrible works of pestilence and famine which were going forward on the earth beneath it. To all this the thunder was constantly adding its angry peals, and the lightning flashing, as if uttering the indignation of heaven against our devoted people ; and what rendered such fearful manifestations ominous and alarming to the superstitious was the fact of their occurrence in the evening and at night —circumstances which are always looked upon with unusual terror and dismay.

To any person passing through the country such a combination of startling and awful appearances was presented as has probably never been witnessed since. Go where you might, every object reminded you of the fearful desolation that was progressing around you. The features of the people were gaunt, their eyes wild and hollow, and their gait feeble and tottering. Pass through the fields, and you were met by little groups bearing home on their shoulders, and that with difficulty, a coffin, or perhaps two of them. The roads were literally black with funerals ; and, as you passed along from parish to parish, the death-bells were pealing forth, in slow but dismal tones, the gloomy triumph which pestilence was achieving over the face of our devoted country—a country that each successive day filled with darker desolation and deeper mourning.

Nor was this all. The people had an alarmed and unsettled aspect, and whether you met them as individuals or crowds, they seemed, when closely observed, to labour under some strong and insatiable want that rendered them almost reckless. The number of those who were reduced to mendicancy was incredible, and if it had not been for the extraordinary and unparelleled exertions of the clergy of all creeds, medical men, and local committees, thousands upon thousands would have perished of disease or hunger on the very highways. Many, indeed, did so perish ; and it was no unusual sight to meet the father and mother, accompanied by their children, going, they knew not whither, and to witness one or other of them lying down on the roadside ; and well were they off who could succeed in obtaining a sheaf of straw on which, as a luxury, to lay down their aching head, that was never more to rise from it, until borne, in a parish shell, to a shallow and hasty grave.

Temporary sheds were also erected on the roadsides, or near them, containing fever-stricken patients, who had no other home ; and when they were released at last from their sorrows, nothing was more common than to place the coffin on the roadside also, with a plate on the lid of it, in order to solicit, from those who passed, such aid as they could afford to the sick or starving survivors.

That, indeed, was the trying and melancholy period in which all the lingering traces of self-respect—all recollection of former independence—all sense of modesty was cast to the winds. Under the terrible pressure of the complex destitution which prevailed, everything like shame was forgotten, and

it was well known that whole families, who had hitherto
been respectable and independent, were precipitated, almost
at once, into all the common cant of importunity and clamour
during this frightful struggle between life and death. Of
the truth of this, the scenes which took place at the public
soup shops, and other appointed places of relief, afforded
melancholy proof. Here were wild crowds, ragged, sickly,
and wasted away to skin and bone, struggling for the dole
of charity like so many hungry vultures about the remnant
of some carcase which they were tearing, amid noise, and
screams, and strife, into very shreds; for, as we have said,
all sense of becoming restraint or shame was now abandoned,
and the timid girl, or modest mother of a family, or decent
farmer, goaded by the same wild and tyrannical cravings,
urged their claims with as much turbulent solicitation and
outcry as if they had been trained since their very infancy
to all the forms of impudent cant and imposture.

This, our readers will admit, was a most deplorable state
of things; but, unfortunately, we cannot limit the truth of
our descriptions to the scenes we have just attempted to
pourtray. The misery which prevailed, as it had more than
one source, so had it more than one aspect. There were, in
the first place, studded over the country, a vast number of
strong farmers, with bursting granaries and immense hag-
gards, who, without coming under the odious denomination
of misers or mealmongers, are in the habit of keeping up
their provisions in large quantities, because they can afford
to do so, until a year of scarcity arrives, when they draw
upon their stock precisely when famine and prices are both
at the highest. In addition to these there was another still
viler class; we mean the hard-hearted and well-known
misers—men who at every time, and in every season, prey
upon the distress and destitution of the poor, and who can
never look upon a promising spring or an abundant harvest
without an inward sense of ingratitude against God for His
goodness, or upon a season of drought, or a failing crop,

unless with a thankful feeling of devotion for the approach-ing calamity.

During such periods, and under such circumstances, these men—including those of both classes—and the famished people, in general, live and act under antagonist principles. Hunger, they say, will break through stone walls; and when we reflect that, in addition to this irresistible stimulus, we may add a spirit of strong prejudice and resentment against these heartless persons, it is not surprising that the starving multitudes should, in the ravening madness of famine, follow up its outrageous impulses, and forget those legal restraints, or moral principles, that protect property under ordinary or different circumstances. It was just at this precise period, therefore, that the people, impelled by hunger and general misery, began to burst out into that excited stupefaction which is, we believe, peculiar to famine riots. And what rendered them still more exasperated than they probably would have been was, the long lines of provision carts which met or intermingled with the funerals on the public thorough-fares whilst on their way to the neighbouring harbours for exportation. Such, indeed, was the extraordinary fact! Day after day vessels laden with Irish provisions, drawn from a population perishing with actual hunger, as well as with the pestilence which it occasioned, were passing out of our ports, whilst, singular as it may seem, other vessels came in freighted with our own provisions, sent back, through the charity of England, to our relief.

It is not our business, any more than it is our inclination, to dwell here upon the state of those sumptuary enactments which reflected such honour upon the legislative wisdom that permitted our country to arrive at the lamentable con-dition we have attempted to describe. We merely mention the facts, and leave to those who possess position and ability the task of giving to this extraordinary state of things a more effectual attention. Without the least disposition, however, to defend or justify any violation of the laws, we may be permitted to observe that the very witnessing of such facts as these by destitute and starving multitudes, was in itself such a temptation to break in upon the provisions thus transmitted as it was scarcely within the strength of men, furious with famine, to resist. Be this as it may, however, it is our duty, as a faithful historian, to state that at the present period of our narrative the famine riots had begun to assume something of an alarming aspect. Several carts had been attacked and pillaged, some strong farmers had been visited, and two or three misers were obliged to become benevolent with rather a bad grace. At the head of these parties were two persons mentioned in these pages—to wit, Thomas Dalton and Red Roddy Duncan, together with several others of various estimation and character, some of them, as might be naturally expected, the most daring and turbulent spirits in the neighbourhood.

Such, then, was the miserable state of things in the country at that particular period. The dreadful typhus was now abroad in all its deadly power, accompanied, on this occasion, as it always is among the Irish, by a panic, which invested it with tenfold terrors. The moment fever was ascertained, or even supposed, to visit a family, that moment the infected persons were avoided by their neighbours and friends as if they carried death, as they often did, about them, so that its presence occasioned all the usual inter-changes of civility and good-neighbourhood to be discon-tinued. Nor should this excite our wonder, inasmuch as this terrific scourge, though unquestionably an epidemic, was also ascertained to be dangerously and fatally contagious. None, then, but persons of extraordinary moral strength, or posses-sing powerful impressions of religious duty, had courage to enter the houses of the sick or dead for the purpose of ren-dering to the afflicted those offices of humanity which their circumstances required, if we except only their nearest relatives, or those who lived in the same family.

Having thus endeavoured to give what we feel to be but a

faint picture of the state of the kingdom at large in this memorable year, we beg our readers to accompany us once more to the cabin of our moody and mysterious friend, the Black Prophet.

Evening was now tolerably far advanced; Donnel Dhu sat gloomily, as usual, looking into the fire, with no agreeable aspect; whilst on the opposite side sat Nelly, as silent and nearly as gloomy-looking as himself. Every now and then his black piercing eye would stray over to her, as if in a state of abstraction, and again with that undetermined kind of significance which made it doubtful whether the subject matter of his cogitations was connected with her at all or not. In this position were they placed when Sarah entered the cabin, and throwing aside her cloak, seated herself in front of the fire, something about half-way between each. She also appeared moody; and if one could judge by her countenance, felt equally disposed to melancholy or illtemper.

"Well, madam," said her father, "I hope it's no offence to ask you where you have been sportin' yourself since? I suppose you went to see Charley Hanlon; or, what is betther, his masther, Young Dick o' the Grange?"

"No," she replied, "I did not. Charley Hanlon! Oh, no!"

"Well, his masther?"

"Don't vex me—don't vex me," she replied, abruptly; "I don't wish to fight about nothin', or about trifles, or to give bad answers; but still, don't vex me, I say."

"There's somethin' in the wind now," observed Nelly; "she's gettin' fast into one of her tantrums. I know it by her eyes; she'd as soon whale me now as cry; and she'd jist as soon cry as whale me. Oh! my lady, I know you. Here, at any rate, will you have your supper?"

The resentment which had been gathering at Nelly's coarse observations, disappeared the moment the question as to supper had been put to her.

"Oh! why don't you," she said—"an' why didn't you always spake to me in a kind voice?"

"But about Young Dick," said the suspicious Prophet; "did you see him since?"

"No," she replied, calmly and thoughtfully; but, as if catching, by reflection, the base import of the query, she replied, in a loud and piercing voice, rendered at once full and keen by indignation—"No! I say; an' don't dare to suspect me of goin' to Dick o' the Grange, or any sich profligate."

"Hullo! there's a breeze!" After a pause: "You won't bate us, I hope. Then, madam, where were you?"

Short as was the period that had passed since her reply and the putting of his last question, she had relapsed or fallen into a mood of such complete abstraction, that she heard him not. With her naturally beautiful and taper hand under her still more finely chiselled chin, she sat looking, in apparent sorrow and perplexity, into the fire, and, whilst so engaged, she sighed deeply two or three times.

"Never mind her, man," said Nelly; "let her alone, an' don't draw an ould house on our heads. She has had a fight with Charley Hanlon, I suppose; maybe he has refused to marry her, if he ever had any notion of it—which I don't think he had."

Sarah rose up, and approaching her, said—

"What is that you wor sayin'?—Charley Hanlon!—never name him an' me together from this minute out. I like him well enough as an acquaintance, but never name us together as sweethearts—mark my words now. I would go any length to sarve Charley Hanlon, but I care nothin' for him beyond an acquaintance, although I did like him a little, or I thought I did."

"Poor Charley!" exclaimed Nelly, "he'll break his heart. *Arrah*, what'll he do for a piece o' black crape to go into murnin'?—eh?—ha! ha! ha!"

"If you had made use of them words to me only yester-day," she replied, "I'd pay you on the spot; but now, you unfortunate woman, you're below my anger. Say what you will, or what you wish, another quarrel with you I will never have."

"What does she mane?" said the other, looking fiercely at the Prophet—"I ax you, you traitor, what she manes?"

"Ay, an' you'll ax me till you're hoarse, before you get an' answer," he replied.

"You're a dark an' deep villain," she uttered, whilst her face became crimson with rage, and the veins of her neck and temples swelled out as if they would burst; "however, I tould you what your fate would be, an' that Providence would be on your bloody trail. Ay, did I, and you'll find it true soon."

The Prophet rose and rushed at her; but Sarah, with the quickness of lightning, flew between them.

"Don't be so mane?" she said—"don't now, father; if you rise your hand to her I'll never sleep a night undher the roof. Why don't you separate yourself from her? Oh, no, the man that would rise his hand to sich a woman—to a woman that must have the conscience she has—especially when he could put the salt seas between himself an' her—is worse an' meaner than she is. As for me, I'm lavin' this house in a day or two, for my mind's made up that the same roof won't cover us."

"The divil go wid you an' sixpence, then," replied Nelly, disdainfully—"an' then you'll want neither money nor com-pany; but, before you go, I'd thank you to tell me what has become o' the ould tobaccy-box that you pulled out o' the wall the other day. I know you were lookin' for it, an' I'm sure you got it—there was no one else to take it: so, before you go, tell me—unless you wish to get a knife put into me by that dark-lookin' ould father of yours."

"I know nothing about your ould box, but I wish I did."

"That's a lie, you sthrap; you know right well where it is."

"No," replied her father, "she does not, when she says she doesn't. Did you ever know her to tell a lie?"

"Ay—did I, fifty."

The Prophet rushed at her again, and again did Sarah interpose.

"You vile ould tarmagint," he exclaimed, "you're statin' what you feel to be false when you say so; right well you know that neither you nor I, nor any one else, ever heard a lie from her lips, an' yet you have the brass to say to the contrairy."

"Father," said Sarah, "there's but the one coorse for you as for me, my mind's made up—in this house I don't stay, if she does."

"If you'd think of what I spoke to you about," he replied, "all would soon be right wid us; but then you're so unraisonable, an' full of foolish notions, that it's hard for me to know what to do, especially as I wish to do all for the best."

"Well," rejoined Sarah, "I'll spake to you again about it; at this time I'm disturbed and unaisy in my mind—I'm unhappy—unhappy—an' I hardly know on what hand to turn. I'm afeard I was born for a hard fate, an' that the day of my doom isn't far from me. All, father, is dark before me—everything—my heart is, indeed, low an' full of sorrow; an' sometimes I could a'most tear any one that 'ud contradict me. Anyway, I'm unhappy."

As she uttered the last words, her father, considerably surprised at the melancholy tenor of her language, looked at her, and perceived that, whilst she spoke, her large black eyes were full of distress, and swam in tears.

"Don't be a fool, Sarah," said he; "it's not a thrifle should make any one cry in sich a world as this. If Charley Hanlon an' you has quarrelled, it was only the case with thousands before you. If he won't marry you, maybe as good or betther will; for sure, as the ould proverb says, there's as good fish in the say as ever was catched. In the mane time, think of what I said to you, an' all will be right."

Sarah looked not at him; but whilst he spoke, she hastily dried her tears, and ere half-a-minute had passed, her face had assumed a firm and somewhat of an indignant expression. Little, however, did her father then dream of the surprising change which one short day had brought about in her existence, nor of the strong passions which one unhappy interview had awakened in her generous but unregulated heart.

CHAPTER XVIII

LOVE WINS THE RACE FROM PROFLIGACY

DONNEL DHU M'GOWAN'S reputation as a prophecy-man arose, in the first instance, as much on account of his mysterious pretensions to a knowledge of the quack prophecies of his day—Pastorini, Columbkille, etc., etc., and such stuff —as from any pretensions he claimed to foretell the future himself. In the course of time, however, by assuming to be a seventh son, he availed himself of the credulity and ignorance of the people, and soon added a pretended insight into futurity to his powers of interpreting Pastorini, and all the catchpenny trash of the kind which then circulated among the people. This imposture, in course of time, produced its effect. Many, it is true, laughed at his impudent assumptions; but, on the other hand, hundreds were strongly impressed with a belief in the mysterious and rhapsodical predictions which he was in the habit of uttering. Among the latter class, we may reckon simple-hearted Jerry Sullivan and his family, all of whom, Mave herself included, placed the most religious confidence in the oracles he gave forth. It was, then, with considerable agitation and a palpitating heart, that, on the day following that of Donnel's visit to her father's, she approached the Grey Stone, where, in the words of the Prophet, she should meet " the young man who was to bring her love, wealth, and happiness, and all that a woman can wish to have with a man." The agitation she felt, however, was the result of a depression that almost amounted to despair. Her faithful heart was fixed but upon one alone, and she knew that her meeting with any other could not, so far as she was concerned, realize the golden visions of Donnel Dhu. The words, however, could not be misunderstood; the first person she met, on the right-hand side of the way, after passing the Grey Stone, was to be the individual; and when we consider her implicit belief in Donnel's prophecy, contrasted with her own impressions, and the state of mind in which she approached the place, we may form a tolerably accurate notion of what she must have experienced. On arriving within two hundred yards or so of the spot mentioned, she observed in the distance, about half-a-mile before her, a gentleman on horseback, approaching her at rapid speed. Her heart, on perceiving him, literally sank within her, and she felt so weak as to be scarcely able to proceed.

"Oh! what," she at length asked herself, "would I not give but for one glance of young Condy Dalton! But it is not to be. The unfortunate murdher of my uncle has prevented that for ever; although I can't get myself to b'lieve that any of the Daltons ever did it; but maybe that's because I wish they didn't. The general opinion is, that his father is the man that did it. May the Lord forgive them, whoever they are, that took his life—for it was a black act to me at any rate!"

Across the road before her, ran one of those little deep valleys, or large ravines, and into this had the horseman disappeared as she closed the soliloquy. He had not, however, at all slackened his pace, but, on the contrary, evidently increased it, as she could hear by the noise of his horse's feet.

At this moment she reached the brow of the ravine, and our readers may form some conception of what she felt when, on looking down it, she saw her lover, young Dalton, toiling up towards her with feeble and failing steps, whilst pressing after him from the bottom, came young Henderson, urging his horse with whip and spur. Her heart, which had that moment bounded with delight, now utterly failed her, on perceiving the little chance which the poor young man had of being the first to meet her, and thus fulfil the prophecy. Henderson was gaining upon him at a rapid rate, and must in a few minutes have passed him, had not woman's wit and presence of mind come to her assistance. " If he cannot run to me up the hill," she said to herself, " I can run to him down it "—and as the thought occurred to her, she started towards him at her greatest speed, which indeed was considerable, as her form was of that light and elastic description which betokens great powers of activity and exertion. The struggle indeed was close; Henderson now plied whip and spur with redoubled energy, and the animal was approaching at full speed. Mave, on the other hand, urged by a thousand motives, forgot everything but the necessity for exertion. Dalton was incapable of running a step, and appeared not to know the cause of the contest between the parties. At length Mave, by her singular activity and speed, reached her lover, into whose arms she actually ran, just as Henderson had come within about half-a-dozen yards of the spot where she met him. This effort on the part of Mave, was in perfect accordance with the simple earnestness of her character ; her youthful figure, her innocence of manner, the glow of beauty, and the crowd of blushing graces which the act developed, together with the joyous exultation of her triumph on reaching her lover's arms, and thus securing to herself and him the completion of so delightful a prediction—all, when taken in at one view, rendered her a being so irresistibly fascinating, that her lover could scarcely look upon the incident as a real one, but for a moment almost persuaded himself that his beloved Mave had undergone some delightful and glorious transformation—such as he had seen her assume in the dreams of his late illness.

Henderson, finding himself disappointed, now pulled up his horse, and addressed her.

" Upon my word, Miss Sullivan—I believe," he added, " I have the pleasure of addressing Jerry Sullivan's daughter, so far famed for her beauty—I say, upon my word, Miss Sullivan, your speed outstrips the wind—those light and beautiful feet of yours scarcely touched the ground—I am certain you must dance delightfully."

Mave again blushed, and immediately extricated herself from her lover's arms ; but before she did, she felt his frame trembling with indignation at the liberty Henderson had taken in addressing her at all.

"Dalton," the latter proceeded, unconscious of the passion he was exciting, "I cannot but envy you at all events—I would myself delight to be a winning-post under such circumstances."

Dalton looked at him, and his eye, like that of his father, when enraged, glared with a deadly light.

" Pass on, sir," he replied ; " Mave Sullivan is no girl for the like of you to address. She wishes to have no conversation with you, and she will not."

" I shan't take your word for that, my good friend," replied Henderson, smiling ; " she can speak for herself—an' will, too, I trust."

" Dear Condy," whispered Mave, " don't put yourself in a passion ; you are too weak to bear it."

" Miss Sullivan," proceeded Young Dick, " is a pretty girl —and as such I claim a portion of her attention, and—should she so far favour me—even of her conversation ; and that with every respect for your very superior judgment, my good Mr. Dalton."

" What is you object, now, in wishin' to spake to her ? " asked the latter, looking him sternly in the face.

" I don't exactly see that I'm bound to answer your cate-chism," said Dick ; " it is to Miss Sullivan I would address myself. I speak to you, Miss Sullivan ; and, allow me to say, that I feel a very warm interest in your welfare, and nothing would give me greater pleasure than to promote it by any means in my power."

Mave was about to reply, but Dalton anticipated her.

"The only favour you can bestow upon Miss Sullivan, as you are plaized to call her, is to pass her by," said Dalton; "she wishes to have no intimacy nor conversation of any kind with sich a noted profligate. She knows your correcther, Mr. Henderson; or if she doesn't, I do—an' that it's as much as a daicent girl's good name is worth to be seen spakin' to you. Now, I tell you again to pass on. Don't force either yourself or your conversation upon her, if you're wise—I'm here to protect her—an' I won't see her insulted for nothing."

"Do you mean that as a threat, my good fellow?"

"If you think it a threat, don't desarve it, an' you won't get it. If right was to take place, our family would have a heavy account to settle with you and yours; an' it wouldn't be wise in you to add this to it."

"Ha! I see—oh, I understand you, I think—more threatening?—eh?"

"As I said before," replied Dalton, "that's as you may desarve it. Your cruelty, and injustice, and oppression to our family, we might overlook; but I tell you, that if you become the means of bringin' a stain—the slightest that ever was breathed—upon the fair name of this girl, it would be a thousand times betther that you never were born."

"Ah! indeed, Master Dalton; but in the mean time, what does Miss Sullivan herself say? We are anxious to hear your own sentiments on this matter, Miss Sullivan."

"I would feel obliged to you to pass on, sir," she replied; "Condy Dalton is ill, and badly able to bear sich a conversation as this."

"Here," said Dalton, fiercely, laying his hand upon Mave's shoulder; "if you cross my path here—or lave but the shadow of a stain, as I said, upon her name, woe betide you!"

"Your wishes are commands to me, Miss Sullivan," replied Henderson, without noticing Dalton's denunciation in the slightest degree; " and I trust that when we meet again, you won't be guarded by such a terrible bow-wow of a dragon as has now charge of you. Good-bye! and accept my best wishes, until then."

He immediately set spurs once more to his horse, and in a few minutes had turned at the cross-roads, and taken that which led to his father's house.

"It is well for him," said Dalton, immediately after he had left them, " that I hadn't a loaded pistol in my hand— but no, dear Mave," he added, checking himself, " the hasty temper and the hasty blow is the fault of our family, an' so far as I am consarned, I'll do everything to overcome it."

Mave now examined him somewhat more earnestly than she had done; and although grieved at his thin and wasted appearance, yet she could not help being forcibly struck by the singular clearness and manly beauty of his features. And yet this beauty filled her heart with anything but satisfaction; for on contemplating it she saw that it was overshadowed by an expression of such settled sorrow and dejection, as it was impossible to look upon without the deepest compassion and sympathy.

"We had betther rest a little, dear Mave," he said; "you must be fatigued, and so am I. Turn back a little, will you, an' let us sit upon the Grey Stone; it's the only thing in the shape of a seat that is now near us. Have you any objection?"

"None in the world," she replied; "I'll be time enough at my uncle's, especially as I don't intend to come home to-night."

They accordingly sauntered back, and took their seat upon a ledge of the stone in question, that almost concealed them from observation; after which the dialogue proceeded as follows :—

"Condy," observed Mave, "I was glad to hear that you recovered from the fever; but I'm sorry to see you look so ill: there is a great deal of care in your face."

" There is, dear Mave—there is," he replied, with a melancholy smile, " an' a great deal of care in my heart. You look thin yourself, and care-worn too, dear."

" We are not without our own struggles at home," she replied, " as, indeed, who is now? But I had more than ourselves to fret for."

" Who ? " he asked ; but on putting the question, he saw a look of such tender reproach in her eye as touched him.

" Kind heart!" he exclaimed—" kindest and best of hearts, why should I ask sich a question? Surely I ought to know you. I am glad I met you, Mave, for I have many things to say to you, an' it's hard to say when I may have an opportunity again."

" I know that is true," said she ; " but I did not expect to meet you here."

" Mave," he proceeded, in a voice filled with melancholy and sadness, " you acknowledged that you loved me."

She looked at him, and that look moved him to the heart.

" I know you do love me," he proceeded, " and now, dear Mave, the thought of that fills my heart with sorrow."

She started slightly, and looked at him again with a good deal of surprise ; but on seeing his eyes filled with tears, she also caught the contagion, and asked with deep emotion—

" Why, dear Condy? Why does my love for you make your heart sorrowful ? "

" Because I have no hope," said he—" no hope that you can ever be mine."

Mave remained silent ; for she knew the insurmountable obstacles that prevented their union ; but she wept afresh.

" When I saw your father last, behind your garden, the day I struck Donnel Dhu," Dalton proceeded, " I tould him what I then believed to be true, that my father never had a hand in your uncle's death. Mave dear, I cannot tell a lie —nor I will not. I couldn't say as much to him now ; I'm afeared that his death is upon my father's sowl."

Mave started, and got pale at the words.

"Great God!" she exclaimed, "don't say so, Con, dear. Oh, no, no—is it your father that was always so good, an' so kind, an' so generous to every one that stood in need of it at his hands, an' who was always so charitable to the poor?"

"Ay," said he, "he was charitable to the poor; but of late I've heard him say things that nobody but a man that has some great crime to answer for could or would say. I believe, too, that what the public says is right—that it's the hand of God Himself that's upon him an' us for that murdher."

"But maybe," said Mave, who still continued pale and trembling—"maybe it was accidental afther all—a chance blow, maybe; but whatever it was, dear Con, let us spake no more about it. I am not able to listen to it—it would sicken me soon."

"Very well, dear, we'll drop it; an' I hope I'm wrong; for I can't think, afther all, that a man with sich a kind an' tendher heart as my father—a pious man, too—could "—he paused a moment, and then added—" oh, no—I'm surely wrong —he never did that act. However, as we said, I'll drop it; for indeed, dear Mave, I have enough that's sorrowful and heart-breakin' to spake about, over and above that unfortunate subject."

"I hope," said Mave, "that there's nothing worse than your own illness—an' you know, thanks be to the Almighty, you're recoverin' fast from that."

"My poor, lovin' sister Nancy," said he, "was laid down yesterday mornin' with this terrible fever; she was our chief dependence; we could stand it out no longer; I could an' can do nothing; an' my mother this mornin' "—his tears fell so fast, and his affliction was so deep, that he was not able, for a time, to proceed.

"Oh! what about her?" asked Mave, participating in his grief; "oh! what about her that every one loves?"

"She was obliged to go out this mornin'," he proceeded, "to beg openly in the face of day among the neighbours! Now, Mave Sullivan, farewell!" said he, rising, whilst his face was crimsoned over with shame; "farewell, Mave Sullivan—all, from this minute, is over between you an' me. The son of a beggar must never become your husband—will never call you his wife—even if there was no other raison against it."

The lovely girl rose with him—she trembled—she blushed and again got pale; then blushed once more—at length she spoke,—

"An' is that, dear Con, all that you yet know of Mave Sullivan's heart, or the love for you that's in it? Your mother! Oh! an' is it come to that with her? but—but—do you think that even that, or anything that wouldn't be a crime in yourself; or, do you think—oh! I know not what to say—I see now, dear Con, the raison for the sorrow that's in your face—the heart-break an' the care that's there—I see, indeed, how low in spirits, an' how hopeless you are; an' I see that, although your eye is clear, still it's heavy—heavy with hard affliction; but then, what is love, Con, dear, if it's to fly away when these things come on us? Is it now, then, that you'd expect me to desert you?—to keep cool with you, or to lave you when you have no other heart to go to for any comfort but mine? Oh, no! Con, dear. Your own Mave Sullivan is none of these. God knows, it's little comfort," she proceeded, weeping bitterly—"it's little comfort's in my poor heart for any one; but there's one thing in it, Con, dear—that, poor as I stand here this minute—an' where, oh! where is there or could there be a poorer girl than I am—still there's one thing in it that I wouldn't exchange for the world's wealth—an' that—that, dear Con, is my love for you! That's the love, dear Con, that neither this world nor its cares, nor its shame, nor its poverty, nor its sorrow, can ever overcome or banish—that's the love that would live with you in wealth—that would keep by your side through good and through evil—that would share your sickness—that would rejoice with you—that would grieve with you—beg with you, starve with you, go where you might, and die by your side. I cannot bid you to throw care and sorrow away; but if it's any consolation to you to know an' to feel how your own Mave Sullivan loves you, then you have that consolation. Dear Con, I am ready to marry you, an' to share your distresses to-morrow—ay, this day, or this minute, if it could be done."

There was a gentle, calm, but firm enthusiasm about her manner, which carried immediate conviction with it, and, as her tears fell in silence, she bestowed a look upon her lover which fully and tenderly confirmed all that her tongue had uttered.

Both had been standing; but her lover, taking her hand, sat down, as she also did; he then turned round and pressed her to his heart, and their tears, in this melancholy embrace of love and sorrow, both literally mingled together.

"I would be ungrateful to God, my beloved Mave," he replied, "and unworthy of you—and indeed, at best I'm not worthy of you—if I didn't take hope an' courage, when I know that sich a girl loves me—as it is, I feel my heart aisier, and my spirits lighter—although at the same time, dear Mave, I'm very wake, and far from being well."

"That's bekase this disturbance of your mind is too much for you yet—but keep your spirits up—you don't know," she continued, smiling sweetly through her tears, "what a delightful prophecy was fulfilled for us this day—ay, awhile ago even when I met you."

"No," he replied, "what was it?"

She then detailed the particulars of Donnel Dhu's prediction, which she dwelt upon with a very cheerful spirit, after which she added—

"And now, Con, dear, don't you think that's a sign we'll be yet happy."

Dalton, who placed no reliance whatsoever on Donnel Dhu's

impostures, still felt reluctant to destroy the hope occasioned by such an agreeable illusion—"Well," he replied, "although I don't much believe in anything that ould scoundrel says, I trust, for all that, that he has tould you thruth for wanst."

"But how did you happen to come here, Con?" she asked —"to be here at the very minute, too?"

"Why," said he, "I was desired to take care to be the first to meet you after you passed the Grey Stone—the very one we're sittin' on—if I loved you, an' wished to sarve you."

"But who on earth could tell you this?" she asked, "bekase I thought no livin' bein' knew of it but myself and Donnel Dhu."

"It was Sarah, his daughter," said Dalton; "but when I asked her why I should come to do so, she wouldn't tell me— she said if I wished to save you from evil, or, at any rate, from trouble. That's a strange girl—his daughter"—he added, "she makes one do whatever she likes."

"Isn't she very handsome?" said Mave, with an expression of admiration. "I think she's, without exception, the purtiest girl I ever seen; an' her beautiful figure beats all; but somehow they say every one's afraid of her, an' durstn't vex her."

"She examined me well yestherday, at all events," replied Con. "I thought them broad, black, beautiful eyes of hers would look through me. Many a wager has been as to which is the handsomest—you or she; an' I know hundreds that 'ud give a great deal to see you both beside one another."

"Indeed an' she has it, then," said Mave, "far an' away, in face, in figure, an' in everything."

"I don't think so," he replied; "but at any rate, not in everything—not in the heart, dear Mave—not in the heart."

"They say she's kind-hearted, then," replied Mave.

"They do," said Con, "an' I don't know how it comes; but somehow every one loves her, and every one fears her at the same time. She asked me yestherday if I thought my father murdhered Sullivan."

" Oh! for God's sake, don't talk about it," said Mave, again getting pale ; " I can't bear to hear it spoken of."

The Grey Stone—on a low ledge of which, nearly concealed from public view, our lovers had been sitting—was, in point of size, a very large rock of irregular shape. After the last words, alluding to the murder, had been uttered, an old man, very neatly but plainly dressed, and bearing a pedlar's pack, came round from behind a projection of it, and approached them. From his position, it was all but certain that he must have overheard their whole conversation. Mave, on seeing him, blushed deeply, and Dalton himself felt considerably embarrassed at the idea that the stranger had been listening, and become acquainted with circumstances that were never designed for any other ears but their own.

The old man, on making his appearance, surveyed our lovers from head to foot with a curious and inquisitive eye— a circumstance which, taken in connection with his eavesdropping, was not at all relished by young Dalton.

" I think you will know us again," said he, in no friendly voice. " How long have you been sittin' behind the corner there ? " he inquired.

" I hope I may know yez agin," replied the pedlar, for he was one; " I was jist long enough behind the corner to hear some of what you were spakin' about last."

" An' what was that ? " said Dalton, putting him to the test.

" You wor talkin' about the murdher of one Sullivan."

" We were," replied Dalton; " but I'll thank you to say nothing further about it ; it's disagreeable to both of us— distressin' to both of us."

" I don't undherstand that," said the old pedlar; " how can it be so to either of you, if you're not consarned in it one way or other ? "

" We are, then," said Dalton, with warmth ; " the man that was killed was this girl's uncle, an' the man that was supposed to take his life is my father. Maybe you undherstand me now ? "

The blood left the cheeks of the old man, who staggered over to the ledge whereon they sat, and placed himself beside them.

"God of heaven!" said he, with astonishment, "can this be thrue?"

"Now that you know what you do know," said Dalton, "we'll thank you to drop the subject."

"Well, I will," said he; "but first, for Heaven's sake, answer me a question or two. What's your name, *avic*?"

"Condy Dalton."

"Ay, Condy Dalton!—the Lord be about us. An' Sullivan—Sullivan was the name of the man that was murdered, you say?"

"Yes, Bartley Sullivan—God rest him!"

"An' whishper—tell me—God presarve us!—was there anything done to your father, *avic*? What was done to him?"

"Why, he was taken up on suspicion soon afther it happened; but—but—there was nothin' done: they had no proof against him, an' he was let go again."

"Is your father alive still?"

"He is livin'," replied Dalton; "but come—pass on, ould man," he added, bitterly, "I'll give you no more information."

"Well, thank you, dear," said the pedlar; "I ax your pardon for givin' you pain—an' the *colleen* here—ay, you are a Sullivan, then—an' a purty but sorrowful lookin' crature you are, God knows. Poor things! God pity you both, an' grant you a betther fate than what appears to be before you! for I did hear a thrifle of your discoorse."

There was something singularly benevolent and kind in the old pedlar's voice, as he uttered the last words, and he had not gone many perches from the stone, when Dalton's heart relented as he reflected on his harsh and unfriendly demeanour towards him.

"That is a good old man," he observed, "and I am now

sorry that I spoke to him so roughly—there was kindness in his voice and in his eye as he looked upon us."

"There was," replied Mave, "and I think him a good old man too. I don't think he would harm any one."

"Dear Mave," said Dalton, "I must now get home as soon as I can ; I don't feel so well as I was—there is a chill upon me, and I'm afeard I won't have a comfortable night."

"And I can do nothing for you ! " added Mave, her eyes filling with tears.

"I didn't thank you for the lock of hair you sent me by Donnel Dhu," he added. "It is here upon my heart, and I needn't say that if anything had happened me, or if anything should happen me, it an' that heart must go to dust together."

"You are too much cast down," she replied, her tears flowing fast, "an' it can't surely be otherwise; but, dear Con, let us hope for better days—an' put our trust in God's goodness."

"Farewell, dear Mave," he replied, "and may God bless and preserve you till I see you again ! "

"And may He send down aid to you all," she added, "and give consolation to your breakin' hearts."

An embrace, long, tender, and mournful, accompanied their words, after which they separated in sorrow and in tears, and with but little hope of happiness on the path of life that then lay before them.

CHAPTER XIX

HANLON SECURES THE TOBACCO-BOX — STRANGE SCENE AT
MIDNIGHT

THE hour so mysteriously appointed by Red Roddy for the delivery of the tobacco-box to Hanlon, was fast approaching, and the night, though by no means so stormy as that which we have described on the occasion of that person's first visit to the Grey Stone, was neverthless dark and rainy, with an occasional slight gust of wind, that uttered a dreary and melancholy moan, as it swept over the hedges. Hanlon, whose fear of supernatural appearances had not been diminished by what he had heard there before as well as on his way home, now felt alarmed at every gust of wind that went past him. He hurried on, however, and kept his nerves as firmly set as his terrors would allow him, until he got out upon the plain old road which led directly to the appointed place. The remarkable interest which he had felt at an earlier stage of the circumstances that compose our narrative, was beginning to cool a little, when it was revived by his recent conversation with Red Roddy concerning the Black Prophet, and the palpable contradictions in which he detected that person, with reference to the period when the Prophet came to reside in the neighbourhood. His anxiety, therefore, about the tobacco-box began, as he approached the Grey Stone, to balance his fears ; so that by the time he arrived there, he found himself cooler and firmer a good deal, than when he first crossed the dark fields from home. Hanlon, in fact, had learned a good deal of the Prophet's real character, from several of those who had never been duped by his impostures ; and the fact of ascertaining that the very article so essential to the completion of his purpose, had been found in the Prophet's house or possession, gave a fresh and still more powerful impulse to his determinations. The night, we have already observed, was dark, and the heavy gloom which covered the sky was dismal and monotonous. Several flashes of lightning, it is true, had shot out from the impervious masses of black clouds that lay against each other overhead. These, however, only added terror to the depression which such a night and such a sky were calculated to occasion.

"I trust," thought Hanlon, as he approached the stone, " that there will be no disappointment, and that I won't have my journey on sich a dark and dismal night for nothing.

How this red ruffian can have any authority over a girl like
Sarah, is a puzzle that I can't make out."

It was just as these thoughts occurred to him that he
arrived at the stone, where he stood anxiously waiting and
listening, and repeating his *pater noster*, as well as he could,
for several minutes, but without hearing or seeing any one.

"I might have known," thought he, "that the rascal could
bring about nothing of the kind, an' I am only a fool for
heedin' him at all."

At this moment, however, he heard the noise of a light
quick footstep approaching, and almost immediately afterwards Sarah joined him.

"Well, I am glad you are come," said he, "for God knows
when I thought of our last stand here, I was anything but
comfortable."

"Why," replied Sarah, "what wor you afeard of? I hate
a cowardly man, Charley, an' you are cowardly."

"Not where mere flesh and blood is consarned," he replied;
"I'm afeard of neither man nor woman—but I wouldn't like
to meet a ghost or spirit, may the Lord presarve us!"

"Why, now? What harm could a ghost or spirit do
you? Did you ever hear that they laid hands on or killed
any one?"

"No; but for all that, it's well known that several persons
have died of fright, in consequence."

"Ay, of cowardliness; but it wasn't the ghost killed
them. Sure the poor ghost only comes to get some relief
for itself—to have masses said; or, maybe, to do justice to
some one that is wronged in this world. There's Jemmy
Beatty, an' he lay three weeks of fright from seein' a ghost,
an' it turned out when all was known, that the ghost was
nothing more or less than Tom Martin's white-faced cow—
ha! ha! ha!"

"At any rate let us change the subject," said Hanlon;
"you heard yourself the last night we were here, what I'll
never forget."

"We heard some noise like a groan, an' that was all; but who can tell what it was, or who cares either?"

"I, for one, do; but, dear Sarah, have you the box?"

"Why does your voice tremble that way? Is it fear? bekase if I thought it was, I wouldn't scruple much to walk home without another word, an' bring the box with me."

"You have it, then?"

"To be sure I have, an' my father an' Nelly is both huntin' the house for it."

"Why, what could your father want with it?"

"How can I tell?—an' only that I promised it to you, I wouldn't fetch it at all."

"I thought you had given it up for lost! how did you get it again?"

"That's nothing to you, an' don't trouble your head about it. There it is now, an' I have kept my word; for while I live, I'll never break it if I can. Dear me, how bright that flash was!"

As Hanlon was taking the box out of her hand, a fearful flash of sheeted lightning opened out of a cloud, almost immediately above them, and discovered it so plainly, that the very letters, P. M., were distinctly legible on the lid of it, and nearly at the same moment a deep groan was heard, as if coming out of the rock.

"Father of heaven!" exclaimed Hanlon; "do you hear that?"

"Yes" she replied, "I did hear a groan—but here—do you go—oh, it would be useless to ask you—so I must only do it myself; stand here, an' I'll go round the rock; at any rate, let us be sure that it is a ghost."

"Don't, Sarah," he exclaimed, seizing her arm; "for God's sake don't—it is a spirit—I know it—don't lave me. I undherstand it all, an' maybe you will some day, too."

"Now," she exclaimed, indignantly, and in an incredulous tone of voice—"in God's name what has a spirit to do with an ould rusty tobaccy-box? It's surely a curious box;

there's my father would give one of his eyes to find it—an' Nelly, that hid it the other day, found it gone when she went to get it for him."

" Do you tell me so ? " said Hanlon, placing it as he spoke in his safest pocket.

" I do," she replied; "and only that I promised it to you, and would not break my word, I'd give it to my father; but I don't see myself what use it can be of to him or anybody."

Hanlon, despite of his terrors, heard this intelligence with the deepest interest—indeed, with an interest so deep, that he almost forget them altogether ; and with a view of eliciting from her as much information in connexion with it as he could, he asked her to accompany him a part of the way home.

" It's not quite the thing," she replied, " for a girl like me to be walkin' with a young fellow at this hour ; but as I'm not afeard of you, and as I know you're afeard of the ghost—if there is a ghost—I will go part of the way with you, although it does not say much for your courage to ax me."

" Thank you, Sarah ; you are a perfect treasure."

" Whatever I was, or whatever I am, Charley, I can never be anything more to you than a mere acquaintance—I don't think ever we were much more—but what I want to tell you is, that if ever you had any serious notion of me, you must put it out of your head."

" Why so, Sarah ? "

"Why so," she replied, hastily; "why, bekase I don't wish it—isn't that enough for you, if you have spirit? "

" Well, but I'd like to know why you changed your mind ? "

" Ay," said she; " well, afther all, that is only natural— it is but raisonable ; an' I'll tell you :—in the first place, then, there's a want of manliness about you that I don't like —I think you have but little heart or feelin'. You toy with the girls—with this one and that one—an' you don't appear

to love any one of them—in short, you're not affectionate,
I'm afeard. Now, here am I, an' I can scarcely say that
ever you coorted me like a man that had feelin'. I think
you're revengeful, too; for I have seen you look black an'
angry at a woman, before now. You never loved me, I know
—I say I know now you did not. There, then, is some of
my reasons—but I'll tell you one more, that's worth them all.
I love another now—ay," she added with a convulsive sigh
—"I love another; and I know, Charley, that he can't love
me—there's more lightnin'—what a flash! Oh, I didn't care
this minute it went through my heart."

"Don't talk so, Sarah."

"I know what's before me—disappointment—disappointment in everything—the people say I'm wild and very
wicked in my temper—an' I am, too—but how could I be
otherwise? for what did I ever see or hear undher our own
miserable roof, but evil talk an' evil deeds? A word of kindness I never got from my father or from Nelly—nothin' but
the bad word an' the hard blow—until now that she is afeard
of me; but little she knew, that many a time when I was
fiercest, an' threatened to put a knife into her, there was a
quiver of affection in my heart—a yearnin', I may say, afther
kindness, that had me often near throwin' my arms around
her neck, an' askin' her why she mightn't as well be kind as
cruel to me; but I couldn't, bekase I knew that if I did,
she'd only tramp on me, an' despise me, an' tyrannize over
me more an' more."

She uttered these sentiments under the influence of deep
feeling, with an occasional burst of wild distraction, that
seemed to originate from much bitterness of heart.

"Is it a fair question," replied Hanlon, whose character
she had altogether misunderstood, having, in point of fact,
never had an opportunity of viewing it in its natural light—
"is it a fair question to ask you who is it you're in love
wid?"

"It's not a fair question," she replied; "for I know he

loves another, an' for that raison I'll never breathe it to mortual."

"Bekase," he added, "if I knew, maybe I might be able to put in a good word for you, now and then, accordin' as I got an opportunity."

"For me!" she replied indignantly—"what!—to beg him to get fond o' me! Oh, it's wondherful the maneness that's in a'most every one you meet. No," she proceeded vehemently, "if he was the king on his throne, sooner than stoop to that, or if he didn't or couldn't love me on my own account, I'd let the last dhrop o' my heart's blood out first. Oh, no! —no, no—he loves another," she added, hastily—"he loves another!"

"An' do you know her?" asked Hanlon.

"Do I know her!" she replied—"do I know her!—it's I that do; ay, an' I have her in my power, too; an' if I set about it, can prevent a ring from ever goin' on them. Ha! ha! Oh, ay—that divil, Sarah M'Gowan—what a fine characther I have got! Well, well, good-night, Charley! Maybe it's a folly to have the bad name for nothin'—at laist they say so. Ha! ha! Good-night; I'll go home. Oh, I had like to forget—Red Roddy tould me he was spakin' to you about somethin' that he says you can't but undherstand yourself; an' he desired me to get you, if I could, to join him in it. I said I would, if it was right an' honest; for I have great doubts of it bein' either the one or the other, if it comes from him. He said that it was both; but that it 'ud be a great piece of roguery to lave it undone. Now, if it is what *he* says it is, help him in it, if you can; but if it isn't, have no hand in it. That's all I tould him, I would say, an' that's all I do say. Keep out of his saicrets, I advise you; an', above all things, avoid everything mane an' dishonest; for, Charley, I have a kind o' likin' for you that I can't explain, although I don't love you as a sweetheart. Good-night again!"

She left him abruptly, and, at a rapid pace, proceeded back

to the Grey Stone, around which she walked, with a view of examining whether or not there might be any cause visible, earthly or otherwise, for the groans which they had heard ; but, notwithstanding a close and diligent search, she could neither see nor hear anything whatsoever to which they might possibly be ascribed.

She reached home about one o'clock, and after having sat musing for a time over the fire, which was raked for the night—that is, covered over with *greeshaugh*, or living ashes —she was preparing to sleep in her humble bed, behind a little partition wall about five feet high, at the lower end of the cabin, when her father, who had been moaning, and starting, and uttering abrupt exclamations in his sleep, at length rose up, and began deliberately to dress himself, as if with an intention of going out.

" Father," said she, " in the name of goodness, where are you goin' at this hour of the night ? "

" I'm goin' to the murdhered man's grave," he replied. " I'm goin' to tell them all how he was murdhered, and who it was that murdhered him."

A girl with nerves less firm would have felt a most deadly terror at such language, on perceiving—as Sarah at once did —that her father, whose eyes were shut, was fast asleep at the time. In her, however, it only produced such a high degree of excitement and interest, as might be expected from one of her ardent and excitable temperament, imbued as it was with a good deal of natural romance.

" In God's name," she said to herself, " what can this mean ?   Of late he hasn't had one hour's quiet rest at night ; nothin' but startin', and shoutin' out, and talkin' about murdher and murdherers !   What can it mane ? for he's now walkin' in his sleep.   Father," she said, " you're asleep ; go back to bed, you had betther."

" No, I'm not asleep," he replied ; " I'm goin' down to the grave here below, behind the rocks down in Glendhu, where the murdhered man is lyin' buried ! "

" An' what brings you there at this time o' the night ? "

" Ha ! ha ! " he replied, uttering an exclamation of caution in a low, guarded voice—" what brings me ?—whisht, hould your tongue, an' I'll tell you."

She really began to doubt her senses, notwithstanding the fact of his eyes being shut.

"Whisht yourself," she replied ; " I don't want to hear anything about it; I have no relish for sich saicrets. I'm ready enough with my own hands, especially when there's a weapon in it—readier than ever I'll be again; but for all that I don't wish to hear sich saicrets. Are you asleep or awake ? "

" I'm awake, of coorse," he replied.

" An' why are your eyes shut then? You're frightful, father, to look at—no corpse had ever sich a face as you have; your heavy brows is knit in sich a way—jist as if you were in agony—your cheeks is so white, too, an' your mouth down at the corners, that a ghost—ay, the ghost of the murdhered man himself—would be agreeable, compared to you. Go to bed, father, if you're awake."

To all this he made no reply, but, having dressed himself, he deliberately, and with great caution, raised the latch and proceeded out at that dismal and lonely hour. Sarah, for a time, knew not how to act. She had often heard of sleep-walking, and she feared now that if she awakened him, he might imagine she had heard matters which he wished no ears whatever to hear ; for the truth was, that some vague suspicions of a dreadful nature had latterly entered her mind—suspicions, which his broken slumbers, his starts, and frequent exclamations during sleep, had only tended to confirm.

" I'll watch him, at all events," said she to herself, " and see that he comes to no danger." She accordingly shut the door after her, and followed him pretty closely into the deep gloom of the silent and solitary glen. With cautious, but steady and unerring steps, he proceeded in the direction

of the loneliest spot of it, which having reached, he went
by a narrow and untrodden circuit—a kind of broken but
natural pathway—to the identical spot where the body,
which Nelly had discovered, lay.

He then raised his hand, as if in caution, and whispered
—" Whisht ! here is where the murdhered man's body
lies."

" I'll not do it," said Sarah. " I'll not do it—it would be
mane an' ungenerous to ax him a question that might make
him bethray himself."

At this moment the moon, which had been for some time
risen, presented a strange and alarming aspect. She seemed
red as blood ; and directly across her centre there went
a black bar—a bar so ominously and intensely black, that
it was impossible to look upon it without experiencing something like what one might be supposed to feel in the presence
of a supernatural appearance ; or at the performance of some
magic or unnatural rite, where the sorcerer, by the wickedness of his spell, forced her, as it were, thus to lend a dreadful and reluctant sanction to his proceedings.

Her father, however, proceeded—" Ay—who murdhered
him, my lord ? Why, my lord—hem—it was—Condy Dalton, an' I have another man to prove it along wid myself—
one Roddy Duncan ; now, Roddy, swear strong—swear
home ; mind yourself, Roddy."

These words were spoken aside, precisely as one would
address them when instructing any person to give a particular
line of evidence. He then stooped down, and placing his
hand upon the grave, he said, as if he were addressing the
dead man—

"Ha—you sleep cool there, you guilty villain ! an' it
wasn't my fault that the unfaithful an' dishonest sthrap
that you got that for, didn't get as much herself—there you
are, an' you'll tell no tales at all events ! You know,
Roddy," he proceeded, " it was Dalton that murdhered him—
mind that—but you're a coward at heart ; as for myself,

there's nothing troubles me but that tobaccy-box; but you
know nothing about that—may the divil confound me, at
any rate, for not destroyin' it! an' that ould sthrap, Nelly,
suspects something—for she's always ringin' Providence into
my ears; but if I had that box destroyed, I'd disregard
Providence—if there is a Providence."

The words had barely proceeded out of his lips, when
a peal of thunder, astonishingly loud, broke, as it were, over
their very heads, having been preceded by a flash of lightning, so bright that the long, well-defined grave was exposed, in all its lonely horrors, to Sarah's eye.

"That's odd, now," said she, "that the thunder should
come as he said them very words; but thank God that
it was Dalton that did the deed, for if it was himself he'd
not keep it back now, when the truth would be sure to come
out."

"It was he, my lord, and gentlemen of the jury," proceeded her father, "an' my conscience, my lord, during all
this long time——"

Here he muttered something which she could not understand, and after stooping down, and putting his hand upon
the grave a second time, he turned about and retraced his
steps home. It appeared, however, that late as the hour
was, there were other persons abroad as well as themselves,
for Sarah could distinctly hear the footsteps of several
persons passing along the adjoining road, past the Grey
Stone, and she also thought that among the rest might be
distinguished the voice of Red Roddy Duncan. The Prophet
quietly opened the door, entered, as usual, and went to bed;
Sarah having also retired to her own little sleeping-place,
lay for some time, musing deeply over the incidents of the
night.

CHAPTER XX

THE next morning opened with all the dark sultry rain and black cloudy drapery, which had, as we have already stated, characterized the whole season. Indeed, during the year we are describing, it was well known that all those visible signs which prognosticate any particular description of weather, had altogether lost their significance. If a fine day came, for instance, which indeed was a rare case, or a clear and beautiful evening, it was but natural that after such a dark and dreary course of weather, the heart should become glad and full, of hope that a permanent change for the better was about' to take place; but, alas! all cheerful hope and expectation were in vain. The morrow's sun arose as before, dim and gloomy, to wade along his dismal and wintry path, without one glimpse of enlivening light from his rising to his setting.

We have already mentioned slightly, those outrages to which the disease and misery that scourged the country in so many shapes had driven the unfortunate and perishing multitudes. Indeed, if there be any violation of the law, that can or ought to be looked upon with the most lenient consideration and forbearance, by the executive authorities, it is that which takes place under the irresistible pressure of famine. And singular as it may appear, it is no less true, that this is a subject concerning which much ignorance prevails, not only throughout other parts of the empire, but even at home here in Ireland, with ourselves. Much, for instance, is said, and has been said, concerning what are termed "Years of Famine," but it is not generally known, that since the introduction of the potato into this country, no year has ever passed which, in some remote locality or other, has not been such to the unfortunate inhabitants.

The climate of Ireland is so unsettled, its soil so various in quality, and the potato so liable to injury from excess of either drought or moisture, that we have no hesitation in stating the startling fact of this annual famine as one we can vouch for, upon our own personal knowledge, and against the truth of which we challenge contradiction. Neither does an autumn pass without a complaint peculiar to those who feed solely upon the new and unripe potato, and which, ever since the year '32, is known by the people as the "potato cholera." With these circumstances the legislature ought to be acquainted, inasmuch as they are calamities that will desolate and afflict the country, so long as the potato is permitted to be, as it unfortunately is, the staple food of the people. That we are subject, in consequence of that fact, to periodical recurrences of dearth and disease, is well known and admitted; but that every season brings its partial scourge of both these evils to various remote and neglected districts in Ireland, has not been, what it ought long since to have been, an acknowledged and established fact in the sanitary statistics of the country. Indeed, one would imagine, that after the many terrible visitations which we have had from destitution and pestilence, a legislature sincerely anxious for the health and comfort of the people, would have devoted itself, in some reasonable measure, to the humane consideration of such proper sumptuary and sanitary enactments, as would have provided not only against the recurrence of these evils, but for a more enlightened system of public health and cleanliness, and a better and more comfortable provision of food for the indigent and poor. As it is at present, provision-dealers of all kinds, mealmongers, forestallers, butchers, bakers, and huxters, combine together, and sustain such a general monopoly in food, as is at variance with the spirit of all law and humanity, and constitutes a kind of artificial famine in the country; and surely these circumstances ought not to be permitted, so long as we have a deliberative legislature, whose duty it is to watch and guard the health and morals of the people.

At the present period of our narrative, and especially on the gloomy morning following the Prophet's unconscious visit to the grave of the murdered man, the popular outrages had risen to an alarming height. Up to the present time occasional outbreaks, by small and detached groups of individuals, had taken place at night or before dawn, and rather in a timid or furtive manner, than with the recklessness of men who assemble in large crowds, and set both law and all consequences at open defiance. Now, however, destitution and disease had wrought such woful work among the general population, that it was difficult to know where or how to prescribe bounds to the impetuous resentment with which they expressed themselves against those who held over large quantities of food in order to procure high prices. At this moment the country, with its waste, unreaped crops, lying in a state of plashy and fermenting ruin, and its desolate and wintry aspect, was in frightful keeping with the appearance of the people when thus congregated together. We can only say, that the famine crowds of that awful year should have been seen in order to be understood and felt. The whole country was in a state of dull but frantic tumult, and the wild crowds, as they came and went in the perpetration of their melancholy outrages, were worn down by such startling evidences of general poverty and suffering, as were enough to fill the heart with fear as well as pity, even to look upon. Their cadaverous and emaciated aspects had something in them so wild and wolfish, and the fire of famine blazed so savagely in their hollow eyes, that many of them looked like creatures changed from their very humanity by some judicial plague, that had been sent down from heaven to punish and desolate the land. And in truth there is no doubt whatsoever, that the intensity of their sufferings, and the natural panic which was occasioned by the united ravages of disease and famine, had weakened the powers of their understanding, and impressed upon their bearing and features an expression which seemed partly the wild excitement of temporary frenzy, and partly the dull, hopeless apathy of fatuity—a state to which it is well known that misery, sickness, and hunger, all together, had brought down the strong intellect and reason of the wretched and famishing multitudes. Nor was this state of feeling confined to those who were goaded by the frightful sufferings that prevailed. On the contrary, thousands became victims of a quick and powerful contagion which spread the insane spirit of violence at a rapid rate, affecting many during the course of the day, who in the early part of the morning had not partaken of its influence. To no other principle than this can we attribute the wanton and irrational outrages of many of the people. Every one acquainted with such awful visitations must know that their terrific realities cause them, by wild influences that run through whole masses, to forget all the decencies and restraints of ordinary life, until fear and shame, and the becoming respect for order, all of which constitute the moral safety of society, are thrown aside or resolved into the great tyrannical instinct of self preservation, which, when thus stimulated, becomes what may be termed the insanity of desolation. We know that the most savage animals, as well as the most timid, will, when impelled by its ravenous clamours, alike forget every other appetite but that which is necessary for the sustainment of life. Urged by it alone, they will sometimes approach and assail the habitations of man, and, in the fury of the moment, expose themselves to his power, and dare his resentment—just as a famine mob will do, when urged by the same instinct, in a year of scarcity.

There is no beast, however, in the deepest jungle of Africa itself, so wild, savage, and ferocious, as a human mob, when left to its own blind and headlong impulses. On the morning in question, the whole country was pouring forth its famished hordes to intercept meal-carts and provision vehicles of all descriptions, on their way to market, or to the next seaport for shipment; or to attack the granaries of contractors or provision-dealers, and all who, having food in large quantities, refused to give it *gratis,* or at a nominal price, to the poor. Carts and cars, therefore, mostly the property of unoffending persons, were stopped on the highways, there broken, and the food which they carried openly taken away, and, in case of resistance, those who had charge of them were severely beaten. Mills were also attacked and pillaged, and in many instances large quantities of flour and grain not only carried off, but wantonly and wickedly strown about the streets and destroyed.

In all these acts of violence there was very little shouting; the fact being, that the wretched people were not able to shout, unless on rare occasions; and sooth to say, their vociferations were then but a faint and feeble echo of the noisy tumults which in general characterize the proceedings of excited and angry crowds. Truly, these pitiable gatherings had their own peculiarities of misery. During the progress of the pillage, individuals of every age, sex, and condition—so far as condition can be applied to the lower classes—might be seen behind ditches, in remote nooks—in porches of houses, and many on the open highways and streets, eating, or rather gobbling up raw flour or oatmeal; others, more fortunate, were tearing and devouring bread, with a fury, to which only the unnatural appetites of so many famished maniacs could be compared. As might be expected, most of these inconsiderate acts of license were punished by the consequences which followed them. Sickness of various descriptions, giddiness, retchings, fainting-fits, convulsions, and, in some cases, death itself, were induced by this wolfish and frightful gluttony on the part of the starving people. Others, however, who possessed more sense, and maintained a greater restraint over their individual sufferings, might be seen in all directions hurrying home, loaded with provisions of the most portable description, under which they tottered and panted, and sometimes fell utterly prostrate from recent illness, or the mere exhaustion of want. Aged people, grey-haired old men, and old women bent with age, exhibited a wild and excited alacrity that was grevious to witness, whilst hirpling homewards—if they had a home, or if not, to the first friendly shelter they could get—a kind of dim exulting joy feebly blazing in their heavy eyes, and a wild sense of unexpected good fortune working in unnatural play upon the muscles of their wrinkled and miserable faces. The ghastly impressions of famine, however, were not confined to those who composed the crowds. Even the children were little living skeletons, wan and yellow, with a spirit of pain and suffering legible upon their fleshless but innocent features; whilst the very dogs, as was well observed, were not able to bark, for, indeed, such of them as survived, were nothing but ribs and skin. At all events, they assisted in making up the terrible picture of general misery which the country at large presented. Both day and night, but at night especially, their hungry howlings could be heard over the country, or mingling with the wailings which the people were in the habit of pouring over those whom the terrible typhus was sweeping away with such wide and indiscriminating fatality.

Our readers may now perceive, that the sufferings of these unhappy crowds, before they had been driven to these acts of violence, were almost beyond belief.[1]   At an earlier period

[1] It is as well to state here that the season described in this tale is the dreadful and melancholy one of 1817; and we may add, that in order to avoid the charge of having exaggerated the almost incredible sufferings of the people in that year, we have studiously kept our descriptions of them within the limits of truth. Doctor Corrigan, in his able and very seasonable pamphlet "ON FEVER AND FAMINE AS CAUSE AND EFFECT IN IRELAND"—a pamphlet, by the way, which has been the means of conveying most important truths to statesmen, and which ought to be looked on as a great public benefit—has confirmed the accuracy of the gloomy pictures I was forced to draw. Here follows an extract or two:—

"It is scarcely necessary to call to recollection the summer of 1816, cold and wet—corn uncut in November, or rotting in the

of the season, when the potatoes could not yet be dug, miserable women might be seen early in the morning, and, in fact, during all hours of the day, gathering weeds of various

sheaves on the ground; potatoes not ripened (and when unripe there cannot be worse food), containing more water than nutriment; straw at such an extravagant price as to render the obtaining of it for bedding almost impossible, and when procured, retaining from its half-fermented state so much moisture, that the use was, perhaps, worse than the want of it. The same agent that destroyed the harvest spoiled the turf. Seldom had such a multiplication of evils come together. In some of the former years, although food and bedding were deficient, the portion saved was of good quality, and fuel was not wanting; but in 1816 every comfort that might have compensated for partial want was absent. This description applies to the two years of 1816 and 1817. In midsummer of 1817, the blaze of fever was over the entire country. It had burst forth almost in a thousand different points. Within the short space of a month, in the summer of 1817, the epidemic sprung forth in Tramore, Youghal, Kinsale, Tralee and Clonmel, in Carrick-on-Suir, Roscrea,Ballina, Castlebar, Belfast, Armagh, Omagh, Londonderry, Monastereven, Tullamore, and Slane. This simultaneous break-out shows that there must have been some universal cause."

Again :—

" The poor were deprived of employment, and were driven from the doors where before they had always received relief, lest they should introduce disease with them. Thus, destitution and fever continued in a vicious circle, each impelling the other, while want of presence of mind aggravated a thousandfold the terrible infliction. Of the miseries that attend a visitation of epidemic fever, few can form a conception. The mere relation of the scenes that occurred in the country, even in one of its last visitations, makes one shudder in reading them. As Barker and Cheyne observe in their Report, ' a volume might be filled with instances of the distress occasioned by the visitation of fever in 1817.'

"' On the road leading from Cork, within a mile of the town (Kanturk), I visited a woman labouring under typhus ; on her left lay a child very ill, at the foot of the bed another child just able to crawl about, and on her right the corpse of a third child who had died two days previously, which the unhappy mother could not get removed.'—*Letter from Dr. O'Leary, Kanturk.*

"' Ellen Fagan, a young woman, whose husband was obliged, in order to seek employment, to leave her almost destitute in a miserable cabin, with three children, gave the shelter of her roof to a

descriptions, in order to sustain life; and happy were they
who could procure a few handfuls of young nettles, chicken-
weed, sorrell, *preshagh*, buglass, or sea-weed, to bring home

poor beggar who had fever. She herself caught the disease, and
from the terror created in the neighbourhood, was, with her three
children, deserted, except that some person left a little water and
milk at the window for the children, one about four, the other about
three years old, and the other an infant at her breast. In this way
she continued for a week, when a neighbour sent her a loaf of
bread, which was left in the window. Four days after this he grew
uneasy about her, and one night, having prepared some tea and
bread, he set off to her relief. When he arrived, the following scene
presented itself: in the window lay the loaf, where it had been deposited four days previously; in one corner of the cabin, on a little
straw, without covering of any kind, lay the wretched mother
actually dying, and her infant dead by her side for the want of
that sustenance which she had not to give; on the floor lay the
children to all appearance dying also of cold and hunger. At
first they refused to take anything, and he had to pour a little
liquid down their throats; with the cautious administration of
food they gradually recovered. The woman expired before the
visitor quitted the house.'—*Letter from Dr. Macartney, Monivae.*

"'A man, his wife, and two children lay together in fever. The
man died in the night; his wife, nearly convalescent, was so terrified with his corpse in the same bed with her, that she relapsed,
and died in two days after; the children recovered from fever, but
the eldest of them lost his reason by the fright. Many other
wretched scenes have I witnessed, which would be too tedious to
relate.'—*Barker and Cheyne's Report.*

"I know not of any visitation so much to be dreaded as epidemic
fever; it is worse than plague, for it lasts through all seasons.
Cholera may seem more frightful, but it is in reality less destructive—it terminates rapidly in death, or in as rapid recovery; its
visitation, too, is short, and it leaves those who recover unimpaired
in health and strength. Civil war, were it not for its crimes, would
be, as far as regards the welfare of a country, a visitation less to be
dreaded than epidemic fever.

*　　　　*　　　　*　　　　*　　　　*

" It is not possible, then, to form an exaggerated picture of the
sufferings *of a million and a half* of people in these countries, in their
convalescence from fever, deprived of, not only the comforts, but
even the necessaries of life, with scanty food, and fuel, and covering, only rising from fever to fall victims slowly to those numerous

as food, either for themselves or their unfortunate children. Others again, were glad to creep or totter to stock-farms, at great distances across the country, in the hope of being able to procure a portion of blood, which, on such melancholy occasions, is taken from the heifers and bullocks that graze there, in order to prevent the miserable poor from perishing by actual starvation and death.

Alas, little do our English neighbours know or dream of the horrors which attend a year of severe famine in this unhappy country. The crowds which kept perpetual and incessant siege to the houses of wealthy, and even of struggling small farmers, were such as scarcely any pen could describe. Neither can we render anything like adequate justice to the benevolence and charity—nay, we ought to say, the generosity and magnanimity of this and the middle classes in general. In no country on earth could such noble instances of self-denial and sublime humanity be witnessed. It has happened, in thousands of instances, that the last miserable morsel, the last mouthful of nourishing liquid, the last potatoe, or the last sixpence, has been divided with wretched and desolate beings who required it more, and this, too, by persons who, when that was gone, knew not to what quarter they could turn with a hope of replacing for themselves that which they had just shared in a spirit of such genuine and exalted piety.

It was to such a state of general tumult that the Prophet and his family arose on the morning of the following day. As usual, he was grim and sullen, but on this occasion his face had a pallid and sunken look in it, which apparently added at least ten years to his age. There was little spoken, and after breakfast he prepared to go out. Sarah, during the

chronic diseases that are sure to seize upon enfeebled constitutions. Death would be to many a more merciful dispensation than such recovery."—*Famine and Fever, as Cause and Effect in Ireland, etc., etc.* By D. J. CORRIGAN, Esq., M.D., M.R.C.S.E. Dublin: J. Fannin & Co., Grafton Street.

whole morning, watched his looks, and paid a marked attention to everything he said. He appeared, however, to be
utterly unconscious of the previous night's adventure, a fact
which his daughter easily perceived, and which occasioned
her to feel a kind of vague compassion for him, in consequence
of the advantage it might give to Nelly over him; for of late
she began to participate in her father's fears and suspicions
of that stubborn but superstitious personage.

"Father," said she, as he was about to go out, "is it fair to
ask where you are goin'?"

"It's neither fair nor foul," he replied; "but if it's any
satisfaction to you to know, I won't tell you."

"Have you any objection, then, that I should walk a piece
of the way with you?"

"Not if you have come to your senses, as you ought, about
what I mentioned to you."

"I have something to say to you," she replied, without
noticing the allusion he had made; "something that you
ought to know."

"An' why not mention it where we are?"

"Bekase I don't wish her there to know it."

"Thank you, ma'am," replied Nelly; "I feel your kindness
—an' dear me, what a sight of wisdom I'll lose by bein' kep'
out o' the saicret—saicret, indeed! A fig for yourself an'
your saicret; maybe I have my saicret as well as you."

"Well, then," replied Sarah, "if yon have, do you keep
yours as I'll keep mine, an' then we'll be aiquil. Come,
father, for I must go from home, too. Indeed, I think this
is the last day I'll be with either of you for some time—maybe ever."

"What do you mane?" said the father.

"Hut!" said the mother, "what a goose you are! Charley
Hanlon, to be sure; I suppose she'll run off wid him. Oh!
thin God pity him, or any one that's doomed to be blisthered
wid you!"

Sarah's eyes flashed like lightning, and her frame began to

work with that extraordinary energy which always accompanied the manifestation of her resentment.

"You will," said she, approaching the other—"you will, after your escape the other day; you—no, ah! no—I won't now; I forgot myself. Come, father—come, come; my last quarrel with her is over."

"Ay," returned Nelly, as they went out, "there you go, an' a sweet pair you are—father and daughter!"

"Now, father," resumed Sarah, after they had got out of hearing, "will you tell me if you slep' well last night?"

"Why do you ax?" he replied; "to be sure I did."

"I tell you why I ax," she answered; "do you know that you went last night—in the middle of the night—to the murdhered man's grave, in the glen there?"

It is impossible to express the look of astonishment and dismay which he turned upon her at these words.

"Sarah!" said he sternly; but she interrupted him.

"It's thruth," said she; "an' I went with you."

"What are you spakin' about? Me go out, an' not know it! Nonsense!"

"You went in your sleep," she rejoined.

"Did I spake?" said he, with a blank and ghastly look.

"You did."

"What, what—tell me—eh? What did I say?"

"You talked a good deal, an' said that it was Condy Dalton that murdhered him, and that you had Red Roddy to prove it."

"That was what I said?—eh, Sarah?"

"That's what you said, an' I thought it was only right to tell you."

"It was right, Sarah; but, at the same time, at the peril of your life, never folly me there again. Of coorse you know now that Sullivan's buried there."

"I do," said she; "but that's no great comfort, although it is to know that you didn't murdher him. At any rate, father, remember what I tould you about Condy Dalton.

Lave him to God; an' jist, that you may feel what you ought
to feel on the subject, suppose you were in his situation—
suppose for a minute that it was yourself that murdhered him
—then ask, would you like to be dragged out from us and
hanged, in your ould age, like a dog—a disgrace to all belongin' to you. Father, I'll believe that Condy Dalton murdhered him, when I hear it from his own lips, but not till
then. Now, good-bye. You won't find me at home when you
come back, I think."

"Why, where are you goin'?"

"There's plenty for me to do," she replied; "there's the
sick an' the dyin' on all hands about me, an' it's a shame for
any one that has a heart in their body, to see their fellow-creatures gaspin' for want of a dhrop of cowld wather to wet their
lips, or a hand to turn them where they lie. Think of how
many poor sthrangers is lyin' in ditches an' in barns, an' in
outhouses, without a livin' bein' a'most to look to them, or
reach them any single thing they want; no, not even to bring
the priest to them, that they might die reconciled to the Almighty. Isn't it a shame, then, for me, an' the likes o' me,
that has health an' strength, an' nothin' to do, to see my
fellow-creatures dyin' on all hands about me, for want of the
very assistance that I can afford them. At any rate, I
wouldn't live in the house with that woman, an' you know
that, an' that I oughtn't."

"But aren't you afeard of catchin' this terrible faver, that's
takin' away so many, if you go among them?"

"Afeard!" she replied; "no, father, I feel no fear either
of that or anything else. If I die, I lave a world that I never
had much happiness in, an' I know that I'll never be happy
again in it. What, then, have I to fear from death? Any
change for me must now be for the betther; at all events, it
can hardly be for the worse. No—my happiness is gone."

"What, in Heaven's name, is the matter with you?" asked
her father; "an' what brings the big tears into your eyes
that way?"

"Good-bye," said she; and as she spoke, a melancholy
smile, at once sad and brilliant, irradiated her features. "It's
not likely, father, that ever you'll see me under your roof
again. Forgive me all my follies now, maybe it's the last
time ever you'll have an opportunity."

"Tut, you foolish girl; go in out o' this, I say; it's enough
to sicken one to hear the like o' you spake that way—sich
stuff!"

She stood and looked at him for a moment, and the light of
her smile gradually deepened, or rather faded away, until
nothing remained but a face of exquisite beauty, deeply
shadowed by anxiety and distress.

The prophet pursued his way to Dick o' the Grange's,
whither, indeed, he was bent; and Sarah, having looked after
him for a moment with a troubled face, proceeded in the
direction of old Dalton's, with the sufferings and pitiable
circumstances of whose family she was already but too well
acquainted. Her journey across the country presented her
with little else than records of death, suffering, and outrage.
Along the roads the funerals were so frequent, that, in general, they excited no particular notice. They could, in fact,
scarcely be termed funerals, inasmuch as they were now nothing more than squalid and meagre-looking knots of those
who were immediately related to the deceased, hurrying onward, with reckless speed and disturbed looks, to the churchyard, where their melancholy burthen was hastily covered up
with scarcely any exhibition of that simple and affecting decorum, or of those sacred and natural sorrows, which in other
circumstances throw their tender but solemn light over the
last offices of death. As she went along, new and more
startling objects of distress attracted her notice. In dry and
sheltered places she observed little temporary sheds, which,
in consequence of the dreadful panic which always accompanies an epidemic in Ireland, had, to a timid imagination,
something fearful about them, especially when it is considered that death and contagion were then at work in them in

such terrible shapes. To Sarah, however, they had no terrors; so far from that, a great portion of the day was spent by her in relieving their wretched, and, in many cases, dying inmates, as well as she could. She brought them water, lit fires for them, fixed up their sheds, and even begged aid for them from the neighbours around, and, as far as she could, did everything to ease their pain, or soothe their last moments by the consolation of her sympathy. If she met a family on the highway, worn with either illness or fatigue— perhaps an unhappy mother, surrounded by a helpless brood, bearing, or rather tottering under a couple of sick children, who were unable to walk—she herself, perhaps, also ill, as was often the case—she would instantly take one of them out of the poor creature's arms, and carry it in her own as far as she happened to go in that direction, utterly careless of contagion or all other consequences.

In this way was she engaged, towards evening, when at a turn of the road she was met by a large crowd of the rioters, headed by Red Roddy, Tom Dalton, and many others in the parish who were remarkable only for a tendency to ruffianism and outrage; for we may remark here, that on occasions such as we are describing, it is generally those who have suffered least, and have but little or nothing to complain of, that lead the misguided and thoughtless people into crime, and ultimately into punishment.

The change that had come over young Dalton was frightful; he was not half his former size; his clothes were now in rags, his hat without a crown, his beard grown, his face half black with dirt, and his whole aspect and appearance that of some miscreant in whom it was difficult to say whether the ruffian or the idiot predominated most. He appeared now in his glory, frantic and destructive; but amidst all this drivelling impetuosity, it was not difficult to detect some desperate and unshaken purpose in his heavy but violent and blood-shot eye.

Far different from him was Red Roddy, who headed his

own section of them with an easy but knowing swagger; now nodding his head with some wonderful purpose which nobody could understand; or winking at some acquaintance with an indefinite meaning, that set them a-guessing at it in vain. It was easy to see that he was a knave, but one of those knaves on whom no earthly reliance could be placed, and who would betray to-morrow, for good reasons, and without a moment's hesitation, those whom he had corrupted to-day.

"Come, Tom," said Roddy, "we have scattered a few of the mealmongerin' vagabonds—weren't you talkin' about that blessed voteen, ould Darby Skinadre? The villain that allowed Peggy Murtagh an' her child to starve to death. Aren't we to pay him a visit?"

Dalton coughed several times to clear his throat; a settled hoarseness having given a frightful hollowness to his voice —"Ay," said he—"ha, ha, ha—by the broken heart she died of, we'll—we'll—eh, Roddy, what are we to do to him?"

Roddy looked significantly at the crowd and grinned, then touched his forehead, and pointed at Dalton.

"That boy's up to everything," said he, "he's the man to head us all—ah, ha!"

"Never mind laughin' at him, any way," observed one of his friends, "maybe if you suffered what he did, poor fellow, an' his family too, that it's not fun you'd be makin' of him."

"Why," asked a new-comer, "what's wrong wid him?"

"He's not *at* himself," replied the other, "ever since he had the faver; that, they say, an' the death of a very purty girl he was goin' to be married to, has put him beside himself, the Lord save us!"

"Come on now," shouted Tom, in his terrible voice, "here's the greatest of all before us still. Who wants meal now? Come on, I say—ha, ha, ha! Is there any of you hungry? Is there any of you goin' to die for want of food? Now's your time—ho, ho! Now, Peggy, now.

Amn't I doin' it? Ay am I, an' it's all for your sake, Peggy dear, for I swore by the broken heart you died of—ay, an' didn't I tell you that last night on your grave where I slep'. No, he wouldn't—he wouldn't—but now —now—he'll see the differ—ay an' feel it too. Come on," he shouted, " whoever's hungry, folly me! ha, ha, ha ! "

This idiotic but ferocious laugh echoing such a dreadful purpose, was appalling; but the people who knew what he had suffered only felt it as a more forceful incentive to outrage. Darby's residence was now quite at hand, and in a few minutes it was surrounded by such a multitude, both of men and women, as no other occasion could ever bring together. The people were, in fact, almost lost in their own garments; some were without coats or waistcoats to protect them from the elements, having been forced, poor wretches, to part with them for food; others had nightcaps or handkerchiefs upon their heads instead of hats; a certain proof that they were only in a state of convalescence from fever—the women stood with dishevelled hair—some of them half naked, and others leading their children about, or bearing them in their arms; altogether they presented such an appearance as was enough to wring the benevolent heart with compassion and sorrow for their sufferings.

On arriving at Darby's house, they found it closed, but not deserted. At first, Tom Dalton knocked, and desired the door to be opened, but the women who were present, whether with shame or with honour to the sex we are at a loss to say, felt so eager on the occasion, probably for the purpose of avenging Peggy Murtagh, that they lost not a moment in shivering in the windows, and attacking the house with stones and missiles of every description. In a few minutes the movement became so general and simultaneous that the premises were a perfect wreck, and nothing was to be seen but meal and flour, and food of every description, either borne off by the hungry crowd, or scattered most wickedly and wantonly through the streets, whilst, in the very midst of the tumult, Tom Dalton was seen dragging poor Darby out by the throat, and over to the centre of the street.

"Now," said he, "here I have you at last—ha, ha, ha!"—his voice, by the way, as he spoke and laughed, had become fearfully deep and hollow—"now, Peggy dear, didn't I swear it—by the broken heart you died of, I said, an' I'll keep that sacred oath, darlin'."

Whilst speaking, the thin fleshless face of the miser was becoming black—his eyes were getting blood-shot, and, in a very short time, strangulation must have closed his wretched existence, when a young and tall female threw herself by a bound upon Dalton, whom she caught by the throat, precisely as he himself had caught Darby. It was Sarah, who saw that there was but little time to lose in order to save the wretch's life. Her grip was so effectual that Dalton was obliged to relax his hold upon the other, for the purpose of defending himself.

"Who is this?" said he—"let me go, you had better, till I have his life; let me go, I say!"

"It's one," she replied, "that's not afeard but ashamed of you. You, a young man, to go to strangle a weak, helpless, ould creature, that hasn't strength or breath to defend himself no more than a child."

"Didn't he starve Peggy Murtagh?" replied Tom, "ha, ha, ha!—didn't he starve her and her child?"

"No," she replied aloud, and with glowing cheeks, "it's false; it wasn't he but yourself that starved her and her child. Who desarted her—who brought her to shame? an' to sorrow in her own heart and in the eyes of the world? Who left her to the bitther and vile tongues of the whole counthry? Who refused to marry her, and kept her so that she couldn't raise her face before her fellow-creatures? Who sent her, without hope, or any expectation of happiness in this life—this miserable life—to the glens and lonely ditches about the neighbourhood, where she did nothing but shed bitther tears of despair and shame at the heartless lot you brought her to? An' when she was desarted by the wide world, and hadn't a friendly face to look to but God's, an' when one kind word from your lips would give her hope, an' comfort, an' happiness, where were you, and where was that kind word that would a' saved her? Let the ould man go, you unmanly coward; it wasn't him that starved her; it was yourself that starved her and broke her heart!"

"Did yez hear that?" said Dalton, "ha, ha, ha; an' it's all thrue—she has tould me nothing but the thruth; here, then, take the ould vagabond away with you, and do what you like with him—

> " 'I am a bold and rambling boy,
> My lodging's in the Isle of Throy;
> A rambling boy although I be,
> I'd lave them all an' folly thee!'

Ha, ha, ha! but come, boys, pull away; we'll finish the wreck of his house, at any rate."

"Wreck away," said Sarah, "I have nothin' to do with that; but I think them women—mad-women I ought to call them—might considher that there's many a starvin' mouth would be glad to have a little of what they're throwin' about so shamefully. Do you come with me, Darby; I'll save you as far as I can, an' as long as I'm able."

"I will, *achora*," replied Darby, " an' may God bless you, for you have saved my life; but why should they attack me? Sure the world knows, an' God knows, that my heart bleeds ——"

"Whisht!" she exclaimed, "the world and God both knows it's a lie, if you say that your heart bleeds for anything but the destruction that you see on your place. If you had given Peggy Murtagh the meal, she might be a livin' woman to-day; so no more falsehoods now, or I'll turn you back to Tom Dalton's clutches."

" No, then," replied the trembling wretch, " I won't ; but between you an' me, then—an' it needn't go farther—throth my heart bleeds for the severity that's——"

" One word more," she replied, " and I lave you to what you'll get."

Sarah's interference had a singular effect upon the crowd. The female portion of it having reflected upon her words, soon felt and acknowledged their truth, because they involved a principle of justice and affection to their sex ; whilst the men, without annexing any moral consideration to the matter, felt themselves influenced by her exquisite figure and great beauty.

" She's the Black Prophet's daughter," exclaimed the women, " and if the devil was in her, she tould Tom Dalton nothing but the truth, at any rate."

" And they say the devil is in her, the Lord save us, if ever he was in any one—keep away from her—my soul to heaven ! but she'd think no more of tearin' your eyes out, or stickin' you wid a case-knife, than you would of aitin' bread and butther."

" Blessed Father ! " exclaimed another, " did you see the brightness of her eyes while she was spakin' ? "

" No matther what she is," said a young fellow beside them, " the devil a purtier crature ever was made ; be my soul I only wish I had a thousand pounds, I wouldn't be long widout a wife, at any rate ! "

The crowd, having wrecked Skinadre's dwelling, and carried off and destroyed almost his whole stock of provisions, now proceeded in a different direction, with the intention of paying a similar visit to some similar character. Sarah and Darby—for he durst not venture, for the present, towards his own house—now took their way to the cabin of old Condy Dalton, where they arrived just in time to find the house surrounded by the officers of justice, and some military.

" Ah," thought Sarah, on seeing them, " it is done then,

and you lost little time about it. May God forgive you, father ! "

They had scarcely entered, when one of the officers, pulling out a paper, looked at it, and asked, " Isn't your name Condy or Cornelius Dalton ? "

" That is my name," said the old man.

" I arrest you, then," he continued, " for the murder of one Bartholomew Sullivan."

" It is the will of God," replied the old man, whilst the tears flowed down his cheeks—" it's God's will, an' I won't consale it any longer. Take me away—I'm guilty—I'm guilty ! "

CHAPTER XXI

CONDY DALTON GOES TO PRISON

THE scene that presented itself in Condy Dalton's miserable cabin was one, indeed, which might well harrow any heart not utterly callous to human sympathy. The unhappy old man had been sitting in the arm-chair we have alluded to, his chin resting on his breast, and his mind apparently absorbed in deep and painful reflection, when the officers of justice entered. Many of our Landlord readers, and all, probably, of our Absentee ones, will, in the simplicity of their ignorance regarding the actual state of the lower classes, most likely take it for granted that the picture we are about to draw exists nowhere but in our own imagination. Would to God that it were so ! Gladly and willingly would we take to ourselves all the shame, acknowledge all the falsehood, pay the highest penalty for all the moral guilt of our mis-representations, provided only any one acquainted with the country could prove to us that we are wrong, change our nature, or, in other words, falsify the evidence of our senses, and obliterate our experience of the truths we are describing.

Old Dalton was sitting, as we have said, in the only memorial of his former respectability now left him—the old arm-chair—when the men bearing the warrant for his arrest presented themselves. The rain was pouring down in that close, dark, and incessant fall which gives scarcely any hope of its ending, and consequently throws the heart into that anxious and gloomy state which every one can feel, and perhaps no one describe.

The cabin in which the Daltons now lived was of the poorest description. When ejected from their large holding by Dick o' the Grange, or, in other words, when auctioned out, they were unhappily at a loss where to find a place in which they could take a temporary refuge. A kind neighbour, who happened to have the cabin in question lying unoccupied, or rather waste, upon his hands, made them an offer of it—not, as he said, in the expectation that they could live in it for any length of time, but merely until they could provide themselves with a more comfortable and suitable abode.

"He wished," he added, "that it was better, for their sakes; and sorry he was to see such a family brought so low as to live in it at all!"

Alas! he knew not at the time how deeply the unfortunate family in question were steeped in distress and poverty. They accepted this miserable cabin; but, in spite of every effort to improve their condition, days, weeks, and months passed, and still found them unable to make a change for the better.

When Darby and Sarah entered, they found young Con, who had now relapsed, lying in one corner of the cabin, on a wretched shake-down bed of damp straw; whilst on another, of the same description, lay his amiable and affectionate sister Nancy. The cabin stood, as we have said, in a low, moist situation, the floor of it being actually lower— which is a common case—than the ground about it outside. It served, therefore, as a receptacle for the damp and under-water which the incessant down-pouring of rain during the whole season had occasioned. It was, therefore, dangerous to tread upon the floor, it was so soft and slippery. The rain, which fell heavily, now came down through the roof in so many places that they were forced to put under it such vessels as they could spare, not even excepting the beds, over each of which were placed old clothes, doubled up under dishes, pots, and little bowls, in order, if possible, to keep them dry. The house—if such it could be called—was almost destitute of furniture, nothing but a few pots, dishes, wooden noggins, horn spoons, and some stools, being their principal furniture, with the exception of one standing, short-posted bed in a corner near the fire. There, then, in that low, damp, dark pestilential *kraal*, without chimney or window, sat the old man, who, notwithstanding its squalid misery, could have looked upon it as a palace had he been able only to say to his own heart, I am not a murderer. There, we say, he sat alone, surrounded by pestilence and famine in their most fearful shapes, listening to the moanings of his sick family, and the ceaseless dripping of the rain, which fell through the roof into the vessels that were placed to receive it. Mrs. Dalton was "out," a term which was used in the bitter misery of the period to indicate that the person to whom it applied had been driven to the last resource of mendicancy; and his other daughter, Mary, had gone to a neighbour's house to beg a little fire.

As the old man uttered the words, no language could describe the misery which was depicted on his countenance.

"Take me!" he exclaimed; "ah, no; for then what will become of these?" pointing to his son and daughter, who were sick.

The very minions of the law felt for him; and the chief of them said, in a voice of kindness and compassion,—

"It's a distressin' case; but if you'll be guided by me, you won't say anything that may be brought against yourself. I was never engaged," said he, looking towards Darby and Sarah, to whom he partly addressed his discourse, "in any-

thing so painful as this. A man of his age, now, afther so
many years! However—well—it can't be helped; we must
do our duty."

"Where is the rest of your family?" asked another of
them; "is this young woman a daughter of yours?"

"Not at all," replied a third; "this is a daughter to the
Black Prophet himself, and, by japers, you hardened gipsey,
it's a little too bad for you to come to see how your blasted
ould father's work gets on. It's his evidence that's bringin'
this daicent ould man from his family to a gaol this miserable evenin'. Be off out o' this, I desire you; I wondher
yu're not ashamed to be present here, above all places in the
world, you brazen divil."

Sarah's whole soul, however, in all its best and noblest
sympathies, had passed into and mingled with the scene of
unparalleled misery which was then before her. She went
rapidly to the bed on which young Con was stretched, stooped
down, and looking closely at him, perceived that he was in a
broken and painful slumber. She then passed to that in
which his sister lay, and saw that she also was asleep. After
a glance at each, she rubbed her hands with a kind of wild
satisfaction, and going up to old Dalton, exclaimed—for she
had not heard a syllable of the language used towards her
by the officer of justice,—

"Ay," said she, laying her hand upon his white hairs,
"you are to be pitied this night, poor ould man! but which
of you, oh, which of you, is to be pitied most, you or them?
an' your wife, too, an' your other daughther, an' your other
son, too; but he's past undherstandin' it; oh, what will they
do? At your age, too—at your age! Oh, couldn't you die?
—couldn't you contrive, some way, to die?—couldn't you
give one great struggle, an' then break your heart at wanst,
an' for ever?"

These words were uttered rapidly, but in a low and
cautious voice, for she still feared to awaken those who
slept.

The old man had also been absorbed in his own misery, for he looked at her inquiringly, and only replied,—

" Poor girl, what is it you're sayin' ? "

" I'm biddin' you to die," she replied, " if you can ; you needn't be afeard of God ; He has punished you enough for the crime you have committed. Try an' die, if you can—or, if you can't—oh ! " she exclaimed, " I pray God that you—that he, there "—and she ran and bent over young Con's bed for a moment—" that you—that you may never recover, or live to see what you must see."

" It's a fact that between hunger and this sickness," continued he who had addressed her last, " they say, an' I know, that there's a great number of people silly ; but I think this lady is downright mad ; what do you mane, you clip ? "

Sarah stared at him impatiently, but without any anger.

" He doesn't hear me," she added, again putting her hand in a distracted manner upon Dalton's grey hair ; " no, no ; but since it can't be so, there's not a minute to be lost. Oh, take him away now," she proceeded, " take him away, while they're asleep, an' before his wife an' daughther comes home; take him away now, and spare him, spare them, spare them all as much sufferin' as you can."

" There's not much madness in that, Jack," returned one of them ; " I think it would be the best thing we could do. Are you ready to come now, Dalton ? " asked the man.

" Who's that," said the old man, in a voice of indescribable woe and sorrow, " who's that was talkin' of a broken heart ? Oh, God ! " he exclaimed, looking up to heaven with a look of intense agony, " support me—support them ; an' if it be your blessed will, pity us all ; but above all things, pity them, oh, heavenly Father, and don't punish them for my sin ! "

" It's false ! " exclaimed Sarah, looking on Dalton, and reasoning apparently with herself ; " he never committed a could-blooded murdher ; an' the Sullivans are—are—oh—take him away," she said, still in a low, rapid voice ; " take

him away. Come, now," she added, approaching Dalton
again, " come, while they're asleep, an' you'll save them an'
yourself much distress. I'm not afeard of your wife, for
she can bear it, if any wife could; but I do your poor
daughther, an' she so wake an' feeble afther her illness—
come."

Dalton looked at her, and said, " Who is this girl that
seems to feel so much for me ? but whoever she is, may God
bless her, for I feel that she's right. Take me away before
they waken! oh, she is right in every word she says, for I
am not afeard of my wife—her trust in God is too firm for
anything to shake. I'm ready; but I fear I'll scarcely be
able to walk all the way—an' sich an evenin', too. Young
woman, will you break this business to these ones, and to
my wife, as well as you can ? "

" Oh, I will, I will," she replied; " as well as I can; you
did well to say so," she added, in a low voice to herself;
"an' I'll stay here with your sick family, an' I'll watch an'
attend them. Whatever can be done by the like o' me for
them, I'll do; I'll—I'll not lave them—I'll nurse them—I'll
take care of them—I'll beg for them—oh, what would I not
do for them ? " and, whilst speaking, she bent over young
Con's bed, and clasping her hands, and wringing them several
times, she repeated, " oh, what wouldn't I do for you ! "

" May God bless you, best of girls, whoever you are.
Come, now, I'm ready."

" Ay," said Sarah, running over to him; " that's right—
I'll break the bitther news to them as well as it can be done;
come, now."

The old man stood in the midst of this desolation, with his
hat in his hand, and he looked towards the beds.

" Poor things ! " he exclaimed; " what a change has come
over you, from what you wanst, an' that not long since, wor.
Never, my darlin' childre—oh, never did one harsh or undutiful word come from your lips to your unhappy father. In
my ould age and misery I'm now lavin' you—maybe for ever

—never, maybe, to see you again in this world; an' oh, my God, if we are never to meet in the other—if the innocent an' the guilty is never to meet, then this is my last look at you, for everlastin', for everlastin'! I can't do it," he added, weeping bitterly; "I must take my lave of them—I must kiss their lips."

Sarah, while he spoke, had uttered two or three convulsive sobs; but she shed no tear; on the contrary, her eyes were singularly animated and brilliant. She put her arms about him, and said, in a soothing and solicitous tone,—

"Oh, no, it's all thrue; but if you kiss them, you'll disturb and waken them—an' then, you know, when they see you taken away in this manner, an' hears what it's for, it may be their death."

"Thrue, *achora*—thrue; well, I will only look at them, then. Let me keep my eyes on them for a little—it is likely the last time—maybe they may go first, and maybe I may go first—the last time, maybe, for everlastin', that I'll see them!"

He went over, as he spoke, Sarah still having her hand upon his arm, as if to intimate her anxiety to keep him under such control as might prevent her from awakening them; and standing first over the miserable bed where Nancy slept, he looked down upon her.

"Ay," said he, whilst the tears showered down his cheeks, "there lies a child that never vexed a parent's heart, or ruffled one of our tempers. May my blessin', if it is a blessin', or can be a blessin'——"

"It is, it is," said Sarah, with a quick, short sob; "it is a blessin', an' a holy blessin'; but bless him—bless him, too!"

"May my blessin' rest upon you, or rather may the blessin' of Almighty God rest upon you, daughter of my heart! And you, too," he proceeded, turning to the other bed, "here is him that among them all I loved the best—my youngest, an' called afther myself. May my blessin' an' the blessin' of God an' my Saviour rest upon you, my darlin' son; an' if I

never see either of you in this unhappy world, grant, oh
merciful Father, that we may meet in the glory of heaven,
when the stain will be taken away from me for that crime
that I have repented for so long an' so bittherly!"

Sarah, whilst he spoke, had let go his arm, and, placing
her two hands over her eyes, her whole breast quivered; and
the men, on looking at her, saw the tears gushing out in torrents from between her fingers. She turned round, however,
for a few moments, as if to compose herself; and when she
again approached the old man, there was a smile—a smile,
brilliant, but agitated, in her eyes and upon her lips.

"There now," she proceeded, "you have said all you can
say; come, go with them. Ah!" she exclaimed, with a
start of pain, "all we've done, or tried to do, is lost, I doubt.
Here's his wife an' daughter. Come out now," said she, addressing him; "say a word or two to them outside."

Just as she spoke, Mrs. Dalton and the poor invalid, Mary,
entered the house: the one with some scanty supply of food,
and the other bearing a live coal between two turf—one
under, and the other over it.

"Wait," said Sarah, "I'll speak to them before they come
in"; and, ere the words were uttered, she met them.

"Come here, Mrs. Dalton," said she; "stop a minute,
spake to this poor girl, an' support her. These sogers an'
the constables inside is come about Sullivan's business, long
ago."

"I know it," replied Mrs. Dalton; "I've just heard all
about it, there beyond; but she," pointing to her daughter,
"has only crossed the ditch from the commons, an' joined me
this minute."

"Give me these," said Sarah to the girl, "and stay here
till I come out again, wet as it is. Your mother will tell
you why."

She took the fire from her as she spoke, and, running in,
laid it upon the hearth, placing, at the same time, two or
three turf about it in a hurried manner, but still in a way

that argued great presence of mind, amidst all her distraction. On going out again, however, the first object she saw was one of the soldiers supporting the body of poor Mary, who had sunk under the intelligence. Mrs. Dalton having entered the cabin, and laid down the miserable pittance of food which she had been carrying, now waved her hand with authority and singular calmness, but at the same time with a face pallid as death itself.

"This is a solemn hour," said she, "an' a woful sight in this place of misery. Keep quiet, all of you. I know what this is about, dear Condy," she said; "I know it; but what is the value of our faith, if it doesn't teach us obedience? Kiss your child here," said she, "an' go—or come, I ought to say, for I will go with you. It's not to be wondhered at that she couldn't bear it, weak, an' worn, an' nearly heart-broken as she is. Bless her, too, before you go. An' this girl," she said, pointing to Mary, and addressing Sarah, "you will spake to her, an' support her as well as you can, an' stay with them all for an hour or two. I can't lave him."

Dalton, whilst she spoke, had taken Mary in his arms, and as in the case of the others, blessed her with a fervour only surpassed by his sorrow and utter despair.

"I will stay with them," said Sarah; "don't doubt that —not for an hour or two, but till they come to either life or death; so I've tould him."

"It's a bitther case," said Mrs. Dalton—"a bitther case; but then it's God's gracious will, an' them that He loves He chastises. Blessed be His name for all He does, an' blessed be His name even for this!"

Mary now recovered in her father's arms; and her mother, in a low but energetic voice, pointing to the beds, said,—

"Think of them, darlin'. There now, part with him. This world, I often tould you, dear Mary, is not our place, but our passage; an' although it's painful, let us not forget that it's God Himself that's guidin' an' directin' us through it. Come, Con dear—come."

A long, mournful embrace, and another sorrowful but fervent blessing, and with a feeble effort at consolation, Dalton parted with the weeping girl; and, placing his hat on his white head, he gave one long look—one indescribable look—upon all that was so dear to him in this scene of unutterable misery, and departed. He had not gone far, however, when he returned a step or two towards the door; and Mary, having noticed this, went to him, and throwing her arms once more about his neck, exclaimed,—

"Oh! father, darlin', an' is it come to this? Oh, did we ever complain or grumble about all we suffered, while we had you with us? no, we wouldn't. What was our sufferin's, father dear? Nothin'. But oh, nothin' ever broke our hearts, or throubled us, but to see you in sich sorrow."

"It's thrue, Mary darlin'; you wor all a blessin' to me; but I feel, threasure of my heart! that my sorrows won't be long before your eyes; my sorrows an' my cares will soon be over. It's about Tom I came back. Och, sure I didn't care what he or we might suffer, if it had plaised God to lave him in his senses; but maybe now he's happier than we are. Tell him—if he can undherstand it, or when he does undherstand it—that I lave my blessin' an' God's blessin' with him for evermore—for evermore; an' with you all; an' with you too, young woman—for evermore, amin! An' now, come; I submit myself to the will of my marciful Saviour!"

He looked up to heaven as he spoke, his two hands raised aloft; after which he covered his venerable head, and, with this pious and noble instance of resignation, did the affectionate old man proceed, as well as his feeble limbs could support him, to the county prison, accompanied by his pious and truly Christian wife.

As the men were about to go, he who had addressed Sarah so rudely, approached her with as much regret on his face as its hardened and habitual indifference to human misery could express, and said, tapping her on the shoulder,—

"I was rather rough to you, jist now, my purty girl—an',

by japers, it's you that is the purty girl—I dunna, by the
way, how the ould Black Prophet came by the likes o' you;
but, then, he was a han'some vagabon' in his day, himself,
an' you are like him."

"What do you want to say?" she asked impatiently;
"but stand outside, I won't spake to you here—your voice
would waken a corpse. Here now," she added, having gone
out upon the causeway, "what is it?"

"Why, divil a thing," he replied; "only that you're a
betther girl than I tuck you to be. It's a pitiful case this
—a woful case, at his time o' life. Be heaventhers, but I'd
rather a thousand times see the Black Boy, your own precious
father, swing, than this poor ould man."

A moment's temporary fury was visible, but she paused,
and it passed away; after which she returned slowly and
thoughtfully into the cabin.

It is unnecessary to say that almost immediately the
general rumour of Dalton's arrest for the murder had gone
through the whole parish, together with the fact, that it was
upon the evidence of the Black Prophet and Red Roddy
Duncan that the proof of it had been brought home to him.
Upon the former occasion there had been nothing against
him but such circumstances of strong suspicion as justified
the neighbouring magistrates in having him taken into cus-
tudy. On this, however, the two men were ready to point
out the identical spot where the body had been buried, and
to identify it as that of Bartholomew Sullivan. Nothing
remained, therefore, now that Dalton was in custody but to
hold an inquest upon the remains, and to take the usual steps
for the trial of Dalton at the following assizes, which were
not very far distant. Indeed, notwithstanding the desolation
that prevailed throughout the country, and in spite of the
care and sorrow which disease and death brought home to
so many in the neighbourhood, there was a very general
feeling of compassion experienced for poor old Dalton and his
afflicted family. And amongst those who sympathized with

them, there was scarcely one who expressed himself more strongly upon the subject than Mr. Travers, the head agent of the property on which they had lived, especially upon contrasting the extensive farm and respectable residence, from which their middleman landlord had so harshly and unjustly ejected them, with the squalid kennel in which they then endured such a painful and pitiable existence. This gentleman had come to the neighbourhood in order to look closely into the condition of the property which had been entrusted to his management, in consequence of a great number of leases having expired, some of which had been held by extensive and wealthy middlemen, among the latter of whom was our friend, Dick o' the Grange. The estate was the property of an English nobleman, who derived an income of thirty-two or thirty-three thousand a year from it, and who, though as landlords went, was not, in many respects, a bad one, yet when called upon to aid in relieving the misery of those from whose toil he drew so large an income, did actually remit back the munificent sum of one hundred pounds![1] The agent himself was one of those men who are capable of a just, but not of a generous action. He could, for instance, sympathize with the frightful condition of the people, but to contribute to their relief was no part of his duty. Yet he was not a bad man. In his transactions with his lordship's tenantry he was fair, impartial, and considerate. Wherever he could do a good turn, or render a service, without touching his purse, he would do it. He had, it is true, very little intercourse with the poorer class of under-tenants; but, whenever circumstances happened to bring them before him, they found him a hard, just man, who paid attention to their complaints, but who, in a case of doubt, always preferred the interests of his employer, or his own, to theirs. He had received many complaints and statements against the middlemen who resided upon the property, and he had duly and carefully considered them.

[1] A recent fact.

His present visit, therefore, proceeded from a determination
to look closely into the state and condition of the general
tenantry, by which he meant as well those who derived
immediately from the head landlord as those who held under
middlemen. One virtue he possessed, which, in an agent,
deserves every praise : he was inaccessible to bribery on the
one hand, or flattery on the other, and he never permitted
his religious or political principles to degenerate into prejudice so far as to interfere with the impartial discharge of
his duty. Such was Robert James Travers, Esq., and we
only wish that every agent in the country at large would
follow his example.

CHAPTER XXII

RE-APPEARANCE OF THE BOX—FRIENDLY DIALOGUE BETWEEN JEMMY BRANIGAN AND THE PEDLAR

THE next morning but one after the committal of Condy
Dalton the strange woman who had manifested such an
anxious interest in the recovery of the tobacco-box was
seated at her humble fireside, in a larger and more convenient cottage than that which we have described, where
she was soon joined by Charley Hanlon, who had already
made it so comfortable and convenient that she was able to
contribute something towards her own support by letting
what are termed in the country parts of Ireland, " Dry
Lodgings." Her only lodger upon this occasion was our
friend the pedlar, who had been domiciled with her ever
since his arrival in the neighbourhood, and whose principal
traffic, we may observe, consisted in purchasing the flowing
and luxuriant heads of hair which necessity on the one hand,
and fear of fever on the other, induced the country maidens
to part with. This traffic, indeed, was very general during
the period we are describing, the fact being that the poor
people, especially the females, had conceived a notion, and

not a very unreasonable one, that a large crop of hair not only predisposed them to the fever which then prevailed, but rendered their recovery from it more difficult. These notions, to be sure, resulted naturally enough from the treatment which medical men found it necessary to adopt in dealing with it, every one being aware that, in order to relieve the head, whether by blister or other application, it is necessary to remove the hair. Be this, however, as it may, it is our duty to state here that the traffic we allude to was very general, and that many a lovely and luxuriant crop came under the shears of the pedlars who then strolled through the country.

" Afther all, aunt," said Hanlon, after having bidden her good-morrow, " I'm afeard it was a foolish weakness to depend upon a dhrame. I see nothing clear in the business yet. Here now we have got the box, an' what are we the nearer to the discovery ? "

" Well," replied his aunt, for in that relation she stood to him, " is it nothing to get even that ? Sure we know now that it was his, an' do you think that M'Gowan, or as they call him, the Black Prophet, would be in sich a state to get it—an' his wife, too, it seems—unless there was some raison on their part beyond the common, to come at it ? "

" It's a dark business altogether ; but aren't we thrown out of all trace of it in the manetime ? Jist when we thought ourselves on the straight road to the discovery, it turns out to be another an' a different murdher entirely— the murdher of one Sullivan."

At this moment the pedlar, who had been dressing himself in another small apartment, made his appearance, just in time to catch his concluding words.

" An' now," Hanlon added, " it appears that Sullivan's body has been found at last. The Black Prophet and Roddy Duncan knows all about the murdher, an' can prove the act home to Condy Dalton, and identify the body, they say, besides."

The pedlar looked at the speakers with a face of much curiosity and interest, then mused for a time, and at length took a turn or two about the floor, after which he sat down and began to drum his fingers on the little table that had been placed for breakfast.

"Afther I get my breakfast," he said at length, "I'll thank you to let me know what I have to pay. It's not my intention to stop undher this roof any longer ; I don't think I'd be overly safe."

"Safe !—*arrah*, why so ? " asked the woman.

"Why," he replied, "ever since I came here you have done nothing but *collogue—collogue* an' whisper, an' lay your heads together, an' divil a syllable can I hear that hasn't murdher at the front an' rair of it ; either spake out or get me my bill. If you're of that stamp, it's time for me to thravel ; not that I'm so rich as to make it worth anybody's while to take the mouthful of wind out o' me that's in me. What do you mane by this discoorse ? "

"May God rest the sowls of the dead ! " replied the woman, " but it's not for nothing we talk as we do, an' if you knew but all, you wouldn't think so."

"Very likely," he replied, in a dry but dissatisfied voice ; " maybe, sure enough, that the more I'd know of it, the less I'd like of it ; here now is a man named Sullivan—Barney, or Bill, or Bartley, or some sich name, that has been murdhered, an' it seems the murdherer was sent to gaol yestherday evenin'—the villain ! Get me my bill, I say ; it's an unsafe neighbourhood, an' I'll take myself out of it while I'm able."

"It's not widout raison we talk of murdher, then," replied the woman.

"Faith maybe so ; get me my bill, then, I bid you, an' in the manetime let me have my breakfast. As it is, I tell you both that I carry no money to signify about me."

"Tell him the truth, aunt," said Hanlon ; "there's no use

in lyin' undher his suspicion wrongfully, or allowin' him to
lave your little place for no raison."

"The truth is, then," she proceeded, throwing the corner
of her apron over her left shoulder, and rocking herself to
and fro, "that this young man had a dhrame some time ago ;
he dreamt that a near an' dear friend of his an' of mine too,
that was murdhered in this neighbourhood, appeared to him,
an' that he desired him to go of a sartin night, at the hour
of midnight, to a stone near this, called the Grey Stone, an'
there he would get a clue to the murdher."

"Well, an' did he ? "

"He went — an'—but you had better tell it yourself,
avillish," she added, addressing Hanlon ; "you know it
best."

The pedlar instantly fixed his anxious and lively eyes on
the young man, intimating that he looked to him for the rest
of the story.

"I went," proceeded Hanlon, "and you shall hear everything that happened."

It is unnecessary for us, however, to go over the same
ground a second time. Hanlon minutely detailed to him all
that had taken place at the Grey Stone, precisely as it
occurred, if we allow for a slight exaggeration occasioned by
his terrors, and the impressions of supernatural manifestation
which they left upon his imagination.

The pedlar heard all the circumstances with an astonishment which changed his whole bearing into that of deep awe
and the most breathless attention. The previous eccen-
tricity of his manner by degrees abandoned him ; and, as
Hanlon proceeded, he frequently looked at him in a state of
abstraction, then raised his eyes towards heaven, uttering,
from time to time, "Marciful Father ! "—" Heaven presarve
us ! "—" Saints above us ! "—and such like, thus accompanying him by a running comment of exclamations as he went
along.

"Well," said he, when Hanlon had concluded, " surely

the hand of God is in this business; you may take that for
granted."

"I would fain hope as much," replied Hanlon; "but, as
matthers stand now, we're nearly as far from it as ever.
Instead of gettin' any knowledge of the murdherer *we* want
to discover, it proves to be the murdherer of Sullivan that
has been found out."

"Of Sullivan!" he exclaimed ; "well, to be sure—oh, ay
—well, sure that same is something ; but, in the manetime,
will you let me look at this box you spoke of? I feel a
curiosity to see it."

Hanlon rose, and, taking the box from a small deal chest
which was strongly locked, placed it in the pedlar's hands.
After examining it closely for about half-a-minute, they
could observe that he got very pale, and his hands began to
tremble, as he held and turned it about in a manner that was
very remarkable.

"Do you say," he asked, in an agitated voice, " that you
have no manes of tracin' this murdher ? "

"None more than we've tould you."

"Did this box belong to the murdhered man ?—I mane, do
you think he had it about him at the time of his death ? "

"Ay, an' for some time before it," replied the woman.
"It's all belongin' to him that we can find now."

"And you got it in the keeping of this M'Gowan, the
Black Prophet, you say ? "

"We did," replied the woman; " from his daughter, at all
events."

"Who is this Black Prophet? " he asked ; "or what is he?
for that comes nearer the mark. Where did he come from,
where does he live, an' what way does he earn his bread ? "

"The boy here," she replied, pointing to Hanlon, " can tell
you that betther than I can ; for, although I've been at his
place three or four times, I never laid eyes on him yet."

"Well," continued the pedlar, " you have both a right to
be thankful that you tould me this. I now see the hand of

God in the whole business. I know this box, an' I can tell you something that will surprise you more than that. Listen —but wait—I hear somebody's foot. No matther—I'll surprise you both by-an'-by."

" God save all here," said the voice of our friend, Jemmy Branigan, who immediately entered. "In throth, this change is for the betther, at any rate," said he, looking at the house. " I gave you a lift wid the masther yesterday," he added, turning to the woman. " I think I'll get him to throw the ten shillings off—he as good as promised me he would."

" Master ! " exclaimed the pedlar, bitterly—" oh, thin, it's he that's the divil's masther, by all accounts, an' the divil's landlord, too. Be me sowl, he'll get a warm corner down here ; " and, as he uttered the words, he very significantly stamped with his heel, to intimate the geographical position of the place alluded to.

" It would be only manners to wait till your opinion's axed of him," replied Jemmy ; " so mind your pack, you poor *sprissaun*, or, when you do spake, endaivour to know something of what you're discoorsin' about. Masther, indeed ! Divil take your impidence ! "

" He's a scourge to the counthry," continued the pedlar ; " a worse landlord never faced the sun."

" That's what we call, in this part of the counthry—a lie," replied Jemmy. " Do you undherstand what that manes ? "

" No man knows what an outrageous ould blackguard he is betther than yourself," proceeded the pedlar ; " an' how he harrishes the poor."

" That's ditto repeated," responded Jemmy ; " you're improvin'—but tell me, now, do you know any one that he harrished ? "

This was, indeed, a hazardous question on the part of Jemmy, who, by the way, put it solely upon the presumption of the pedlar's ignorance of Dick's proceedings as a landlord in consequence of his (the pedlar) being a stranger.

" Who did you ever know that he harrished, i' you plase?"

" Look at the Daltons," replied the other ; " what do you call his conduct to them ? "

Jemmy, who, whenever he felt himself deficient in truth, always made up for the want of it by warmth of temper, now turned shortly upon his antagonist, and replied, in a spirit very wide of the argument,—

" What do I call his conduct to them ? What do you call the nose on your face, my codger? Divil a sich an impident crature ever I met."

" It would be no wondher that the curse o' God would come on him for his thratement of that unfortunate and respectable family," responded the pedlar.

"The curse o' God knows where to fall best," replied Jemmy, " or it's not in the county jail ould Condy Dalton 'ud be for murdher this day."

" But," returned the other, " isn't it a disgraceful thing to be, as they say he and yourself is, a pair o' scourges in the hands o' God for your fellow-cratures ; an' in throth you're both fit for it, by all accounts."

" Troth," replied Jemmy, whose gall was fast rising, " it's a scourge wid nine tails to it ought to go to your back. The Daltons desarved all they got at his hands; an' the same pack was never anything else than a hot-brained crew, that 'ud knock you on the head to-day and groan over you to-morrow. He sarved them right, an' he's a liar that says to the contrary ; so, if you have a pocket for that, put it in it."

Jemmy, in fact, was now getting rapidly into a towering passion, for it mattered little how high in violence his own pitched battles with Dick ran, he never suffered, nor could suffer, a human being to abuse his master behind his back, but himself. So confirmed, however, by habit, was his spirit of contradiction, that, had the pedlar begun to praise Dick, Jemmy would immediately have attacked him without remorse, and scarcely left a rag of his character together.

" It's a shame for you," proceeded the pedlar, " to defend

an ould sinner like him ; but, then, as there's a pair of you,
that's not unnatural—every rogue will back his brother. I
could name the place, anyway, that'll be apt to hould you
both yet."

" An' I could," replied Jemmy, "name the piece o'
machinery that'll be apt to hould you, if you give the
masther any more abuse. Whether you'll grow in it or not
is more than I know, but, be me sowl, we'll plant you there
anyhow. Do you know what the stocks means? Faith,
many a spare hour you've sarved there, I go bail, that is,
when you had nothing else to do—an' by way of raycreation
jist."

" Ah," said the pedlar, " listen how he sticks to the ould
villain—but, sure, if you put any other two blisters together,
they'll do the same."

" My own opinion is," observed Hanlon's aunt, " that it's
a pity of the Dalton's, at any rate. Every one feels for them
—but still the hand o' God an' his curse, I'm afeard, is upon
them."

" An' that's more, maybe, than you know," replied Jemmy.
" Maybe God's only punishin' them bekase He loves them.
It's good to have our sufferin's in this world."

" Afther all," said the pedlar, " I'm afeard myself, too,
that the wrath o' the Almighty has marked them out. Indeed, I'm sure of it."

" An' maybe that's not the only lie you're sure of," replied
Jemmy. " It's a subject, anyway, you don't undherstand.
No," he proceeded, " by all accounts, Charley, it would wring
any one's heart to see him taken away in his ould age from
his miserable family an' childre ; and then he's so humble,
too, and so resigned to the will an' way o' God. He's lyin'
ill in the jail. I seen him yesterday—I went to see him,
an' to say whatever I could to comfort him. God pity his
grey hairs ! an'—hem—have compassion on him and his
this day ! "

The poor fellow's heart could stand the sudden contempla-

tion of Dalton's sorrows no longer, and on uttering the last
words he fairly wept.

"If I had known what it was about," he proceeded; "but
that ould scoundrel of a Prophet—ay, an' that other ould
scoundrel of a masther of mine—hem—ay—whish—but—
what am I sayin'?—but, if I had known it, it 'ud go hard
but I'd give him a lift—so as that he might get out o' the
way, at any rate."

"Ay," said the pedlar, "at any rate, indeed—faith, you
may well say it; but I say, that at any rate he'll be hanged
as sure as he murdhered Sullivan, and as sure as he did, that
he may swing, I pray this day!"

"I'll hould no more discoorse wid that circulatin' vagabone," replied Jemmy; "I'm a Christian man—a peaceable
man; an' I know what my religion ordhers me to do when I
meet the likes of him—an' that is, when he houlds the one
cheek towardst me to give him a sound Christian rap upon
the other. So to the devil I pitch you, you villain, sowl and
body, an' that's the worst I wish you. If you choose to be
unchristian, be so ; but, be me sowl, I'll not set you the
example. Charley," he proceeded, addressing Hanlon, "I
was sent for you in a hurry. Master Dick wants you, and
so does Red Roddy—the villain! and I tell you to take care
of him, for, like that vagabone Judas, he'd kiss you this
minute and betray you the next."

"I b'lieve you're purty near the truth," replied Hanlon,
"an' I'll surely have my eye about me."

"Do," replied Jemmy, "but I was near forgettin'—it
seems the crowner of the county is sick, an' there can't be an
inquest till he recovers, if he ever does recover; an' if it 'ud
sarve poor ould Dalton, that he never may, I pray God this
day!—come away, you'll be killed for stayin'."

Just then, young Henderson himself called Hanlon forth,
who, after some conversation with him, turned towards the
garden, where he held a second conference with Red Roddy,
who, on leaving him, appeared in excellent spirits, and kept

winking and nodding, with a kind of burlesque good humour, at every one whom he knew, until he reached home.

In this state stood the incidents of our narrative, suspended for some time by the illness of the coroner, when Mr. Travers, himself a magistrate, came to the head inn of the county town in which he always put up, and where he held his office. He had, for several days previously, gone over the greater portion of the estate, and inspected the actual condition of the tenantry on it. It is unnecessary to say that he was grieved at the painful consequences of the middleman system, and of sub-letting in general. Wherever he went, he found the soil in many places covered with hordes of pauper occupants, one holding under another in a series that diminished from bad to worse in everything but numbers, until he arrived at a state of destitution that was absolutely disgraceful to humanity. And what rendered this state of things doubly painful and anomalous was the fact, that whilst these starving wretches lived upon his employer's property, they had no claim on him as a landlord, nor could he recognize them as tenants. It is true that these miserable creatures, located upon small patches of land, were obliged to pay their rents to the little tyrant who was over them, and he again, probably, to a still more important little tyrant, and so on; but whenever it happened that the direct tenant, or any of the series, neglected to pay his or their rent, of course the landlord had no other remedy than to levy it from off the soil, thus rendering it by no means an unfrequent case that the small occupiers who owed nothing to him or those above them, were forced to see their property applied to the payment of the head rent, in consequence of the inability, neglect, or dishonesty of the middleman, or some other subordinate individual from whom they held. This was a state of things which Mr. Travers wished to abolish, but to do so, without inflicting injury, however unintentional, or occasioning harshness to the people, was a matter not merely difficult, but impossible.

As we are not, however, writing a treatise upon the management of property, we shall confine ourselves simply to the circumstances only of such of the tenants as have enacted a part in our narrative.

About a week had now elapsed since the abusive contest between Jemmy Branigan and the pedlar, the coroner was beginning to recover, and Charley Hanlon's aunt had disappeared altogether from the neighbourhood. Previous to her departure, however, she, her nephew, and the pedlar, had several close and apparently interesting conferences, into which their parish priest, the Rev. Anthony Devlin, was ultimately admitted. It was clear, indeed, that whatever secret the pedlar communicated had inspired both Hanlon and his aunt with fresh energy in their attempts to discover the murderer of their relative; and there could be little doubt that the woman's disappearance from the scene of its perpetration was in some way connected with the steps they were taking to bring everything connected with it to light.

Travers, already acquainted with the committal of old Dalton, as he was with all the circumstances of his decline and eviction from his farm, was sitting in his office, about twelve o'clock, when our friend, the pedlar, bearing a folded paper in his hand, presented himself, with a request that he might be favoured with a private interview. This, without any difficulty was granted, and the following dialogue took place between them:—

"Well, my good friend," said the agent, "what is the nature of this private business of yours?"

"Why, plaise your honour, it's a petition in favour of ould Condy Dalton."

"A petition! Of what use is a petition to Dalton? Is he not now in gaol, on a charge of murder? You would not have me attempt to obstruct the course of justice, would you? The man will get a fair trial, I hope."

"I hope so, your honour; but this petition is not about

the crime the unfortunate man is in for; it's an humble prayer to your honour, hopin' you might restore him; or, I ought rather to say, his poor family, to the farm that they wor so cruelly put out of. Will your honour read it, sir, and look into it? bekase, at any rate, it sets forth too common a case."

"I am partly acquainted with the circumstances already; however, let me see the paper."

The pedlar placed it in Mr. Travers's hands, who, on looking over it, read, somewhat to his astonishment, as follows :—

"The humble Petition of Cornelius Dalton, to his Honour, Mr. John Robert Travers, Esq., on behalf of himself, his wife, and his afflicted family : now lying in a state of almost superhuman destitution—by Eugenius M'Grane, philomath and classical instructor in the learned languages of Latin, English, and the Hibernian Vernacular, with an inceptive initiation into the rudiments of Greek, as far as the Gospel of St. John the Divine, attended with copious disquisitions on the relative merits of moral and physical philosophy, as contrasted with the pusillanimous lectures of that ignoramus of the first water, Phadrick M'Swagger, falsely calling himself philomath—*cum multis aliis quos enumerare longum est* :

" HUMBLY SHOWETH—

" That Cornelius Dalton, late of Cargah, gentleman agriculturist, held a farm of fifty-six Irish acres, under the Right Honourable (the reverse could be proved with sound and legitimate logic) Lord Mollyborough, an absentee nobleman, and proprietor of the Tully-stretchem estate. That the said Cornelius Dalton entered upon the farm of Cargah, with a handsome capital and abundant stock, as became a man bent on improving it, for both the intrinsic and external edification and comfort of himself and family. That the rent was originally very high, and, upon complaint of this, several well-indited remonstrances, urged with most persuasive and enthusiastic eloquence, as the inditer hereof can testify, were most insignificantly and superciliously disregarded. That the said Mr. Cornelius Dalton persisted, notwithstanding this great act of contemptuosity and discouragement to his creditable and industrious endeavours, to expend, upon the aforesaid farm, in solid and valuable improvements, a sum of seven hundred pounds and upwards, in building, draining, enclosing, and manuring, all of which im-

provements transcendantly elevated the value of the farm in question, as the whole rational population of the country could depose
to—*me ipso teste quoque.* That when this now highly emendated
tenement was brought to the best condition of excellence of which
it was susceptible, the middleman landlord—*væ miseris agricolis!*—
called upon him for an elevation of rent, which was reluctantly
complied with, under the tyrannical alternative of threatened
ejection, incarceration of cattle, etc., etc., and many other proceedings equally inhuman and iniquitous. That this rack-rent, being
now more than the land could pay, began to paralyze the efforts
and deteriorate the condition of the said Mr. Cornelius Dalton; and
which, being concatenated with successive failures in his crops, and
mortality among his cattle, occasioned him, as it were, to retro-
gradate from his former state; and, in the course of a few calamitous years, to decline, by melancholy gradations and oppressive
treatment from Richard Henderson, Esq., J.P., his landlord, to a
state of painful struggle and poverty. That the said Richard
Henderson, Esq., J.P., his unworthy landlord, having been offered
a still higher rent from a miserable disciple, named Darby Skinadre,
among others, unfeelingly availed himself of Dalton's *res angustæ*—
and under plea of his privileges as a landlord, levied an execution
upon his property, auctioned him out, and expelled him from the
farm; thus turning a respectable man and his family, hopeless and
houseless, beggars upon the world, to endure misery and destitution. That the said Mr. Cornelius Dalton, now plain Corney
Dalton—for vile poverty humilifies even the name—or rather his
respectable family, among whom, *facile princeps*, for piety and unshaken trust in her Redeemer, stands his truly unparalleled wife,
are lying in a damp, wet cabin within about two hundred perches
of his former residence, groaning with the agonies of hunger, destitution, dereliction, and disease, in such a state of complicated and
multiform misery as rarely falls to the lot of human eyes to witness.
That the burthen and *onus* of this petition is, to humbly supplicate
that Mr. Cornelius Dalton, or rather his afflicted and respectable
family, may be reinstated in their farm aforesaid, or if not, that
Richard Henderson, Esq., senior, J.P., may be compelled to swallow
such a titillating emetic from the head landlord as shall compel
him to eructate to this oppressed and plundered man all the money
he expended in making improvements, which remain to augment
the value of the farm; but which, at the same time, were the means
of ruining himself and his most respectable family; for, as the bard
says, 'sic vos non vobis,' etc., etc. Of the remainder of this appro-

priate quotation, your honour cannot be incognizant, or any man who has had the advantage of being college-bred, as every true gentleman, or 'homo factus ad unguem,' must have, otherwise he fails to come under this category. And your petitioner will ever pray."

"Are you the Mr. Eugenius M'Grane," asked the agent, "who drew up this extraordinary document?"

"No, your honour; I'm only merely a friend to the Daltons, although a stranger in the neighbourhood."

"But what means have Dalton or his family, granting that he escapes from this charge of murder that's against him, of stocking or working so large a farm? I am aware myself that the contents of this petition, with all its pedantry, are too true."

"But, consider, sir, that he sunk seven hundre' pounds in it, an' that, according to everything like fair play, he ought either to get his farm again, at a raisonable rate, or the money that raised its value for the landlord, back again; sure that's but fair, your honour?"

"I am not here to discuss the morality of the subject, my good friend, neither do I question the truth of your argument, simply as you put it. I only say, that what you ask is impracticable. You probably know not Dick o' the Grange, for you say you are a stranger—if you did, you would not put yourself to the trouble of getting even a petition for such a purpose written."

"It's a hard case, your honour."

"It is a hard case; but the truth is, I see nothing that can be done for the Daltons. To talk of putting a family, in such a state as they are now in, back again on such a farm, is stark nonsense—without stock or capital of any kind —the thing is ridiculous."

"But suppose they had stock and capital?"

"Why, then they certainly would have the best right to the farm—but where's the use of talking about stock or capital, so far as they are concerned."

" I wish your honour would interfare for an oppressed and ill-treated family against as great a rogue, by all accounts, as ever broke bread—I wish you would make me first sure that they'd get their farm."

" To what purpose, I say ? "

" Why, sir, for a raison I have. If your honour will make me sure that they'll get their land again, that's all I want."

" What is your reason ? Have you capital, and are you willing to assist them ? "

The pedlar shook his head.

" Is it the likes o' me, your honour ? No, but maybe it might be made up for them some way."

" I believe," said the agent, " that your intentions are good ; only that they are altogether impracticable. However, a thought strikes me. Go to Dick o' the Grange, and lay your case before him. Ask a new lease for your friends, the Daltons—of course, he won't give it ; but at all events, come back to me, and let me know, as nearly in his words as you can, what answer he will give you ; go now, that is all I can do for you in the matter."

" Barrin' this, your honour, that set in case the poor heart-broken Daltons wor to get capital some way——"

" Perhaps," said Travers, interrupting him, " you can assist them."

" Oh! if I could!—no, but set in case, as I said, that it was to be forthcomin', you persave. Me!—oh, would to the Lord that *I* was able! "

" Very well," replied the other, anxious to rid himself of the pedlar, " that will do now. You are, I perceive, one of those good-natured, speculating creatures, who are anxious to give hope and comfort to every one. The world has many like you ; and it often happens, that when some good fortune does throw the means of doing good into your power, you turn out to be a poor, pitiful, miserable crew, without actual heart or feeling. Good-bye, now. I have no more time to

spare—try Dick o' the Grange himself, and let me know his
answer."

So saying, he rang the bell, and our friend the pedlar, by
no means satisfied with the success of his interview, took his
leave.

CHAPTER XXIII

DARBY IN DANGER—NATURE TRIUMPHS

THE mild and gentle Mave Sullivan, with all her natural
grace and unobtrusive modesty, was yet like many of the
fair daughters of her country, possessed of qualities which
frequently lie dormant in the heart until some trying calamity
or startling event of more than ordinary importance awakens
them into life and action.   Indeed, any one in the habit of
observing the world may have occasionally noticed, that,
even within the range of his own acquaintances, there has
been many a quiet and apparently diffident girl, without
pretence or affectation of any kind, who, when some unexpected and stunning blow has fallen either upon herself or
upon some one within the circle of her affections, has manifested a spirit so resolute or a devotion so heroic, that she
has at once constituted herself the lofty example whom all
admire and endeavour to follow.   The unrecorded calamities
of ordinary life and the annals of human affection, as they
occur from day to day around us, are full of such noble
instances of courage and self-sacrifice on the part of woman
for the sake of those who are dear to her.   Dear, holy, and
heroic woman! how frequently do we, who too often sneer at
your harmless vanities and foibles, forget the light by which
your love so often dispels the darkness of our affliction, and
the tenderness with which your delicious sympathy charms
our sorrows and our sufferings to rest, when nothing else can
succeed in giving us one moment's consolation !

The situation of the Daltons, together with the awful blow

which fell upon them at a period of such unexampled misery, had now become the melancholy topic of conversation among their neighbours, most, if not all, of whom were, however, so painfully absorbed in their own individual afflictions either of death, or famine, or illness, as to be able to render them no assistance.   Such as had typhus in their own families were incapable of attending to the wants or distresses of others, and such as had not, acting under the general terror of contagion which prevailed, avoided the sick houses as they would a plague.

On the morning after old Dalton's removal to prison, Jerry Sullivan and his family were all assembled around a dull fire, the day being, as usual, so wet that it was impossible to go out unless upon some matter of unusual importance; there was little said, for although they had hitherto escaped the fever, still their sufferings and struggles were such as banished cheerfulness from among them.   Mave appeared more pale and dejected than they had ever yet seen her, and it was noticed by one or two of the family that she had been occasionally weeping in some remote corner of the house where she thought she might do so without being observed.

"Mave, dear," said her father, "what is the matter wid you ?   You look, darlin', to be in very low spirits to-day. Were you cryin' ? "

She raised her large innocent eyes upon him, and they instantly filled with tears.

"I can't keep it back from you, father," she replied, "let me do as I will—an' oh, father dear, when we look out upon the world that's in it, an' when we see how the hand o' God is takin' away so many from among us, and when we see how the people everywhere is sufferin' and strugglin' with so much—how one is here this day, and in a week to come in the presence of their Judge !   Oh, surely, when we see all the doin's of death and distress about us, we ought to think that it's no time to harbour hatred or any other bad or unchristian feelin' in our hearts ! "

" It is not indeed, darlin' ; an' I hope nobody here does."

"No," she replied ; and as she spoke the vibrations of sorrow and of sympathy shook her naturally sweet voice into that tender expression which touches the heart of the hearer with such singular power—" no, father," she proceeded, " I hope not ; religion teaches us a different lesson—not only to forgive our enemies, but to return good for evil."

" It does, *achora machree*," replied her father, whose eyes expressed a kind of melancholy pride, as he contemplated his beautiful but sorrowful-looking girl, giving utterance to truths which added an impressive and elevated character to her beauty.

" Young and ould, *acushla machree*, is fallin' about us in every direction ; but may the Father of Mercy spare you to us, my darlin' child, for if anything was to happen you, where—oh, where, could we look upon your aiquil, or find anything that could console us for your loss ? "

"If it's my fate to go, father, I'll go, an' if it isn't, God will take care of me ; whatever comes, I'm resigned to His will."

" Ay, dear, an' you ever wor, too ; and for the same raison, God's blessin' will be upon you ; but what makes you look so low, *avourneen?* I trust in my Saviour, you're not unwell, Mave, dear ? "

"Thanks be to God, no, father ; but there's a thing on my mind that's distressin' me very much, an' I hope you'll allow me my way in it."

" I may say so, dear ; because I know you wouldn't ax me for anything that 'ud be wrong to grant you. What is it, Mave ? "

" It's the unhappy an' miserable state that these poor Daltons is in," she replied. "Father, dear, forgive me for what I'm about to say ; for, although it may make you angry, there's nothin' farther from my heart than to give you offence."

" You needn't tell me so, Mave—you need not, indeed ;

but sure you know, darlin', that, unfortunately we have nothing in our power to do for them? I wish to the Lord we had! Didn't we do all that people in our poor condition could do for them? Didn't you, yourself, *achora*, make us send them sich little assistance as we could spare—ay, even to sharin', I may say, our last morsel wid them; an' now, darlin', you know we haven't it."

" I know that," she replied, as she wiped away the tears; " where is there a poorer family than we are, sure enough? but, father dear, we can assist them—relieve them—ay, maybe save them—for all that."

" God be praised then!" exclaimed Sullivan; " only show me how, an' we'll be glad to do it; for I can forget everything now, Mave, but their distress."

" But do you know the condition they're in at this moment?" she asked; " do you know, father, that they're stretched on the bed of sickness?—I mean Nancy, an'—an' young Con, who has got into a relapse; poor Mary is scarcely able to go about, she's so badly recovered from the fever—an' Tom, the wild, unfortunate young man, is out of his senses, they say. Then, there's nobody to look to them but Mrs. Dalton herself; an' she, you know, has to go ' out ' to ask their poor bit from the neighbours. Only think," she proceeded, with a fresh burst of sorrow—" oh, only think, father, of sich a woman bein' forced to this!"

" May the Lord pity her an' them, this woful day!" exclaimed Sullivan.

" Now, father," proceeded Mave; " I know—oh, who knows betther or so well—what a good, an' a kind, an' forgivin' heart you have; an' I know, that even in spite of the feelin' that was, an' that maybe is, upon your mind against them, you'll grant me my wish in what I'm goin' to ask."

" What is it, then?—let me hear it."

" It's this: you know that here, in our own family, I can do nothing to help ourselves—that is, there is nothing for me to do—an' I feel the time hang heavy on my hands. I have

been thinkin', father dear, of this miserable state the poor
Daltons is in, without any one to attend them in their sickness—to say a kind word to them, or to hand them even a
drink of clean water, if they wanted it. Them that hasn't
got the fever yet won't go near them, for fear of catchin' it.
What, then, will become of them? There they are, without
the face, or hand, or voice of kindness about them. Oh, what
on God's blessed earth will become of them? They may die
—an' they must die, for want of care and assistance."

"But sure that's not our fault, dear Mave; we can't help
them."

"We can, father—an' we must; if we don't, they'll die.
Father," she added, laying her wasted hand on his; "it is
my intention to go over to them—an' as I have nothing that
I can do at home, to spend the greater part of the day with
them, in taking care of them—an'—an' in doin' what I can
for them. Yes, father dear—it is my intention—for there
is none but me to do for them."

"Saviour of earth, Mave dear, is it mad you are? You,
achora machree, that's dearer to us all than the apple of our
eye, or the pulse of our hearts—to let you into a plague-
house—to let you near the deadly faver that's upon them—
where you'd be sure to catch it; an' then—oh, blessed
Father, Mave, what's come over you, to think of sich a
thing?—ay, or to think that we'd let you expose yourself?
But, poor girl, it's all the goodness and kindness of your
affectionate heart; put it out of your head, however—don't
name it, nor let us hear of it again."

"But, father, it's a duty that our religion teaches us."

"Why, what's come over you, Mave?—all at wanst, too—
you, that was so much afeard of it that you wouldn't go on
the windy side of a feverish house, nor walk near any one
that was even recoverin' from it. Why, what's come over
you?"

"Simply, father, the thought that if I don't go to them
and help them, they will die. I was afeard of the fever,

and I am afeard of it—but am I to let my own foolish fears
prevent me from doin' the part of a Christian to them? Let
us put ourselves in their place—an' who knows—although,
may God forbid!—but it may be our own before the season
passes—suppose it was our own case—an' that all the world
was afeard to come near us, and deserted us—oh, what would
we think of any one, man or woman, that, trustin' in God,
would set their own fears at defiance, an' come to our
relief?"

"Mave, I couldn't think of it; if anything happened you,
an' that we lost you, I never would lay my head down
widout the bitther thought that I had a hand in your
death."

At this moment the mother, who had been in another
room, came into the kitchen—and having listened for a
minute to the subject of their conversation, she immediately
joined her husband—but still with feelings of deep and
almost tearful sympathy for the Daltons.

"It's like her, poor, affectionate girl," she exclaimed,
looking tenderly at her daughter; "but it's a thing, Mave,
we could never think of; so put it out of your head."

She approached her mother, and, seizing her hands, exclaimed,—

"Oh, mother, for the sake of the livin' God, make it our
own case!—think of it—bring it home to you—look into the
frightful state they're in. Are they to die in a Christian
country for want only of some kind person to attend upon
them? Is it not our duty when we know how they are
sufferin'? I cannot rest, nor be at ease; an' I am not
afeard of fever here. You may say that I love young Condy
Dalton, an' that it is on his account I am wishin' to go.
Maybe it is; an' I will now tell you at wanst that I do love
him, and that if it was the worst plague that ever silenced
the noise of life in a whole country, it wouldn't prevent me
from goin' to his relief, nor to the relief of any one belonging to him."

" I knew," said her father, " that was at the bottom of it."

" I do love him," she continued, " an' this is more than ever I had courage to tell you openly before ; but, father, I feel that I am called upon here to go to their assistance, and to see that they don't die from neglect in a Christian country. I have trust an' confidence in the Almighty God. I am not afeard of fever now ; and even if I take it an' die, you both know that I'll die in actin' the part of a Christian girl ; an' what brighter hope could anything bring to us than the happiness that such a death would open to me ? But here I feel that the strength and protection of God is upon me, and I will not die."

" That's all very well, Mave," said her mother ; " but if you took it, and did die—oh, darlin'——"

" In God's name, then, I'll take my chance, an' do the duty that I feel myself called upon to do ; and, father dear, just think for a minute—the thrue Christian doesn't merely forgive the injury, but returns good for evil ; and then, above all things, let us make it our own case. As I said before, if we were as they are—lyin' racked with pain, burnin' with *druth*, the head splittin', the whole strength gone—not able, maybe, to spake, and hardly able to make a sign—too wake ourselves to put a drink to our lips ;—suppose, I say, we wor lyin' in this state, an' that all the world had deserted us—oh, wouldn't we say that any fellow-crature that had the kindness and the courage to come and aid us— wet our lips, raise our heads, and cheer our sinkin' hearts by the sound of their voice alone—oh, wouldn't we say that it was God that in His mercy put it into their heart to come to us, and relieve us, and save us ? "

The mother's feeling gave way at this picture ; and she said, addressing her husband,—

" Jerry, maybe it's right that she should go, bekase, afther all, what if it's God Himself that has put it into her heart ? "

He shook his head, but it was clear that his opposition began to waver.

"Think of the danger," he replied; "think of that. Still, if I thought it was God's own will that was settin' her to it——"

"Father," she replied, "let us do what is right, and lave the rest to God Himself. Surely you aren't afread to trust in *Him?* I may take the fever here at home, without goin' at all, and die; for if it's His blessed will that I should die of it, nothing can save me, let me go or stay where I plaise; and if it's not, it matthers little where I go: His divine grace and goodness will take care of me and protect me. It's to God Himself, then, you're trustin' me, an' that ought to satisfy you."

Her parents looked at each other—then at her; and, with tears in their eyes, as if they had been parting with her as for a sacrifice, they gave a consent, in which that humble confidence in the will of God which constitutes the highest order of piety, was blended with a natural yearning and terror of the heart, lest they were allowing her to place herself rashly within the fatal reach of the contagion which prevailed. Having obtained their permission, she lost very little time in preparing for the task she had proposed to execute. A very small portion of meal, and a little milk, together with one or two jugs for gruel, whey, etc., she put under her cloak; and, after getting the blessing of her parents, and kissing them and the rest of the family, she departed upon her pious—her sublime mission, followed by the tears and earnest prayers of her whole family.

How anomalous, and full of mysterious and inexplicable impulses is the human heart! Mave Sullivan, who, in volunteering to attend at the contagious beds of the unfortunate Daltons, gave a singular and noble proof of the most heroic devotedness, absolutely turned from the common road, on her way to their cabin, rather than meet the funeral of a person who had died of fever, and on one or two occasions kept aloof from men whom she knew to be invalids by the fact of their having handkerchiefs about their heads—a proof, in general, that they had been shaved or blistered, whilst labouring under its severest form.

When she had gone within about a quarter of a mile of her destination, she met two individuals, whose relative position indicated anything but a state of friendly feeling between them. The persons we allude to were Thomas Dalton and the miserable object of his vengeance, Darby Skinadre. Our readers are aware that Sarah caused Darby to accompany her, for safety, to the cabin of the Daltons, as she feared that, should young Dalton again meet him at the head of his mob, and he in such a furious and unsettled state, the hapless miser might fall a victim to his vengeance. No sooner, therefore, had the mealmonger heard Tom's name mentioned by his father, when about to proceed to prison, than he left a dark corner of the cabin, into which he had slunk, and, passing out, easily disappeared, without being noticed, in the state of excitement which prevailed.

The very name of Tom reminded him that he was then in his father's house, and that should he return, and find him there, he might expect little mercy at his hands. Tom, however, amidst the melancholy fatuity under which he laboured, never forgot that he had an account to settle with Skinadre. It ran through his unsettled understanding like a sound thread through a damaged web; for ever and anon his thought and recollection would turn to Peggy Murtagh, and the miser's refusal to give her credit for the food she asked of him. During the early part of that day he had gone about with a halter in his hand, as if seeking some particular individual; and whenever he chanced to be questioned as to his object, he always replied, with a wild and ferocious chuckle,—

"The fellow that killed her!—the fellow that killed her!"

Upon the present occasion, Mave was surprised by meeting him and the miser, whom he must have met accidentally, walking side by side, but in a position which gave fearful intimation of Dalton's purpose respecting him. Around the unfortunate wretch's neck was the halter aforesaid, made into a running noose, whilst, striding beside him, went his wild and formidable companion, holding the end of it in his hand, and eyeing him from time to time with a look of stupid but determined ferocity. Skinadre's appearance and position were ludicrously and painfully helpless. His face was so pale and thin that it was difficult to see, even in those frightful times of sickness and famine, a countenance from which they were more significantly reflected. He was absolutely shrunk up with terror into half his size, his little, thin, corded neck appearing as if it were striving unsuccessfully to work its way down into his trunk, and his small ferret eyes looking about in every direction for some one to extricate him out of the deadly thrall in which he was held. Mave, who had been aware of the enmity which his companion bore him, as well as of its cause, and fearing that the halter was intended to hang the luckless mealman, probably upon the next tree they came to, did not, as many another female would do, avoid or run away from the madman. On the contrary, she approached him with an expression singularly winning and sweet on her countenance, and in a voice of great kindness, laid her hand upon his arm to arrest his attention, and asked him how he did. He paused a moment, and looking upon her with a dull but turbid eye, exclaimed with an insane laugh, pointing, at the same time, to the miser—" This is the fellow that killed her—ha, ha, ha, but I have him now—here he is in the noose—in the noose. Ay, an' I swore it, an' there's another, too, that's to get it, but I won't rob anybody, nor join in that at all—I'll hang him here, though—ha, Skinadre, I have you now."

As he spoke, poor Skinadre received a chuck of the halter which almost brought his tongue out as far as in the throttling process which we have before described.

" Mave, *achora*," said he, looking at her after his recovery from the powerful jerk he had just got, "for the sake of heaven, try an' save my life ; if you don't he'll never let me out of his hands a livin' man."

"Don't be alarmed, Darby," she replied, "poor Tom won't injure you ; so far from that, he'll take the halter from about your neck, an' let you go. Won't you let poor Darby go, Tom ? "

"I will," he replied, "afther I hang him—ha, ha, ha ; 'twas he that killed her ; he let her die wid hunger, but now he'll swing for it, ha, ha, ha ! "

These words were accompanied by another chuck, which pulled miserable Skinadre almost off his legs.

"Tom, for shame ! " said Mave, "why would you do sich an unmanly thing with this poor ould crature ?—be a man, and let him go."

"Ay, when he's hangin', wid his tongue out, ha, ha, ha ; wait till we get to the Rabbit Bank, where there's a tree to be had ; I've sworn it, ay, on her very grave, too ; so good-bye, Mave ! Come along, Darby."

"Mave, as you hope to have the gates of heaven opened to your sowl, don't lave me," exclaimed the miser, with clasped hands.

Mave looked up and down the road, but could perceive no one approach who might render the unfortunate man assistance.

"Tom," said she, "I must insist upon your settin' the poor man at liberty ; I insist upon it. You cannot, an' must not take his life in a Christian country ; if you do, you know you'll be hanged yourself. Let him go immediately."

"Oh, ay," he replied, "you insist, Mave—but I'll tell you what,—I'll put Peggy in a coach yet, when I come into my fortune ; an' so you'll insist, will you ;—just look at that wrist of yours," he replied, seizing hers, but with gentleness, "and then look at that of mine ; an' now will you tell me that you'll insist ? Come, Darby, we're bound for the Bank ; there's not a beech there but's a hundre' feet high, and that's higher than ever I'll make you swing from. Your heart bled for her, didn't it? but how will you look when I lave you facin' the sun, wid your tongue out!"

"Tom," replied the wretch, "I go on my knees to you, an' as you hope, Tom——"

"Hope, you hard-hearted hound! isn't her father's curse upon me? ay, an' in me? wasn't she destroyed among us? and you bid me hope; by the broken heart she died of, you'll get a double tug for that," and he was about to drag him on in a state of great violence, when Mave again placed her hand upon his arm and said,—

"I am sure, Tom, you are not ungrateful; I am sure you would not forget a kind act done to poor Peggy that's gone."

"Peggy!" he replied, "what about her? gone—Peggy gone—is she gone?"

"She is gone," replied Mave, "but not lost; an' it is most likely that she is now lookin' down with displeasure at your conduct and intentions towards this poor man; but listen."

"Are you goin' to spake about Peggy, though?"

"I am, and listen. Do you remember one evenin' in the early part of this summer, it was of a Sunday, there was a crowd about ould Brian Murtagh's house, and the report of Peggy's shame had gone abroad, and couldn't be kept from people's eyes any longer. She was turned out of her father's house—she was beaten by her brother, who swore that he would take the life of the first person, whether man or woman, young or old, that would give her one hour's shelter. She was turned out, poor, young, misled, and mistaken creature, and no one would resave her, for no one durst. There was a young girl then passin' through the village, on her way home, much about Peggy's own age, but barrin' in one respect, neither so good nor so handsome; poor Peggy ran to that young girl, and she was goin' to throw herself into her arms, but she stopped. 'I am not worthy,' she said, cryin' bitterly—'I am not worthy; but, oh, I have no roof to shelter me, for no one dares to take me in. What will become of me ? ' "

While she spoke, Dalton's mind appeared to have been stirred into something like a consciousness of his situation, and his memory to have been brought back, as it were, from the wild and turbulent images which had impaired its efficacy, to a personal recollection of circumstances that had ceased to affect him. His features, for instance, became more human, his eye more significant of his feelings, and his whole manner more quiet and restored. He looked upon the narrator with an awakened interest, surveyed Darby as if he scarcely knew how or why he came there, and then sighed deeply.

" ' I am an outcast now,' said poor Peggy ; ' I have neither house nor home ; I have no father, no mother, no brother, an' he that I loved, an' that said he loved me, has desarted me. Oh,' said she, 'I have nothing to care for, an' nobody to care for me now, an' what was dearest of all—my good name—is gone : no one will shelter me, although I thought of nothing but my love for Tom Dalton ! ' She was scorned, Tom Dalton, she was insulted and abused by women who knew her innocence and her goodness till she met him ; every tongue was against her, every hand was against her, every door was closed against her ; no, not every one—the young woman she spoke to, with tears in her eyes, out of compassion to one so young and unfortunate, brought Peggy Murtagh home, and cried with her, and gave her hope, and consoled her, and pleaded with her father and mother for the poor deluded girl in sich a way that they forgot her misfortune and sheltered her, till, afther her brother's death, she was taken in again to her own father's house. Now, Tom, wouldn't you like to oblige that girl that was kind to poor Peggy Murtagh ? "

" It was in Jerry Sullivan's—it was into your father's house she was taken."

" It was, Tom ; and the young woman who befriended

Peggy Murtagh, is now standin' by your side, and asks you to let Darby Skinadre go ; do, then, let him go, for the sake of that young woman ! "

Mave, on concluding, looked up into his face, and saw that his eyes were moist ; he then smiled moodily, and placing his hand upon her head in an approving manner, said,—

" You wor always good, Mave—here, set Darby free ; but my mind's unaisy ; I'm not right, I doubt, nor as I ought to be ; but I'll tell you what—I'll go back towards home wid you, if you'll tell me more about Peggy."

" Do so," she replied, delighted at such a proposal ; " an' I will tell you many a thing about her ; an' you, Darby ——" she added, turning round to that individual. Short, however, as the time was, the exulting but still trembling usurer was making his way, at full speed, towards his own house ; so that she was spared the trouble of advising him, as she had intended, to look to his safety as well as he could. Such was the gentle power with which Mave softened and sub-dued to her wishes this ferocious and unsettled young man ; and, indeed, so forcible in general was her firm but serene enthusiasm, that wherever the necessity for exerting it occurred, it was always crowned with success.

Thomas Dalton, as might be expected, swayed by the capricious impulses of his unhappy derangement, did not accompany her to his father's cabin. When within a few hundred yards of it, he changed his intention, and struck across the country like one who seemed uncertain as to the course he should take. Of late, indeed, he rambled about, sometimes directing, or otherwise associating himself with, such mobs as we have described ; sometimes wandering, in a solitary manner, throughout the country at large ; and but seldom appearing at home. On the present occasion he looked at Mave, and said,—

" I hate sick people, Mave, an' I won't go home ; but, whisper, when you see Peggy Murtagh's father, tell him that I'll have her in a coach yet, plaise God ; an' he'll take the curse off o' me, when he hears it, maybe, an' all will be right."

He then bid her good-bye, turned from the road, and bent his steps in the direction of the Rabbit Bank, on one of the beeches of which he had intended to hang the miser.

CHAPTER XXIV

RIVALRY

IF the truth were known, the triumph which Mave Sullivan achieved over the terror of fever, which she felt in common with almost every one in the country around her, was the result of such high-minded devotion, as would have won her a statue in the times of old Greece, when self-sacrifice for human good was appreciated and rewarded. In her case, indeed, the triumph was one of almost unparalleled heroism; for amongst all the difficulties which she had to overcome, by far the greatest was her own constitutional dread of contagion. It was only on reaching the miserable pest-house in which the Daltons lived, and on witnessing, with her own eyes, the clammy atmosphere which, in the shape of dark heavy smoke, was oozing in all directions from its roof, that she became conscious of the almost fatal step she was about to take, and the terrible test of Christian duty, and exalted affection, to which she was in the act of subjecting herself.

On arriving at the door, and when about to enter, even the resolution she had come to, and the lofty principle of trust in God, on which it rested, were scarcely able to support her against the host of constitutional terrors, which, for a moment, rushed upon her heart. The great act of self-sacrifice, as it may almost be termed, which she was about to perform, became so diminished in her imagination, that all sense of its virtue passed away; and instead of gaining strength from a consciousness of the pure and unselfish motive by which she was actuatad, she began to contemplate her conduct as the result of a rash and unjustifiable presumption upon the providence of God, and a wanton exposure of the life he had given her. She felt herself tremble ; her heart palpitated, and for a minute or two her whole soul became filled with a tumultuous and indistinct perception of all she had proposed to do, as well as of everything about her. Gradually, however, this state of feeling cleared away; by-and-by the purity and Christian principle that were involved in her conduct, came to her relief.

" What," she asked herself, " if they should die without assistance ? In God's name, and with His strength to aid me, I will run all risks, and fulfil the task I have taken upon me to do. May He support and protect me through it ! "

Thus resolved, and thus fortified, she entered the gloomy scene of sickness and contagion.

There were but four persons within : that is to say, her lover, his sister Nancy, Mary, the invalid, and Sarah M'Gowan. Nancy and her brother were now awake, and poor Mary occupied her father's arm-chair, in which she sat with her head reclined upon the back of it, somewhat, indeed, after his own fashion ; and Sarah sat opposite young Con's bed, having her eye fixed, with a mournful expression, on his pale and almost death-like countenance. Mave's appearance occasioned the whole party to feel much surprise, and Mary rose from her arm-chair, and greeting her affectionately said,—

" I cannot welcome you, dear Mave, to sich a place as this, and indeed I am sorry you came to see us ; for I needn't tell you what I'd feel—what we'd all feel," and here she looked quickly, but with the slightest possible significance, at her brother, " if anything happened you in consequence ; which may God forbid ! How are you all at home ? "

" We are all free from sickness, thank God," said Mave, whom the presence of Sarah caused to blush deeply ; " but how are you all here ? I am sorry to find that poor Nancy is ill, and that Con has got a relapse."

She turned her eyes upon him as she spoke, and, on contemplating his languid and sickly countenance, she could only by a great effort repress her tears."

"Do not come near us, dear Mave," said he, "and, indeed, it was wrong to come here at all.

"God bless you an' guard you, Mave," said Nancy, "an' we feel your goodness; but, as Con says, it was wrong to put yourself in the way of danger; for God's sake, and as you hope to escape this terrible sickness, lave the house at wanst. We're sensible of your kindness: but lave us—lave us—for every minute you stop may be death to you."

Sarah, who had never yet spoken to Mave, turned her black mellow eyes from her to her lover, and from him to her alternately. She then dropped them for a time on the ground, and again looked round her with something like melancholy impatience. Her complexion was high and flushed, and her eyes sparkled with unaccustomed brilliancy.

"It's not right that two people should run sich risk on our account," said Con, looking towards Sarah; "here's a young woman who has come to nurse-tend and take care of us, for which, may God bless her and protect her!—it's Sarah M'Gowan, Donnel Dhu's daughter."

"Think of Mave Sullivan," said Sarah, "think only of Mave Sullivan; she's in danger—ha—but as for me—suppose I should take the faver and die?"

"May God forbid, poor girl," exclaimed Con; "it would lave us all a sad heart. Dear Mave, don't stop here—every minute is dangerous."

Sarah went over to the bedside, and putting her hand gently upon his forehead, said,—

"Don't spake to pity me—I can't bear pity; anything at all but pity from you. Say you don't care what becomes of me, or whether I die or not—but don't pity me."

It is extremely difficult to describe Sarah's appearance and state of mind, as she spoke this. Her manner towards Con was full of tenderness, and the most earnest and anxious

interest ; whilst at the same time there ran through her voice
a tone of bitter feeling, an evident consciousness of something
that pressed strongly on her heart, which gave a marked and
startling character to her language.

Mave for a moment forgot everything but the interest
which Sarah, and the mention of her, excited. She turned
gently round from Mary, who had been speaking to her, and
fixing her eyes on Sarah, examined her with pardonable curiosity, from head to foot ; nor will she be blamed, we trust,
if, even then and there, the scrutiny was not the less close,
in consequence of its having been known to her, that, in point
of beauty and symmetry of figure, they had stood towards
each other, for some time past, in the character of rivals.
Sarah, who had on, without stockings, a pair of small slip-
pers, a good deal the worse for wear, had risen from the bedside, and now stood near the fire, directly opposite the only
little window in the house, and, consequently, in the best
light it afforded. Mave's glance, though rapid, was comprehensive ; but she felt it was sufficient ; the generous girl, on
contemplating the wild grace and natural elegance of Sarah's
figure, and the singular beauty and wonderful animation of
her features, instantly, in her own mind, surrendered all
claim to competition, and admitted to herself that Sarah was,
without exception, the most perfectly beautiful girl she had
ever seen. Her last words, too, and the striking tone in
which they were spoken, arrested her attention still more
so that she passed naturally from the examination of her
person to the purport of her language.

This examination of Sarah, upon the part of Mave Sullivan,
was altogether an involuntary act, and one which occurred in
less time than we have taken to write any one of the lines in
which it is described.

Mave, who perceived at once that the words of Sarah were
burdened by some peculiar distress, could not prevent her
admiration from turning into pity, without exactly knowing
why ; but in consequence of what Sarah had just said, she

feared to express it, either by word or look, lest she might occasion her unnecessary pain. She consequently, after a slight pause, replied to her lover,—

"You must not blame me, dear Con, for being here. I came to give whatever poor attendance I could to Nancy, here, and to sich of ¦you as want it, while you're sick. I came, indeed, to stay and nurse you all, if you will let me ; an' you won't be sorry to hear it, in spite of all that has happened, that I have the consent of my father an' mother for so doin'."

A faint smile of satisfaction lit up her lover's features, but this was soon overshadowed by his apprehension for her safety.

Sarah, who had for about half-a-minute been examining Mave, on her part, now started, and exclaimed, with flashing eyes, and we may add, a bursting and distracted heart,—

"Well, Mave Sullivan, I have often seen you, but never so well as now. You have goodness an' truth in your face. Oh, it's a purty face—a lovely face. But why do you state a falsehood here ?—for what you've just said is false ; I know it."

Mave started, and in a moment her pale face and neck were suffused by one burning blush, at the idea of such an imputation. She looked around her, as if inquiring from all those who were present the nature of the falsehood attributed to her ; and then with a calm but firm eye, she asked Sarah what she could mean by such language.

"You're afther sayin'," replied Sarah, " that you're come here to nurse Nancy there. Now, that's not true, and you know it isn't. You came here to nurse young Con Dalton ; and you came to nurse him bekase you love him. Now, I don't blame you for that, but I do for not sayin' so, without fear or disguise—for I hate both."

"That wouldn't be altogether true either," replied Mave, " if I said so ; for I did come to nurse Nancy, and any others of the family that might stand in need of it. As to Con,

I'm neither ashamed to love him nor afeard to acknowledge it; and I had no notion of statin' a falsehood when I said what I did. I tell you, then, Sarah M'Gowan, that you've done me injustice. If there appeared to be a falsehood in my words, there was none in my heart."

" That's truth; I know, I feel that that's truth," replied Sarah, quickly; " but oh, how wrong I am," she exclaimed, " to mention that or anything else here that might distract him! Ay," she proceeded, addressing Mave, " I did you injustice—I feel I did; but don't be angry with me, for I acknowledge it."

" Why should I be angry with you?" replied Mave, "you only spoke what you thought, an' this, by all accounts, is what you always do."

" Let us talk as little as possible here," replied Sarah, the whole absorbing object of whose existence lay in Dalton's recovery. " I will speak to you on your way home, but not here—not here;" and whilst uttering the last words she pointed to Dalton, to intimate that further conversation might disturb him.

" Dear Mave," observed Mary, now rising from the chair, " you are stayin' too long; oh, for God's sake, don't stop; you can't dhrame of the danger you're in."

" But," replied Mave, calmly, " you know, Mary, that I came to stop and to do whatever I can do till the family comes round. You are too feeble to undertake anything, and might only get into a relapse if you attempted it."

" But then we have Sarah M'Gowan," she replied, " who came, as few would—none livin' this day, I think, barrin' yourself and her—to stay with us, and to do anything that she can do for us all. May God for ever bless her! for short as the time is, I think she has saved some of our lives— Condy's, without a doubt."

Mave turned towards Sarah, and, as she looked upon her, the tears started to her eyes.

" Sarah M'Gowan," said she, " you are fond of truth, an'

you are right; I can't find words to thank you for doin' what you did. God bless and reward you!"

She extended her hand as she spoke, but Sarah put it back. "No," said she, indignantly, "never from you; above all that's livin', don't you thank me. You, you, why you aren't his wife yet," she exclaimed, in a suppressed voice of deep agitation, "an' maybe you never will. You don't know what may happen—you don't know——"

She immediately seemed to recollect something that operated as a motive to restrain any exhibition of strong feeling or passion on her part, for all at once she composed herself, and sitting down, merely said,—

"Mave Sullivan, I'm glad you love truth, and I believe you do; I can't, then, resave any thanks from you, nor I won't; an' I would tell you why any place but here."

"I don't at all understand you," replied Mave, "but for your care an' attention to him, I'm sure it's no harm to say, may God reward you! I will never forget it to you."

"While I have life," said Dalton, feebly, and fixing his eyes upon Sarah's face, "I, for one, won't forget her kindness."

"Kindness!" she re-echoed—"ha, ha!—well, it's no matter—it's no matter!"

"She saved my life, Mave; I was lyin' here, an' hadn't even a drink of water, an' there was no one else in the house; Mary, there, was out, an' poor Nancy was ravin' an' ragin' with illness an' pain; but she, Sarah, was here to settle us, to attend to us, to get us a drink whenever we wanted it— to raise us up, an' to put it to our lips, an' to let us down with as little pain as possible. Oh, how could I forget all this? Dear, dear Sarah, how could I forget this, if I was to live a thousand years?"

Con's face, whilst he spoke, became animated with the enthusiasm of the feeling to which he gave utterance, and, as his eyes were fixed on Sarah with a suitable expression, there appeared to be a warmth of emotion in his whole manner which a sanguine person might probably interpret into something beyond gratitude.

Sarah, after he had concluded, looked upon him with a long, earnest, but uncertain gaze; so long, indeed, and so intensely penetrating was it, that the whole energy of her character might, for a time, be read clearly in the singular expression of her eyes. It was evident that her thoughts were fluctuating between pleasure and pain, cheerfulness and gloom; but at length her countenance lost, by degrees, its earnest character, the alternate play of light and shadow over it ceased, and the gaze changed, almost imperceptibly, into one of settled abstraction.

"It might be," she said, as if thinking aloud—"it might be—but time will tell; and, in the manetime, everything must be done fairly—fairly; still, if it shouldn't come to pass —if it should not—it would be betther if I had never been born; but it may be, an' time will tell."

Mave had watched her countenance closely, and without being able to discover the nature of the conflict that appeared in it, she went over, and, placing her hand gently upon Sarah's arm, exclaimed,—

"Don't blame me for what I am goin' to say, Sarah—if you'll let me call you Sarah; but the truth is, I see that your mind is troubled. I wish to God I could remove that trouble, or that any one here could! I am sure they all would, as willingly as myself."

"She is troubled," said Mary; "I know by her manner that there's something distressin' on her mind. Any earthly thing that we could do to relieve her, we would; but I asked her, an' she wouldn't tell me."

It is likely that Mary's kindness, and especially Mave's, so gently but so sincerely expressed, touched her as they spoke. She made no reply, however, but approached Mave with a slight smile on her face, her lips compressed, and her eyes, which were fixed and brilliant, floating in something that looked like moisture, and which might as well have been

occasioned by the glow of anger as the impulse of a softer
emotion, or perhaps—and this might be nearer the truth—
as a conflict between the two states of feeling. For some
moments she looked into Mave's very eyes; and after a little,
she seemed to regain her composure, and sat down without
speaking. There was a slight pause occasioned by the expectation that she had been about to reply, during which
Dalton's eyes were fixed upon her. In her evident distress,
she looked upon him. Their eyes met, and the revelation
that that glance of anguish, on the part of Sarah, gave to
him, disclosed the secret.

"Oh, my God!" he exclaimed, involuntarily and unconsciously, "is this possible?"

Sarah felt that the discovery had been made by him at
last; and seeing that all their eyes were still upon her, she
rose up, and, approaching Mave, said,—

"It is true, Mave Sullivan, I am troubled—Mary, I am
troubled;" and, as she uttered the words, a blush so deep
and so beautiful spread itself over her face and neck, that the
very females present were, for the moment, lost in admiration
of her radiant youth and loveliness. Dalton's eyes were still
upon her, and, after a little time, he said,—

"Sarah, come to me."

She went to his bedside, and, kneeling, bent her exquisite
figure over him, and, as her dark, brilliant eyes looked into
his, he felt the fragrance of her breath mingling with his own.

"What is it?" said she.

"You are too near me," said he.

"Ah, I feel I am," she said, shaking her head.

"I mane," he added, "for your own safety. Give me your
hand, dear Sarah."

He took her hand, and, raising himself a little on his right
side, he looked upon her again; and, as he did so, she felt a
few warm tears falling upon it.

"Now," he said, "lay me down, dear Sarah."

A few moments of ecstatic tumult, in which Sarah was unconscious of anything about her, passed. She then rose, and, sitting down on the little stool, she wept for some minutes in silence. During this quiet paroxysm no one spoke; but when Dalton turned his eyes upon Mave Sullivan, she was pale as ashes.

Mary, who had noticed nothing particular in the incidents just related, now urged Mave to depart; and the latter, on exchanging glances with Dalton, could perceive that a feeble hectic had overspread his face. She looked on him earnestly for a moment, then paused as if in thought, and, going round to his bedside, knelt down, and, taking his hand, said,—

"Con, if there's any earthly thing that I can do to give ease and comfort to you mind, I am ready to do it. If it would relieve you, forget that you ever saw me, or ever—ever—knew me at all. Suppose I am not living—that I am dead. I say this, dear Con, to relieve you from any pain or distress of mind that you may feel on my account. Believe me, I feel everything for you, an' nothing now for myself. Whatever you do, I tell you that a harsh word or thought from me you will never have."

Mave, whilst she spoke, did not shed a tear; nor was her calm, sweet voice indicative of any extraordinary emotion. Sarah, who had been weeping until the other began to speak, now rose up, and, approaching Mave, said,—

"Go, Mave Sullivan—go out of this dangerous house; an' you, Condy Dalton, heed not what she has said. Mave Sullivan, I think I understand your words, an' they make me ashamed of myself, an' of the thoughts that has been troublin' me. Oh, what am I, when compared to you?—nothing—nothing."

Mave had, on entering, deposited the little matters she had brought for their comfort; and Mary now came over, and placing her hand on her shoulder, said,—

"Sarah is right, dear Mave; for God's sake, do not stay here. Oh, think—only think if you tuck this faver, an' that anything happened you."

" Come," said Sarah, " lave this dangerous place ; I will see you part of the way home—you can do nothing here that I won't do, and everything that I can do will be done."

Her lover's eyes had been fixed upon her, and with a feeble voice—for the agitation had exhausted him—he added his solicitations for her departure to theirs.

" I hope I will soon be betther, dear Mave, and able to get up too—but may God bless you and take care of you till then ! "

Mave again went round, and took his hand, on which he felt a few tears fall.

" I came, dear Con," she said, " to take care of you all, and why need I be ashamed to say so—to do all I could for yourself. Sarah here wishes me to spake the truth an' why shouldn't I ? Think of my words then, Con, and don't let me or the thoughts o' me occasion you one moment's unhappiness. To see you happy is all the wish I have in this world."

She then bade him and them an affectionate farewell, and was about to take her departure, when Sarah, who had been musing for a moment, went to Dalton, and having knelt on one knee, was about to speak, and to speak, as was evident from her manner, with great earnestness, when she suddenly restrained herself, clasped her hands with a vehement action, looked distractedly from him to Mave, and then suddenly rising, took Mave's hand and said—

" Come away—it's dangerous to stop where this faver is— *you* ought to be careful of yourself—you have friends that loves you, and that would feel for you if you were gone. You have a kind, good father—a lovin' mother—a lovin' mother, that you could turn to, an' may turn to, if ever you should have a sore heart—a mother—oh, that blessed word—what wouldn't I gave to say that I have a mother ? Many an outrage—many a wild fit of passion—many a harsh word too—oh, what mightn't I be now if I had a mother ! All the world thinks I have a bad heart—that I'm wicked—

that I'm without feelin'; but, indeed, Mave Sullivan, I am not without feelin', an' I don't think I have a bad heart."

"You have not a bad heart," replied Mave, taking her hand; "no one, dear Sarah, could look into your face and say so; no, but I think so far from that, your heart is both kind and generous."

"I hope so," she replied, "I hope I have—now come—and lave this dangerous house; besides I have something to say to you."

Mave and she proceeded along the old causeway that led to the cabin, and having got out on the open road, Sarah stood.

"Now, Mave Sullivan," said she, "listen—you do me only justice to say that I love truth, an' hate a lie or consalement of any kind. I ax you now this—you discovered awhile ago that I love Condy Dalton? Isn't that thrue?"

"I wasn't altogether certain," replied Mave; "but I thought I did—an' I now think you do love him."

"I do love him—oh, I do—an' why, as you said, should I be ashamed of it?—ay, an' it was my intention to tell you so the first time I'd see you, an' to give you fair notice that I did, an' that I'd lave nothing undone to win him from you."

"Well," replied the other, "this is open and honest at all events."

"That was my intention," pursued Sarah; "an' I had for a short time, other thoughts—ay, an' worse thoughts; my father was persuadin' me—but I can't spake on that—for he has my promise not to do so. Oh, I'm nothing, dear Mave —nothing at all to you. I can't forget your words awhile ago—bekase I knew what you meant at the time, when you said to Con, 'any earthly thing that I can do to give aise an' comfort to your mind I am ready to do it. If it would relieve you, forget that you ever saw me or ever knew me.' Now, Mave, I've confessed to you that I love Con Dalton— but I tell you not to trouble your heart by any thoughts of me, my mind's made up as to what I'll do—don't fear me,

I'll never cross you here. I'm a lonely creature," she proceeded, bursting into bitter tears—" I'm without friends or relations, or any one that cares at all about me——"

" Don't say so," replied Mave, " I care about you, an' it's only now that the people is beginnin' to know you—but that's not all, Sarah, if it's any consolation to you to know it— know it—Condy Dalton loves you; ay, loves you, Sarah M'Gowan; you may take my word for that—I am certain this day that what I say is true."

" Loves me !" she exclaimed.

" Loves you," repeated Mave, " is the word, and I have said it."

" I didn't suspect that when I spoke," she replied.

Each looked upon the other, and both as they stood were pale as death itself. At length Mave spoke—

" I have one only thought, Sarah, an' that is, how to make him happy—to see him happy."

" I can scarcely spake," replied Sarah; " I wouldn't know what to say if I did. I'm all confused; Mave dear, forgive me ! "

" God bless you," replied Mave, " for you are truth an' honesty itself. God bless you, an' make him happy ! Goodbye, dear Sarah."

She put her hand into Sarah's, and felt that it trembled excessively—but Sarah was utterly passive, she did not even return the pressure which she had received, and when Mave departed, she was standing in a reverie incapable of thought, deadly pale, and perfectly motionless.

CHAPTER XXV

SARAH WITHOUT HOPE

How Sarah returned to Dalton's cabin, she herself knew not. Such was the tumult which the communication then made to her by Mave had occasioned in her mind, that the

scene which had just taken place altogether appeared to her
excited spirit like a troubled dream, whose impressions were
too unreal and deceptive to be depended on for a moment.
The reaction from the passive state in which Mave had left
her, was, to a temperament like hers, perfectly overwhelm-
ing. Her pulse beat high, her cheek burned, and her eye
flashed with more than its usual fire and overpowering brilliancy, and, with the exception of one impression alone, all
her thoughts were so rapid and indistinct as to resemble the
careering clouds which fly in tumult and confusion along the
troubled sky, with nothing stationary but the sun far above,
and which, in this case, might be said to resemble the bright
conviction of Dalton's love for her, that Mave's assurance
had left behind it. On re-entering the cabin, without being
properly conscious of what she either did or said, she once
more knelt by the side of Dalton's bed, and hastily taking
his unresisting hand, was about to speak; but a difficulty
how to shape her language held her in a painful and troubled
suspense for some moments, during which Dalton could
plainly perceive the excitement or rather rapture by which
she was actuated. At length, a gush of hot and burning
tears enabled her to speak, and she said—

"Con Dalton—dear Con, is it true?—can it be true?—oh,
no—no—but then she says it—is it true that you like me
—like me!—no, no—that word is too wake—is it true that
you love me?—but no—it can't be—there never was so much
happiness intended for me; and then, if it should be true—
oh, if it was possible, how will I bear it?—what will I do?
—what—what is to be the consequence?—for my love for
you is beyond all belief—beyond all that tongue could tell.
I can't stand this struggle—my head is giddy—I scarcely
know what I'm sayin'—or is it a dhrame that I'll waken
from, and find it false—false?"

Dalton pressed her hand, and looking tenderly upon her
face, replied—

"Dear Sarah, forgive me; your dhrame is both true and

false. It is true that I like you—that I pity you.; but you
forbid me to say that; well, it is true, I say, that I like you,
but I can't say more. The only girl I love in the sense *you*
mane, is Mave Sullivan. I could not tell you an untruth,
Sarah; nor don't desave yourself. I like you, but I love
her."

She started up, and in an instant dashed the tears from
her cheeks; after which she said—

"I am glad I know it; you have said the truth—the bitther truth—ay, bitther it will prove, Condy Dalton, to more
than me. My happiness in this world is now over for ever.
I never was happy; an' it's clear that the doom is against
me; I never will be happy. I am now free to act as I like.
No matther what I do, it cannot make me feel more than I
feel now. I might take a life—ay, twenty, an' I couldn't feel
more miserable than I am. Then, what is there to prevent
me from workin' out my own will, an' doin' what my father
wishes? I may make myself worse an' guiltier, but unhap-
pier I cannot be. That poor, weak hope was all I had in
this world; but that hope is gone, an' I have no other hope
now."

"Compose yourself, dear Sarah; calm yourself," said Dalton.

"Don't call me dear Sarah," she replied; "you were
wrong ever to do so. Oh, why was I born? an' what has
this world an' this life been to me but hardship an' sorrow?
But still," she added, drawing herself up, "I will let you all
see what pride can do. I now know my fate, and what I
must suffer; an' if one tear would gain your love, I wouldn't
shed it—never, never."

"Sarah," said Mary, in a soothing voice, "I hope you
won't blame poor Con. You don't know, maybe, that himself an' Mave Sullivan has loved one another ever since they
were——"

"No more about Mave Sullivan," she replied, almost
fiercely; "lave her to me. As for me, I'll not brake my

word either for good or evil; I was never the one to do an ungenerous—an ungenerous—no——" She paused, however, as if struck by some latent conviction that pressed upon her conscience, and in a panting voice, she added, "I must lave you for awhile, but I will be back in an hour or two—oh, yes, I will—an' in the mean time, Mary, anything that is to be done, you can do it for me till I come agin. Mave Sullivan!—lave Mave Sullivan to me!"

She then threw an humble garment about her, and in a few minutes was on her way to have an interview with her father. On reaching home she found that he had arrived only a few minutes before, and to her surprise he expressed something like good humour, or, perhaps, gratification at her presence there. On looking into her face more closely, how- ever, he had little trouble in perceiving that something ex- traordinary had disturbed her. He then glanced at Nelly, who, as usual, sat gloomily by the fire, knitting her brows, and groaning with suppressed ill-temper, as she had been in the habit of doing ever since she suspected that Donnel had made a certain disclosure, connected with her, to Sarah.

"Well," said he, "has there been another battle?—have you been *ding dust* at it as usual? What's wrong, Sally?— eh? Did it go to blows wid you, for you look raised?"

"You're all out of it," replied Nelly, "her blood's up now —an' I'm not prepared for a sudden death. She's dangerous this minute, an' I'll take care of her. Blessed man, look at her eyes."

She repeated these words with that kind of low, dogged ridicule and scorn which so frequently accompany stupid and wanton brutality; and which are, besides, provoking almost beyond endurance, when the mind is chafed by considerations of an exciting nature.

Sarah flew like lightning to the old knife, which we have already mentioned, and snatching it from the shelf of the dresser on which it lay, exclaimed—

"I have now no earthly thought, nor any hope of good in

this world, to keep my hand from evil; an' for all ever you made me suffer, take this——"

Her father had not yet sat down, and it was indeed well that he had not; for it required all his activity and strength united, to intercept the meditated blow, by seizing his daughter's arm.

"Sarah," said he, "what is this?—are you mad, you murdhering jade, to attempt the vagabond's life?—for she is a vagabond, and an ill-tongued vagabond. Why do you provoke the girl by sich language, you double-distilled ould sthrap? You do nothing but growl, an' snarl, an' curse, an' pray—ay, pray, from mornin' to night, in sich a way, that the very devil himself couldn't bear you, or live with you. Begone out o' this, or I'll let her at you; an' I'll engage she'll give you what'll settle you."

Nelly rose, and putting on her cloak, went out.

"I'm goin'," she replied, looking at and addressing the Prophet; "an' plaise God, before long I'll have the best wish o' my heart fulfilled, by seein' you hanged; but, until then, may my curse, an' the curse o' God, light on you and pursue you. I know you have tould her everything, or she wouldn't act towards me as she has done of late."

Sarah stood like the Pythoness, in a kind of savage beauty, with the knife firmly grasped in her hand.

"I'm glad she's gone," she said; "but it is not her, father, that I ought to rise my hand against."

"Who, then, Sarah?" he asked with something like surprise.

"You asked me," she proceeded, "to assist in a plan to have Mave Sullivan carried off by Young Dick o' the Grange —I'm now ready for anything, an' I'll do it. This world, father, has nothing good or happy in it for me—now I'll be aiquil to it; if it gives me nothing good, it'll get nothing good out of me. I'll give it blow for blow; kindness, good fortune, if it was to happen—but it can't now—would soften me; but I know, an' I feel that ill-treatment, crosses, disappointments, an' want of all hope in this life, has made, an' will make me a devil—ay, an' oh! what a different girl I might be this day!"

"What has vexed you?" asked the father; "for I see that something has."

"Isn't it a cruel thing," she proceeded, without seeming to have attended to him; "isn't it a cruel thing to think that every one you see about you has some happiness except yourself; an' that your heart is burstin', an' your brain burnin', and no relief for you: no one point to turn to for consolation—but everything dark and dismal, and fiery about you!"

"I felt all this, myself," said the Prophet; "so don't be disheartened, Sarah; in the coorse o' time your heart will get so hardened that you'll laugh at the world—ay, at all that's either bad or good in it, as I do."

"I never wish to come to that state," she replied; "an' you never felt what I feel—you never had that much of what was good in your heart. No," she proceeded, "sooner than come to that state—that is, to your state—I'd put this knife into my heart, father. You never loved one of your own kind yet."

"Didn't I?" he replied, whilst his eyes lightened into a glare like those of a provoked tiger; "ay, I loved one of our kind—of your kind; loved her—ay, an' was happy wid her—oh, how happy. Ay, Sarah M'Gowan, an' I loved my fellow-creatures then, too, like a fool as I was: loved, ay, loved; an' she that I so loved, proved false to me—proved an adulteress; an' I tell you now, that it may harden your heart against the world, that that woman—my wife—that I so loved, an' that so disgraced me, was your mother."

"It's a lie—it's as false as the devil himself," she replied, turning round quickly, and looking him, with frantic vehemence of manner, in the face. "My mother never did what you say. She's now in her grave, an' can't spake for or defend herself; but if I was to stand here till judgment-day, I'd say it was false. You were misled or mistaken, or your

own bad, suspicious nature made you do her wrong; an'
even if it was thrue—which it is not, but false as hell—why
would you crush and wring her daughter's heart by a knowledge of it? Couldn't you let me get through the short but
bitther passage of life that's before me, without addin' this to
the other thoughts that's distractin' me?"

"I did it, as I said," he replied, "to make you harden
your heart, an' to prevent you from puttin' any trust in the
world, or expectin' anything either of thruth or goodness
from it."

She started, as if some new light had broken in upon her,
and turning to him, said—

"Maybe I undherstand you, father—I hope I do. Oh,
could it be that you wor wanst a—a—a betther man—a man
that had a heart for your fellow-creatures, and cared for
them? I'm lookin' into my own heart now, and I don't
doubt but I might be brought to the same state yet. Ha,
that's terrible to think of; but again, I can't believe it.
Father, you can stoop to lies and falsity—that I could not
do; but no matther; you wor wanst a good man, maybe.
Am I right?"

The Prophet turned round, and fixing his eyes upon his
daughter, they stood each gazing upon the other for some
time. He then looked for a moment on the ground, after
which he sat down upon a stool, and covering his face with
both his hands, remained in that position for two or three
minutes.

"Am I right, father?" she repeated.

He raised his eyes, and looking upon her with his usual
composure, replied—

"No—you are wrong—you are very wrong. When I
was an innocent child I was a villain. When I was a light-
hearted affectionate boy, playing with my brothers and
sisters, I was a villain. When I grew into youth, Sarah,
an' thought every one full of honesty an' truth, an' the
world all kindness, an' nothing about me but goodness,

an' generosity, an' affection, I was, of coorse, a villain.
When I loved the risin' sun—when I looked upon the stars
of heaven with a wonderin' and happy heart—when the
dawn of mornin' and the last light of the summer evening
filled me with joy, and made me love every one and everything about me—the trees, the runnin' rivers, the green
fields, and all that God—ha, what am I sayin'?—I was a
villain.   When I loved an' married your mother, an' when
she—but no matther—when all these things happened, I
was, I say, a villain ; but now that things is changed for the
betther, I am an honest man ! "

"Father, there is good in you yet," she said, as her eye
sparkled in the very depth of her excitement, with a hopeful
animation that had its source in a noble and exalted benevolence, " you're not lost."

" Don't I say," he replied, with a cold and bitter sneer,
" that I am an honest man ? "

"Ah," she replied, " that's gone too, then—look where I
will, everything's dark—no hope—no hope of any kind; but
no matther now ; since I can't do betther, I'll make them
think o' me, ay, an' feel me, too. Come, then, what have
you to say to me ? "

" Let us have a walk, then," replied her father. " There
is a *weeny* glimpse of sunshine, for a wondher. You look
heated—your face is flushed too, very much, an' the walk
will cool you a little."

" I know my face is flushed," she replied, " for I feel it
burnin,' an' so is my head ; I have a pain in it, and a pain in
the small o' my back too."

" Well, come," he continued, " and a walk will be of sar-
vice to you."

They then went out in the direction of the Rabbit Bank,
the Prophet, during their walk, availing himself of her evident excitement to draw from her the history of its origin.
Such a task, indeed, was easily accomplished, for this singular creature, in whom love of truth, as well as a detesta-

tion of all falsehood and subterfuge, seemed to have been
a moral instinct, at once disclosed to him the state of her
affections, and, indeed, all that the reader already knows of
her love for Dalton, and her rivalry with Mave Sullivan.
These circumstances were such precisely as he could have
wished for, and he failed not to aggravate her jealousy of
Mave, nor to suggest to her the necessity on her part, if she
possessed either pride or spirit, to prevent her union with
Dalton by every means in her power.

"I'll do it," she replied, "I'll do it; to be sure I feel that
it's not right, an' if I had one single hope in this world I'd
scorn it; but I'm now desperate : I tried to be good, but I'm
only a cobweb before the wind—everything is against me, an'
I think I'm like some one that never had a guardian angel to
take care of them."

The Prophet then gave her a detailed account of their plan
for carrying away Mave Sullivan, and of his own subsequent
intentions in life.

" We have more than one iron in the fire," he proceeded,
" an' as soon as everything comes off right and to our wishes,
we'll not lose a single hour in going to America."

" I didn't think," said Sarah, " that Dalton ever murdered
Sullivan till I heard himself confess it; but I can well understand it now.   He was hasty, father, and did it in a passion,
but so itself, he has and had a good heart.   Father, don't
blame me for what I say, but I'd rather be that pious, affectionate ould man, wid his murdher on his head, than you in
the state you're in.   An' that's thrue, I must turn back and
go to them—I'm too long away; still, something ails me—
I'm all sickish, my head and back especially."

" Go home to our own place," he replied ; " maybe it's the
sickness you're takin'."

" Oh, no," she replied, "I felt this way wanst or twice
before, an' I know it'll go off me—good-bye."

" Good - bye, Sarah, an' remember, honour bright and
saicresy."

" Saicresy, father, I grant you, but never honour bright for
me again. It's the world makes me do it—the wicked, dark,
cruel world, that has me as I am, widout a livin' heart to
love me—that's what makes me do it."

Then they separated, he to pursue his way to Dick o' the
Grange's, and she to the miserable cabin of the Daltons.
They had not gone far, however, when she returned, and
calling after him, said—

" I have thought it over again, and won't promise altogether till I see you again."

" Are you goin' back o' your word so soon ? " he asked,
with a kind of sarcastic sneer. " I thought you never broke
your word, Sarah."

She paused, and after looking about her as if in perplexity,
she turned on her heel, and proceeded in silence.

CHAPTER XXVI

THE PEDLAR RUNS A CLOSE RISK OF THE STOCKS

NELLY'S suspicions, apparently well founded as they had
been, were removed from the Prophet, not so much by the
disclosure to her and Sarah of his having been so long cogni-
zant of Sullivan's murder by old Dalton as by that unhappy
man's own confession of the crime. Still, in spite of all that
had yet happened, she could not divest herself of an impression that something dark and guilty was associated with the
tobacco-box—an impression which was strengthened by her
own recollection of certain incidents that occurred upon a
particular night, much about the time of Sullivan's disappearance. Her memory, however, being better as to facts
than to time, was such as prevented her from determining
whether the incidents alluded to had occurred previous to
Sullivan's murder or afterwards. There remained, however,
just enough of suspicion to torment her own mind, without
enabling her to arrive at any satisfactory conclusion as to

Donnel's positive guilt arising from the mysterious incidents in question. A kind of awakened conscience, too, resulting not from any principle of true repentance, but from superstitious alarm and a conviction that the Prophet had communicated to Sarah a certain secret connected with her which she dreaded so much to have known, had, for some time past, rendered her whole life a singular compound of weak terror, ill-temper, gloom, and a kind of conditional repentance, which depended altogether upon the fact of her secret being known. In this mood it was that she left the cabin as we have described.

"I'm not fit to die," she said to herself, after she had gone —" an' that's the second offer for my life she has made. Any way, it's the best of my play to lave them; an', above all, to keep away from her. That's the second attempt; an' I know, to a sartinty, that if she makes a third one, it'ill do for me. Oh, no doubt of that—the third time's always the charm!—an' into my heart that unlucky knife 'ill go, if she ever thries it a third time! They tell me," she proceeded, soliloquizing, as she was in the habit of doing, " that the inquest is to be held in a day or two, an' that the crowner was only unwell a thrifle, an' hadn't the sickness afther all. No matther—not all the wather in the say 'ud clear my mind that there's not villainy joined wid that tobaccy-box, though where it could go, or what could come of it (barrin' the divil himself or the fairies tuck it), I don't know."

So far as concerned the coroner, the rumour of his having caught the prevailing typhus was not founded on fact. A short indisposition, arising from cold caught by a severe wetting, but by no means of a serious or alarming nature, was his only malady; and when the day to which the inquest had been postponed had arrived, he was sufficiently recovered to conduct that important investigation. A very large crowd was assembled upon the occasion, and a deep interest prevailed throughout that part of the country. The circumstances, however, did not, as it happened, admit of any particular difficulty. Jerry Sullivan and his friends attended, as was their duty, in order to give evidence touching the identity of the body. This, however, was a matter of peculiar difficulty. On disinterring the remains, it was found that the clothes worn at the time of the murder had not been buried with them—in other words, that the body had been stripped of all but the under garment previous to its interment. The evidence, nevertheless, of the Black Prophet and of Red Roddy was conclusive. The truth, however, of most, if not of all the details, but not of the fact itself, was denied by old Dalton, who had sufficiently recovered from his illness to be present at the investigation. The circumstances deposed to by the two witnesses were sufficiently strong and home to establish the fact against him, although he impugned the details as we have stated, but admitted that after a hard battle with weighty sticks, he did kill Sullivan by an unlucky blow, and left him dead in a corner of the field for a short time, near the Grey Stone. He said that he did not bury the body, but that he carried it soon afterwards from the field in which the unhappy crime had been committed to the roadside, where he laid it for a time in order to procure assistance. He said he then changed his mind, and, having become afraid to communicate the unhappy accident to any of the neighbours, he fled in great terror across the adjoining mountains, where he wandered nearly frantic until the approach of daybreak the next morning. He then felt himself seized with an uncontrollable anxiety to return to the scene of conflict, which he did, and found, not much to his surprise indeed, that the body had been removed, for he supposed at the time that Sullivan's friends must have brought it home. This he declared was the truth, neither more nor less, and he concluded by solemnly stating that he knew no more than the child unborn of what had become of the body, or how it disappeared. He also acknowledged that he was very much intoxicated at the time of the quarrel, and that were it not for the shock he received by perceiving that the man was dead, he thought he would not have had anything beyond a confused and indistinct recollection of the circumstances at all. He admitted also that he had threatened Sullivan in the market, and followed him closely for the purpose of beating him, but maintained that the fatal blow had not been given with an intention of taking his life.

The fact, on the contrary, that the body had been privately buried, and stripped before interment, was corroborated by the circumstance of Sullivan's body-coat having been found the next morning in a torn and bloody state, together with his great-coat and hat ; but, indeed, the impression upon the minds of many was, that Dalton's version of the circumstances was got up for the purpose of giving to what was looked upon as a deliberate assassination the character of simple homicide or manslaughter, so as that he might escape the capital felony, and come off triumphantly by a short imprisonment. The feeling against him too was strengthened and exasperated by the impetuous resentment with which he addressed himself to the Prophet and Roddy Duncan whilst giving their evidence, for it was not unreasonable to suppose that the man who, at his years, and in such awful circumstances, could threaten the lives of the witnesses against him, as he did, would not hesitate to commit, in a fit of that ungovernable passion that had made him remarkable through life, the very crime with which he stood charged through a similar act of blind and ferocious vengeance. Others, on the contrary, held different opinions, and thought that the old man's account of the matter was both simple and natural, and bore the stamp of sincerity and truth upon the very face of it. Jerry Sullivan only swore that, to the best of his opinion, the skeleton found was much about the size of what his brother's would be ; but as the proof of his private interment by Dalton had been clearly established by the evidence of the Prophet and Roddy, constituting, as it did, an unbroken chain of circumstances which nothing could resist,

the jury had no hesitation in returning the following verdict :—

" We find a verdict of wilful murder against Cornelius
Dalton, senior, for that he, on or about the night of the four-
teenth of December, in the year of grace 1798, did follow and
waylay Bartholomew Sullivan, and deprive him of his life
by blows and violence, having threatened him to the same
effect on the aforesaid day."

During the progress of the investigation our friend the
pedlar and Charley Hanlon were anxious and deeply attentive spectators. The former never kept his eyes off the
Prophet, but surveyed him with a face in which it was
difficult to say whether the expression was one of calm conviction or astonishment. When the investigation had come
to a close, he drew Hanlon aside and said—

" That swearin', Charley, was too clear, an', if I was on
the jury myself, I would find the same verdict. May the
Lord support the poor ould man in the mane time ! for, in
spite of all that happened, one can't help pityin' him, or, at
any rate, his unfortunate family. However, see what comes
by not havin' a curb over one's passions when the blood's up."

" God's a just God," replied Hanlon—" the murderer deserves his punishment, an' I hope will meet it."

" There is little doubt of it," said the pedlar. " The hand
of God is in it all."

" That's more than I see, or can at the present time,
then," replied Hanlon. " Why should my aunt stay so
long ?—but I dare say the truth is, she is either sick or dead,
an' if that's the case, what's all you have said or done worth?
You see it's but a chance still."

" Trust in God," replied the pedlar ; " that's all either of
us can do or say now. There's the coffin. I'm tould they're
goin' to bury him, and to have the greatest funeral that ever
was in the counthry ; but, God knows, there's funerals enough
in the neighbourhood widout their making a show of themselves wid this."

"There's no truth in that report, either," said Hanlon. "I was spakin' to Jerry Sullivan this mornin', an' I have it from him that they intend to bury him as quietly as they can. He's much changed from what he was—Jerry is—an' doesn't wish to have the ould man hanged at all, if he can prevent it."

"Hanged or not, Charley, I must go on with my petition to Dick o' the Grange. Of coorse, I have no chance, but maybe the Lord put something good into Travers's heart, when he bid me bring it to him ; at any rate it can do no harm."

"Nor any earthly good," replied the other. "The farm is this minute the property of Darby Skinadre, an' to my own knowledge Masther Dick has a good hundre' pounds in his pocket for befriendin' the mealmonger."

"Still an' all, Charley, I'll go to the father, if it was only bekase the agent wishes it ; I promised I would, an' who knows, at any rate, but he may do somethin' for the poor Daltons himself, when he finds that the villain that robbed and ruined them won't."

"So far you may be right," said Hanlon, "an' as you say, if it does no good it can do no harm ; but for my part, I can scarcely think of anything but my poor aunt. What, in God's name, except sickness or death, can keep her away, I don't know."

"Put your trust in God, man—that's my advice to you."

"And a good one it is," replied the other, "if we could only follow it up as we ought. Every one here wondhers at the change that's come over me—I that was light and airy, and so fond of every divarsion that was to be had, am now as grave as a parson ; but, indeed, no wondher, for ever since that awful night at the Grey Stone—since both nights, indeed—I'm not the same man, an' I feel as if there was a weight over me that nothing will remove, unless we trace the murdher, an' I hardly know what to say about it, now that my aunt isn't forthcomin'."

"Trust in God, I tell you, for as sure as you live, truth will come to light yet."

The conversation then took various changes as they proceeded, until they reached the Grange, where the first person they met was Jemmy Branigan, who addressed his old enemy, the pedlar, in that peculiarly dry and ironical tone which he was often in the habit of using when he wished to disguise a friendly act in an ungracious garb—a method of granting favours, by the way, to which he was proverbially addicted. In fact, a surly answer from Jemmy was as frequently indicative of his intention to serve you with his master as it was otherwise; but so adroitly did he disguise his sentiments, that no earthly penetration could develop them until proved by the result. Jemmy, besides, liked the pedlar at heart for his open, honest scurrility—a quality which he latterly found extremely beneficial to himself, inasmuch as now that increasing infirmity had incapacitated his master from delivering much of the alternate abuse that took place between them, he experienced great relief every morning from a fresh breathing with his rather eccentric opponent.

"Jemmy," said Hanlon, "is the master in the office?"

"Is he in the office?—who wants him?" and as he put the query he accompanied it by a look of ineffable contempt at the pedlar.

"Your friend, the pedlar, wants him; and so now," added Hanlon, "I leave you both to fight it out between you."

"You're comin' wid your petition, an' a purty object you are, goin' to look afther a farm for a man that'll be hanged (may God forbid — this day, amin!" he exclaimed in an earnest undertone which the other could not hear)—"an' what can you expect but to get kicked out or put in the stocks for attemptin' to take a farm over another man's head."

"What other man's head?—nobody has it yet."

"Ay, has there—a very daicent, respectable man has it,

by name one Darby Skinadre (may he never warm his
hungry nose in the same farm, the miserable *keowt* that he is
this day," he added in another soliloquy, which escaped the
pedlar)—"a very honest man is Darby Skinadre, so you may
save yourself the trouble, I say."

"At any rate, there's no harm in tryin'—worse than fail
we can't, an' if we succeed it'll be good to come in for anything from the ould scoundrel, before the divil gets him."

Jemmy gave him a look.

"Why, what have you to say against the Ould Boy?
Sure it's not castin' reflections on your own masther you'd
be."

"Oh, not at all," replied the pedlar, "especially when I'm
expectin' a favour from one of his sarvints. Throth he'll
soon, by all accounts, have his hook in the ould Clip o' the
Grange—an' afther that some of his friends will soon folly
him. I wouldn't be manin' one Jemmy Branigan. Oh, dear
no—but's a sure case that it's the Black Boy's intention to
take the whole family by instalments, an' wid respect to the
sarvints to place them in their ould situations. Faith you'll
have a warm berth of it, Jemmy, an' well you desarve it."

"Why, then, you circulating vagabone," replied Jemmy;
"if you weren't a close friend to him, you'd not know his
intentions so well. Don't let out on yourself, man alive,
unless you have the face to be proud of your acquaintances,
which in throth is more than any one, barrin' the *same set*,
could be of you."

"Well, well," retorted the pedlar, "sure blood alive, as
we're all of the same connexion, let us not quarrel now, but
sarve another if we can. Go an' tell the ould blackguard I
want to see him about business."

"Will I tell him you're itchy about the houghs?—eh?
However, the truth is, that they"—and he pointed to the
stocks—"might be justice, but no novelty to you. The iron
garthers is an ornament you often wore, an' will agin, plaise
goodness."

"Throth, an' your ornament is one you'll never wear a second time—the hemp collar will grace your neck yet; but never mind, you're leadin' the life to desarve it. See now if I can spake a word wid your masther for a poor family."

"Why, then, to avoid your tongue, I may as well tell you that, himself, Masther Richard, and Darby Skinadre's in the office; an' if you can use the same blackguard tongue as well in a good cause as you can in a bad one, it would be well for the poor craythers. Go in now, an'," he added in another soliloquy, "may the Lord prosper his virtuous endayvours, the vagabone; although all hope o' that's past, I doubt; for hasn't Skinadre the promise, and Masther Richard the bribe. However, who can tell; so God prosper the vagabone, I say again!"

The pedlar, on entering, found old Henderson sitting in an arm-chair, with one of his legs, as usual, bandaged and stretched out before him on another chair. He seemed much worn and debilitated, and altogether had the appearance of a man whose life was not worth a single week's purchase. Skinadre was about taking leave of his patron, the son, who had been speaking to him as the pedlar entered.

"Don't be uneasy, Darby," he said; "we can't give you a lease for about a week or fortnight; but the agent is now here, an' we must first take out new leases ourselves. As soon as we do you shall have yours."

"If you only knew, your honour, the scrapin' I had, in these hard times, to get together that hundre'——"

"Hush—there," said the other, clapping his hand, with an air of ridicule and contempt, upon the miser's mouth; "that will do now; be off, and depend upon—mum, you understand me! Ha, ha, ha,—that's not a bad move, father," he added; "however, I think we must give him the farm."

The pedlar had been standing in the middle of the floor, when young Dick, turning round suddenly, asked him, with a frown, occasioned by the fact of his having overheard this short dialogue, what he wanted.

"God save your honours, gintleman," said the pedlar, in a loud, straightforward voice. "I'm glad to see your honour looking so well," he added, turning to the father; "it's fresh an' young you're gettin', sir, glory be to God!"

"Who is this fellow, Dick? Do you think I look better, my man?"

"Says Jemmy Branigan to me afore I came in," proceeded the pedlar — "he's a thrue friend o' mine, your honour, Jemmy is, an' 'ud go to the well o' the world's end to sarve me—says he, you'll be delighted Harry, to see the masther look so fresh and well."

"And the cursed old hypocrite is just after telling me, Dick, to prepare for a long journey, adding, for my consolation, that it won't be a troublesome one, inasmuch that it will be all down hill."

"Why," replied the son, "he has given you that information for the ten thousandth time, to my own knowledge. What does this man want?   What's your business, my good fellow?"

"Beggin' your pardon, sir," replied the pedlar, "will you allow me to ax you one question—were you ever in the forty-seventh foot?   Oh, begad, it must be him to a sartainty," he added, as if to himself.

"No," replied Dick; why so?"

"Take care, your honour," said the pedlar, smiling roguishly; "take care now. If it wasn't you——"

"What are you speaking about?—what do you mean?" asked the young man.

The pedlar went over to him, and said, in a low voice, looking cautiously at the father, as if he didn't wish that he should hear him,—

"It was surely your honour took away Lord Handicap's daughter when you wor an ensign—the handsome ensign, as they called you in the forty-seventh?   Eh? faix I knew you the minute I looked at you."

"Ha, ha, ha—do you know what, father?   He says I'm

the handsome ensign of the forty-seventh, that took away
Lord Handicap's daughter."

"The greatest beauty in all England," added the pedlar ;
" an' I knew him at wanst, your honour."

"Well, Dick, that's a compliment, at any rate," replied
the father."

"Were *you* ever in the forty-seventh ? " asked the son,
smiling.

" Ah, ha," returned the pedlar, with a knowing wink,
" behave yourself, captain ; I'm not so soft as all that comes
to ; but sure as I have a favour to ax from his honour, your
father, I'm glad to have your assistance. Faix, by all
accounts, you pleaded your own cause well, at any rate ; an'
I hope you'll give me a lift now wid his honour here."

Dick the younger laughed heartily, but really had not
ready virtue enough about him to disclaim the compliment.

"Come, then," he added, "let us hear what your favour is."

"Oh, thin, thank you, an' God bless you, captain ! It's
this, only to know if you'd be good enough to grant a new
lease of Cargah farm to young Condy Dalton ; for the ould
man, by all accounts, isn't long for this world."

Both turned their eyes upon him with a look of singular
astonishment.

" Who are you at all, my good fellow ? " asked the father ;
" or what the devil drove you here on such an impudent
message ? A lease to the son of that old murderer and his
crew of beggars ! That's good, Dick !—well done, soger !—
will you back him in that, captain ? Ha, ha, ha ! D——n
me, if ever I heard the like of it ! "

" I hope you will back me, captain," said the pedlar.

"Upon what grounds, comrade ? Ha, ha, ha ! Go on !
Let us hear you ! "

" Why, your honour, bekase he's best entitled to it.
Think of what it was when he got it, an' think of what it is
now, and then ax yourselves—' Who raised it in value, an'
made it worth twiste what it was worth ? ' Wasn't it the

Daltons? Didn't they lay out near eight hundre' pounds upon it? An' didn't you, at every renewal, screw them up— beggin' your pardon, gintlemen—until they found that the more they improved it the poorer they were gettin'? An' now that it lies there, worth double its value, and they that made it so (to put money into your pockets) beggars—widin' a few hundred yards of it—wouldn't it be rather hard to let them die an' starve in destitution, and them wishin' to get it back at a raisonable rint?"

"In this country, brother soldier," replied Dick, ironically, "we generally starve first an' die afterwards."

"You may well say so, your honour; an' God knows, there's not upon the face of the earth a counthry where starvation is so much practised, or so well undherstood. Faith, unfortunately, it's the national divarsion wid us. However, is what I'm sayin' raisonable, gintlemen?"

"Exceedingly so," said Dick; "go on."

"Well, then, I wish to know, will you give them a new lease of their farm?"

"You do!—do you?"

"Throth I do, your honour."

"Well, then," replied the son, "I beg to inform you that we will not."

"Why so, your honour?"

"Simply, you knave," exclaimed the father, in a passion, "because we don't wish it. Kick him out, Dick!"

"My good friend and brother soldier," said Dick, "the fact is, that we are about to introduce a new system altogether upon our property. We are determined to manage it upon a perfectly new principle. It has been too much sub-let under us, and we have resolved to rectify this evil. That is our answer. You get no lease. Provide for yourself, and your friends, the Daltons, as best you can, but on this property you get no lease. That is your answer."

"Begone, now, you scoundrel," said the father, "and not a word more out of your head."

"Gentlemen! gentlemen!" exclaimed the pedlar, "have you no consciences? Is there no justice in the world? The misery, and sorrow, and sufferin's of this unfortunate family will be upon you, I doubt, if you don't do them justice."

"Touch the bell, Dick! Here, some one! Jemmy Branigan! Harry Lowry! Jack Clinton!—where are you all, you scoundrels? Here, put this rascal in the stocks, immediately! —in with him!"

Jemmy, who, from an adjoining room, had been listening to every word that passed, now entered.

"Here, you, sir; clap this vagabond in the stocks for his insolence. He has come here purposely to insult myself and my son—to the stocks with him, at once!"

"No!" replied Jemmy; "the divil resave the stock will go on him this day. Didn't I hear every word that passed? An' what did he say but the thruth, an' what every one knows to be the thruth?"

"Put him in the stocks, I desire you, this instant!"

"Throth if you wor to look at your mug in the glass, you'd feel that you'll soon be in a worse stocks yourself than ever you put any poor craythur into," replied the redoubtable Jemmy. "Do you be off about your business, in the mane-time, you good-natured vagabone, or this ould firebrand will get some one wid less conscience than I have, that'll clap you in them."

"Never mind, father," observed the son; "let the fellow go about his business—he's not worth your resentment."

The pedlar took the hint, and withdrew, accompanied by Jemmy, on whose face there was a grin of triumph that he could not conceal.

"I tould you," he added, as they went down the steps, "that the same stocks was afore you; an' in the mane time God pardon me for the injustice I did in keepin' you out o' them."

"Go on ' replied the other ; " divil a harsh word ever I'll say to you again."

"Throth will you," said Jemmy ; " an' both of us will be as fresh as a daisy at it in the mornin', plaise goodness. I have scarcely any one to abuse me, or to abuse either, now that the ould masther is so feeble."

Jemmy extended his hand as he spoke, and gave the pedlar a squeeze, the cordiality of which was strongly at variance with the abuse he had given him.

" God bless you ! " said the pedlar, returning the pressure ; " your bark is worse than your bite. I'm off now to mention the reception they gave me and the answers I got to a man that will, maybe, bring themselves to their marrowbones afore long."

" Ay, but don't abuse them for all that," replied Jemmy, " for I won't hear it."

" Throth," returned the other, " you're a quare Jemmy— an' so, God bless you ! "

Having uttered these words in an amicable and grateful spirit, our friend the pedlar bent his steps to the head inn of the next town—being that of the assizes—where Mr. Travers, the agent, kept his office.

CHAPTER XXVII

SARAH ILL—MAVE AGAIN TO THE RESCUE

YOUNG Henderson, whose passion for Mave Sullivan was neither virtuous nor honourable, would not have lent himself, notwithstanding, to the unprincipled projects of the Prophet, had not that worthy personage gradually and dishonestly drawn him into a false position. In other words, he led the vain and credulous young man to believe that Mave had been seized with a secret affection for him, and was willing, pro- vided everything was properly managed, to consent to an elopement. For this purpose it was necessary that the plan

should be executed without violence, as the Prophet well
knew, because, on sounding Young Dick upon that subject,
in an early stage of the business, he had ascertained that the
proposal of anything bordering upon outrage or force, would
instantly cause him to withdraw from the project altogether.
For this reason then he found it necessary, if possible, to
embark Sarah as an accomplice, otherwise he could not effect
his design without violence, and he felt that her co-operation
was required to sustain the falsehood of his assertions to
Henderson with regard to Mave's consent to place herself
under his protection. This was to be brought about so as to
hoodwink Henderson, in the following manner. The Prophet
proposed, that Sarah should, by his own or her ingenuity,
contrive to domicile herself in Jerry Sullivan's house for a
few days previous to the execution of their design; not only
for the purpose of using her influence, such as it was, to
sway the young creature's mind and principles from the path
of rectitude and virtue, by dwelling upon the luxury and
grandeur of her future life with Henderson, whose intentions
were to be represented as honourable, but if necessary, to
leave a free ingress to the house, so as that, under any circumstances, and even with a little violence, Mave should be
placed in Henderson's hands. Should the Prophet, by his
management, effect this, he was to receive a certain sum of
money from his employer the moment he or his party had
her in their possession—for such were the terms of the agree-
ment—otherwise Donnel Dhu reserved to himself the alternative of disclosing the matter to her friends, and acquainting
them with her situation. This, at all events, was readily
consented to by Henderson, whose natural vanity and extraordinary opinion of his own merits in the eyes of the sex
prevented him from apprehending any want of success with
Mave, provided he had an opportunity of bringing the
influence of his person, and his wonderful powers of persua-
sion, to bear upon such a simple country girl, as he considered
her to be. So far, then, he had taken certain steps to secure

himself, whilst he left Henderson to run the risk of such
contingencies as might in all probability arise from the
transaction.

This, however, was but an underplot of the Prophet, whose
object was indeed far beyond that of becoming the paltry in-
strument in a rustic intrigue.   It was a custom with Dick o'
the Grange, for a few years previous to the date of our story,
to sleep, during the assizes, in the head inn of the town,
attended by Jemmy Branigan.   This was rendered in some
degree necessary by the condition of his leg, and his extraordinary devotion to convivial indulgence—a propensity to
which he gave full stretch during the social license of the
grand-jury dinners.   Now, the general opinion was that
Henderson always kept large sums of money in the house,
an opinion which we believe to have been correct, and which
seemed to have been confirmed by the fact that on no occasion were both father and son ever known to sleep out of the
house at the same time, to which we may also add another,
viz., that the whole family were well provided with fire-arms
which were freshly primed and loaded every night.

The Prophet, therefore, had so contrived it, that Young
Dick's design upon Mave Sullivan, or, in other words, the
Prophet's own design upon the money coffers of the Grange,
should render his absence from home necessary whilst his
father was swilling at the assizes, by which arrangements,
added to others that will soon appear, the house must, to a
certain degree, be left unprotected, or altogether under the
care of dissolute servants, whose habits, caught from those
of the establishment, were remarkable for dissipation and
neglect.

The Prophet, indeed, was naturally a plotter.   It is not
likely, however, that he would ever have thought of projecting the robbery of the Grange, had he not found himself, as
he imagined, foiled in his designs upon Mave Sullivan, by
the instinctive honour and love of truth which shone so
brilliantly in the neglected character of his extraordinary

daughter. Having first entrapped her into a promise of secrecy—a promise which he knew death itself would scarcely induce her to violate—he disclosed to her the whole plan in the most plausible and mitigated language. Effort after effort was made to work upon her principles, but in vain. Once or twice, it is true, she entertained the matter for a time; but a momentary deliberation soon raised her naturally noble and generous spirit above the turpitude of so vile a project.

It was, then, in this state of things, that the failure of the one, and the lesser plan, through the incorruptible honour of his daughter, drove him upon the larger and more tempting one of the burglar. In this latter he took unto himself as his principal accomplice, Red Roddy Duncan, whose anxiety to procure the driver's situation arose from the necessity that existed to have a friend in the house, who might aid them in effecting a quiet entrance, and by unloading or wetting the fire-arms, neutralize the resistance which they might otherwise expect.

Sarah's excitement and distraction, however, resulting from her last interview with young Dalton, giving, as it did, a fatal blow to her passion and her hopes, vehement and extraordinary as they were, threw her across her father's path at the precise moment when her great but unregulated spirit, inflamed by jealousy and reckless from despair, rendered her most accessible to the wily and aggravating arguments with which he tempted and overcame her. Thus did he, so far as human means could devise, or foresight calculate, provide for the completion of two plots instead of one.

It is true, Mave Sullivan was not left altogether without having been forewarned. Nobody, however, had made her acquainted with the peculiar nature of the danger that was before her. Nelly M'Gowan, as she was called, had strongly cautioned her against both Donnel and Sarah, but then Nelly herself was completely in the dark as to the character of the injury against which she warned her, so that her friendly

precautions were founded more upon · the general and unscrupulous profligacy of Donnel's principles, and his daughter's
violence, than upon any particular knowledge she possessed
of their intentions towards her. Mave's own serene and
innocent disposition was such, in fact, as to render her not
easily impressed by suspicion ; and our readers may have
perceived, by the interview which took place between her
and Sarah, that from the latter, at all events, she apprehended no injury.

It was on the following day after that interview, about
two o'clock, that whilst she was spreading some clothes upon
the garden hedge, during a sickly gleam of sunshine, our
friend the pedlar made his appearance, and entered her
father's house. Mave having laid her washing before the
sun, went in and found him busily engaged in showing his
wares, which consisted principally of cutlery and trinkets.
The pedlar, as she entered, threw a hasty glance at her, and
perceived that she shook down her luxuriant hair, which had
been disarranged by a branch of thorn that was caught in it
while stretching over the hedge. She at once recognized
him, and blushed deeply ; but he seemed altogether to have
forgotten her.

" Ha ! " he exclaimed, " well, that I may be blest but it's
many a long day since I seen such a head o' hair as that !
Holy St. Countryman, but it's a beauty. *Musha, a Gra
Gal*, maybe you'll dispose of it, for, in troth, if ever a face
livin' could afford to part wid its best ornament, an' yours
is that one."

Mave smiled and blushed at the compliment, and the
pedlar eyed her apparently with a mixed feeling of admiration and compassion.

" No," she replied, " I haven't any desire to part with it."

" You had the sickness, maybe ? "

" Thanks be to the mercy of God," she fervently exclaimed,
" no one in this family has had it yet."

" Well, *achora*," he continued, " if you take my advice

you'll dispose of it, in regard that if the sickness—which may God prevint—should come, it will be well for you to have it off you. If you sell it, I'll give you either money or value for it; for indeed an' truth it flogs all I've seen this many a day."

"They say," observed her mother, "that it's not lucky to sell one's hair, and whether it's thrue or not I don't know; but I'm tould for a sartinty, that there's not a girl that ever sould it but was sure to catch the sickness."

"I know that there's truth in that," said Jerry himself. "There's Sally Hacket, and Mary Geoghegan, and Katty Dowdall, all sould it, and not one of them escaped the sickness. And, moreover, didn't I hear Misther Cooper, the bleedin' docthor, say, myself, in the market, on Sathurday, that the people couldn't do a worse thing than cut their hair close, as it lets the sickness in by the head, and makes it tin times as hard upon them when it comes."

"Well, well, there's no arguin' wid you," said the pedlar; "all I say is, that you ought to part wid it, *acushla*—by all manner o' manes you ought."

"Never mind him, Mave darlin'," said her mother, whose motive in saying so was altogether dictated by affectionate apprehension for her health.

"No," replied her daughter, "it is not my intention, mother, to part with what God has given me. I have no notion of it."

At this stage of the dialogue her eldest brother, who had been getting a horse shod at the next forge, entered the house, and threw himself carelessly on a chair. His appearance occasioned a slight pause in the conversation.

"Well, Denny," said the father, "what's the news?"

"Bad news wid the Daltons," replied the boy.

"With the Daltons!" exclaimed Mave, trembling, and getting paler, if possible, than she was, "for God's mercy, Dennis, what has happened among them?"

"I met Mrs. Dalton a while ago," he replied, "and she

tould me that they had no one now to take care o' them.
Sarah M'Gowan, the Black Prophet's daughter, has catched
the sickness, and is lyin' in a shed there beyant, that a poor
thravellin' family was in about a week ago. Mrs. Dalton
says her own family isn't worse wid the sickness, but betther,
she thinks; but she was cryin', the daicent craythur, and
she says they'll die wid neglect and starvation, for she must
be out, and there's no one to attend to them, and they have
nothing but the black wather, God help them! "

Whilst he spoke, Mave's eyes were fastened upon him, as
if the sentence of her own life or death was about to issue
from his lips. Gradually, however, she breathed more freely;
a pale red tinged her cheek for a moment, after which a
greater paleness settled upon it again.

The pedlar shook his head.

" Ah," he exclaimed, " they are hard times, sure enough;
may the Lord bring us all safe through them! Well, I see
I'm not likely to make my fortune among you," he added,
smiling, " so I must tramp on, but, any way, I thank you for
your houseroom and your civility."

" I'd offer something to ait," said Mrs. Sullivan, with
evident pain, " but the truth is——"

" Not a morsel," replied the other, " if the house was
overflowin'. God bless you all—God bless you."

Mave, almost immediately after her brother had concluded,
passed to another room, and returned just as the old pedlar
had gone out. She instantly followed him with a hasty
step; whilst he, on hearing her foot, turned round.

" You tould me that you admired my hair," she said, on
coming up with him. " Now, supposin' I'm willin' to sell it
to you, what ought I to get for it? "

" Don't be alarmed by what they say inside," replied the
pedlar; " any regular docthor would tell you that, in these
times, it's safer to part wid it—that I may be happy but
I'm tellin' you thruth. What is it worth? What are you
axin'? "

"I don't know; but for God's sake cut it off, an' give me the most you can afford for it. Oh! believe me, it's not on account of the mere value of it, but the money may save lives."

"Why, *achora*, what do you intend doin' wid the money, if it's a fair question to ax?"

"It's not a fair question for a stranger; it's enough for me to tell you that I'll do nothing with it without my father and mother's knowledge. Here, Denny," she said, addressing her brother, who was on his way to the stable, "slip a stool through the windy, an' stay with me in the barn; I want to send you of a message in a few minutes."

It is only necessary to say that the compensation was a more liberal one than Mave had at all expected, and that the pedlar disencumbered her of as rich and abundant a mass of hair as ever ornamented a female head. This he did, however, in such a way as to render the absence of it as little perceptible as might be; the side-locks he did not disturb, and Mave, when she put on a clean night-cap, looked as if she had not undergone any such operation.

As the pedlar was going away he called her aside, so that her brother might not hear.

"Did you ever see me afore?" he asked.

"I did," she replied, blushing.

"Well, *achora*," he proceeded, "if ever you happen to be hard set, either for yourself or your friends, send to me in Widow Hanlon's house at the Grange, an' maybe I may befriend either you or them; that is, as far as I can, which, dear knows, is not far; but, still an' all, send. I'm known as the Cannie Sugah, or Merry Pedlar, an' that'll do. God mark you, ahagur!"

Her brother's intelligence respecting the situation of the Daltons, as well as of Sarah M'Gowan, saved Mave a longer explanation to her parents for the act of having parted with her hair.

" We are able to live—barely able to live," she exclaimed ; " an', thanks be to God, we have our health ; but the Daltons —oh ! they'll never get through what they're sufferin'; an' that girl—oh ! mother, sich a girl as that is—how little does the world know of the heart that beautiful craythur has. May the mercy of God rest upon her ! This money is for the poor Daltons an' her ; we can do without it—an', mother dear, my hair will grow again. Oh ! father dear, think of it —lyin' in a cowld shed by the roadside, an' no one to help or assist her—to hand her a drink—to ease her on her hard bed—bed !—on the cowld earth, I suppose ! Oh ! think if I was in that desolate state. May God support me, but she's the first I'll see ; an' while I have life an' strength, she musn't want attendance ; an', thank God, that her shed's on my way to the Daltons ! "

She then hastily sent her brother into Ballynafail for such comforts as she deemed necessary for both parties, and, in the meantime, putting a bonnet over her clean night-cap, she proceeded to the shed in which Sarah M'Gowan lay.

On looking at it, ere she entered, she could not help shuddering. It was not such a place as the poorest pauper in the poorest cabin would willingly place an animal in for shelter. It simply consisted of a few sticks laid up against the side of a ditch ; over these sticks were thrown a few scraws, that is, the sward of the earth cut thin ; in the inside was the remnant of some loose straw, the greater part having been taken away either for bedding or for firing.

When Mave entered, she started at the singular appearance of Sarah. From the first moment her person had been known to her until the present she had never seen her look half so beautiful. She literally lay stretched upon a little straw, with no other pillow than a sod of earth under that rich and glowing cheek, whilst her raven hair had fallen down, and added to the milk-white purity of her shining neck and bosom.

"Father of Mercy!" exclaimed Mave, mentally, "how will she live—how can she live here? An' what will become of her? Is she to die in this miserable way in a Christian land?"

Sarah lay groaning with pain, and starting from time to time with the pangs of its feverish inflictions. Mave spoke not when she entered the shed, being ignorant whether Sarah was asleep or awake; but a very few moments soon satisfied her that the unhappy and deserted girl was under the influence of delirium.

"I won't break my promise, father, but I'll break my heart; an' I can't even give her warnin'. Ah! but it's threacherous—an' I hate that. No, no—I'll have no hand in it—manage it your own way—it's threacherous. She has crossed my happiness, you say—ay, an' there you're right —so she has—only for her I might—amn't I as handsome, you say, an' as well shaped—hav'n't I as white a skin?—as beautiful hair, an' as good eyes?—people say betther—an' if I have, wouldn't he come to love me in time?—only for her—or if there wasn't that bar put between us. You're right, you're right. She's the cause of all my sufferin' an' sorrow—she is—I agree—I agree—down with her—out o' my way with her—I hate her—I hate the thoughts of her— an' I'll join it—for mark me, father, wickeder I may be, but more miserable I can't—so I'll join you in it. What need I care now?"

Mave felt her heart sink, and her whole being disturbed with a heavy sense of terror as Sarah uttered the incoherent rhapsody which we have just repeated. The vague but strongly expressed warnings which she had previously heard from Nelly, and the earnest admonitions which that person had given her to beware of evil designs on the part of Donnel Dhu and his daughter, now rushed upon her mind, and she stood looking upon the desolate girl with feelings that it is difficult to describe. She also remembered that Sarah herself had told her, in their last interview, that she had other thoughts, and worse thoughts than the fair battle of rivalry between them would justify ; and it was only now, too, that the unconscious allusion to the Prophet struck her with full force.

Her sweet and gentle magnanimity, however, rose over every consideration but the frightfully desolate state of her unhappy rival. Even in this case, also, her own fears of contagion yielded to the benevolent sense of duty by which she was actuated.

" Come what will," she said to her own heart, " we ought to return good for evil, an' there's no use in know'n' what is right unless we strive to put it in practice. At any rate, poor girl, poor generous Sarah, I'm afeard that you're never likely to do harm to me, nor any one else, in this world. May God, in His mercy, pity and relieve you, and restore you wanst more to health ! "

Mave, unconsciously, repeated the last words aloud, and Sarah, who had been lying with her back to the unprotected opening of the shed, having had a slight mitigation, and but a slight one, of the paroxysm under which she had uttered the previous incoherencies, now turned round, and fixing her eyes upon Mave, kept sharply, but steadily, gazing at her for some time. It was quite evident, however, that consciousness had not returned, for, after she had surveyed Mave for a minute or two, she proceeded,—

" The devil was there a while ago, but I wasn't afeard of him, because I knew that God was stronger than him ; and then there came an angel—another angel, not you—an' put him away ; but it wasn't my guardian angel, for I never had a guardian angel—oh, never, never—no, nor any one to take care o' me, or make me love them."

She uttered the last words in a tone of such deep and distressing sorrow that Mave's eyes filled with tears, and she replied,—

" Dear Sarah, let me be your guardian angel; I will do what I can for you ; you do not know me ? "

" No, I don't ; aren't you one o' the angels that come about me ? The place is full o' them."

" Unhappy girl—or, maybe, happy girl," exclaimed Mave, with a fresh gush of tears, " who knows but the Almighty has your could and deserted—bed I can't call it—surrounded with beings that may comfort you, an' take care that no evil thing will harm you. Oh, no, dear Sarah, I am far from that ; I'm a wake, sinful mortal."

" Bekase they're about me continually ; an'—let me see— who are you ? I know you. One o' them said, a while ago, ' may God relieve you, and restore you wanst more to health ' ; I heard the voice."

" Dear Sarah, don't you know me ? " reiterated Mave ; " look at me ; don't you know Mave Sullivan—your friend, Mave Sullivan, that knows your value, and loves you ? "

" Who," she asked, starting a little ; " who—what name is that ?—who is it ?—say it again."

" Don't you know Mave Sullivan ? I am Mave Sullivan, that loves you, an' feels for your miserable situation, my dear Sarah."

" I never had a guardian angel, nor any one to take care o' me—nor a mother, many a time—often—often—the whole world—jist to look at her face—and to know—feel—love me. Oh, a dhrink, a dhrink—is there no one to give me a dhrink ? I'm burnin', I'm burnin'—is there no one to get me a dhrink ? Mave Sullivan, Mave Sullivan, have pity on me ! I heard some one name her—I heard her voice—I'll die without a dhrink."

Mave looked about the desolate shed, and, to her delight, spied a tin porringer, which Sarah's unhappy predecessors had left behind them ; seizing this, she flew to a little stream that ran by the place, and filling the vessel, returned and placed it to Sarah's lips. She drank it eagerly, and looking piteously and painfully up into Mave's face, she laid back her head, and appeared to breathe more freely. Mave hoped that the drink of cold water would have cooled her fever and

assuaged her thirst, so as to have brought her to a rational
state—such a state as would have enabled the poor girl to
give some account of the extraordinary situation in which
she found herself, and of the circumstances which occasioned
her to take shelter in such a place. In this, however, she
was disappointed. Sarah, having drunk the cold water, once
more shut her eyes, and fell into that broken and oppressive
slumber which characterizes the terrible malady which had
stricken her down. For some time she waited with this
benign expectation, but perceiving that there was no likelihood of her restoration to consciousness, she again filled the
tin vessel, and placing it upon a stone by her bedside, composed the poor girl's dress about her, and turned her steps
toward a scene in which she expected to find equal misery.

It is not our intention, however, to dwell upon it. It is
sufficient to say that she found the Daltons—who, by the
way, had a pretty long visit from the Pedlar—as her
brother had said, beginning to recover, and so far this was
consolatory; but there was not within the walls of the house
earthly comfort, or food, or nourishment of any kind. Poor
Mary was literally gasping for want of sustenance, and a few
hours more might have been fatal to them all. There was no
drink, no fire, no gruel, milk, or anything that could in the
slightest possible degree afford them relief. Her brother,
Denny, however, who had been desired by her to fetch his
purchases directly to their cabin, soon returned, and almost
at a moment that might be called the crisis, not of their
malady, for that had passed, but of their fate itself, his voice
was heard shouting from a distance that he had discharged
his commission; for we may observe that no possible induce-
ment could tempt him to enter that, or any other house where
fever was at work. Mave lost little time in administering to
their wants and weaknesses. With busy and affectionate
hands she did all that could be done for them at that particular juncture. She prepared food for Mary, made whey and
gruel, and left as much of her little purse as she thought
could be spared from the wants of Sarah M'Gowan.

In the course of two or three days afterwards, however, Sarah's situation was very much changed for the better; but until that change was effected, Mave devoted as much time to the poor girl as she possibly could spare. Nor was the force of her example without its beneficial effects in the neighbourhood, especially as regarded Sarah herself. The courage she displayed, despite her constitutional timidity, communicated similar courage to others, in consequence of which Sarah was scarcely ever without some one in her bleak shed to watch and take care of her. Her father, however, on hearing of her situation, availed himself of what some of the neighbours considered a mitigation of her symptoms, and with as much care and caution as possible, she was conveyed home on a kind of litter, and nursetended by an old woman from the next village, Nelly having disappeared from the neighbourhood.

The attendance of this old woman, by the way, surprised the Prophet exceedingly. He had not engaged her to attend on Sarah, nor could he ascertain who had. Upon this subject she was perfectly inscrutable. All he could know or get out of her was, that she had been engaged; and he could perceive also that she was able to procure for her many general comforts, not usually to be had about the sick bed of a person in her condition of life.

Mave, during all her attendance upon Sarah, was never able to ascertain whether, in the pauses of delirium, she had been able to recognize her. At one period, while giving her a drink of whey, she looked up into her eyes with something like a glance of consciousness, mingled with wonder, and appeared about to speak; but in a moment it was gone, and she relapsed into her former state.

This, however, was not the only circumstance that astonished Mave. The course of a single week also made a very singular change in the condition of the Daltons. Their miserable cabin began to exhibit an abundance of wholesome food, such as fresh meat, soup, tea, sugar, white bread, and

even wine to strengthen the invalids. These things were to
Mave equally a relief and a wonder ; nor were the neighbours
less puzzled at such an unaccountable improvement in the
circumstances of this pitiable and suffering family. As in the
case of Sarah, however, all these comforts, and the source
from whence they proceeded, were shrouded in mystery. It
is true, Mrs. Dalton smiled in a melancholy way when any
inquiries were made about the matter, and shaking her head,
declared, that although she knew, it was out of her power to
break the seal of secrecy, or violate the promise she had made
to their unknown benefactor.

Sarah's fever was dreadfully severe, and for some time after
her removal from the shed, there was little hope of her
recovery. Our friend, the pedlar, paid her a visit in the
very height of her malady, and without permission given or
asked, took the liberty, in her father's absence, of completely
removing her raven hair, with the exception, as in Mave's
case, of those locks which adorn the face and forehead.

CHAPTER XXVIII

DOUBLE TREACHERY

THE state of the country at this period of our narrative was
indeed singularly gloomy and miserable. Some improvement,
however, had taken place in the statistics of disease ; but the
destitution was still so sharp and terrible, that there was
very little diminution in the character and violence of the
tumults which still prevailed. Indeed, the rioting, in some
districts, had risen to a frightful extent. The cry of the
people was for either bread or work ; and to still, if possible,
this woful clamour, local committees, by large subscriptions,
aided, in some cases, by loans from government, contrived to
find them employment on useful public works. Previous to

this, nothing could surpass the prostration and abject subserviency with which the miserable crowds solicited food or labour. Only give them labour at any rate—say sixpence a day—and they do not wish to beg or violate the laws. No, no; only give them peaceable employment, and they would rest not only perfectly contented, but deeply grateful. In the meantime, the employment they sought for was provided, not at sixpence, but one-and-sixpence a day; so that for a time they appeared to feel satisfied, and matters went on peaceably enough. This, however, was too good to last. There are ever, amongst such masses of people, unprincipled knaves, known as " politicians "—idle vagabonds, who hate all honest employment themselves, and ask no better than to mislead and fleece the ignorant and unreflecting people, however or whenever they can. These fellows read and expound the papers on Sundays and holidays; rail not only against every government, no matter what its principles are, but, in general, attack all constituted authority, without feeling one single spark of true national principle, or independent love of liberty. It is such corrupt scoundrels that always assail the executive of the country, and at the same time supply the official staff of spies and informers with their blackest perjurers and traitors. In truth, they are always the first to corrupt, and the first to betray. You may hear these men denouncing government this week, and see them strutting about the castle, its pampered instruments, and insolent with its patronage, the next. If there be a strike, conspiracy, or cabal of any kind, these " patriots " are at the bottom of it; and wherever Ribbonism and other secret societies do not exist, there they are certain to set them a-going.

For only a short time were those who had procured industrial employment permitted to rest satisfied with the efforts which had been made on their behalf. The " patriots " soon commenced operations.

" Eighteenpence a day was nothing; the government had plenty of money, and if the people wished to hear a truth, it

could be told them by those who knew—listen hether "—as
the Munster men say—" the country gentlemen and the committees are putting half the money into their own pockets "—
this being precisely what the knaves would do themselves if
they were in their places—" and for that reason we'll strike
for higher wages."

In this manner were the people led first into folly, and ultimately into rioting and crime ; for it is not, in point of fact,
those who are suffering most severely that take a prominent
part in these senseless tumults, or who are the first to trample
upon law and order.   The evil example is set to those who
do suffer by these factious vagabonds ; and, under such circumstances, and betrayed by such delusions, the poor people
join the crowd, and find themselves engaged in the outrage
before they have time to reflect upon their conduct.

At the time of which we write, however, the government
did not consider it any part of its duty to take a deep interest in the domestic or social improvement of the people.
The laws of the country, at that period, had but one aspect—
that of terror ; for it was evident that the legislature of the
day had forgotten that neither an individual nor a people can
both love and fear the same object at the same time.   The
laws checked insubordination, and punished crime ; and,
having done this, the great end and object of all law was
considered to have been attained.   We hope, however, the
day has come when education, progress, improvement, and
reward, will shed their mild and peaceful lustre upon our
statute-books, and banish from these those Draconian enactments, that engender only fear and hatred, breathe of cruelty,
and have their origin in a tyrannical love of blood.

We have said that the aspect of the country was depressing
and gloomy ; but we may add here, that these words convey
but a vague and feeble idea of the state to which the people
at large were reduced.   The general destitution, the famine,
sickness, and death, which had poured such misery and desolation over the land, left, as might be expected, their terrible

traces behind them. Indeed the sufferings which a year of famine and disease—and they usually either accompany or immediately succeed each other—inflicts upon the multitudes of poor, are such as no human pen could at all describe, so as to portray a picture sufficiently faithful to the dreary and death-like spirit which should breathe in it. Upon the occasion we write of, nothing met you, go where you might, but sorrow, and suffering, and death, to which we may add, tumult, and crime, and bloodshed. Scarcely a family but had lost one or more. Every face you met was an index of calamity, and bore on it the unquestionable impressions of struggle and hardship. Cheerfulness and mirth had gone, and were forgotten; all the customary amusements of the people had died away. Almost every house had a lonely and deserted look; for it was known that one or more beloved beings had gone out of it to the grave. A dark, heartless spirit was abroad. The whole land, in fact, mourned, and nothing on which the eye could rest bore a green or thriving look, or any symptom of activity, but the churchyards, and here the digging and the delving were incessant—at the early twilight, during the gloomy noon, the dreary dusk, and the still more funereal-looking light of the midnight taper.[1]

The first day of the assizes was now near, and among all those who awaited them there was none whose fate excited so profound an interest as that of old Condy Dalton. His family had now recovered from their terrible sufferings, and were able to visit him in his prison—a privilege which was awarded to them as a mark of respect for their many virtues, and of sympathy for their extraordinary calamities and trials. They found him resigned to his fate, but stunned with wonder at the testimony on which he was likely to be convicted. The pedlar, who appeared to take so singular an interest in the fortunes of his family, sought and obtained a short interview with him, in which he requested him to state, as

[1] A fact—the sextons were frequently obliged to dig graves by candlelight.

accurately as he could remember, the circumstances on which the prosecution was founded, precisely as they occurred. This he did, closing his account by the usual burthen of all his conversation ever since he went to gaol.

" I know I must suffer; but I think nothing of myself, only for the shame it will bring upon my family."

Sarah's unexpected illness disconcerted at least one of the projects of Donnel Dhu. There were now only two days until the assizes, and she was as yet incapable of leaving her bed, although in a state of convalescence. This mortified the Prophet very much, but his subtlety and invention never abandoned him. It struck him that the most effectual plan now would be—as Sarah's part in aiding to take away Mave was out of the question—to merge the violence to which he felt they must resort, into that of the famine riots; and under the character of one of these tumults, to succeed, if possible, in removing Mave from her father's house, ere her family could understand the true cause of her removal. Those who were to be engaged in this were, besides, principally strangers, to whom neither Mave nor any of her family were personally known; and as a female cousin of hers—an orphan—had come to reside with them until better times should arrive, it would be necessary to have some one among the party who knew Mave sufficiently to make no mistake as to her person. For this purpose he judiciously fixed upon Tom Dalton as the most appropriate individual to execute an act of violence against the very family who were likely to be the means of bringing his father to a shameful death. This young man had not yet recovered the use of his reason, so as to be considered sane. He still roved about as before, sometimes joining the mobs, and leading them on to outrage, and sometimes sauntering in a solitary mood, without seeming altogether conscious of what he did or said. To secure his co-operation was a matter of little or no difficulty, and the less so as he heard, with infinite satisfaction, that Dalton was perpetually threatening every description of vengeance against the Sullivans, ever since he had come to understand that his father was about to be tried, and likely to suffer, for the murder.

It was now the day but one previous to the commencement of the assizes, and our readers will be kind enough to accompany us to the Grange, or rather to the garden of the Grange, at the gate of which our acquaintance, Red Roddy, is knocking. He has knocked two or three times, and sent, on each occasion, Hanlon, old Dick, young Dick, together with all the component parts of the establishment, to a certain territory, where, so far as its legitimate historians assure us, the coldness of the climate has never been known to give any particular offence.

"I know he's inside, for didn't I see him goin' in?—well, may all the devils—hem—oh, good-morrow, Charley—throth you'd make a good messenger to send for death. I'm knocking here till I have lost the use of my arm wid downright fatigue."

"Never mind, Roddy, you'll recover it before you're twiste married—come in."

They then entered.

"Well, Roddy, what's the news?"

"What's the news is it? Why then is anything in the shape of news—of good news I mane—to be had in sich a counthry as this? Troth it's a shame for any one that has health an' limbs to remain in it. An' now that you're answered, what's the news yourself, Charley? I hope the drivership's safe at last. I thought I was to sleep at home in my comfortable berth last night."

"Not now till afther the 'sizes, Roddy."

"The masther's goin' to them, thin? bekase I hard he wasn't able."

"He's goin', he says, happen what may; he thinks it's his last visit to them, an' I agree wid him—he'll soon have a greater 'sizes and a different Judge to meet."

"Ay, Charley, think of that now; an' tell me, he sleeps in Ballynafail as usual; eh, now?"

" He does, of course."

" An' Jemmy Branigan goes along wid him ? "

" Are you foolish, Roddy ? do you think he could live wid-out him ? "

" Well, I b'lieve not. Troth, whenever the ould fellow goes in the next world, there'll be no keepin' Jemmy from him. Howandever, to dhrop that. Isn't these poor times, Charley, an' isn't this a poor counthry to live in—or it would be nearer the truth to say starve in ? "

" No, but it would be the thruth itself," replied the other. " What is there over the whole counthry but starvation and misery ? "

" Any dhrames about America since, Charley ? eh, now ? "

" Maybe ay, an' maybe no, Roddy. Is it thrue that Tom Dalton threatens all kinds o' vengeance on the Sullivans ? "

" Ay, is it, an' the whole counthry says, that he's as ready to knock one o' them on the head as ever the father before him was. They don't think the betther of the ould fellow for it ; but what do you mane by ' maybe ay, an' maybe no,' Charley ? "

" What do you mane by axin' me ? "

Each looked keenly for some time at the other as he spoke, and after this there was a pause. At length, Hanlon, placing his hand upon Roddy's shoulder, replied,—

" Roddy, it won't do, I know the design—and I tell you now that one word from my lips could have you brought up at the assizes—tried—and—I won't say the rest. You're betrayed ! "

The ruffian's lip fell, his voice faltered, and he became pale.

" Ay !" proceeded the other, " you may well look astonished —but listen, you talk about goin' to America—do you wish to go ? "

" Of coorse I do," replied Roddy ; " of coorse—not a doubt of it."

" Well," proceeded Hanlon again, " listen still ; your plan's discovered—you're betrayed—but I can't tell you who betrayed you; I'm not at liberty. Now, listen, I say—come this way. Couldn't you an' I ourselves do the thing—couldn't we make the haul, and couldn't we cut off to America widout any danger to signify—that is, if you can be faithful?"

"Faithful!" he exclaimed. "By all the books that ever was opened an' shut, I'm thruth an' honesty itself, so I am; howandiver, you said I was betrayed?"

"But I can't tell you the man that tould me. Whether you're able to guess at him or not I don't know; but the thruth is, Roddy, I've taken a likin' to you, an' if you'll jist stand the thrial I'm goin' to put you to, I'll be a friend to you—the best you ever had, too."

"Well, Charley," said the other, plucking up courage a little, for the fellow was a thorough coward, "what is the thrial?"

"The man," continued Hanlon, "that betrayed you gave me one account of what you're about; but whether he tould me thruth or not I don't know till I hear another, an' that's yours. Now, you see clearly, Roddy, that I'm up to all, as it is, so that you needn't be a bit backward in tellin' the whole thruth. I say you're in danger, an' it's only by trustin' to me—mark that—by trustin' faithfully to me that you'll get out of it; an', plaise the fates, I hope that, before three months is over, we'll be both safe an' comfortable in America. Do you undherstand that? I had my dhrames, Roddy; but if I had, there must be nobody but yourself and me to know them."

"It wasn't I that first thought of it, but Donnel Dhu," replied Roddy; "I never dhreamt that he'd turn thrator, though."

"Don't be sayin', to-morrow or next day, that I said he did," replied Hanlon. "Do you mind me, now? A nod's as good as a wink to a blind horse."

Roddy, though cowardly and treacherous, was extremely cunning, and upon turning the matter over in his mind, he began to dread, or rather to feel, that Hanlon had so far

overreached him. Still, it might be possible, he thought, that
the Prophet had betrayed him, and he resolved to put a query
to his companion that would test his veracity; after which
he would leave himself at liberty to play a double game, if
matters should so fall out as to render it necessary.

"Did the man that tould you everything," he asked, "tell
you the night that was appointed for this business?"

Hanlon felt that this was a puzzler, and that he might
possibly commit himself by replying in the affirmative.

"No," he replied, "he didn't tell me that."

"Ah, ha!" thought his companion, "I see whereabouts you
are."

He disclosed, however, the whole plot, with the single exception of the night appointed for the robbery, which, in point
of date, he placed in his narrative exactly a week after the
real time.

"Now," he said to himself, "so far I'm on the safe side;
still, if he has humbugged me, I've paid him in his own coin.
Maybe the whole haul, as he calls it, may be secured before
they begin to prepare for it."

Hanlon, however, had other designs. After musing a little,
they sauntered along the garden walks, during which he proposed a plan of their own for the robbery of Henderson; and
so admirably was it concocted, and so tempting to the villan-
ous cupidity of Duncan, that he expressed himself delighted
from the commencement of its fancied execution until their
ultimate settlement in America.

"It was a treacherous thing, I grant, to betray you, Roddy," said Hanlon; "an' if I was in your place, I'd give him
tit for tat. An', by the way, talkin' of the Prophet—not that
I say it was he betrayed you; for indeed, now, it wasn't;
bad cess to me if it was—I think you wanst said you knew
more about him than I thought."

"Ah, ha!" again thought Roddy, "I think I see what
you're afther at last; but no matther, I'll keep my eye on you.
Hut, ay did I," he replied; "but I forget now what's this it

was. However, I'll thry if I can remimber it; if I do I'll
tell you."

" You an' he will hang that murdherin' villain, Dalton."

" I'm afeard o' that," replied the other; " an' for my part,
I'd as soon be out of the thing altogether; however, it can't
be helped now."

" Isn't it strange, Roddy, how murdher comes out at last ? "
observed Hanlon; "now, there's that ould man, an' see,
afther twenty years or more, how it comes against him.
However, it's not a very pleasant subject, so let it dhrop.
Here's Masther Richard comin' through the private gate," he
added; " but if you slip down to my aunt's to-night, we'll
have a glass of something that'll do us no harm at any rate,
an' we can talk more about the other business."

" Very well," replied Roddy, " I'll be down, so good-bye ;
an' whisper, Charley," he added, putting on a broad grin,
"don't be too sure that I tould you a single word o' thruth
about the rob—hem—ha, ha, ha! take care of yourself—good
people is scarce, you know—ha, ha, ha! "

He then left Hanlon in a state of considerable doubt as to
the discovery he had made touching the apprehended burglary; and his uncertainty was the greater, inasmuch as he
had frequently heard the highest possible encomiums lavished
upon Duncan's extraordinary powers of invention and humbug.

Young Henderson, on hearing these circumstances, did not
seriously question their truth ; neither did they in the slightest
degree shake his confidence in the intentions of the Prophet
with respect to Mave Sullivan. Indeed, he argued very
reasonably and correctly, that the man who was capable of
the one act would have little hesitation to commit the other.
This train of reflection, however, he kept to himself, for it is
necessary to state here that Hanlon was not at all in the
secret of the plot against Mave. Henderson had, on an
earlier occasion, sounded him upon it, but perceived at once
that his scruples could not be overcome, and that, of course,
it would be dangerous to repose confidence in him.

The next evening was that immediately preceding the assizes, and it was known that Dalton's trial was either the second or third on the list, and must consequently come on the following day. The pedlar and Hanlon sat in a depressed and melancholy mood at the fire; an old crone belonging to the village, who had been engaged to take care of the house during the absence of Hanlon's aunt, sat at the other side, occasionally putting an empty *dudeen* into her mouth, drawing it hopelessly, and immediately knocking the bowl of it in a fretful manner against the nail of her left thumb.

" What's the matther, Ailey ? " asked the pedlar; " are you out o' tobaccy ? "

" Throth it's time for you to ax—ay am I; since I ate my dinner sorra puff I had."

" Here, then," he replied, suiting the action to the word, and throwing a few halfpence into her lap, " go to Peggy Finigan's, an' buy yourself a couple of ounces, an' smoke rings round you; an' listen to me, go down, before you come back, to Barney Keeran's, an' see whether he has my shoes done or not ; an' tell him from me, that if they're not ready for me to-morrow mornin', I'll get him exkumnicated."

When the crone had gone out, the pedlar proceeded—

" Don't be cast down yet, I tell you; there's still time enough, an' they may be here still."

" Be here still !—why, good God ! isn't the thrial to come on to-morrow, they say ? "

" So itself ; you may take my word for it, that even if he's found guilty, they won't hang him, or any man of his years."

" Don't be too sure o' that," replied Hanlon; " but indeed what could I expect afther dependin' upon a foolish dhrame ? "

" Never mind ; I'm still of opinion that everything may come about yet. The Prophet's wife was with Father Hanratty, tellin' him something, an' he's to call here early in the mornin' ; he bid me tell you so."

" When did you see him ? "

" To-day at the cross roads, as he was goin' to a sick call."

" But where's the use o' that, when they're not here ? My own opinion is, that she's either sick, or if God hasn't said it, maybe dead. How can we tell if ever she seen or found the man you sent her for ? Sure if she didn't, all's lost."

" Throth I allow," replied the pedlar, " that things is in a distressin' state with us ; however, while there's life there's hope, as the docthor says. There must be something extraordinary wrong to keep them away so long, I grant—or herself at any rate ; still, I say again, trust in God. You have secured Duncan, you say ; but can you depend on the ruffian ? "

" If it was on his honesty, I could not one second, but I do upon his villainy and love of money. I have promised him enough, and it all depends on whether he'll believe me or not."

" Well, well," observed the other, " I wisht things had a brighter look up. If we fail, I won't know what to say. We must only thry an' do the best we can ourselves."

" Have you seen the agint since you gave him the petition ? " asked Hanlon.

" I did, but he had no discoorse with the Hendhersons ; and he bid me call on him again."

" I dunna what does he intend to do ? "

" Hut, nothing. What 'id he do ? I'll go bail, he'll never throuble his head about it more ; at any rate, I tould him a thing."

" Very likely he won't," replied Hanlon ; " but what I'm thinkin' of now is the poor Daltons. May God in His marcy pity an' support them this night ! "

The pedlar clasped his hands tightly as he looked up, and said, Amen !

" Ay," said he, " it's now, Charley, when I think of *them*, that I get frightened about our disappointment, and the way that everything has failed with us. God pity them, I say too ! "

The situation of this much-tried family was, indeed, on the night in question, pitiable in the extreme! It is true, they had now recovered, or nearly so, the full enjoyment of their health, and were—owing, as we have already said, to the bounty of some unknown friend—in circumstances of considerable comfort. Dalton's confession of the murder had taken away from them every principle upon which they could rely, with one only exception. Until the moment of that confession, they had never absolutely been in possession of the secret cause of his remorse—although it must be admitted that, on some occasions, the strength of his language and the melancholy depth of his sorrow, filled them with something like suspicion. Still, such they knew to be the natural affection and tenderness of his heart, his benevolence and generosity, in spite of his occasional bursts of passion, that they could not reconcile to themselves the notion that he had ever murdered a fellow-creature. Every one knows how slow the heart of a wife or child is to entertain such a terrible suspicion against a husband or a parent, and that the discovery of their guilt comes upon the spirit with a weight of distress and agony that is great in proportion to the confidence felt in them.

The affectionate family in question had just concluded their simple act of evening worship, and were seated around a dull fire, looking forward in deep dejection to the awful event of the following day. The silence that prevailed was only broken by an occasional sob from the girls, or a deep sigh from young Con, who, with his mother, had not been long returned from Ballynafail, where they had gone to make preparations for the old man's defence. His chair stood by the fire in its usual place, and as they looked upon it from time to time, they could not prevent their grief from bursting out afresh. The mother, on this occasion, found the usual grounds for comfort taken away from both herself and them —we mean, the husband's innocence. She consequently had but one principle to rely on—that of simple dependence upon

God, and obedience to His sovereign will, however bitter the task might be, and so she told them.

"It's a great thrial to us, children," she observed ; "and it's only natural we should feel it. I do not bid you to stop cryin', my poor girls, because it would be very strange if you didn't cry. Still, let us not forget that it's our duty to bow down humbly before whatever misfortune—an' this is, indeed, a woful one—that it pleases God, in His wisdom (or, maybe, in His mercy), to lay in our way. That's all we can do now, God help us—an' a hard trial it is ; for when we think of what he was to us—of his kindness—his affection !——"

Her own voice became infirm, and instead of proceeding, she paused a moment, and then giving one long convulsive sob, that rushed up from her very heart, she wept out long and bitterly. The grief now became a wail ; and were it not for the presence of Con, who, however, could scarcely maintain a firm voice himself, the sorrow-worn mother and her unhappy daughters would have scarcely known when to cease.

"Mother dear ! " he exclaimed, "what use is in this ? You began with givin' us a good advice, an' you ended with settin' us a bad example—a bad example ! Oh, mother, darlin', forgive me the word—never, never since we remember anything, did you ever set us a bad example."

"Con, dear, I bore up as long as I could," she replied, wiping her eyes ; " but you know, after all, nature's nature, an' will have its way. You know, too, that this is the first tear I shed since he left us."

"I know," replied her son, laying her careworn cheek over upon his bosom, "that you are the best mother that ever breathed, an' that I would lay down my life to save your heart from bein' crushed as it is, an' as it has been."

She felt a few warm tears fall upon her face as he spoke ; and the only reply she made was, to press him affectionately to her heart.

"God's merciful, if we're obedient," she added, in a few

moments; "don't you remember, that when Abraham was commanded to kill his only son, he was ready to obey God, and to do it; and don't you remember that it wasn't until his very hand was raised, with the knife in it, that God interfered? Whisht," she continued, "I hear a step; who is it? Oh, poor Tom!"

The poor young man entered as she spoke, and after looking about him for some time, placed himself in the arm-chair.

"Tom, darlin'," said his sister Peggy, "don't sit in that; that's our poor father's chair, an' until he sits in it again, none of us ever will."

"Nobody has sich a right to sit in it as I have," he replied; "I'm a murdherer."

His words, his wild figure, and the manner in which he uttered them, filled them with alarm and horror.

"Tom, dear," said his brother, approaching him, "why do you spake that way?—you're not a murdherer."

"I am," he replied; "but I haven't done wid the Sullivans yet, for what they're goin' to do—ha, ha, ha—oh, no. It's all planned; an' they'll suffer, never doubt it."

"Tom," said Mary, who began to fear that he might, in some wild paroxysm, have taken the life of the unfortunate miser, or some one else; "if you murdhered any one, who was it?"

"Who was it?" he replied; "if you go up to Curraghbeg churchyard, you'll find her there; the child's wid her—but I didn't murdher the child, did I?"

On finding that he alluded only to the unfortunate Peggy Murtagh, they recovered from the shock into which his words had thrown them. Tom, however, appeared exceedingly exhausted and feeble, as was evident from his inability to keep himself awake. His head gradually sank upon his breast, and in a few minutes he fell into a slumber.

"I'll put him to bed," said Con; "help me to raise him."

They lifted him up, and a melancholy sight it was to see that face, which had once been such a noble specimen of manly beauty, now shrunk away into an expression of gaunt and haggard wildness, that was painful to contemplate. His sisters could not restrain their tears, on looking at the wreck which was before them ; and his mother, with a voice of deep anguish, exclaimed—

"My brave, my beautiful boy, what, oh, what has become of you? Oh, Tom, Tom," she added, "maybe it's well for you that you don't know the breakin' hearts that's about you this night, or the bitter fate that's over him that loved you so well."

As they turned him about to take off his cravat, he suddenly raised his head, and looking about him, asked—

"Where's my father gone? I see you all about me but him ; where's my father?—where's my fath——"

Ere the words were pronounced, however, he was once more asleep, and free for a time from the wild and moody malady which oppressed him.

Such was the night, and such were the circumstances and feelings that ushered in the fearful day of Condy Dalton's trial.

CHAPTER XXIX

A PICTURE FOR THE PRESENT—SARAH BREAKS HER WORD

THE gray of a cold frosty morning had begun to dawn, and the angry red of the eastern sky gradually to change into that dim but darkened aspect which marks a coming tempest of snow, when the parish priest, the Rev. Father Hanratty, accompanied by Nelly M'Gowan, passed along the Ballyna-fail road, on their way to the Grange, for the purpose of having a communication with Charley Hanlon. It would, indeed, be impossible to describe a morning more strongly marked than the one in question, by that cold and shivering impression of utter misery which it is calculated to leave on any mind, especially when associated with the sufferings of our people. The breeze was keen and so cutting, that one felt as if that part of the person exposed to it had undergone the process of excoriation, and when a stronger blast than usual swept over the naked and desolate-looking fields, its influence actually benumbed the joints, and penetrated the whole system with a sensation that made one imagine the very marrow within the bones was frozen. They had not proceeded far beyond the miserable shed where Sarah, in the rapid prostration of typhus, had been forced to take shelter, when, on passing a wretched cabin by the roadside, which, from its open door and ruinous windows, had all the appearance of being uninhabited, they heard the moanings of some unhappy individual within, accompanied, as it were, with something like the low, feeble wail of an infant.

" Ah," said the worthy priest, " this, I fear, is another of these awful cases of desertion and death that are too common in this terrible and scourging visitation. We must not pass here without seeing what is the matter, and rendering such assistance as we can."

" Wid the help o' God, my foot won't cross the threshel," replied Nelly—" I know it's the sickness—God keep it from us !—an' I won't put myself in the way of it."

" Don't profane the name of the Almighty, you wretched woman," replied the priest, alighting from his horse, " it is always His will and wish, that in such trials as these you should do whatever you can for your suffering fellow-creatures."

" But if I should catch it," the other replied, " what 'ud become o' me ? Mightn't I be as bad as they are in there ; an' maybe in the same place too ; an' God knows I'm not fit to die."

" Stay where you are," said the priest, " until I enter the house, and if your assistance should be necessary, I shall command you to come in."

" Well, if you ordher me," replied the superstitious creature, " that changes the case. I'll be then undher obadience to my clargy."

" If you had better observed the precepts of your religion and the injunctions of your clergy, wretched woman, you would not be the vile creature you are to-day," he replied, as he hooked his horse's bridle upon a staple in the doorpost, and entered the cabin.

" Oh, merciful Father, support me ! " he exclaimed ; " what a sight is here ! Come in at once," he added, addressing himself to Nelly ; " and if you have a woman's heart within you, aid me in trying what can be done."

Awed by his words, but with timidity and reluctance, she approached the scene of appalling misery which there lay before them. But how shall we describe it ? The cabin in which they stood had been evidently for some time deserted, a proof that its former humble inmates had been all swept off by typhus ; for in these peculiar and not un-common cases, no other family would occupy the house thus left desolate, so that the cause of its desertion was easily understood. The floor was strewed in some places with little stopples of rotten thatch, evidently blown in by the wind of the previous night ; the cheerless fireplace was covered with clots of soot, and the floor was all spattered over with the black shining moisture, called soot-drops, which want of heat and habitation caused to fall from the roof. The cold, strong blast, too, from time to time, rushed in with wild moans of desolation, that rose and fell in almost supernatural tones, and swept the dead ashes and soot from the fireplace, and the rotten thatch from the floor, in little eddies that spun about until they had got into some nook or corner where the fiercer strength of the blast could not reach them. Stretched out in this wretched and abandoned hut, lay before the good priest and his companion a group of misery, con-sisting of both the dying and the dead—to wit, a mother and her three children. Over in the corner, on the right hand side of the fireplace, the unhappy and perishing creature lay, divided or rather torn asunder, as it were, by the rival claims of affection. Lying close to her cold and shivering breast was an infant of about six months old, striving feebly, from time to time, to draw from that natural source of affec-

tion the sustenance which had been dried up by chilling
misery and want. Beside her, on the left, lay a boy—a pale,
emaciated boy—about eight years old, silent and motionless,
with the exception that, ever and anon, he turned round his
heavy blue eyes, as if to ask some comfort or aid, or even
some notice from his unfortunate mother, who, as if conscious
of these affectionate supplications, pressed his wan cheek
tenderly with her fingers, to intimate to him that, as far as
she could, she responded to, and acknowledged these last
entreaties of the heart; whilst, again, she felt her affections
called upon by the apparently dying struggles of the infant
that was, in reality, fast perishing at the now exhausted
fountain of its life. Between these two claimants was the
breaking heart of the woful mother divided, but the alternations of her love seemed now almost wrought up to the
last terrible agonies of mere animal instinct, when the sufferings are strong in proportion to that debility of reason which
supervenes in such deaths as arise from famine, or under
these feelings of indescribable torture which tore her affection, as it were, to pieces, and paralyzed her higher powers
of moral suffering. Beyond the infant again, and next the
wall, lay a girl, it might be about eleven, stretched, as if in
sleep, and apparently in a state of composure that struck
one forcibly, when contrasted, from its utter stillness, with
the yet living agonies by which she was surrounded. It
was evident from the decency with which the girl's thin,
scanty covering was arranged, and the emaciated arms placed
by her side, that the poor parent had endeavoured, as well as
she could, *to lay her out*; and oh, great God! what a task
for a mother, and under what circumstances must it have
been performed! There, however, did the corpse of this fair
and unhappy child lie; her light and silken locks blown
about her still and deathlike features by the ruffian blast,
and the sweetness which had evidently characterized her
countenance when in life, now stamped by death, with the
sharp and worn expression of misery and the grave. Thus

surrounded lay the dying mother, and it was not until the priest had taken in, at more than one view, the whole terrors of this awful scene, that he had time to let his eyes rest upon her countenance and person. When he did, however, the history, though a fearful one, was, in her case, as indeed in too many, legible at a glance, and may be comprised in one word—*starvation*.

Father Hanratty was a firm-minded man, with a somewhat rough manner, but a heart natural and warm. After looking upon her face for a few moments, he clasped his hands closely together, and, turning up his eyes to heaven, exclaimed—

" Great God, guide and support me in this trying scene ! "

And, indeed, such an exclamation is not to be wondered at. There lay in the woman's eyes—between her knit and painful eyebrows, over her shrunken upper forehead,. upon her sharp cheek-bones, and along the ridge of her thin, wasted nose—there lay upon her skeleton arms, pointed elbows, and long-jointed fingers, a frightful expression, at once uniform and varied, that spoke of gaunt and yellow famine in all its most hideous horrors. Her eyeballs protruded even to sharpness, and as she glared about her with a half-conscious and half-instinctive look, there seemed a fierce demand in her eye that would have been painful were it not that it was occasionally tamed down into something mournful and imploring by a recollection of the helpless beings that were about her. Stripped, as she then was, of all that civilised society presents to a human being on the bed of death—without friends, aid of any kind, comfort, sympathy, or the consolations of religion—she might be truly said to have sunk to the mere condition of animal life—whose uncontrollable impulses had thus left their startling and savage impress upon her countenance, unless, as we have said, when the faint dawn of consciousness threw a softer and more human light into her wild features.

" In the name and in the spirit of God's mercy," asked the

priest, "and if you have the use of your tongue or voice, tell me what the matter is with you or your children? Is it sickness or starvation?"

The sound of a human voice appeared to arrest her attention and rouse her a little. She paused, as it were, from her sufferings, and looked, first at the priest and then at his companion, but she spoke not. He then repeated the question, and after a little delay he saw that her lips moved.

"She is striving to speak," said he, "but cannot. I will stoop to her."

He repeated the question a third time, and, stooping so as to bring his ear near her mouth, he could catch, expressed very feebly and indistinctly, the word—*hunger.* She then made an effort, and bent down her mouth to the infant which now lay still at her breast. She felt for its little heart, she felt its little lips, but they were now chill and motionless; its little hands had ceased to gather any longer around her breast; it was cold—it was breathless—it was dead! Her countenance now underwent a singular and touching change —a kind of solemn joy—a sorrowful serenity was diffused over it. She seemed to remember their position, and was in the act, after having raised her eyes to heaven, of putting round her hand to feel for the boy who lay on the other side, when she was seized with a short and rather feeble spasm, and, laying down her head in its original position between her children, she was at last freed from life and all the sufferings which its gloomy lot had inflicted upon her and those whom she loved.

The priest, seeing that she was dead, offered up a short but earnest prayer for the repose of her soul, after which he turned his attention to the boy.

"The question now is," he observed to his companion, "can we save this poor but interesting child?"

"I hardly think it possible," she replied; "doesn't your reverence see that death's workin' at him—and an aisy job he'll have of the poor thing now."

" Hunger and cold have here done awful work," said Father Hanratty, " as they have and will in many other conditions similar to this. I shall mount my horse, and if you lift the poor child up, I will wrap him as well as I can in my great coat "—which he stripped off him as he spoke. He then folded it round the boy, and, putting him into Nelly's arms, was about to leave the cabin, when the child, looking around him for a moment, and then upon his mother, made a faint struggle to get back.

" What is it, asthore? " asked the woman ; " what is it you want ? "

" Lave me wid my mother," he said ; " let me go to her ; my poor father's dead, an' left us—oh ! let me stay wid her."

The poor boy's voice was so low and feeble that it was with difficulty she heard the words, which she repeated to the priest.

" Dear child," said the latter, " we are bringing you to where you will get food and drink, and a warm bed to go to, and you will get better, I hope."

And as he took the helpless and innocent sufferer into his arms, after having fixed himself in the saddle, the tears of strong compassion ran down his cheeks.

" He is as light as a feather, poor thing," exclaimed the kind-hearted man ; " but I trust in Heaven we may save him yet."

And they immediately hurried onward to the next house, which happened to be that of our friend Jerry Sullivan, to the care of whose humane and affectionate family they consigned him. The boy with care recovered ; his unfortunate mother, with her two children, received an humble grave in the nearest churchyard, beyond the reach of the storms and miseries of life for ever.

On reaching the Grange, or, rather, the house now occupied by Widow Hanlon, the priest, having sent for Charley, into whose confidence he had for some time been admitted, had a private conference, of considerable length, with him and the pedlar; after which Nelly was called in, as it would seem, to make some disclosure connected with the subject they were discussing. A deep gloom, however, rested upon both Hanlon and the pedlar; and it was sufficiently evident that whatever the import of Nelly M'Gowan's communication may have been, it was not of so cheering a nature as to compensate for the absence of Widow Hanlon and the party for which she had been sent. Father Hanratty having left them, they took an early breakfast, and proceeded to Ballynafail—which we choose to designate as the assize town—in order to watch, with disappointed and heavy hearts, the trial of Condy Dalton, in whose fate they felt a deeper interest than the reader might suppose.

All the parties attended, the Prophet among the rest; and it might have been observed that his countenance was marked by an expression of peculiar determination. His brow was, if possible, darker than usual; his eye was quicker and more circumspect; but his complexion, notwithstanding this, was not merely pale, but absolutely white as ashes. The morning came, however, and the assizes were opened with the usual formalities. The judge's charge to the grand jury, in consequence of the famine outrages, which had taken place to such an extent, was unusually long; nor was "the King against Dalton," for the murder of Sullivan, left without due advice and comment. In this way a considerable portion of the day passed. At length a trial for horse-stealing came on, but closed too late to allow them to think of commencing any other case during that day; and, as a natural consequence, that of Condy Dalton was postponed until the next morning.

It is an impressive thing, and fills the mind with a reverent sense of the wisdom manifested by an over-ruling Providence, to reflect upon the wondrous manner in which the influence of slight incidents is made to frustrate the subtlest designs of human ingenuity, and vindicate the justice of the Almighty in the eyes of His creatures, some-

times for the reward of the just, and as often for the punishment of the guilty. Had the trial of Dalton, for instance,
gone on, as had been anticipated, during the first day, it is
impossible to say how many of the characters in our humble
drama might have grievously suffered or escaped in consequence. At all events, it is not likely that the following
dialogue would have ever taken place, or been made instrumental in working out purposes and defeating plans, with
which the reader, if he is not already, will very soon be made
acquainted.

Donnel Dhu had returned from the assizes, and was sitting, as usual, poring over the fire, when he asked the old
woman who nursed Sarah if there had been any persons inquiring for him since nightfall.

"Three or four," she replied ; "but I said you hadn't
come home yet ; an' divil a one o' them but was all on the
same tune, an' bid me to tell you that it was a safe night."

"Well, I hope it is, Biddy," he replied ; "but not so safe,"
he added to himself, "as I could wish it to be. How is
Sarah ? "

"She's better," replied the woman, " an' was up to-day for
an hour or two ; but still she's poorly, and I think her brain
isn't right yet."

"Very likely it isn't," said the Prophet. " But, Biddy,
when were you at Shanco ? "

" Not this week past."

" Well, then, if you like to slip over for an hour or so now,
you may, an' I'll take care of Sarah till you come back ; only
don't be longer."

"Long life to you, Donnel ; throth an' I want to go, if it
was only to set the little matthers right for them poor orphans, my granchildre."

"Well, then, go," he replied ; " but don't be more than an
hour away, mind. I'll take care of Sarah for you till you
come back."

At this moment a tap came to the door, and Donnel, on

hearing it, went out, and in a minute or two returned again, saying—

"Hurry, Biddy; make haste, if you wish to go at all; but remimber not to be more than an hour away."

The old creature accordingly threw her cloak about her, and made the best of her way to see her grandchildren, both of whose parents had been swept off by the first deadly ravages of the typhus fever.

She had not been long gone, when another tap was given, and Donnel, on opening the door, said—

"You may come in now; she's off to Shanco. I didn't think it safe that she should see us together on this night, at all events. Sit down. This girl's illness has nearly spoiled all; however, we must only do the best we can. Thank God the night's dark, that's one comfort."

"If we could a' had Dalton found guilty," replied Roddy, "all would be well over this night, an' we might be on our way out o' this to America; but what 'ud you do wid Sarah, if we had? Sure she wouldn't be able to thravel, nor she won't, I doubt, as it is."

"Sarah," replied the Prophet, who suspected the object of the question, "is well fit to take care of herself. We must only go without her, if she's not able to come the day afther to-morrow. Where are the boys for the Grange?"

"Undher shelther of the Grey Stone, waiting to start."

"Well, then, as it is," said Donnel, "they know their business, at any rate. The Grange folk don't expect them this week to come, you think?"

Roddy looked at the Prophet very keenly, as he thought of the conversation that took place between himself and Charley Hanlon, and which, upon an explanation with Donnel, he had detailed. The fellow, however, as we said, was both cowardly and suspicious, and took it into his head that his friend might feel disposed to play him a trick, by sending him to conduct the burglary, of which Hanlon had spoken with such startling confidence—a piece of cowardice which, indeed, was com-

pletely gratuitous and unfounded on his part; the truth being
that it was the Prophet's interest, above all things, to keep
Roddy out of danger, both for that worthy individual's sake
and his own. Roddy, we say, looked at him; and of a certainty it must be admitted, that the physiognomy of our friend
the Seer, during that whole day, was one from which no very
high opinion of his integrity or good faith could be drawn.

"It's a very sthrange thing," replied Roddy, in a tone of
thought and reflection, "how Charley Hanlon came to know
of this matther at all."

"He never heard a word of it," replied Donnel, "barrin'
from yourself."

"From me!" replied Roddy, indignantly; "what do you
mane by that?"

"Why, when you went to sound him," said Donnel, "you
let too much out; and Charley was too cute not to see what
you wor at."

"All *feasthalagh* an' nonsense," returned Roddy, who, by
the way, entertained a very high opinion of his own sagacity;
"no mortal could suspect that there was a plot to rob the
house from what I said; but hould," he added, slapping his
knee, as if he had made a discovery, "*ma chorp an diauol*,
but I have it all!"

"What is it?" said the Prophet, calmly.

"You tould the matther to Sarah, an' she, by coorse, tould
it to Charley Hanlon, that she tells everything to."

"No sich thing," replied the other. "Sarah knows nothing
about the robbery that's to go on to-night at the Grange, but
she did about the plan upon Mave Sullivan, and promised to
help us in it, as I tould you before."

"Well, at any rate," replied Duncan, "I'll have nothing
to do wid this robbery—divil a thing; but I'll make a bargain wid you—if you manage the Grange business, I'll lend a
hand in Mave Sullivan's affair."

The Prophet looked at him, fastening his dark, piercing
eyes upon his face.

"I see," he proceeded, "you're suspicious or you're cowardly, or maybe both; but to make you feel that I am neither the one nor the other, and that you have no raison to be so either, I say I'll take you at your word. Do manage Mave Sullivan's business, and I'll see what can be done with the other. An' listen to me now, it's our business, in case of a discovery of the robbery, to have Masther Dick's neck as far in the noose for Mave's affair as ours may be for the other thing; an' for the same raison you needn't care how far you drive him. He doesn't wish to have violence; but do you take care that there will be violence, and then maybe we may manage him if there's a discovery in the other affair."

"Donnel, you're a great headpiece—the divil's not so deep as you are; but as the most of them all is sthrangers, an' they say there's two girls in Sullivan's instead o' one—how will the sthrange boys know the right one?"

"If it goes to that," said the Prophet, "you'll know her by the clipped head. The minute they seize upon the girl with the clipped head, let them make sure of her. Poor foolish Tom Dalton, who knows nothing about our scheme, thinks the visit is merely to frighten the Sullivans; but when you get the girl, let her be brought to the cross-roads of Tulnavert, where Masther Dick will have a chaise waitin' for her, an' wanst she's with him your care's over. In the main time, while he's waitin' there, I an' the others will see what can be done at the Grange."

"But tell me, Donnel, you don't intend, surely, to lave poor Sarah behind us?"

"Eh?—Sarah?" returned the Prophet.

"Ay; bekase you said so awhile agone."

"I know I said so awhile ago; but regardin' Sarah, Roddy, she's the only livin' thing on this earth that I care about. I have hardened my heart, thank God, against all the world but herself; an' although I have never much showed it to her, an' although I've neglected her, an' sometimes thought I hated her for her mother's sake—well, no matther—she's the only thing I love or care about for all that. Oh, no—go without Sarah—come what will—we must not."

"Bekase," continued Roddy, "when we're all safe, an' out o' the raich o' danger, I have a thing to say to you about Sarah."

"Very well, Roddy," said the Prophet, with a grim but bitter smile, "it'll be time enough then. Now, go an' manage these fellows, an' see you do things as they ought to be done."

"She's fond o' Charley Hanlon, to my own knowledge."

"Who is?"

"Sarah; an', betune you an' me, it's not a *brinoge* like him that's fit for her. She's a hasty an' an unsartain kind of a girl—a good dale wild or so—an' it isn't, as I said, the likes o' that chap that 'ud answer her, but a steady, experienced, sober——"

"Honest man, Roddy. Well, I'm not in a laughin' humour now; be off, an' see that you do yourself an' us all credit."

When he was gone, the Prophet drew a long breath—one, however, from its depth, evidently indicative of anything but ease of mind. He then rose, and was preparing to go out, when Sarah, who had only laid herself on the bed, without undressing, got up, and, approaching him, said, in a voice tremulous with weakness—

"Father, I have heard every word you and Roddy said."

"Well," replied her father, looking at her, "I supposed as much. I made no secret of anything; however, keep to your bed—you are not able to rise yet."

"Father, I have changed my mind; you have neither my heart nor wish in anything you're bent on this night."

"Changed your mind!" replied the Prophet, bitterly. "Oh, you're a real woman, I suppose, like your mother; you'll drive some unfortunate man to hate the world an' all that's in it yet."

"Father, I care as little about the world as you do; but still I never will lay myself out to do anything that's wrong."

"You promised to assist us then in Mave Sullivan's business, for all that," he replied. "You can break your word, too. Ah! a real woman again."

"Sooner than keep that promise, father, *now*, I would willingly let the last dhrop o' blood out o' my heart—my unhappy heart. Father, you're provin' yourself to be what I can't name. Listen to me—you're on the brink o' destruction. Stop in time, an' fly, for there's a fate over you. I dreamt since I lay down—not more than a couple of hours ago—that I saw the tobaccy-box you were lookin' for, in the hands of——"

"Don't bother or vex me with your d—d nonsense about dhrames," he replied, in a loud and excited voice. "The curse o' heaven on all dhrames, an' every stuff o' the kind. Go to bed."

He slapped the door violently after him, as he spoke, and left her to her own meditations.

CHAPTER XXX

SELF-SACRIFICE—VILLAINY DEFEATED

TIME passes now as it did on the night recorded in the preceding chapter. About the hour of two o'clock on that same night, a chaise was standing at the cross roads of Tulnavert, in which a gentleman, a little the worse of liquor, sat in a mood redolent of anything but patience. Many ejaculations did he utter, and some oaths, in consequence of the delay of certain parties, whom he expected to meet there. At length, the noise of many feet was heard, and in the course of a few minutes a body of men advanced in the darkness, one of whom approached the chaise, and asked—

"Is that Masther Dick?"

" Masther Dick, sirrah ? No, it's not."

"Then there must be some mistake," replied the fellow, who was a stranger; " and as it's a runaway match, by gorra it would never do to give the girl to the wrong person. It was Masther Dick that Hanlon desired us to inquire for."

" There is a mistake, my friend ; there is—my name, my good fellow, happens to be Masther Richard, or rather Mister Richard. In all other respects everything is right. I expect a lady ; and I am the gentleman, but not Masther Dick ; Richard is the correct reading."

"Then, sir," replied the fellow, " here she is "; and whilst speaking, a horseman, bearing a female before him, came forward, and in a few minutes she was transferred, without any apparent resistance, to the inside of the vehicle which awaited her.

The night, as we said, was dark, but it was also cold and stormy. The driver, who had received his instructions, proceeded in the direction of the Grange ; so many cross roads branched off from that which they took, that it was impossible to say when or where Master or Mister Richard may have intended to stop. In the mean time, that enterprising and gallant young gentleman commenced a dialogue, somewhat as follows :—

" My dear Miss Sullivan, I must be satisfied that these fellows have conducted this business with all due respect to your feelings. I hope they have not done anything to insult you."

" I am very weak," replied the lady ; you needn't expect me to spake much, for I'm not able ; I only wish I was in heaven, or anywhere out of this world."

" You speak as if you had been agitated or frightened ; but compose yourself, you are now under my protection at last, and you shall want for nothing that can contribute to your ease and comfort. Upon my honour—upon my sacred honour, I say—I would not have caused you even this annoyance, were it not that you yourself expressed a willingness—very natural, indeed, considering our affection—to meet me here to-night."

"Who tould you that I was willin' to meet you?"

"Who? why who but our mutual friend, the Black Prophet; and, by the way, he is to meet us at the Grey Stone by-and-by."

"He tould you false, then," replied his companion, feebly.

"Why," asked Henderson, "are you not here with your own consent?" .

"I am—oh, indeed, I am; it's altogether my own act that brings me here—my own act—an' I thank God that I had strength for it!"

"Admirable girl! that is just what I have been led to expect from you, and you shall not regret it; I have, as I said, everything provided that can make you happy."

"Happy!—I can't bear this, sir; I'm desavin' you; I'm not what you think me."

"You are ill, I fear, my dear Miss Sullivan; the bustle and disturbance have agitated you too much, and you are ill."

"You are speaking truth—I am very ill, but I'll soon be better—I'll soon be better. She feared nothing from me," added his companion, in low soliloquy; "an' could I let her outdo me in generosity and kindness? Is this fire—is there fire in the coach?" she asked, in a loud voice; "or is it lightenin'? Oh, my head, my head! but it will soon be over."

"Compose yourself, I entreat of you, my dearest girl. What! good heavens, how is this? You have not been ill for any time? Your hand—pardon me, you need not withdraw it so hastily—is quite burning and fleshless; what is wrong?"

"Everything, sir, is wrong, unless that I am here, an' that is as it ought to be. Ha, ha!"

"Good, my dearest girl—that consoles me again. Upon my honour, the old Prophet shall not lose by this; on the contrary, I shall keep my word like a prince, and at the Grey Stone shall he pocket, ere half-an-hour, the reward of his allegiance to his liege lord. I have for a long time had my eye on you, Miss Sullivan, an' when the Prophet assured me that you had discarded Dalton for my sake, I could scarcely credit him until you confirmed the delightful fact by transmitting me a tress of your beautiful hair."

His companion made no reply to this, and the chaise went on for some minutes without any further discourse. Henderson at length ventured to put over his hand towards the corner in which his companion sat, but it no sooner came in contact with her person, than he felt her shrinking, as it were, from his very touch. With his usual complacent confidence, however, in his own powers of attraction, and strongly impressed besides with a belief in his knowledge of the sex, he at once imputed all this to caprice on the behalf of Mave, or rather to that assumption of extreme delicacy which is often resorted to, and over-acted, when the truthful and modest principle from which it should originate has ceased to exist.

" Well, my dear girl," he proceeded, " I grant that all this is natural enough—quite so—I know the step you have taken shows great strength of character; for indeed it requires a very high degree of moral courage and virtue in you, to set society and the whole world at perfect defiance for my sake ; but, my dearest girl, don't be cast down—you are not alone in this heroic sacrifice; not at all, believe me. You are not the first who has made it for me ; neither, I trust, shall you be the last. This I say of course to encourage you, because I see that the step you have taken has affected you very much, as it is natural it should."

A low moan, apparently of great pain, was the only reply Henderson received to this eloquent effort at consolation. The carriage again rolled onward in silence, and nothing could be heard but the sweep of the storm without—for it blew violently—and deep breathings, or occasional moanings, from his companion within. They drove it might be for a quarter of an hour in this way, when Henderson felt his companion start, and the next moment her hand was placed upon his arm.

"Ha! ha! my dearest," thought he, "I knew, notwith-standing all your beautiful startings and fencings, that mat-ters would come to this. There is nothing, after all, like leaving you to yourselves a little, and you are sure to come round. My dear Miss Sullivan," he added aloud, "be com-posed; say but what it is you wish, and if man can accom-plish it, it must be complied with."

"Then," said she, "if you are a human being, let me know when we come to the Grey Stone."

"Undoubtedly I shall. The grim old Prophet promised to meet us there; and for a reason I have, I know he will keep his word. We shall be there in less than a quarter of an hour. But, my precious creature, now that you understand how we are placed with relation to each other, I think you might not, and ought not, object to allowing me to support you after the fatigue and agitation of the night—hem! Do repose your head upon my bosom, like a pretty, trembling, agitated dear, as you are."

"Hould away!" exclaimed his companion; "don't dare to lay a hand upon me. If your life is worth anything—an' it's not worth much—keep your distance. You'll find your mis-take soon. I didn't put myself in your power without the manes of defindin' myself, and punishin' you, if you should desarve it."

"Beautiful caprice! But, my dearest girl, I can under-stand it all—it is well done; and I know, besides, that a little hysterics will be necessary in their proper place; but for that you must wait till we get to our destination; and then you will be most charmingly affected with a fit— a de-lightful, sweet, soft, sobbing fit—which will render it neces-sary for me to soothe and console you; to wipe your lovely eyes; and then, you know, to kiss your delicious lips. All this, my darling girl, will happen as a natural consequence, and in due time everything will be well."

There was no reply given to this; but the moaning was deeper, and apparently more indicative of pain and distress

than before. A third silence ensued, during which they
arrived at the Grey Stone, of whose proximity the driver had
received orders to give them intimation.

"Hallo!" exclaimed Henderson, "what's the matter?
Why do you stop, my good fellow?"

"We are at the Grey Stone, your honour," replied the
man.

"Oh, very well; pull up a moment," he added. "My
dear Miss Sullivan, we are at the Grey Stone now," said he,
addressing her.

She moaned again, and started.

"Whisht," said she; "I don't hear his voice."

At this moment a man approached the driver, and desired
him to let Mr. Henderson know that a person wished to speak
with him. The female in the carriage no sooner heard the
voice, even although the words were uttered in whispers,
than she called out—

"Father, come to me—help me home—I'm dyin'! You've
been desaved, Mr. Henderson," she added. "It wasn't Mave
Sullivan, but the Prophet's own daughter, you took away.
Blessed be God, I've saved her that disgrace. Father, help
me home; I won't be long a throuble to you now."

"What's this?" exclaimed Henderson. "Are you not
Miss Sullivan?"

"Am I in a dhrame," said the Prophet, approaching the
door of the chaise; "surely—now—what is it? It's my
daughter's voice! Is that Sarah, that I left in her bed of
typhus faver this night? Or am I in a dhrame still, I say?
Sarah, is it you? Spake."

"It is me, father; help me home. It will be your last
throuble with me, I think; at laste I hope so—oh, I hope
so!"

"Who talks about typhus fever?" asked Henderson, starting out of the chaise with alarm. "What means this?
Explain yourself."

"I can no more explain it," replied the prophet, "than you

can. I left my daughter lyin' in a bed of typhus faver, not more than three or four hours ago; an', if I'm to believe my ears, I find her in the carriage with you now ! "

" I'm here," she replied ; " help me out."

" Oh, I see it all now," observed Henderson, in a fit of passion, aggravated by the bitterness of his disappointment— " I see your trick ; an' so, you old scoundrel, you thought to impose your termagant daughter upon me instead of Miss Sullivan, and she reeking with typhus fever, too, by your own account. For this piece of villainy I shall settle with you, however, never fear. Typhus fever ! Good God ! and I so dreadfully afraid of it all along that I couldn't bear to look near a house in which it was, nor approach any person even recovering out of it. Driver, you may leave the girl at home. As for me I shall not enter your chaise again, contaminated, as it probably is, with that dreadful complaint that is carrying off half the country. Call at the Grange in the morning, and you shall be paid. Good night, you prophetical old impostor ; I shall mark you for this piece of villainy ; you may rest assured of that. A pretty trudge I shall have to the Grange, such a vile and tempestuous night ; but you shall suffer for it, I say again."

Donnel Dhu was not merely disappointed at finding Sarah in such a situation, he was literally stupified with amazement, and could scarcely believe the circumstances to be real. It had been agreed between him and Henderson that should the latter succeed in fetching Mave Sullivan as far as the Grey Stone, he (the Prophet) should be considered to have fulfilled the conditions of the compact entered into between them, and the wages of his iniquity were to have been paid him on that spot. It is unnecessary to say, therefore, that his disappointment and indignation were fully equal to those of Henderson himself.

" Where am I to go now ? " asked the driver.

" To hell," replied the Prophet, " an' you may bring your fare with you."

" You must take the reins yourself, then," replied the man, " for I don't know the way."

" Drive across the river here, then," continued the other, " and up the little road to the cottage on the right; yes, to the right—till we get that—that—I can't find words to name her—into the house."

A few minutes brought them to the door, and poor Sarah found herself once more in her own cabin, but in such a state as neutralized most of her father's resentment. When the driver had gone, Donnel came in again, and was about to wreak upon her one of those fits of impetuous fury, in which, it is true, he seldom indulged, but which, when wrought to a high state of passion, were, indeed, frightful.

"Now," he began, "in the name of all that's "—he paused, however, for, on looking closely at her, there appeared something in her aspect so utterly subversive of resentment, that he felt himself disarmed at once. Her face was pale as his own, but the expression of it was so chaste, so mournful, and yet so beautiful, that his tongue refused its office.

" Sarah," said he, "what is the matther with you?— account for all this—I don't understand it."

She rose with great difficulty, and, tottering over towards him, laid her head upon his bosom, and looking up with a smile of melancholy tenderness into his face, burst into tears.

" Father," said she, "it is not worth your while to be angry with Sarah, now. I heard words from your lips this night that would make me forgive you a thousand crimes. I heard you say that you loved me—loved me betther than anything else in this world. I'm glad I know it, for that will be all the consolation I will have on my bed of death—an' there it is, father," she said, pointing to that which she always occupied; " help me over to it now, for I feel that I will never rise from it more."

Her father spoke not, but assisted her to the bed from which the old nurse, who had fallen asleep in it, now arose. He then went into the open air for a few minutes, but soon returned, and going over to the bedside where she lay, he looked upon her long and earnestly.

"Father," said she, "I only did my duty this night. I knew, indeed, I would never recover it—but then she risked her life for me, an' why shouldn't I do as much for her?"

The Prophet still looked upon her, but spoke not a word; his lips were closely compressed, his hands tightly clasped, and his piercing eyes almost immovable. Minute after minute thus passed, until nearly half an hour had elapsed, and Sarah, dreadfully exhausted by what she had undergone, found her eyes beginning to close in an unsettled and feverish slumber. At length, he said, in a tone of voice which breathed of tenderness itself—

"Sleep, dear Sarah—dear Sarah, sleep."

She apparently was asleep, but not so as to be altogether unconscious of his words, for, in spite of illness and fatigue, a sweet and serene smile stole gently over her pale face— rested on it for a little, and, again, gradually, and with a mournful placidity, died away. Her father sighed deeply, and, turning from the bedside, said—

"It is useless to ask her anything this night, Biddy. Can you tell me what became of her, or how she got out?"

"Oh, the sorra word," replied the old woman; "I'm sure such a start was never taken out o' mortal as I got when I came here, and found her gone. I searched all the neighbourhood, but no use—devil a sowl seen her—so, after trottin' here an' there, an' up an' down, I came in not able to mark the ground, and laid myself down on the bed, where I fell asleep till you an' she came back; but where, in the name of all that's wonderful, was she?"

Donnel sat down in silence, and the crone saw that he was in no mood for answering questions, or entering into conversation; she accordingly seated herself on her hunkers, and commenced sucking her dudeen, without at all seeming to expect a reply.

We, however, shall avail ourselves of the historian's privilege, in order to acquaint our readers, very briefly, with that, of which we presume, so far as Sarah is concerned, they can scarcely plead ignorance. Having heard the conversation between Roddy Duncan and her father, which satisfied her that the plot for taking away Mave Sullivan was to be brought about that very night, Sarah, with her usual energy and disregard for herself, resolved to make an effort to save her generous rival, for we must here acquaint our readers that during the progress of her convalescence, she had been able to bring to her recollection the presence of Mave Sullivan in the shed on more than one occasion. She did not, however, depend upon her own memory or impressions for this, but made inquiries from her nurse, who, in common with the whole neighbourhood, had heard of Mave's humanity and attention towards her, to which, it was well known, she owed her life. The generous girl, therefore, filled with remorse at having, for one moment, contemplated any act of injury towards Mave, now determined to save her from the impending danger, or lose her life in the attempt. How she won her way in such an enfeebled state of health, and on such a night, cannot now be known; it is sufficient here to say, that she arrived only a few minutes before the attack was made upon Sullivan's house, and just in time to have Mave and her cousin each concealed under a bed. Knowing, however, that a strict search would have rendered light of some kind necessary, and enabled the ruffians to discover Mave besides, she at once threw herself in their way, under a feigned attempt at escape, and the next moment three or four voices exclaimed, exultingly, " we have her—the cropped head—here she is— all's right—come away, you darlin', you'll be a happy girl before this day week ! "

" I hope so," she replied ; " oh, I hope so—bring me away ! "

The Prophet's own adventure was not less disastrous. Roddy Duncan's sudden withdrawal from the robbery surprised him very much. On seriously and closely reconsidering the circumstances, it looked suspicious, and ere a single hour had passed, Donnel felt an impression that, on that business at least, Roddy had betrayed him. Acting upon this conviction—for it amounted to that—he soon satisfied himself that the house was secured against the possibility of any successful attack upon it. This he discovered in the village of Grange, when, on inquiring, he found that most of the young men were gone to sit up all night in the " big house." So much being known, any additional information to Donnel was now unnecessary. He accordingly relinquished the enterprise ; and remembering the engagement with young Henderson at the Grey Stone, met him, there to receive the wages of his iniquity ; but with what success the reader is already acquainted.

This double failure of his projects threw the mind of the Prophet into a train of deep and painful reflection. He began to think that his views of life and society might not, after all, be either the safest or the best. He looked back over his own past life, and forward to the future, and he felt as if the shadow of some approaching evil was over him. He then thought of his daughter, and pictured to himself what she might have been, had he discharged, as he ought to have done, the duties of a Christian parent towards her. This and other recollections pressed upon him, and his heart was once or twice upon the point of falling back into the fresh impulses of its early humanity, when the trial of to-morrow threw him once more into a gloom, that settled him down into a resentful but unsatisfactory determination to discharge the duty he had imposed upon himself.

CHAPTER XXXI

A DOUBLE TRIAL—RETRIBUTIVE JUSTICE

WITH beating and anxious hearts did the family of the Daltons rise upon the gloomy morning of the old man's trial. Deep concern prevented them from eating, or even feeling inclined to eat; but when about to sit down to their early and sorrowful repast, Mrs. Dalton, looking around her, asked—

"Where is poor Tom from us this morning?"

"He went out last night," replied one of his sisters, "but didn't come back since."

"That poor boy," said his mother, "won't be long with us; he's gone every way—health and strength, and reason —he has no appetite—and a child has more strength. After this day he must be kept in the house, if possible, or looked to when he goes out; but indeed I fear that in a day or two he will not be able to go anywhere. Poor affectionate boy! he never recovered the death of that unhappy girl, nor ever will; an' it would be well for himself that he was removed from this world, in which indeed he's now not fit to live."

Little time was lost in the despatch of their brief meal, and they set out, with the exception of Mary, to be present at the trial of their aged father.

The court was crowded to excess, as was but natural, for the case had excited a very deep interest throughout almost the whole country.

At length the judge was seated, and in a few minutes Cornelius Dalton was put to the bar, charged with the wilful murder of Bartholomew Sullivan, by striking him on the head with a walking-stick, in the corner of a field near a place called the Grey Stone, etc., etc., situate and being in the barony of, etc., etc. When the reverend-looking old man stood up at the bar, we need scarcely say that all eyes were immediately turned on him with singular interest. It was clear, however, that there was an admission of guilt in his very face; for, instead of appearing with the erect and independent attitude of conscious innocence, he looked towards the judge and around the court with an expression of such remorse and sorrow, and his mild blue eye had in it a feeling so full of humility, resignation, and contrition, that it was impossible to look on his aged figure and almost white hairs with indifference, or, we should rather say, without sympathy. Indeed, his case appeared to be one of those in which the stern and unrelenting decree of human law comes to demand its rights, long after the unhappy victim has washed away his crime by repentance, and made his peace with God, a position in connection with conventional offences that is too often overlooked in the administration of justice and the distribution of punishment.

It was not without considerable difficulty that they succeeded in prevailing on him to plead not guilty; which he did at length, but in a tone of voice that conveyed anything but a conviction of his innocence to the court, the jury, and those about him.

The first witness called was Jeremiah Sullivan, who deposed that he was present in one of the Christmas *Margamores*,[1] in the year 1798, when an altercation took place between his late brother Bartle and the prisoner at the bar, respecting the price of some barley, which the prisoner had bought from his brother. The prisoner had bought it, his brother maintained, for the sum of thirty-five pounds fifteen shillings, whilst the prisoner asserted that it was only for thirty-five pounds thirteen, upon which they came to blows; his brother, when struck by the prisoner, having returned the blow, and knocked the prisoner down. They were then separated by their friends, who interposed, and, as the cause of dispute was so trifling, it was proposed that it should be spent in drink, each contributing one-half. To this both assented, and

---

[1] Big markets.

the parties having commenced drinking, did not confine themselves to the amount disputed, but drank on until they became somewhat tipsy, and were, with difficulty, kept from quarrelling again. The last words he heard from them that night were, as far as he can remember—" Dalton," said his brother, " you have no more brains than the pillar of a gate." Upon which the other attempted to strike him, and, on being prevented, he shook his stick at him, and swore that " before he slept he'd know whether he had brains or not." Their friends then took them different ways ; he was separated from them, and knows nothing further about what happened. He never saw his brother alive afterwards. He then deposed to the finding of his coat and hat, each in a crushed and torn state. The footmarks in the corner of the field were proved to have been those of his brother and the prisoner, as the shoes of each exactly fitted them when tried. He was then asked how it could be possible, as his brother had altogether disappeared, to know whether his shoes fitted the footprints or not, to which he replied, that one of his shoes was found on the spot the next morning, and that a second pair which he had at home were also tried, and fitted precisely.

The next witness was Roddy Duncan, who deposed that on the night in question he was passing on a car, after having sold a load of oats in the market. On coming to the corner of the field he saw a man drag or carry something heavy like a sack, which, on seeing him, Roddy, he (the man) left hastily inside the ditch, and stooped, as if to avoid being known. He asked the person what he was about, who replied that, " he hoped he was no gauger " ; by which he understood that he was concerned in private distillation, and that it might have been malt, an opinion in which he was confirmed on hearing the man's voice, which he knew to be that of the prisoner, who had been engaged in the poteen work for some years. One thing struck him, which he remembered afterwards, that the prisoner had a hat in his hand; and when it was observed in the cross-examination that the hat might have been his own, he replied that he did not think it could, as he had his own on his head at the time. He then asked was that Condy Dalton, and the reply was, "it is *unfortunately*"; upon which he wished him good-night, and drove homewards. He remembers the night well, as he lived at that time down at the Long Ridge, and caught a severe illness on his way home, by reason of a heavy shower that wet him to the skin. He wasn't able to leave the house for three months afterwards. It was an unlucky night, anyway.

Next came the Prophet. It was near daybreak on the morning of the same night, and he was on his way through Glendhu. He was then desired to state what it was that brought him through Glendhu at such an hour. He would tell the truth, as it was safe to do so *now*—he had been making United Irishmen that night; and, at all events, he was on his keeping, for the truth was, he had been reported to Government, and there was a warrant out for him. He was then desired to proceed in his evidence, and he did so On his way through Glendhu he come to a very lonely spot, where he had been obliged to hide, at that time, more than once or twice himself. Here, to his surprise, he found the body of a man lying dead, and he knew it at once to be that of the late Bartholomew Sullivan; beside it was a grave dug about two feet deep. He was astonished and shocked, and knew not what to say; but he felt that murder had been committed, and he became dreadfully afraid. In his confusion and alarm he looked about to try if he could see any person near, when he caught a glimpse of the prisoner, Condy Dalton, crouched among a clump of blackthorn bushes, with a spade in his hands. It instantly came into his head that he, the prisoner, on finding himself discovered, might murder him also; and, in order to prevent the other from supposing that he had seen him, he shouted out and asked, Is there anybody near? and hearing no answer, he was glad to get off safe. In less than an hour he was on his way out of the country, for, on coming within sight of his own house, he saw it surrounded with soldiers, and he lost no time in going to England, where, in about a month afterwards, he heard that the prisoner had been hanged for the murder, which was an untrue account of the affair, as he, the prisoner, had only been imprisoned for a time, which, he supposed, led to the report.

When asked why he did not communicate an account of what he had seen to some one in the neighbourhood before he went, he replied, " that at that hour the whole country was in bed, and when a man is flying for his life he is not very anxious to hould conversation with anybody."

On the cross-examination, he said, " that the reason why he let the matter rest until now was, that he did not wish to be the means of bringin' a fellow-creature to an untimely death, especially such a man as the prisoner, nor to be the means of drawing down disgrace upon his decent and respectable family. His conscience, however, always kept him uneasy, and, to tell the truth, he had neither peace nor rest for many a long year, in consequence of concealing his knowledge of the murder ; and he now came forward to free his own mind from what he had suffered by it. He wished both parties well, an' he hoped no one would blame him for what he was doing, for, indeed, of late, he could not rest in his bed at night. Many a time the murdhered man appeared to him, and threatened him, he thought, for not disclosing what he knew."

At this moment there was a slight bustle at that side of the court where the counsel for the defence sat, which, after a little time, subsided, and the evidence was about to close, when the latter gentleman, after having closely cross-examined him to very little purpose, said—" So you tell us that in consequence of your very tender conscience you have not, of late, been able to rest in your bed at night?"

" I do."

" And you say the murdered man appeared to you, and threatened you?"

" I do."

"Which of them?"

"Peter Magennis—what am I sayin'?—I mean Bartle Sullivan."

"Gentlemen of the jury, you will please to take down the name of *Peter Magennis*—will your Lordship also take a note of that. Well," he proceeded, "will you tell us what kind of a man this Bartle or Bartholomew Sullivan was?"

"He was a very remarkable man in appearance; very stout, with a long face, a slight scar on his chin, and a cast in his eye."

"Do you remember which of them?"

"Indeed, I don't, an' it wouldn't be raisonable that I should, afther such a distance of time."

"And you saw that man murdered?"

"I seen him dead after havin' been murdered."

"Very right—I stand corrected. Well, you saw him buried?"

"I didn't see him buried, but I saw him dead, as I said, an' the grave ready for him."

"Do you think now if he were to rise again from that grave that you would know him?"

"Well, I'm sure I can't say. By all accounts the grave makes great changes, but if it didn't change him very much entirely, it wouldn't be hard to know him again—for, as I said, he was a remarkable man."

"Well, then, we shall give you an opportunity of refreshing your memory. Here," he said, addressing himself to some person behind him, "come forward—get up on the table, and stand face to face with that man."

The stranger advanced, pushed over to the corner of the table, and mounting it, stood, as he had been directed, confronting the Black Prophet.

"Whether you seen me dead," said the stranger, "or whether you seen me buried, is best known to yourself; all I can say is, that here I am—by name Bartle Sullivan, alive an' well, thanks be to the Almighty for it!"

"What is this?" asked the judge, addressing Dalton's counsel; "who is this man?"

"My lord," replied that gentlemen, "this is the individual, for the murder of whom, upon the evidence of these two villains, the prisoner at the bar stands charged. It is a conspiracy as singular as it is diabolical, but one which, I trust, we shall clear up by-and-by."

"I must confess I do not see my way through it at present," returned the judge. "Did not the prisoner at the bar acknowledge his guilt?—had you not some difficulty in getting him to plead *not* guilty? Are you sure, Mr. O'Hagan, that this stranger is not a counterfeit?"

The reply of the counsel could not now be heard—hundreds in the court-house, on hearing his name, and seeing him alive and well before them, at once recognized his person, and testified their recognition by the usual manifestations of wonder, satisfaction and delight. The murmur, in fact, gradually gained strength, and deepened until it fairly burst forth in one loud and astounding cheer, and it was not, as usual, until the judge threatened to commit the first person who should again disturb the court that it subsided. There were two persons present, however—we mean Condy Dalton and the Prophet—on both of whom Sullivan's unexpected appearance produced very opposite effects. When old Dalton first noticed the strange man getting upon the table, the appearance of Sullivan, associated as it had been by the language of his counsel with some vague notion of his resurrection from the grave, filled his mind with such a morbid and uncertain feeling of everything about him, that he began to imagine himself in a dream, and that his reason must soon awaken to the terrible reality of his situation. A dimness of perception, in fact, came over all his faculties, and for some minutes he could not understand the nature of the proceedings around him. The reaction was too sudden for a mind that had been broken down so long, and harassed so painfully by impressions of remorse and guilt.

The consequence was, that he forgot, for a time, the nature of his situation—all appeared unintelligible confusion about him, he could see a multitude of faces, and of people all agitated by some great cause of commotion, and that was, then, all he could understand about it.

" What is this ? " said he to himself ; " am I on my trial, or is it some dhrame that I'm dhramin' at home in my own poor place among my heart-broken family ? "

A little time, however, soon undeceived him, and awoke his honest heart to a true perception of his happiness.

" My lord," said the strange man, in reply to the judge's last observation, " I am no counterfeit, an' I thank my good an' gracious God that I have been able to come in time to save this worthy and honest man's life ! Condy Dalton," said he, " I can explain all; but in the manetime let me shake hands wid you, and ax your pardon for the bad treatment and provocation I gave you on that unlucky day—well may I say so, so far as you are consarned—for as I hear, an' as I see, indeed it has caused you an' your family bitther trouble and sorrow."

" Bartle Sullivan ! Marciful Father, is this all right ?—is it real ? No dhrame, then ! an' I have my ould friend by the hand—let me see—let me feel you !—it is—it's truth—but, there now—I don't care who sees me—I must offer one short prayer of thanksgivin' to my marciful God, who has released me from the snares of my enemies, an' taken this great weight off o' my heart ! " As he spoke, he clasped his hands, looked up with an expression of deep and fervent gratitude to heaven, then knelt down in a corner of the dock and returned thanks to God.

The Prophet, on beholding the man, stood more in surprise than astonishment, and seemed evidently filled with mortification rather than wonder. He looked around the court with great calmness, and then, fastening his eyes upon Sullivan, studied, or appeared to study, his features for a considerable time. A shadow, so dark, or, we should rather say, so fearfully black, settled upon his countenance, that it gave him an almost supernatural aspect; it looked, in fact, as if the gloom of his fate had fallen upon him in the midst of his plans and iniquities. He seemed for a moment to feel this himself, for whilst the confusion and murmurs were spreading through the court, he muttered to himself,—

"I am doomed; I did this as if something drove me to it; however, if I could only be sure that that cursed box was really lost, I might laugh at the world still."

He then looked around him with singular composure, and ultimately at the judge, as if to ascertain whether he might depart or not. At this moment a pale, sickly-looking female, aided, or rather supported, by the pedlar and Hanlon, was in the act of approaching the place where Dalton's attorney stood, as if to make some communication to him, when a scream was heard, followed by the exclamation,—

"Blessed heaven! it's himself!—it's himself!"

Order and silence were immediately called by the crier, but the Prophet's eyes had been already attracted to the woman, who was no other than Hanlon's aunt, and for some time he looked at her with an apparent sensation of absolute terror. Gradually, however, his usual indomitable hardness of manner returned to him; he still kept his gaze fixed upon her, as if to make certain that there could be no mistake, after which his countenance assumed an expression of rage and malignity that no language could describe; his teeth became absolutely locked, as if he could have ground her between them, and his eyes literally blazed with fury, which resembled that of a rabid beast of prey. The shock was evidently more than the woman could bear, who, still supported by the pedlar and Hanlon, withdrew in a state almost bordering on insensibility.

A very brief space now determined the trial. Sullivan's brother and several of the jurors themselves clearly established his identity, and, as a matter of course, Condy Dalton was instantly discharged. His appearance in the street was

hailed by the cheers and acclamations of the people, who are
in general delighted with the acquittal of a fellow-creature,
unless under circumstances of very atrocious criminality.

"I suppose I may go down," said the Prophet; "you have
done with me?"

"Not exactly," replied Dalton's counsel.

"Let these two men be taken into custody," said the
judge, "and let an indictment for perjury be prepared against
them and sent up to the grand jury forthwith."

"My lord," proceeded the counsel, "we are, we think, in
a capacity to establish a much graver charge against M'Gowan
—a charge of murder, my lord, discovered under circumstances
little short of providential."

In short, not to trouble the reader with the dry details of
the court, after some discussion it was arranged that two
bills should be prepared and sent up, one for perjury, and the
other for the murder of a carman, named Peter Magennis,
almost at the very spot where it had, until then, been supposed that poor Dalton had murdered Bartholomew Sullivan.
The consequence was that Donnel, or Donald M'Gowan, the
Black Prophet, found himself in the very dock where Dalton
had stood the preceding day. His case, whether as regarded
the perjury or the murder, was entitled to no clemency
beyond that which the letter of the law strictly allowed.
The judge assigned him counsel, with whom he was permitted to communicate; and he himself, probably supposing that
his chance of escape was then greater than if more time were
allowed to procure and arrange evidence against him, said he
was ready and willing, without further notice, to be brought
to trial.

We beg to observe here that we do not strictly confine ourselves to the statements made during the trial, inasmuch as
we deem it necessary to mention circumstances to the reader
which the rules of legitimate evidence would render inadmis-
sible in a court of justice. We are not reporting the case,
and consequently hold ourselves warranted in adding what-

ever may be necessary to making it perfectly clear, or in withholding circumstances that do not bear upon our narrative. With this proviso, we now proceed to detail the *denouement*.

The first evidence against him was that of our female friend, whom we have called the Widow Hanlon, but who, in fact, was no other than the Prophet's wife, and sister to the man Magennis, whom he had murdered. The Prophet's real name, she stated, was M'Ivor, but why he changed it she knew not. He had been a man, in the early part of his life, of rather a kind and placid disposition, unless when highly provoked, and then his resentments were terrible. He was all his life the slave of a dark and ever-wakeful jealousy, that destroyed his peace, and rendered his life painful both to himself and others. It happened that her brother, the murdered man, had prosecuted M'Ivor for taking forcible possession of a house, for which he, M'Ivor, received twelve months' imprisonment. It happened also, about that time, that is, a little before the murder, that he had become jealous of her and a neighbour, who had paid his addresses to her before marriage. M'Ivor, at this period, acted in the capacity of a plain land-surveyor among the farmers and cottiers of the barony, and had much reputation for his exactness and accuracy. Whilst in prison, he vowed deadly vengeance against her brother, Magennis, and swore that if she ever spoke to him, acknowledged him, or received him into her house during her life, she should never live another day under his roof.

In this state matters were when her brother, having heard that her husband was in a distant part of the barony surveying, or subdividing a farm, came to ask her to her sister's wedding, and whilst in the house, the Prophet, most unexpectedly, was discovered within a few perches of the door, on his return. Terror on her part, from a dread of his violence, and also an apprehension lest he and her brother should meet, and, perhaps, seriously injure each other, even to bloodshed, caused her to hurry the latter into another room, with instructions to get out of the window as quietly as possible and go home. Unfortunately he did so, but had scarcely escaped when a poor mendicant woman, coming in to ask alms, exclaimed, " Take care, good people, that you have not been robbed. I saw a man comin' out of the windy, and runnin' over towards Jemmy Campbell's house "—Campbell being the name of the young man of whom her husband was jealous. M'Ivor, now furious, ran towards Campbell's, and meeting the servant-maid at the door, asked " if her master was at home."

She replied, " Yes, he just came in this minute."

" What direction did he come from ? "

" From the direction of your own house," she answered.

It should be stated, however, that his wife, at once recollecting his jealousy, told him immediately that the person who had left the house was her brother ; but he rushed on, and paid no attention whatsoever to her words.

From this period forward he never lived with her, but she had heard recently—no longer ago than the previous night—that he had associated himself with a woman named Eleanor M'Guirk, about thirty miles farther west from their original neighbourhood, near a place called Glendhu, and it was at that place her brother was murdered.

Neither her anxieties nor her troubles, however, ended here. When her husband left her, he took a daughter, their only child, then almost an infant, away with him, and contrived to circulate a report that he and she had gone to America. After her return home, she followed her nephew to this neighbourhood, and that accounted for her presence there. So well, indeed, did he manage this matter, that she received a very contrite and affectionate letter, that had been sent, she thought, from Boston, desiring her to follow himself and the child there. The deceit was successful. Gratified at the prospect of joining them, she made the due preparations, and set sail. It is unnecessary to say, that on arriving at Boston she could get no tidings whatsoever of either the one or the other; but, as she had some relations in the place, she made them out, and resided there until within a few months before, when she set sail for Ireland, where she arrived only a short time previous to the period of the trial. She has often heard M'Ivor say, that he would settle accounts with her brother some fine night, but he usually added, "I will take my time, and kill two birds with one stone when I go about it," by which she thought he meant robbing him, as well as murdering him, as her brother was known mostly to have a good deal of money about him.

We now add here, although the fact was not brought out until a later stage of the trial, that she proved the identity of the body found in the grave of Glendhu, as being that of her brother very clearly. His right leg had been broken, and having been mismanaged was a little crooked, which occasioned him to have a slight halt in his walk. The top joint also of the second toe, on the same foot, had been snapped off by the tramp of a horse, while her brother was a schoolboy—two circumstances which were corroborated by the Coroner, and one or two of those who had examined the body, at the previous inquest, and which they could then attribute only to injuries received during his rude interment, but which were now perfectly intelligible and significant.

The next witness called was Bartholomew Sullivan, who deposed—"That about a month before his disappearance from the country he was one night coming home from a wake, and within about half a mile of the Grey Stone he met a person, evidently a carman, accompanying a horse and cart, who bade him the time of night, as he passed. He noticed that the man had a slight halt as he walked, but could not remember his face, although the night was by no means dark. On passing onwards, towards home, he met another person walking after the carman, who, on seeing him (Sullivan) approach, hastily threw some weapon or other into the ditch. The hour was about three o'clock in the night (morning), and on looking closely at the man, for he seemed to follow the other in a stealthy way, he could only observe that he had a very pale face, and heavy black eyebrows ; indeed he has little doubt but that the prisoner is the man, although he will not actually swear it after such a length of time." This was the evidence given by Sullivan.

The third witness produced was Theodosius M'Mahon, or, as he was better known, Toddy Mack, the pedlar, who deposed to the fact of having, previously to his departure for Boston, given to Peter Magennis a present of a steel tobacco-box as a keepsake, and as the man did not use tobacco, he said, on putting it into his pocket—" This will do nicely to hould my money in on my way home from Dublin."

Upon which Toddy Mack observed, laughing, " that if he put either silver or brass in it, half the country would know by the jingle."

" I'll take care of that, never fear," replied Magennis, " for I'll put nothing in this but the soft, comfortable notes."

He was asked if the box had any peculiar mark by which it might be known.

" Yes, he had himself punched upon the lid of it the initials of the person to whom he gave it—to wit, P. M., for Peter Magennis."

" Would you know the box if you saw it ? "

" Certainly."

" Is that it ? " asked the prosecuting counsel, placing the box in his hands.

" That is the same box I gave him, upon my oath ; it is a good deal rusted now, but there's the holes as I punched them ; and, by the same token, there's in the letter P. the very place yet where the two holes broke into one, as I was punchin' it."

" Pray how did the box turn up ? " asked the judge—" in whose possession has it been ever since ? "

" My lord, we have just come to that—crier, call Eleanor M'Guirk."

The woman hitherto known as Nelly M'Gowan, and

supposed to be the Prophet's wife, now made her appearance.

"Will you state to the gentlemen of the jury what you know about this box?"

Our readers are partially aware of her evidence with respect to it; we shall, however, briefly recapitulate her account of the circumstance.

"The first time she ever saw it," she said, "was the night the carman was murdered, or that he disappeared, at any rate. She resided by herself, in a little house at the mouth of Glendhu—the same she and the Prophet had lived in ever since. They had not been long acquainted at that time—but still longer than was right or proper. He had been very little in the country then, and any time he did come was principally at night, when he stopped with her, and went away again, generally before dawn. He passed himself on her as an unmarried man, and said his name was M'Gowan. On that evening he came about dusk, but went out again, and she did not see him till far in the night, when he returned, and appeared to be fatigued and agitated—his clothes, too, were soiled and crumpled, especially the collar of his shirt, which was nearly torn off, as if in a struggle of some kind. She asked him what was the matter with him, and said he looked as if he had been fighting."

He replied, "No, Nelly, but I've killed two birds with one stone this night."

She asked him what he meant by these words, but he would give her no further information.

"I'll give no explanation," said he, "but this"; and turning his back to her he opened a tobacco-box, which, by stretching her neck, she saw distinctly, and, taking out a roll of bank-notes, he separated one of them from the rest, and handing it to her exclaimed—"there's all the explanation you can want; a close mouth, Nelly, is the sign of a wise head, an' by keepin' a close mouth you'll get more explanations of *this* kind. Do you understand that?" said he.

" I do," she replied.

" Very well, then," he observed, " let that be the law and the gospel between us."

When he fell asleep, she got up, and lookiñg at the box, saw that it was stuffed with bank-notes, had a broken hinge —the hinge was freshly broken—and something like two letters on the lid of it.

"She then did not see it," she continued, " until some weeks ago, when his daughter and herself having had a quarrel, in which the girl cut her—she (his daughter) on stretching up for some cobwebs on the wall, to stanch the bleeding, accidentally pulled the box out of a crevice, in which it had probably been hid. About this time," she added, " the prisoner became very restless at night, indeed she might say by day and night, and after a good deal of gloomy ill-temper, he made inquiries for it, and on hearing that it had again appeared, even threatened her life if it were not produced."

She closed her evidence by stating that she had secreted it, but could tell nothing of its ultimate and mysterious disappearance.

Hanlon's part in tracing the murder is already known to the reader. He dreamt, but his dream was not permitted to go to the jury, that his father came to him, and said that if he repaired to the Grey Stone at Glendhu, on a night which he named, at the hour of twelve o'clock, he would get such a clue to his murder as would enable him to bring the murderer to justice.

" Are you the son, then, of the man who is said to have been murdered ? " asked the judge.

" He was his son," he replied, " and came first to that part of the country, in consequence of having been engaged in a ' party fight' in his native place. It seems a warrant had been issued against him and others, and he thought it more prudent to take his mother's name, which was Hanlon, in order to avoid discovery, the case being a very common one under circumstances of that kind."

Roddy Duncan's explanation, with respect to the tobacco-box, was not called for on the trial, but we shall give it here in order to satisfy the reader. He saw Nelly M'Gowan, as we may still call her, thrusting something under the thatch of the cabin, and feeling a kind of curiosity to ascertain what it could be, he seized the first opportunity of examining, and finding a tobacco-box, he put it in his pocket, and thought himself extremely fortunate in securing it, for reasons which the reader will immediately understand. The truth is, that Roddy, together with about half-a-dozen virtuous youths in the neighbourhood, were in the habit of being out pretty frequently at night, for what purposes we will not now wait to enquire. Their usual place of *rendezvous* was the Grey Stone, in consequence of the shelter and concealment which its immense projections afforded them. On the night of the first meeting between Sarah and Hanlon, Roddy had heard the whole conversation by accident, whilst waiting for his companions, and very judiciously furnished the groans, as he did also upon the second night, on both occasions for his own amusement. His motives for ingratiating himself, through means of the box, with Sarah and Hanlon, are already known to the reader, and require no further explanation from us.

In fact, such a chain of circumstantial evidence was produced, as completely established the Prophet's guilt, in the opinion of all who had heard the trial, and the result was a verdict of guilty by the jury, and a sentence of death by the judge.

" Your case," said the judge, as he was about to pronounce sentence, " is another proof of the certainty with which Providence never, so to speak, loses sight of the man who deliberately sheds his fellow-creature's blood. It is an additional and striking instance, too, of the retributive spirit with which it converts all the most cautious disguises of guilt, no matter how ingeniously assumed, into the very manifestations by which its enormity is discovered and punished."

After recommending him to a higher tribunal, and impressing upon him the necessity of repentance, and seeking peace with God, he sentenced him to be hanged by the neck on the fourth day after the assizes, recommending his soul, as usual, to the mercy of his Creator.

The Prophet was evidently a man of great moral intrepidity and firmness. He kept his black, unquailing eye fixed upon the judge while he spoke, but betrayed not a single symptom of a timid or vacillating spirit. When the sentence was pronounced, he looked with an expression of something like contempt upon those who had broken out, as usual, into those mingled murmurs of compassion or satisfaction, which are sometimes uttered under circumstances similar to his.

"Now," said he to the gaoler, "that everything is over, and the worst come to the worst, the sooner I get to my cell the betther. I have despised the world too long to care a single curse what it says or thinks of me, or about me. All I'm sorry for is, that I didn't take more out of it, and that I let it slip through my hands so aisily as I did. My curse upon it and its villainy! Bring me in."

The gratification of the country for a wide circle around, was now absolutely exuberant. There was not only the acquittal of the good-hearted and generous old man to fill the public with a feeling of delight, but also the unexpected resurrection, as it were, of honest Bartholomew Sullivan, which came to animate all parties with a double enjoyment. Indeed the congratulations which both parties received were sincere and fervent. Old Condy Dalton had no sooner left the dock than he was surrounded by friends and relatives, each and all anxious to manifest their sense of his good fortune in the usual way of "treating" him and his family. Their gratitude, however, towards the Almighty for His unexpected interposition in their favour, was too exalted and pious to allow them to profane it by convivial indulgences. With as little delay, therefore, as might be, they sought their humble cabin, where a scene awaited him that was cal-

culated to dash with sorrow the sentiments of justifiable
exultation which they felt.

Our readers may remember that owing to Sarah's illness,
the Prophet, as an afterthought, had determined to give to
the abduction of Mave Sullivan the colour of a famine outrage; and for this purpose he had resolved also to engage
Tom Dalton to act as a kind of leader—a circumstance which
he hoped would change the character of the proceeding altogether to one of wild and licentious revenge on the part of
Dalton.   Poor Dalton lent himself to this, as far as its aspect
of a mere outbreak had attractions for the melancholy love of
turbulence, by which he had been of late unhappily animated.
He accordingly left home with the intention of taking a part
in their proceedings; but he never joined them. Where he
had gone to, or how he had passed the night, nobody knew.
Be this as it may, he made his appearance at home about
noon on the day of his father's trial, in evidently a dying
state, and in this condition his family found him on their
return. 'Tis true they had the consolation of perceiving that
he was calmer and more collected than he had been since the
death of Peggy Murtagh. His reason, indeed, might be said
to have been altogether restored.

They found him sitting in his father's arm-chair, his head
supported—oh, how tenderly supported!—by his affectionate
sister, Mary.

Mrs. Dalton herself had come before, to break the joyful
tidings to this excellent girl, who, on seeing her, burst into
tears, exclaiming in Irish,—

"Mother dear, I'm afraid you're bringing a heavy heart to
a house of sorrow!"

"A light heart, dear Mary—a light and a grateful heart.
Your father, *acushla machree*—your father, my dear unhappy
Tom, is not a murderer."

The girl had one arm around her brother's neck, but she
instinctively raised the other, as if in ecstatic delight; but in
a moment she dropped it again, and said sorrowfully,—

"Ay; but, mother dear, didn't he say himself he was guilty?"

"He thought so, dear! but it was only a rash blow; and oh, how many a deadly accident has come from rash blows! The man was not killed at all, dear Mary, but is alive and well, and was in the court-house this day. Oh! what do we not owe to a good God for His mercy towards us all! Tom, dear, I am glad to see you at home; you must not go out again."

"Oh, mother dear," said his sister, kissing him, and bursting into tears, "Tom's dying!"

"What!" exclaimed his mother—"what's this!—death's in my boy's face!"

He raised his head gently, and, looking at her, replied with a faint smile,—

"No, mother, I will not go out any more; I will be good at last—it's time for me."

At this moment old Dalton and the rest of the family entered the house, but were not surprised at finding Mary and her mother in tears; for they supposed, naturally enough, that the tears were those of joy for the old man's acquittal. Mrs. Dalton raised her hand to enjoin silence; and then, pointing to her son said,—"We must keep quiet for a little."

They all looked upon the young man, and saw, at a glance that death, immediate death, was stamped upon his features, gleamed wildly out of his eyes, and spoke in his feeble and hollow voice.

"Father," said he, "let me kiss you, or come and kiss me. Thank God for what has happened this day. Father," he added, looking up into the old man's face, with an expression of unutterable sorrow and affection—"father, I know I was wild; but I will be wild no more. I was wicked too, but I will be wicked no more. There is now an end to all my follies and to all my crimes; an' I hope—I hope that God will have mercy upon me, an' forgive me."

The tears rained fast upon his pale face from the old man's eyes, as he exclaimed,—

" He will have mercy upon you, my darlin' son; look to Him. I know, darlin', that whatever crimes or follies you committed, you are sorry for them, an' God will forgive you."

"I am," he replied; "kiss me, all of you; my sight is gettin' wake, an' my tongue isn't—isn't so strong as it was."

One after one they all kissed him, and as each knew that this tender and sorrowful embrace must be the last that should ever pass between them, it is impossible adequately to describe the scene which then took place.

"I have a request to make," he said, feebly; "an' it is, that I may sleep with Peggy an' our baby. Maybe I'm not worthy of that; but still I'd like it, an' my heart's upon it; an' I think she would like it, too."

"It can be done, an' we'll do it," replied his mother; "we'll do it, my darlin' boy—my son, my son, we'll do it."

"Don't you all forgive me—forgive me everything?"

They could only, for some time, reply by their tears; but at length they did reply, and he seemed satisfied.

"Now," said he, "there was an ould Irish air that Peggy used to sing for me—I thought I heard her often singin' it of late—did I?"

"I suppose so, darlin'," replied his mother; "I suppose you did."

" Mary, here," he proceeded, "sings it; I would like to hear it before I go; it's the air of *Gra Gal Machree.*"

" Before you go, *alanna !* " exclaimed his father, pressing him tenderly to his breast. " Oh! but they're bitther words to us, my darlin', my lovin' boy. But the air, Mary, darlin', strive an' sing it for him as well as you can."

It was a trying task for the affectionate girl, who, however, so far overcame her grief, as to be able to sing it with the very pathos of nature itself.

" Ay," said he, as she proceeded, " that's it—that's what Peggy used to sing for me, bekase she knew I liked it."

Tender and full of sorrow were the notes as they came from the innocent lips of that affectionate sister. Her task, however, was soon over; for scarcely had she concluded the air, when her poor brother's ears and heart were closed to the melody and affection it breathed, for ever.

"I know," said she, with tears, "that there's one thing will give comfort to you all respecting poor Tom. Peter Rafferty, who helped him home, seein' the dyin' state he was in, went over to the Carr, and brought one of Father Hanratty's curates to him, so that he didn't depart without resaving the rites of the Church, thank God!"

This took the sting of bitterness out of their grief, and infused into it a spirit that soothed their hearts, and sustained them by that consolation which the influence of religion and its ordinances, in the hour of death and sorrow, never fail to give to an Irish family.

Old Dalton's sleep was sound that night, and when he awoke the next morning the first voice he heard was that of our friend Toddy Mack, which, despite of the loss they had sustained, and its consequent sorrow, diffused among them a spirit of cheerfulness and contentment.

"You have no raison," said he, "to fly in the face of God—I don't mane you, Mrs. Dalton—but these youngsters. If what I heard is thrue, that that poor boy never was himself since the girl died, it was a mercy for God to take him; and, afther all, He is a betther judge of what's fit for us than we are ourselves. Bounce, now, Mr. Dalton, you have little time to lose. I want you to come wid me to the agent, Mr. Travers. He wishes, I think, to see yourself, for he says he has heard a good account o' you, an' I promised to bring you. If we're there about two o'clock, we'll hit the time purty close."

"What can he want with him, do you think?" asked Mrs. Dalton.

"Dear knows—fifty things—maybe to stand for one of his childre'—or—but ah! forgive me—I could be merry anywhere else; but here—here—forgive me, Mrs. Dalton."

In a short time Dalton and he mounted a car, which Toddy had brought with him, and started for the office of Mr. Travers.

Whilst they are on their way we shall return to our friend, young Dick, who was left to trudge home from the Grey Stone on the night set apart for the abduction of Mave Sullivan. Hanlon, or Magennis, as we ought now to call him, having, by his shrewdness, and Roddy Duncan's loose manner of talking, succeeded in preventing the burglarious attack upon his master's house, was a good deal surprised at young Dick's quick return, for he had not expected him at all that night. The appearance of the young gentleman was calculated to excite impressions of rather a serio-comic character.

"Hanlon," said he, "is all right?—every man at his post?"

"All right, sir; but I did not expect you back so soon. Whatever you've been engaged on to-night is a saicret you kep' me out of."

"D——e, I was afraid of you, Hanlon; you were too honest for what I was about to-night. You wouldn't have stood it; I probed you on it once before, and you winced."

"Well, sir, I assure you I don't wish to know what it is."

"Why, as the whole thing has failed, there can be no great secret in it now. The old Prophet hoaxed me cursedly to-night. It was arranged between us that he should carry off Sullivan's handsome daughter for me, and what does the mercenary old scoundrel do but put his own in her place, with a view of imposing her on me."

"Faith, an' of the two she is thought to be the finest an' handsomest girl; but, my God! how could he do what you say, an' his daughter sick of the typhus?"

"There's some d——d puzzle about it, I grant; he seemed puzzled, his daughter seemed sick, sure enough, and I am sick. Hanlon, I fear I've caught the typhus from her. I can think of nothing else."

"Go to bed, sir; I tould you as you went out that you had taken rather much. You've been disappointed, an' you're vexed, that's what ails you; but go to bed, an' you'll sleep it off."

" Yes, I must. In a day or two it's arranged that I and Travers are to settle about the leases, and I must meet that worthy gentleman with a clear head."

" Is Darby Skinadre, sir, to have Dalton's farm ? "

" Why, I've pocketed a hundred of his money for it, and I think he ought. However, all this part of the property is out of lease, and you know we can neither do nor say anything till we get the new leases."

" Oh, yes, you can, sir," replied Hanlon, laughing; " it's clear you can do, at any rate."

" How is that ? What do you grin at, confound you ? "

" You can take the money, sir; that's what I mane by doin' him. Ha, ha, ha ! "

" Very good, Charley; but I'm sick, and I very much fear that I've caught this confounded typhus."

The next day being that on which the trial took place, he did not rise from his bed, and when the time appointed for meeting Travers came he was not at all in anything of an improved condition. His gig was got ready, however, and, accompanied by Hanlon, he drove to the agent's office.

Travers was a quick, expert man of business, who lost but little time and few words in his dealings with the world. He was clear, rapid, and decisive, and having once formed an opinion, there was scarcely any possibility of changing it. This, indeed, was the worst and most impracticable point about him, for as it often happened that his opinions were based upon imperfect or erroneous data, it consequently followed that his inflexibility was but another name for obstinacy, and not unfrequently for injustice.

As Henderson entered the office, he met our friend the pedlar and old Dalton going out.

" Dalton," said Travers, " do you and your friend stay in the next room; I wish to see you again before you go. How do you do, Henderson ? "

" I am not well," replied Henderson, " not at all well; but it won't signify."

"How is your father?"

"Much as usual; I wonder he didn't call on you."

"No, he did not; I suppose he's otherwise engaged; the assizes always occupy him. However, now to business, Mr. Henderson," and he looked inquiringly at Dick, as much as to say, I am ready to hear you.

"We had better see, I think," proceeded Dick, "and make arrangements about these new leases."

"I shall expect to be bribed for each of them, Mr. Richard."

"Bribed!" exclaimed the other, "ha, ha, ha! that's good."

"Why, do you think there's anything morally wrong or dishonourable in a bribe?" asked the other, with a very serious face.

"Come, come, Mr. Travers," said Dick, "a joke's a joke, only don't put so grave a face on you when you ask such a question. However, as you say yourself, now to business—about these leases."

"I trust," continued Travers, "that I am both an honest man and a gentleman, yet I expect a bribe for every lease."

"Well, then," replied Henderson, "it is not generally supposed that either an honest man or a gentleman——"

"Would take a bribe?—eh?"

"Well, d——n it, no; not exactly that either; but come, let us understand each other. If you be wilful on it, why a wilful man, they say, must have his way. Bribery, however, rank bribery is a——"

"Crime to which neither an honest man nor a gentleman would stoop. You see, I anticipate what you are about to say; you despise bribery, Mr. Henderson?"

"Sir," replied the other, rather warmly, "I trust that I am a gentleman and an honest man, too."

"But still a wilful man, Mr. Henderson, must have his way, you know. Well of course you are a gentleman and an honest man." He then rose, and touching the bell, said to the servant who answered it,—

" Send in the man named Darby Skinadre."

If that miserable wretch was thin and shrivelled-looking when first introduced to our readers, he appeared at the present period little else than the shadow of what he had been. He not only had lost heavily even by the usurious credit he had given, in consequence of the widespread poverty and crying distress of the wretched people, who were mostly insolvent, but he suffered severely by the outrages which had taken place, and doubly so in consequence of the anxiety which so many felt to wreak their vengeance on him, under that guise, for his heartless and blood-sucking extortions upon them.

" Your name," proceeded the agent, " is Darby Skinadre ? "

" Yes, sir."

" And you have given this gentleman the sum of a hundred pounds as a bribe for promising you a lease of Cornelius Dalton's farm ? "

" I gave him a hundre' pounds, but not at all as a bribe, sir ; I'm an honest man, I trust, an' the Lord forbid I'd have anything to do wid a bribe ; an' if you an' he knew, both o' you, the hard strivin', an' scrapin', and sweepin' I had to get it together——"

" That will do, sir ; be silent. You received this money, Mr. Henderson ? "

" Tut, Travers, my good friend ; that is playing too high a card about such a matter. Don't you know, devilish well, that these things are common, ay, and among gentlemen and honest men, too, as you say ? "

" Well, then," continued Henderson, smiling, " if *you* have no objection, I am willing that you should take Skinadre's affair and mine as a precedent between you and me. Let us not be fools, Mr. Travers ; it is every one for himself in this world."

" What is it you expect, in the first place ? " asked the agent.

" Why, new leases," replied the other ; " upon reasonable terms, of course."

" Well, then," said Travers, " I beg to inform you that you shall not have them, with only one exception. You shall have a lease of sixty-nine acres attached to the Grange, being the quantity of land which you actually farm."

" Pray, why not all the property ? " asked Dick.

"My good friend," replied the agent, nearly in his own words to the pedlar, " the fact is, that we are about to introduce a new system altogether upon our property. We are determined to manage it upon a perfectly new principle. It has been too much sub-let under us, and we have resolved, Mr. Henderson, to rectify this evil. That is my answer. With the exception of the Grange Farm, you get no leases. We shall turn over a new leaf, and see that a better order of things be established upon the property. As for you, Skinadre, settle this matter of your hundred pounds with Mr. Henderson as best you may. That was a private transaction altogether between yourselves; between yourselves, then, does the settlement of it lie."

He once more touched the bell, and desired Cornelius Dalton and the pedlar to be sent in.

" Mr. Henderson," he proceeded, " I will bid you goodmorning; you certainly look ill. Skinadre, you may go. I have sent for Dalton, Mr. Henderson, to let him know that he shall be re-instated in his farm, and every reasonable allowance made him for the oppression and injustice which he and his respectable family have suffered, at—I will not say *whose* hands."

" Travers," replied Henderson, "your conduct is harsh— and—however, I cannot now think of leases—I am, every moment, getting worse—I am very ill—good morning." He then went.

" An' am I to lose my hundre' pounds, your honour, of my hard-earned money, that I squeezed——"

" Out of the blood and marrow and life of the struggling and industrious people, you cruel and heartless extortioner ! Begone, sirrah ; a foot of land upon the property for which I am agent you shall never occupy. You and your tribe, whether you batten upon the distress of struggling industry in the deceitful Maelstrooms of the metropolis, or in the dirty, dingy, shops of a private country village, are each a scorpion curse to the people. Your very existence is a libel upon the laws by which the rights of civil society are protected."

"Troth, your honour does me injustice; I never see a case of distress that my heart doesn't bleed——"

"With a leech-like propensity to pounce upon it—begone." The man slunk out. "Dalton," he proceeded, when the old man, accompanied by the pedlar, came in, "I sent for you to say that I am willing you should have your farm again."

"Sir," replied the other, "I am thankful and grateful to you for that kindness, but it is now too late; I am not able to go back upon it; I have neither money nor stock of any kind. I am deeply and gratefully obliged to you; but I have not sixpence worth in the world to put on it. An honest heart, sir, an' a clear fame is all that God has left me, blessed be His name!"

"Don't b'lieve a word of it," replied the pedlar. "Only let your honour give him a good lease, at a raisonable rint, makin' allowances for his improvements——"

"Never mind conditions, my good friend," said the agent, "but proceed; for, if I don't mistake, you will yourself give him a lift."

"Maybe we'll fin' him stock an' capital a thrifle, any way," replied the pedlar, with a knowing wink. "I haven't carried a pack all my life for nothing, I hope."

"I understand," said the agent to Dalton, "that one of your sons is dead. I leave town to-day, but I shall be here this day fortnight; call then, and we shall have everything arranged. Your case was a very hard one, and a very common one; but it was one with which *we* had nothing to do, and in which, until now, we could not interfere. I have looked clearly into it, and regret to find that such cases do exist upon Irish property to a painful extent, although I am

glad to find that public opinion, and a more enlightened experience are every day diminishing the evil."

He then rang for some one else, and our friends withdrew,
impressed with a grateful sense of his integrity and justice.

CHAPTER XXXII

CONCLUSION

WHEN Mrs. M'Ivor—whom we may now, without any error,
style the wife of Donnel Dhu—recognized in the court-house
the man called the Black Prophet, as her husband, she knew
also, without having been aware of it, that she had seen and
conversed with her own daughter. To most women, her
position would have been one of indescribable and distracting
agony. Here had she been aiding her nephew to trace the
murderer of his father—her own brother—and now that they
had found him, he turns out to be no other than her own
husband, and the father of her child. She was, however,
as we have said at an early stage of our narrative, a woman
of much firmness, if not obstinacy of character; or to come
still nearer to the truth, it would be difficult to find on Irish
soil a female who possessed such a stoical ascendency over
her own feelings.

The interest excited by the trial, involving as it did so
much that concerned the Sullivans, especially the hopes and
affections of their daughter Mave, naturally induced them—
though not on this latter account—young and old, to attend
the assizes, not excepting Mave herself; for her father, much
against her inclination, had made a point to bring her with
them. On finding, however, how matters turned out, a
perfect and hearty reconciliation took place between the two
families, in the course of which Mave and the Prophet's
wife once more renewed their acquaintance. Some necessary
and brief explanation took place, in the course of which
allusion was made to Sarah and her state of health.

"I hope," said Mave, "you will lose no time in goin' to see her. I know her affectionate heart; an' that when she hears an' feels that she has a mother alive an' well, an' that loves her as she ought to be loved, it will put new life into her."

"She is a fine lookin' girl," replied her mother, "an' while I was spakin' to her I felt my heart warm to her, sure enough; but she's a wild creature, they say."

"Hasty a little," said Mave; "but then such a heart as she has. You ought to go see her at wanst."

"I would, dear, an' my heart is longin' to see her; but I think it's betther that I should not till afther his thrial to-morrow. I'm to be a witness against the unfortunate man."

"Against her father!—against your own husband!" exclaimed Mave, looking aghast at this intimation.

"Yes, dear; for it was my brother he murdhered, an' he must take the consequences, if he was my husband an' her father ten times over. My brother's blood musn't pass for nothin'. Besides, the hand of God is in it, an' I must do my duty."

The heart of the gentle and the heroic Mave, which could encounter contagion and death, from a principle of unconscious magnanimity and affection that deserved a garland, now shrunk back with pain at the sentiments so coolly expressed by Sarah's mother. She thought for a moment of young Dalton, and that if she were called upon to prosecute him—but she hastily put the fearful hypothesis aside, and was about to bid her acquaintance good-bye, when the latter said,—

"To-morrow, or rather the day afther, I'd wish to see her, for then I'll know what will happen to him, and how to act with her; an' if you'd come wid me, I'd be glad of it, an' you'd oblage me."

Mave's gentle and affectionate spirit was disquieted within her by what she had already heard; but a moment's reflection convinced her that her presence on the occasion might be serviceable to Sarah, whose excitable temperament and delicate state of health required gentle and judicious treatment.

" I'm afeard," said Mrs. M'Ivor, " that by the time the thrial's over to-morrow, it'll be too late ; but let us say the day afther, if it's the same to you ? "

" Well, then," replied Mave, " you can call to our place, as it's on your way, an' we'll both go together."

" If she knew her," said Mave to her friends, on her way home, " as I do ; if she only knew the heart she has—the lovin', the fearless, the great heart ;—oh, if she did, no earthly thing would prevent her from goin' to her without the loss of a minute's time. Poor Sarah !—brave and generous girl—what wouldn't I do to bring her back to health ! But ah, mother, I'm afeard ; " and as the noble girl spoke, the tears gushed to her eyes—" ' It's my last act for you,' she whispered to me, on that night when the house was surrounded by villains—' I know what you risked for me in the shed ; I know it, dear Mave, and I'm now sthrivin' to pay back my debt to you.' Oh, mother ! " she exclaimed, " where—where could one look for the like of her ? an' yet, how little does the world know about her goodness, or her greatness, I may say. Well," proceeded Mave, " she paid that debt, but I'm afeard, mother, it'll turn out that it was with her own life she paid it."

At the hour appointed, Mrs. M'Ivor and Mave set out on their visit to Sarah, each now aware of the dreadful and inevitable doom that awaited her father, and of the part which one of them at least had taken in bringing it about.

About half-an-hour before their arrival, Sarah, whose anxiety touching the fate of old Dalton could endure no more, lay awaiting the return of her nurse—a simple, good-hearted, matter-of-fact creature, who had no notion of ever concealing the truth, under any circumstances. The poor girl had sent her to get an account of the trial the best way she could, and, as we said, she now lay awaiting her return. At length she came in.

" Well, Biddy, what's the news—or have you got any ?"

The old woman gently and affectionately put her hand over on Sarah's forehead, as if the act was a religious cere- mony, and accompanied an invocation, as indeed she intended it to do,—

" May God in His mercy soon relieve you from your thrials, my poor girl, an' bring you to Himself! but it's the black news I have for you this day."

Sarah started.

" What news ? " she asked hastily—" what black news ? "

" Husth, now, an' I'll tell you ;—in the first place, your mother is alive, an' has come to the counthry."

Sarah immediately sat up in the bed, without assistance, and fastening her black, brilliant eyes upon the woman, exclaimed,—

"My mother—my mother—my own mother! an' do you dare to tell me that this is black news ? Lave the house, I bid you. I'll get up—I'm not sick—I'm well! Great God !—yes, I'm well—very well ; but how dare you name black news an' my mother—my blessed mother—in the same breath, or on the same day ? "

" Will you hear me out, then ? " continued the nurse.

" No," replied Sarah, attempting to get up. " I want to hear no more ; now I wish to live—now I am sure of one, an' that one my mother—my own mother—to love me—to guide me—to taiche me all that I ought to know ; but, above all, to love me. An' my father—my poor unhappy father— an' he *is* unhappy—he loves me, too. Oh, Biddy, I can forgive you now for what you said—I will be happy still— an' my mother will be happy—an' my father—my poor father—will be happy yet ; he'll reform—he'll repent, may- be ; an' he'll wanst more get back his early heart—his heart, when it was good, an' not hardened, as he says it was, by the world. Biddy, did you ever see any one cry with joy before—ha—ha—did you now ? "

" God strengthen you, my poor child," exclaimed the nurse,

bursting into tears; " for what will become of you ? Your
father, Sarah, dear, is to be hanged for murdher, an' it was
your mother's evidence that hanged him. She swore against
him on the thrial, an' his sentence is passed. Bartle Sullivan
wasn't murdhered at all, but another man was, an' it was
your father that done it. On next Friday he's to be hanged,
an' your mother, they say, swore his life away ! If that's
not black news, I don't know what is."

Sarah's face had been flushed to such a degree by the first
portion of the woman's intelligence, that it's expression
was brilliant and animated beyond belief. On hearing its
conclusion, however, the change from joy to horror was
instantaneous, shocking, and pitiable, beyond all power of
language to express. She was struck perfectly motionless
and ghastly; and as she kept her large lucid eyes fixed
upon the woman's face, the powers of life, that had been
hitherto in such a tumult of delight within her, seemed
slowly, and with a deadly and scarcely perceptible motion, to
ebb out of her system. The revulsion was too dreadful ; and
with the appearance of one who was anxious to shrink or
hide from something that was painful, she laid her head
down on the humble pillow of her bed.

" Now, *asthore*," said the woman, struck by the woful
change—" don't take it too much to heart ; you're young, an'
please God, you'll get over it all yet."

" No," she replied, but in a voice so utterly changed and
deprived of its strength, that the woman could with difficulty
hear or understand her.

" There is but one good bein' in the world," she said to herself, " an' that is Mave Sullivan. I have no mother, no father
—all I can love now is Mave Sullivan—that's all."

" Every one that knows her does," said the nurse.

" Who ? " said Sarah, inquiringly.

" Why, Mave Sullivan," replied the other ; " worn't you
spakin' about her ? "

" Was I ? " said she, " maybe so—what was I sayin' ? "

She then put her hand to her forehead, as if she felt pain and confusion; after which she waved the nurse towards her, but on the woman stooping down, she seemed to forget that she had beckoned to her at all.

At this moment Mave and her mother entered, and after looking towards the bed on which she lay, they inquired in a whisper from the attendant how she was.

The woman pointed hopelessly to her own head, and then looked significantly at Sarah, as if to intimate that her brain was then unsettled.

"There's something wrong here," she added, in an under-tone, and, touching her head, "especially since I tould her what happened."

"Is she acquainted with everything?" asked her mother.

"She is," replied the other; "she knows that her father is to die on Friday, and that you swore agin' him."

"But what on earth," said Mave, "could make you be so mad as to let her know anything of that kind?"

"Why, she sent me to get word," replied the simple crea-ture, "an' you wouldn't have me tell her a lie, an' the poor girl on her death-bed, I'm afeard."

Her mother went over and stood opposite where she lay, that is, near the foot of her bed, and putting one hand under her chin, looked at her long and steadily. Mave went to her side, and taking her hand gently up, kissed it, and wept quietly but bitterly.

It was, indeed, impossible to look upon her without a feeling of deep and extraordinary interest. Her singularly youthful aspect—her surprising beauty, to which disease and suffering had given a character of purity and tenderness almost etherial—the natural symmetry and elegance of her very arms and hands—the wonderful whiteness of her skin, which contrasted so strikingly with the raven black of her glossy hair, and the soul of thought and feeling which lay obviously expressed by the long silken eyelashes of her closed eyes— all, when taken in at a glance, were calculated to impress a beholder with love, and sympathy, and tenderness, such as no human heart could resist.

Mave, on glancing at her mother, saw a few tears stealing, as it were, down her cheeks.

"I wish to God, my dear daughter," exclaimed the latter, in a low voice, "that I had never seen your face, lovely as it is, an' it surely would be betther for yourself that you had never been born."

She then passed to the bedside, and taking Mave's place, who withdrew, she stooped down, and placing her lips upon Sarah's white, broad forehead, exclaimed — "May God bless you, my dear daughter, is the heartfelt prayer of your unhappy mother."

Sarah suddenly opened her eyes, and started : "What is this?" she exclaimed, "What is wrong? There is something wrong. Didn't I hear some one callin' me daughter? Here's a strange woman — Charley Hanlon's aunt — Biddy, come here!"

"Well, *acushla*, here I am—keep yourself quiet, *achora*— what is it?"

"Didn't you tell me that my mother swore my father's life away?"

"It's what they say," replied the matter-of-fact nurse.

"Then it's a lie—a lie that comes from hell itself," she replied. "Oh, if I was only up and strong as I was, let me see the man or woman that durst say so. My mother! to become unnatural and treacherous, an' I have a mother—ha, ha—oh, how often have I thought of this—thought of what a girl I would be if I was to have a mother—how good I would be too—how kind to her—how I would love her, an' how she would love me, and then my heart would sink when I'd think of home—ay, an' then when Nelly would spake cruelly an' harshly to me I'd feel as if I could kill her or any one."

Her eye here caught Mave Sullivan, and she again started.

"What is this?" she exclaimed, "am I still in the shed? Mave Sullivan!—help me up, Biddy."

" I am here, dear Sarah," replied the gentle girl—" I am here ; keep yourself quiet, and don't attempt to sit up ; you're not able to do it."

The composed and serene aspect of Mave, and the kind touching tones of her voice seemed to operate favourably upon her, and to aid her in collecting her confused and scattered thoughts into something like order.

" Oh, dear Mave," said she, " what is this? What has happened? Isn't there something wrong? I'm confused. Have I a mother? Have I a *livin'* mother that will *love* me ? "

Her large dark eyes suddenly sparkled with singular animation as she asked the last question, and Mave thought this was the most appropriate moment to make the mother known to her.

" You have, dear Sarah, an' here she is, waiting to clasp you to her heart an' give you her blessin'."

" Where? " she exclaimed, starting up in her bed, as if in full health ; " my mother! where ?—where? "

She held her arms out towards her, for Mave had again assumed the mother's station at the bedside, and the latter stood at a little distance. On seeing her daughter's arms wildly extended towards her, she approached her, but, whether checked by Sarah's allusion to her conduct or from a wish to spare her excitement, or from natural coldness of disposition, it is difficult to say, she did it with so little appearance of the eager enthusiasm that the heart of the latter expected, and with a manner so singularly cool and unexcited, that Sarah, whose feelings were always decisive and rapid as lightning, had time to recognize her features as Hanlon's aunt, whom she had seen and talked to before ; but that was not all; she perceived not in her these external manifestations of strong affection and natural tenderness for which her own heart yearned almost convulsively ; there was no sparkling glance—no precipitate emotion—no gushing of tears—no mother's love—in short, nothing of what her noble and loving spirit could recognize as kindred to itself and to her warm and impulsive heart. The moment—the glance—that sought and found not what it looked for—were decisive ; the arms that had been extended remained extended still, but the spirit of their attitude was changed, as was that eager and tumultuous delight which had just flashed from her countenance. Her thoughts, as we said, were quick, and in almost a moment's time she appeared to be altogether a different individual.

"Stop!" she exclaimed, now repelling instead of soliciting the embrace; "there isn't the love of a mother in that woman's heart—an' what did I hear? that she swore my father's life away—her husband's life away! No, no; I'm changed—I see my father's blood, shed by her, too, his own wife! Look at her features, they're hard and harsh—there's no love in her eyes—they're cowld and sevare. No, no; there's something wrong there—I feel that—I feel it—it's here—the feelin's in my heart—oh, what a dark hour this is! You were right, Biddy, you brought me black news this day—but it won't—it won't—trouble me long—it won't disturb this poor brain long—it won't pierce this poor heart long—I hope not. Oh," she exclaimed, turning to Mave, and extending her arms towards her, " Mave Sullivan, let me die ! "

The affectionate but disappointed girl had all Mave's sympathies, whose warm and affectionate feelings recoiled from the coldness and apparent want of natural tenderness which characterized the mother's manner, under circumstances in themselves so affecting. Still, after having soothed Sarah for a few minutes, and placed her head once more upon the pillow, she whispered to the mother, who seemed to think more than to feel,—

"Don't be surprised; when you consider the state she's in —and, indeed, it isn't to be wondered at after what she has heard—you must make every allowance for the poor girl."

Sarah's emotions were now evidently in incessant play.

"Biddy," said she, " come here again ; help me up."

"Dear Sarah," said Mave, "you are not able to bear all

this; if you could compose yourself, an' forget everything unpleasant for a while, till you grow strong."

"If I could forget that my mother has no heart to love me with—that she's could and strange to me—if I could forget that she's brought my father to a shameful death—my father's heart wasn't altogether bad; no, an' he was wanst —I mane in his early life—a good man. I know that—I feel that—' dear Sarah, sleep,—sleep, dear Sarah '—no, bad as he is, there was a thousand times more love and nature in the voice that spoke them words than in a hundred women like my mother, that hasn't yet kissed my lips. Biddy, come here, I say—here, lift me up again."

There was such energy, and fire, and command in her voice and words now that Mave could not remonstrate any longer, nor the nurse refuse to obey her. When she was once more placed sitting she looked about her.

"Mother," she said, come here."

And, as she pronounced the word mother, a trait so beautiful, so exquisite, so natural, and so pathetic accompanied it that Mave once more wept. Her voice, in uttering the word quivered, and softened into tenderness, with the affection which nature itself seems to have associated with it. Sarah herself remarked this, even in the anguish of the moment.

"My very heart knows and loves the word," she said. "Oh! why is it that I am to suffer this? Is it possible that the empty name is all that's left me afther all? Mother, come here—I am pleadin' for my father now—you pleaded against him, but I always took the weakest side—here is God now among us—you must stand before Him—look your daughter in the face, an' answer her as you expect to meet God, when you leave this throubled life; truth—truth now, mother, an' nothin' else. Mother, I am dyin'. Now, as God is to judge you, did you ever love my father as a wife ought?"

There was some irresistible spirit, some unaccountable power, in her manner and language—such command and such wonderful love of candour in her full, dark eye—that it was impossible to gainsay or withstand her.

"I will spake the thruth," replied her mother, evidently borne away and subdued, "although it's against myself—to my shame an' to my sorrow I say it—that when I married your father another man had my affections; but, as I'm to appear before God, I never wronged him. I don't know how it is that you've made me confess it; but, at any rate, you're the first that ever wrung it out o' me."

"That will do," replied her daughter, calmly; "that sounds like murdher from my mother's lips! Lay me down now, Biddy."

Mave, who had scarcely ever taken her eyes from off her varying and busy features, was now struck by a singular change which she observed to come over them—a change that was nothing but the shadow of death, and cannot be described.

"Sarah!" she exclaimed, "dear, darling Sarah, what is the matter with you? Have you got ill again?"

"Oh! my child," exclaimed her mother, "am I to lose you this way at last? Oh! dear Sarah, forgive me—I'm your mother, and you'll forgive me."

"Mave," said Sarah, "take this—I remember seein' yours and mine together not very long ago—take this lock of my hair—I think you will get a pair of scissors on the corner of the shelf—cut it off with your own hands; let it be sent to my father, an' when's he's dyin' a disgraceful death, let him wear it next his heart; and wherever he's to be buried, let him have this buried with him. Let whoever will give it to him, say that it comes from Sarah, an' that if she was able, she would be with him through shame, an' disgrace, an' death; that she'd support him as well as she could in his trouble; that she'd scorn the world for him; an' that because he said once in his life that he loved her; she'd forgive him all a thousand times, an' would lay down her life for him."

"You would do that, my noble girl," exclaimed Mave, with a choking voice.

"And above all things," proceeded Sarah, "let him be tould if it can be done, that Sarah said to him to die without fear— to bear it up like a man and not like a coward—to look manfully about him on the very scaffold—an'—an' to die as a man ought to die—bravely an' without fear—bravely an' without fear ! "

Her voice and strength were, since the last change that Mave observed, both rapidly sinking, and her mother, anxious, if possible, to have her forgiveness, again approached her and said,—

"Dear Sarah, you are angry with me ?   Oh! forgive me— am I not your mother ? "

The great girl's resentments, however, had all passed, and the business of her life and its functions she felt were now over—she said so,—

"It's all over, at last now, mother," she replied; "I have no anger now—come and kiss me.   Whatever you have done, you are still my mother.   Bless me—bless your daughter Sarah.   I have nothing now in my heart but love for everybody ; tell Nelly, dear Mave, that Sarah forgave her, an' hoped that she'd forgive Sarah.   Mave, I trust you an' he will be happy—that's my last wish, an' tell him so.   Mave, there's sweet faces about me, sich as I seen in the shed ; they're smilin' upon me— smilin' upon Sarah—upon poor hasty Sarah M'Gowan, that would have loved every one.   Mave, think of me sometimes ; an' let him, when he thinks of the wild girl that loved him, look upon you, dearest Mave, an' love you, if possible, betther for her sake.   These sweet faces is about me again.   Father, I'll be before you ; but die—die like a man."

Whilst uttering the last few sentences, which were spoken with great difficulty, she began to pull the bedclothes about with her hands, and whilst uttering the last word, her beautiful hand was slightly clenched, as if helping out a sentiment so completely in accordance with her brave spirit.   These motions, however, ceased suddenly ; she heaved a deep sigh, and the troubled spirit of the kind, the generous, the erring but affectionate Sarah M'Gowan—as we shall call her still—passed away to another and, we trust, a better life. The storms of her heart and brain were at rest for ever.

Thus perished in early life one of those creatures, that sometimes seem as if they were placed by mistake in a wrong sphere of existence. It is impossible to say to what a height of moral grandeur and true greatness, culture and education might have elevated her, or to say with what brilliancy her virtues might have shown, had her heart and affections been properly cultivated. Like some beautiful and luxuriant flower, however, she was permitted to run into wildness and disorder for want of a guiding hand; but no want, no absence of training, could ever destroy its natural delicacy, nor prevent its fragrance from smelling sweet, even in the neglected situation where it was left to pine and die.

There is little now to be added. "Time, the consoler," passes not in vain even over the abodes of wretchedness and misery. The sufferings of that year of famine we have endeavoured to bring before those who may have the power in their hands of assuaging the similar horrors which have revisited our country in this. The pictures we have given are not exaggerated, but drawn from memory and the terrible realities of 1817.

It is unnecessary to add, that when "sickness," and the severity of winter passed away, our lovers, Mave and young Condy Dalton, were happily married, as they deserved to be, and occupied the farm from which the good old man had been so unjustly expelled.

It was on the first social evening that the two families, now so happily reconciled, spent together subsequent to the trial, that Bartle Sullivan gratified them with the following account of his history :—

"I remimber fightin'," he proceeded, " wid Condy on that night, and the devil's own *bulliah battha* he was. We went into a corner of the field near the Grey Stone, to decide it. All at wanst I forgot what happened, till I found myself lyin' upon a car wid the M'Mahons of Edenberg, that lived ten or twelve miles beyant the mountains, at the foot of Carnmore. They knew me, and good right they had, for I had been spakin' to their sisther Shibby, but she wasn't for me at the time, although I was ready to kick my own shadow about her, God knows. Well, you see, I felt disgraced at bein' beaten by Con Dalton, and I was fond of her, so what 'ud you have of us but off we went together to America, for you see she promised to marry me if I'd go. They had taken me up on one of their carts, thinkin' I was dhrunk, to lave me, for safety, in the next neighbour's house we came to. Well, she an' I married when we got to Boston; but God never blessed us wid a family; and Toddy here, who tuk to the life of a pedlar, came back afther many a long year, with a good purse, and lived wid us. At last I begun to long for home, and so we all came together. The Prophet's wife was wid us, an' another passenger tould me that Con, here, had been suspected of murdherin' me. I got unwell in Liverpool, but I sent Toddy on before me to make their minds aisy. As we wor talkin' over these matthers, I happened to mention to the woman what I had seen the night the carman was murdhered, and I wondhered at the way she looked on hearin' it. She went on, but afther a time came back to Liverpool for me, an' took the typhus on her way home; but, thank God! we were all in time to clear the innocent and punish the guilty; ay, an' reward the good, too eh, Toddy?"

"I'll give Mave away," replied Toddy, "if there wasn't another man in Europe; an' when I'm puttin' your hand into Con's, Mave, it won't be an empty one. Ay, an' if your friend Sarah, the wild girl, had lived—but it can't be helped—death takes the young as well as the ould, an' may God prepare us all to meet Him."

Young Richard Henderson's anticipations were unfortunately too true. On leaving Mr. Travers's office, he returned home, took his bed, and in the course of one short week had paid, by a kind of judicial punishment, the fatal penalty of his contemplated profligacy. His father survived him only a few months, so that there is not, at this moment, one of the name or blood of Henderson in the Grange. The old man died of a quarrel with Jemmy Branigan, to whom he left a pension of fifty pounds a year; and truly the grief of his aged servant after him was unique and original.

"What's to become of me?" said Jemmy, with tears in his eyes; "I have nothing to do, nobody to attend to, nobody to fight with, nothing to disturb me or put me out of timper : I knew, however, that he would stick to his wickedness to the last, an' so he did, for the devil tempted him, out of sheer malice, when he could get at me no way else, to lave me fifty pounds a year to keep me aisy! Sich revenge an' villany by a dyin' man was never heard of. God help me, what am I to do now, or what hand will I turn to? What is there before me but peace and quietness for the remainder of my life? but I won't stand *that* long—an' to lave me fifty pounds a-year to keep me aisy! God forgive him!"

The Prophet suffered the sentence of the law, but refused all religious consolation. Whether his daughter's message ever reached him or not, we have had no means of ascertaining. He died, however, as she wished, firmly, but sullenly, and as if he despised and defied the world and its laws. He neither admitted his guilt, nor attempted to maintain his innocence, but passed out of existence like a man who was already wearied with its cares, and who now felt satisfied, when it was too late, that contempt for the laws of God and man never leads to safety, much less to happiness. His only observation was the following:—"When I dreamt that young Dalton drove a nail in my coffin, little I thought it would end this way."

We have simply to conclude by saying that Roddy Duncan was transported for perjury; and that Nelly became a *voteen* or devotee, and, as far as one could judge, exhibited something like repentance for the sinful life she had led with the Prophet.